WILLIAM AND THE LOST SPIRIT

GWEN DE BONNEVAL & MATTHIEU BONHOMME

COLORS BY WALTER

TRANSLATION AND COMMENTARY BY
ANNE AND OWEN SMITH

GRAPHIC UNIVERSE™ ◆ MINNEAPOLIS ◆ NEW YORK

Story by Gwen de Bonneval
Art by Matthieu Bonhomme
Colors by Walter
Translation by Anne and Owen Smith

First American edition published in 2013 by Graphic Universe™.
Published by arrangement with MEDIATOON LICENSING — France.

Messire Guillaume 1 – *Les contrées lointaines*
© DUPUIS 2006 — De Bonneval, Bonhomme

Messire Guillaume 2 – *Le pays de vérité*
© DUPUIS 2007 — De Bonneval, Bonhomme

Messire Guillaume 3 – *Terre et mère*
© DUPUIS 2009 — De Bonneval, Bonhomme

www.dupuis.com

Graphic Universe™
A division of Lerner Publishing Group, Inc.
241 First Avenue North
Minneapolis, MN 55401 U.S.A.

Website address: www.lernerbooks.com

Library of Congress Cataloging-in-Publication Data

Bonneval, Gwen de.
    [Messire Guillaume, l'esprit perdu. English]
      William and the lost spirit / Gwen de Bonneval ; illustrated by Matthieu Bonhomme—1st
    American ed.
        p. cm.
      ISBN 978-0-7613-8567-7 (lib. bdg. : alk. paper)
      1. Graphic novels. [1. Graphic novels. 2. Middle Ages—Fiction.
    3. Knights and knighthood—Fiction. 4. Voyages and travels—Fiction. 5. Families—Fiction.
    6. Mythology—Fiction. 7. Folklore—Fiction.] I. Bonhomme, Matthieu, ill. II. Smith, Anne Collins.
    III. Smith, Owen (Owen M.) IV. Title.
    PZ7.7.B66Wi 2013
    741.5'944—dc23   2012008115

Manufactured in the United States of America
1 – BP – 12/31/12

PART 1:
THE FAR-OFF LANDS

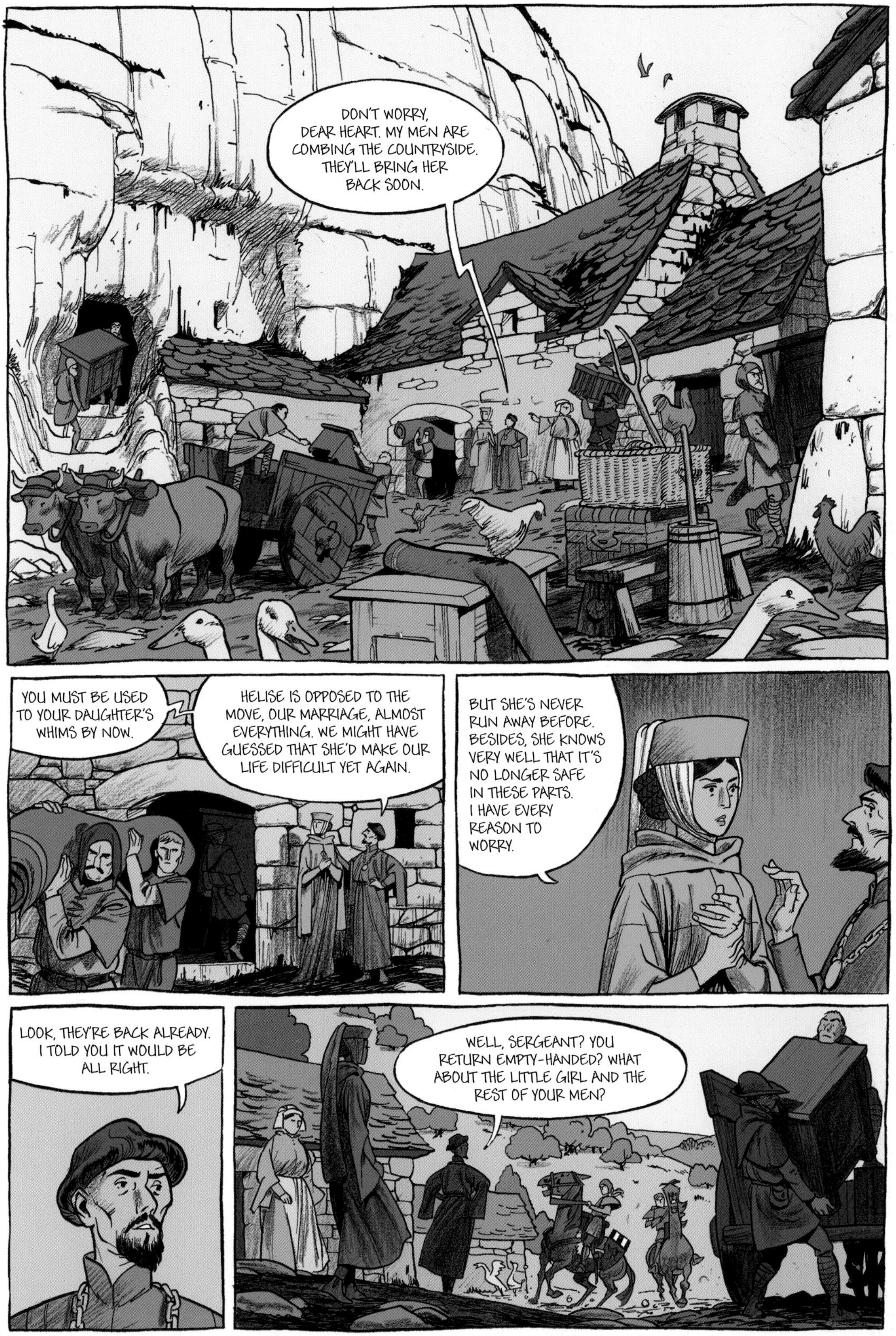
DON'T WORRY, DEAR HEART. MY MEN ARE COMBING THE COUNTRYSIDE. THEY'LL BRING HER BACK SOON.
YOU MUST BE USED TO YOUR DAUGHTER'S WHIMS BY NOW.
HELISE IS OPPOSED TO THE MOVE, OUR MARRIAGE, ALMOST EVERYTHING. WE MIGHT HAVE GUESSED THAT SHE'D MAKE OUR LIFE DIFFICULT YET AGAIN.
BUT SHE'S NEVER RUN AWAY BEFORE. BESIDES, SHE KNOWS VERY WELL THAT IT'S NO LONGER SAFE IN THESE PARTS. I HAVE EVERY REASON TO WORRY.
LOOK, THEY'RE BACK ALREADY. I TOLD YOU IT WOULD BE ALL RIGHT.
WELL, SERGEANT? YOU RETURN EMPTY-HANDED? WHAT ABOUT THE LITTLE GIRL AND THE REST OF YOUR MEN?

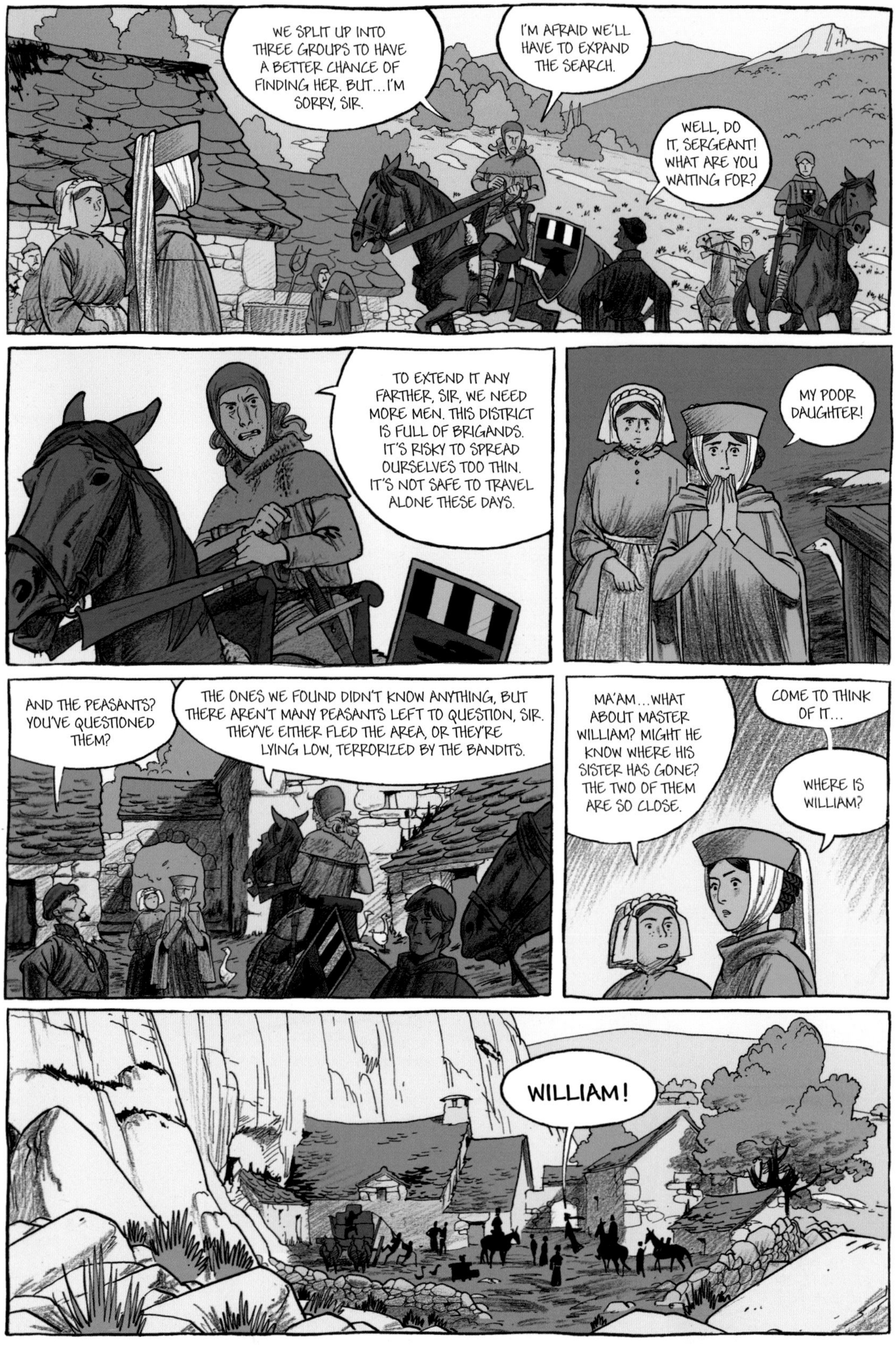
WE SPLIT UP INTO THREE GROUPS TO HAVE A BETTER CHANCE OF FINDING HER. BUT…I'M SORRY, SIR.
I'M AFRAID WE'LL HAVE TO EXPAND THE SEARCH.
WELL, DO IT, SERGEANT! WHAT ARE YOU WAITING FOR?
TO EXTEND IT ANY FARTHER, SIR, WE NEED MORE MEN. THIS DISTRICT IS FULL OF BRIGANDS. IT'S RISKY TO SPREAD OURSELVES TOO THIN. IT'S NOT SAFE TO TRAVEL ALONE THESE DAYS.
MY POOR DAUGHTER!
AND THE PEASANTS? YOU'VE QUESTIONED THEM?
THE ONES WE FOUND DIDN'T KNOW ANYTHING, BUT THERE AREN'T MANY PEASANTS LEFT TO QUESTION, SIR. THEY'VE EITHER FLED THE AREA, OR THEY'RE LYING LOW, TERRORIZED BY THE BANDITS.
MA'AM…WHAT ABOUT MASTER WILLIAM? MIGHT HE KNOW WHERE HIS SISTER HAS GONE? THE TWO OF THEM ARE SO CLOSE.
COME TO THINK OF IT…
WHERE IS WILLIAM?
WILLIAM!

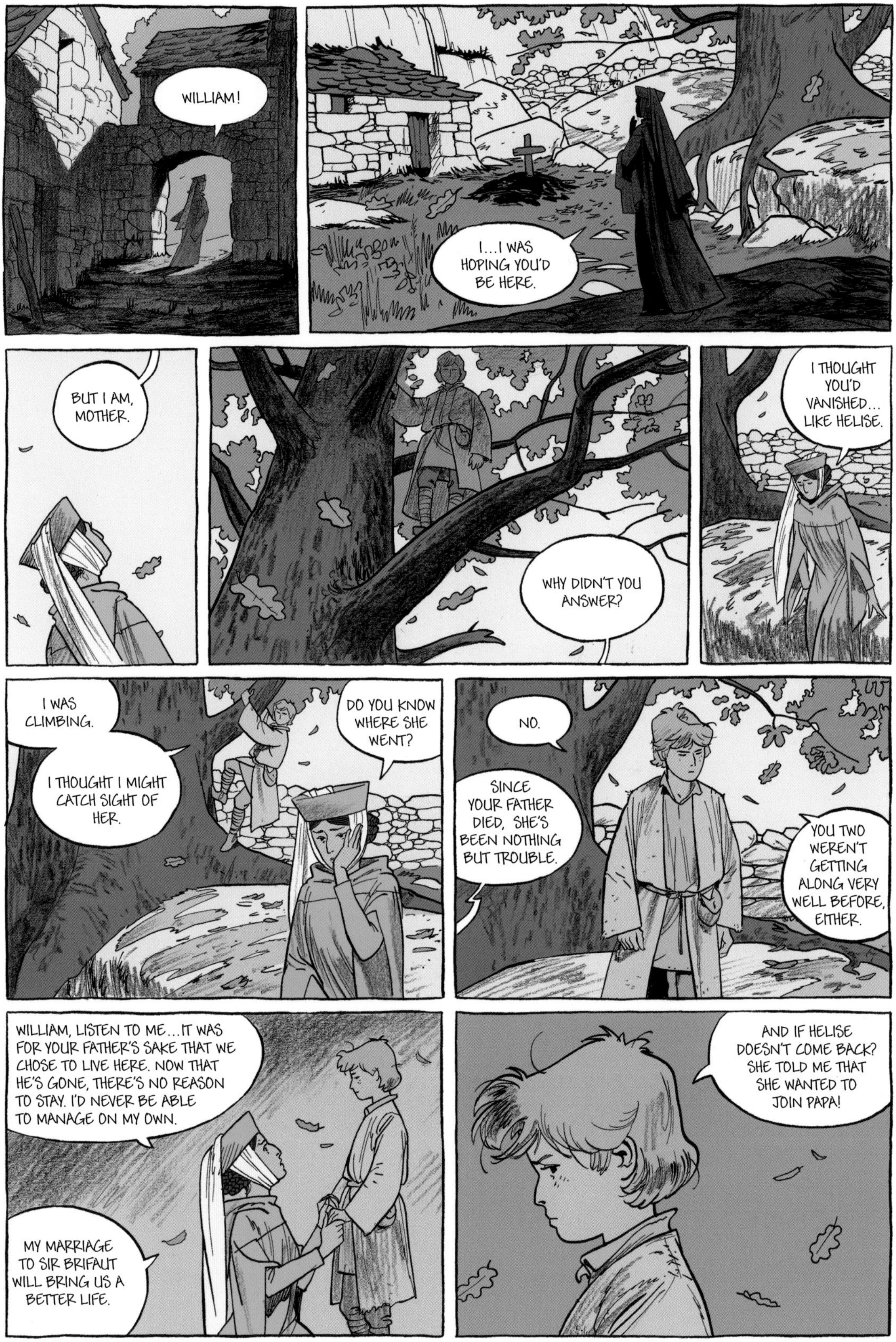
WILLIAM!
I...I WAS HOPING YOU'D BE HERE.
BUT I AM, MOTHER.
WHY DIDN'T YOU ANSWER?
I THOUGHT YOU'D VANISHED... LIKE HELISE.
I WAS CLIMBING.
I THOUGHT I MIGHT CATCH SIGHT OF HER.
DO YOU KNOW WHERE SHE WENT?
NO.
SINCE YOUR FATHER DIED, SHE'S BEEN NOTHING BUT TROUBLE.
YOU TWO WEREN'T GETTING ALONG VERY WELL BEFORE, EITHER.
WILLIAM, LISTEN TO ME... IT WAS FOR YOUR FATHER'S SAKE THAT WE CHOSE TO LIVE HERE. NOW THAT HE'S GONE, THERE'S NO REASON TO STAY. I'D NEVER BE ABLE TO MANAGE ON MY OWN.
MY MARRIAGE TO SIR BRIFAUT WILL BRING US A BETTER LIFE.
AND IF HELISE DOESN'T COME BACK? SHE TOLD ME THAT SHE WANTED TO JOIN PAPA!

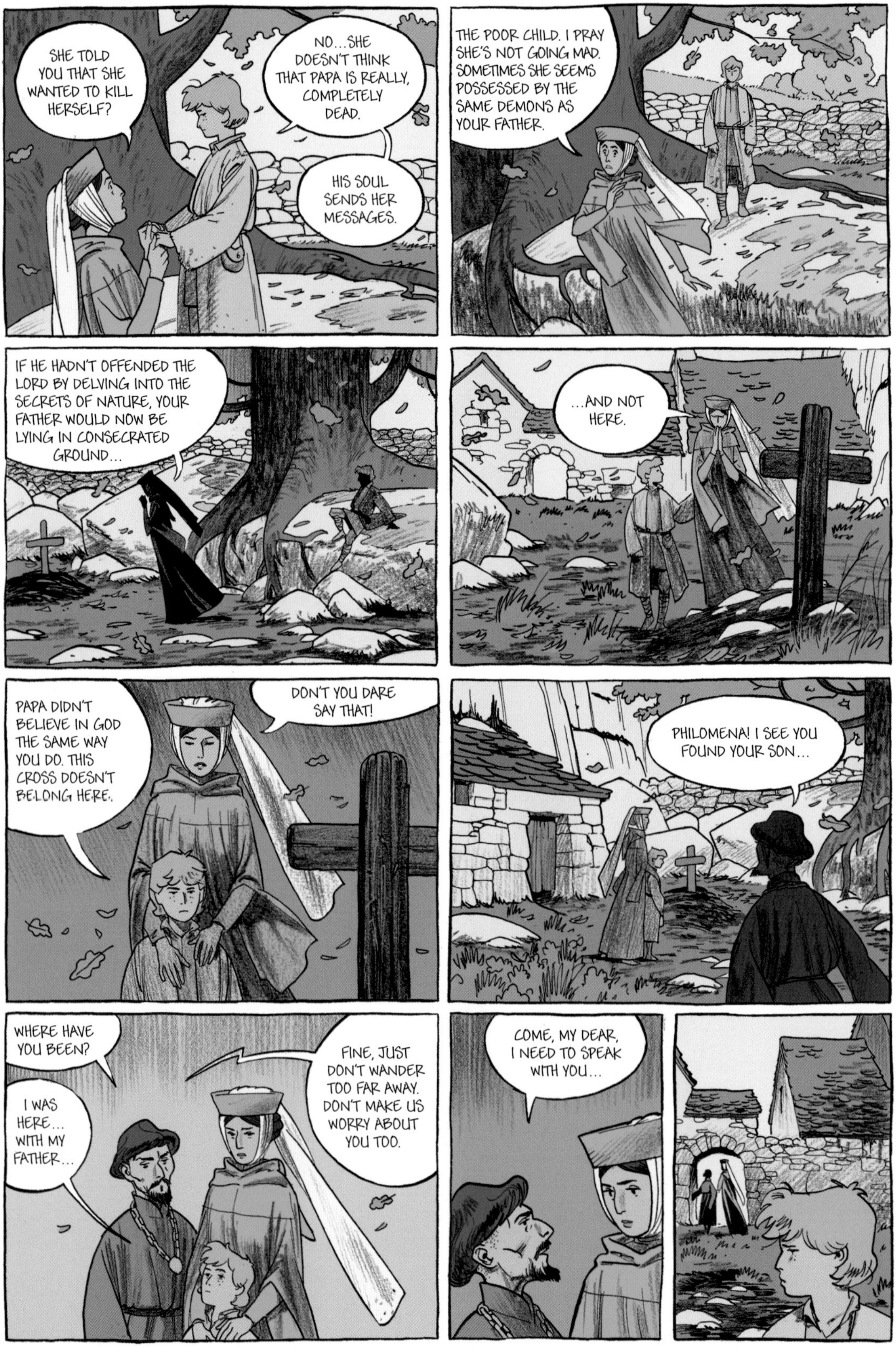
SHE TOLD YOU THAT SHE WANTED TO KILL HERSELF?
NO... SHE DOESN'T THINK THAT PAPA IS REALLY, COMPLETELY DEAD.
HIS SOUL SENDS HER MESSAGES.
THE POOR CHILD. I PRAY SHE'S NOT GOING MAD. SOMETIMES SHE SEEMS POSSESSED BY THE SAME DEMONS AS YOUR FATHER.
IF HE HADN'T OFFENDED THE LORD BY DELVING INTO THE SECRETS OF NATURE, YOUR FATHER WOULD NOW BE LYING IN CONSECRATED GROUND...
...AND NOT HERE.
PAPA DIDN'T BELIEVE IN GOD THE SAME WAY YOU DO. THIS CROSS DOESN'T BELONG HERE.
DON'T YOU DARE SAY THAT!
PHILOMENA! I SEE YOU FOUND YOUR SON...
WHERE HAVE YOU BEEN?
I WAS HERE... WITH MY FATHER...
FINE, JUST DON'T WANDER TOO FAR AWAY. DON'T MAKE US WORRY ABOUT YOU TOO.
COME, MY DEAR, I NEED TO SPEAK WITH YOU...

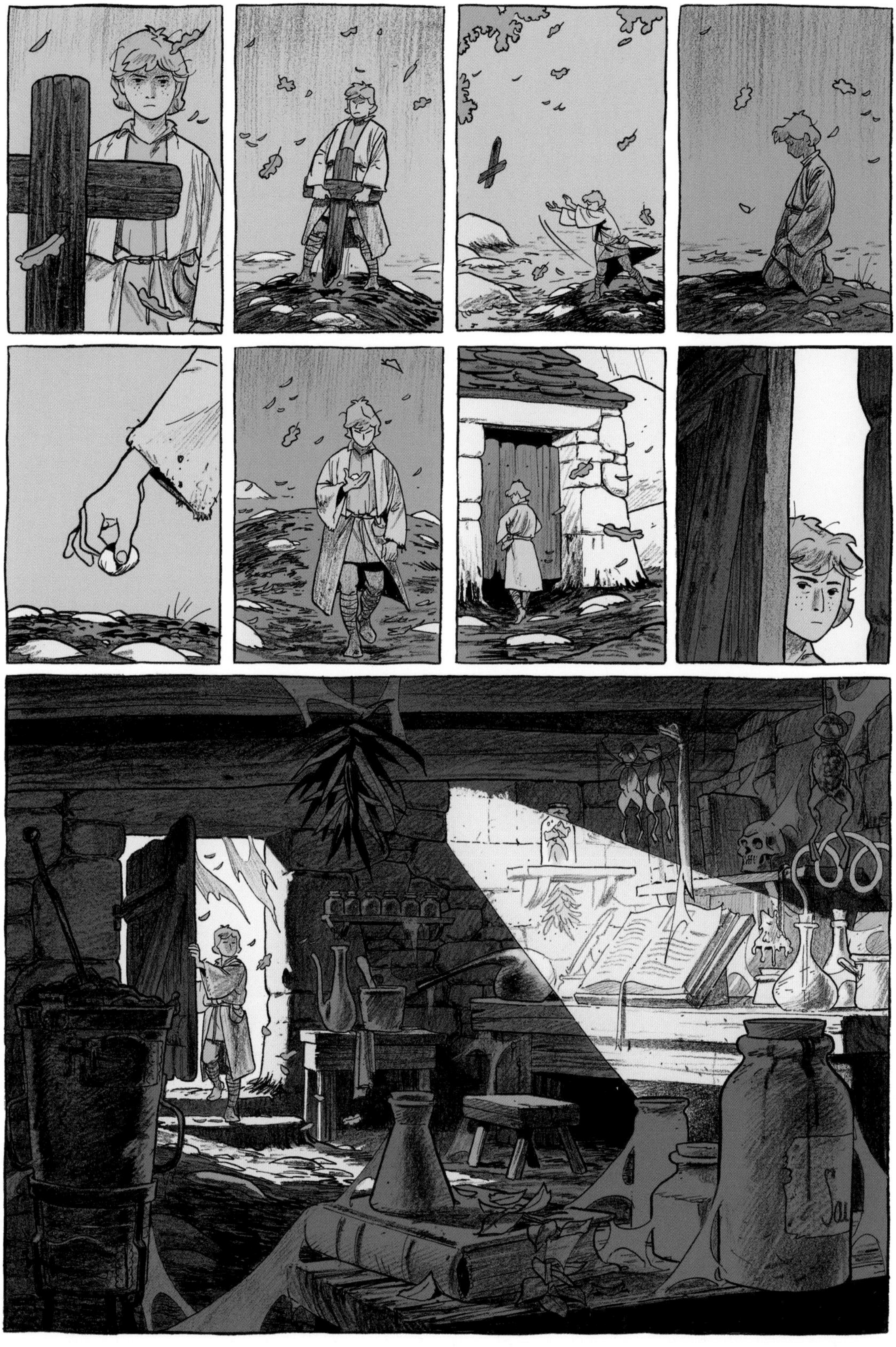

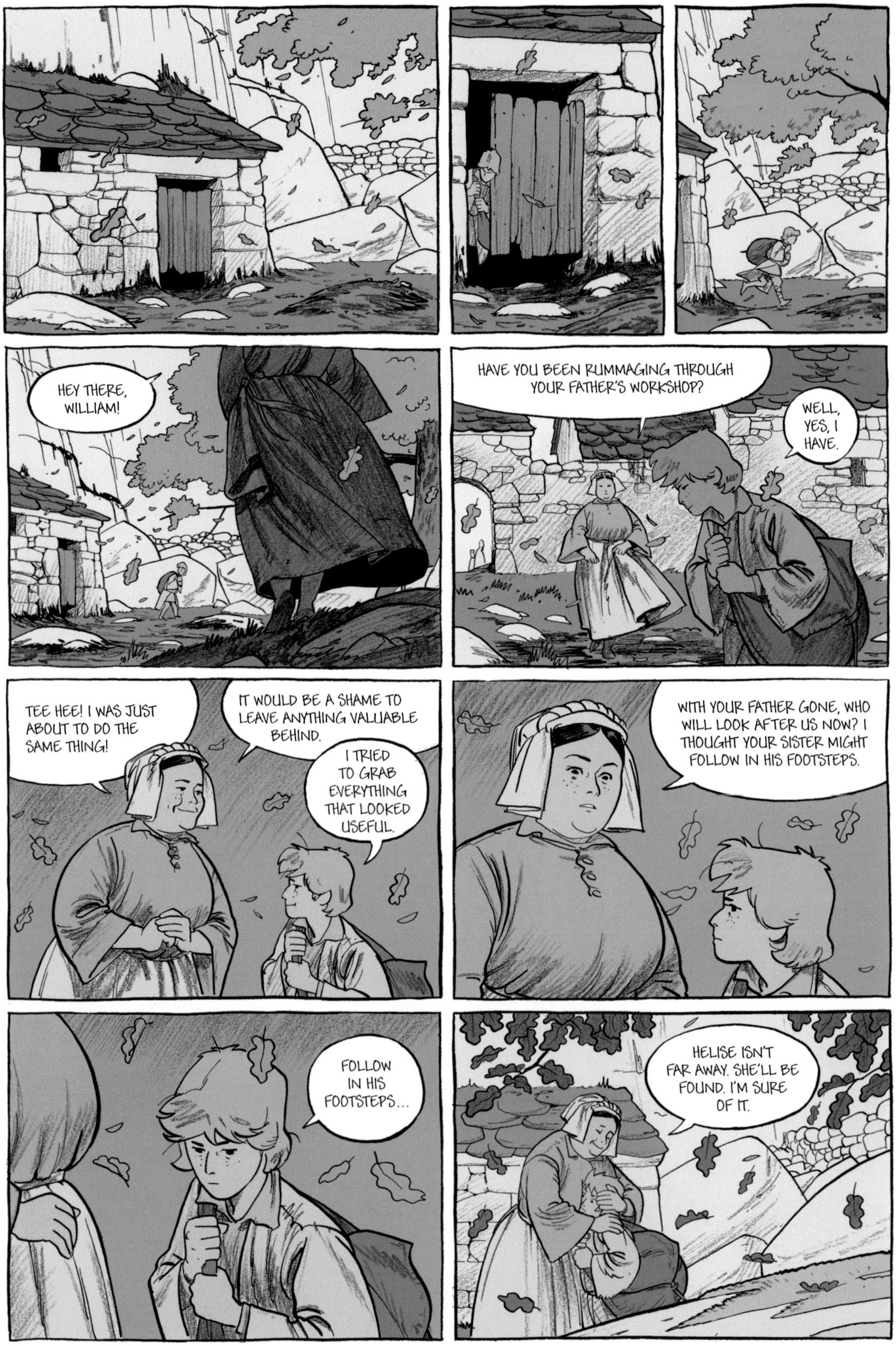
HEY THERE, WILLIAM!
HAVE YOU BEEN RUMMAGING THROUGH YOUR FATHER'S WORKSHOP?
WELL, YES, I HAVE.
TEE HEE! I WAS JUST ABOUT TO DO THE SAME THING!
IT WOULD BE A SHAME TO LEAVE ANYTHING VALUABLE BEHIND.
I TRIED TO GRAB EVERYTHING THAT LOOKED USEFUL.
WITH YOUR FATHER GONE, WHO WILL LOOK AFTER US NOW? I THOUGHT YOUR SISTER MIGHT FOLLOW IN HIS FOOTSTEPS.
FOLLOW IN HIS FOOTSTEPS...
HELISE ISN'T FAR AWAY. SHE'LL BE FOUND. I'M SURE OF IT.

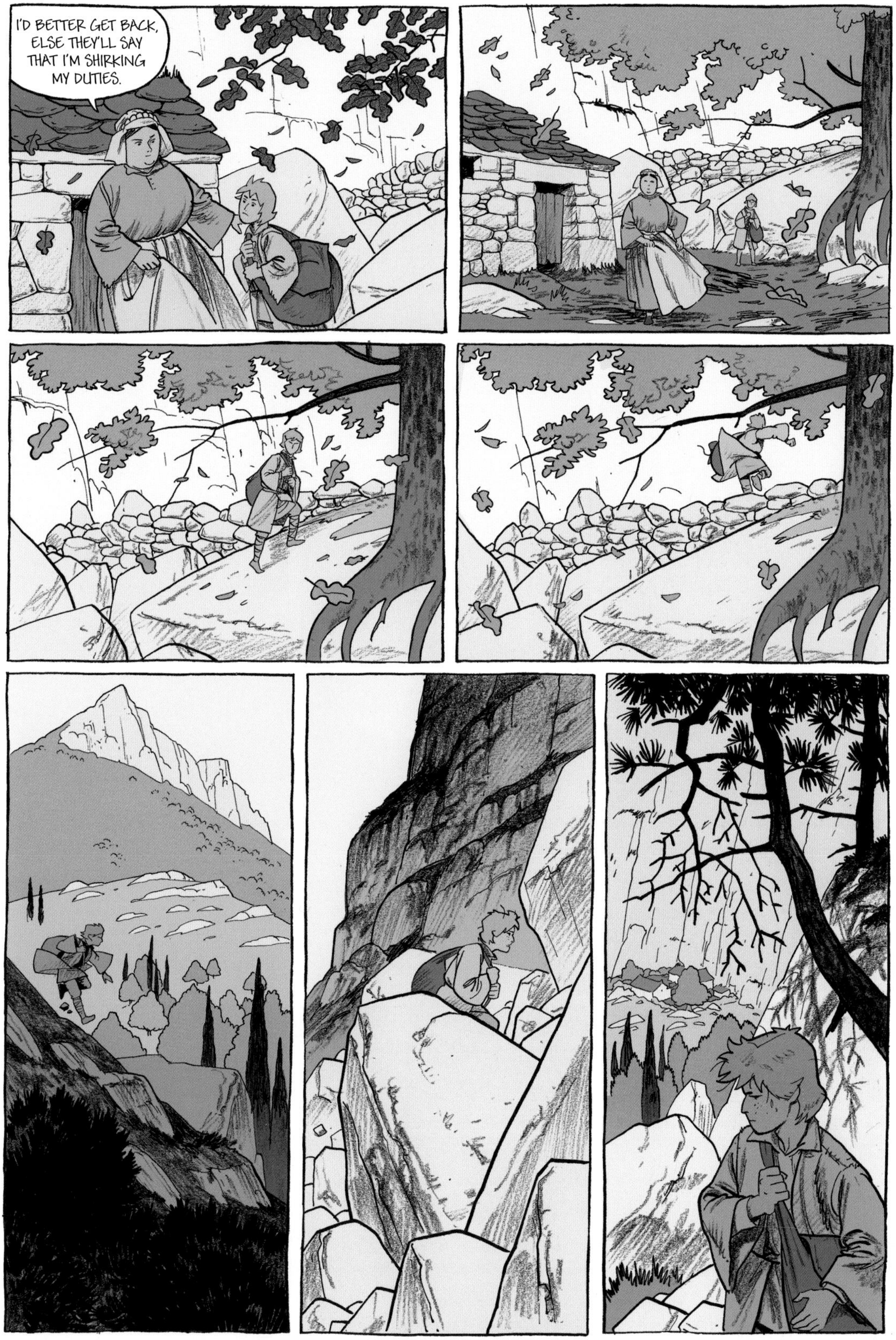
I'D BETTER GET BACK, ELSE THEY'LL SAY THAT I'M SHIRKING MY DUTIES.

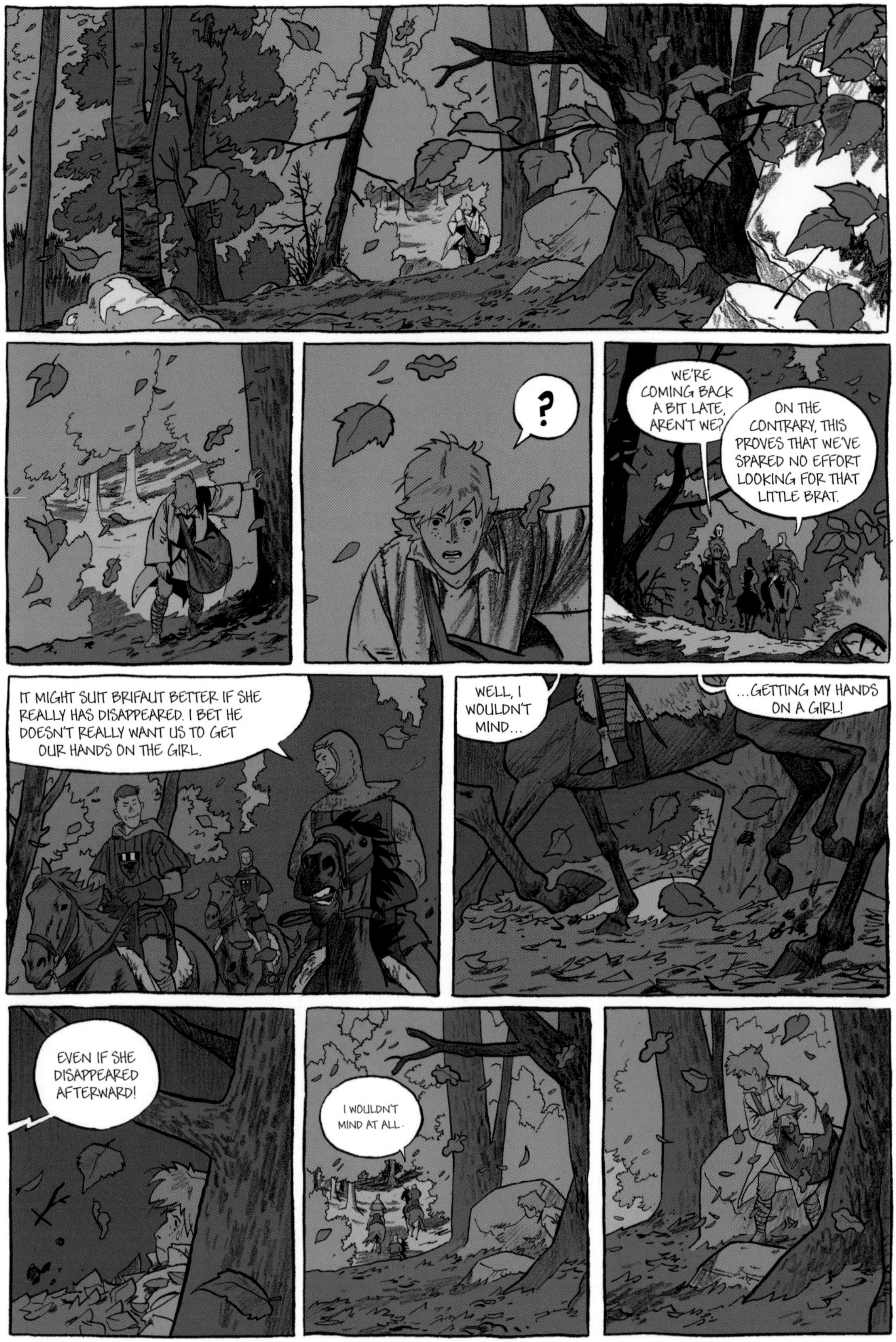
?
WE'RE COMING BACK A BIT LATE, AREN'T WE?
ON THE CONTRARY, THIS PROVES THAT WE'VE SPARED NO EFFORT LOOKING FOR THAT LITTLE BRAT.
IT MIGHT SUIT BRIFAUT BETTER IF SHE REALLY HAS DISAPPEARED. I BET HE DOESN'T REALLY WANT US TO GET OUR HANDS ON THE GIRL.
WELL, I WOULDN'T MIND...
...GETTING MY HANDS ON A GIRL!
EVEN IF SHE DISAPPEARED AFTERWARD!
I WOULDN'T MIND AT ALL.

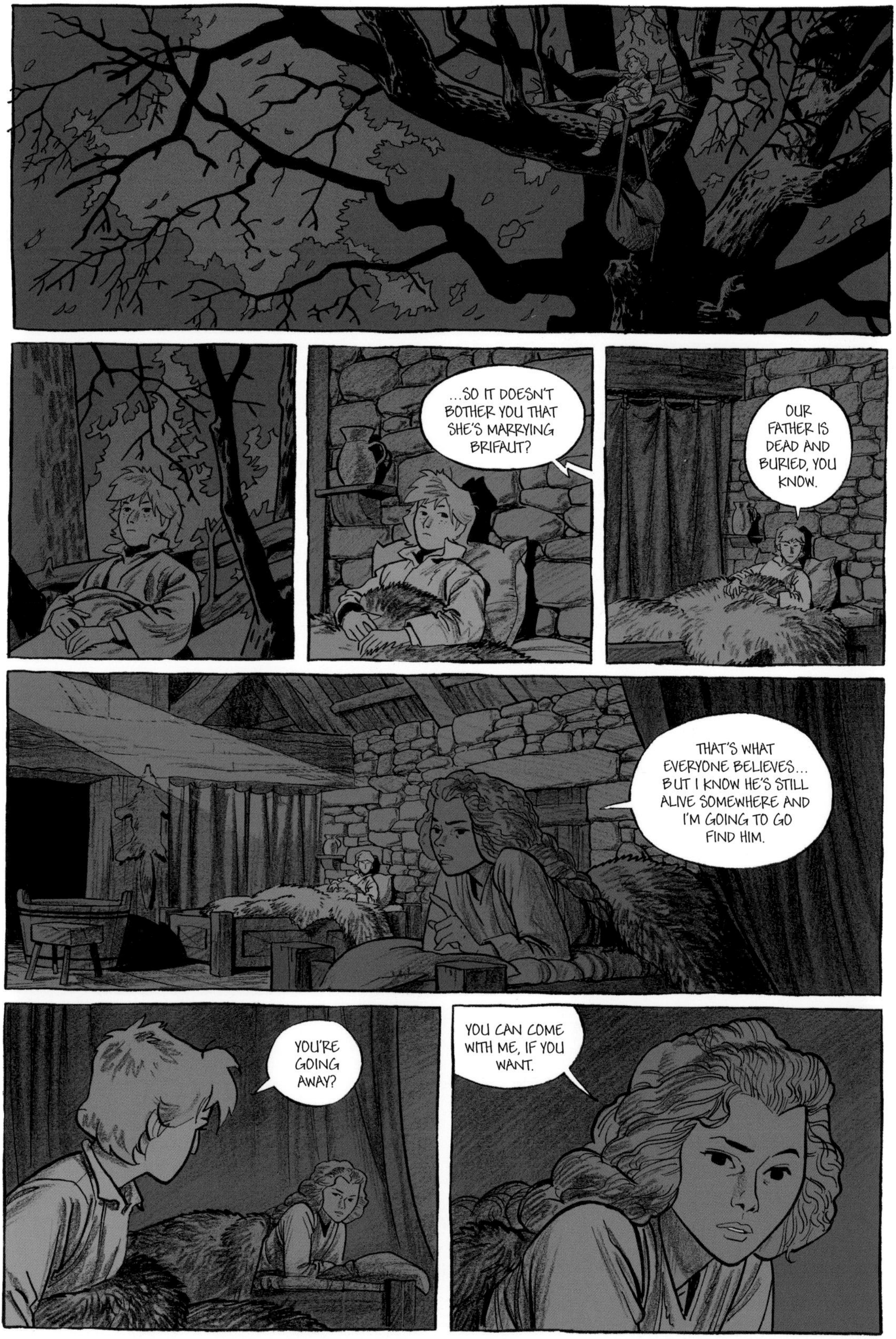
…SO IT DOESN'T BOTHER YOU THAT SHE'S MARRYING BRIFAUT?
OUR FATHER IS DEAD AND BURIED, YOU KNOW.
THAT'S WHAT EVERYONE BELIEVES… BUT I KNOW HE'S STILL ALIVE SOMEWHERE AND I'M GOING TO GO FIND HIM.
YOU'RE GOING AWAY?
YOU CAN COME WITH ME, IF YOU WANT.

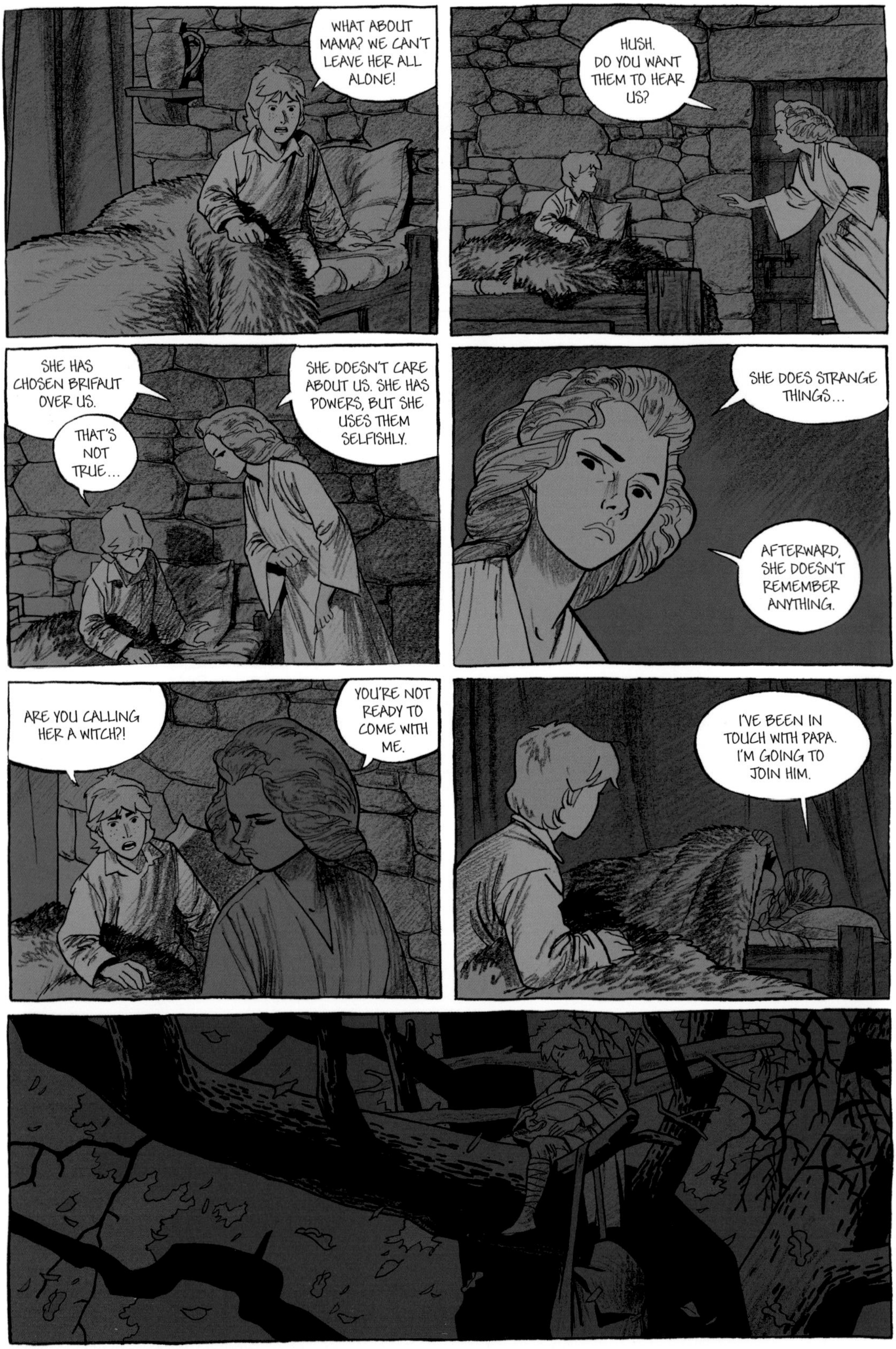
WHAT ABOUT MAMA? WE CAN'T LEAVE HER ALL ALONE!
HUSH. DO YOU WANT THEM TO HEAR US?
SHE HAS CHOSEN BRIFAUT OVER US.
THAT'S NOT TRUE…
SHE DOESN'T CARE ABOUT US. SHE HAS POWERS, BUT SHE USES THEM SELFISHLY.
SHE DOES STRANGE THINGS…
AFTERWARD, SHE DOESN'T REMEMBER ANYTHING.
ARE YOU CALLING HER A WITCH?!
YOU'RE NOT READY TO COME WITH ME.
I'VE BEEN IN TOUCH WITH PAPA. I'M GOING TO JOIN HIM.

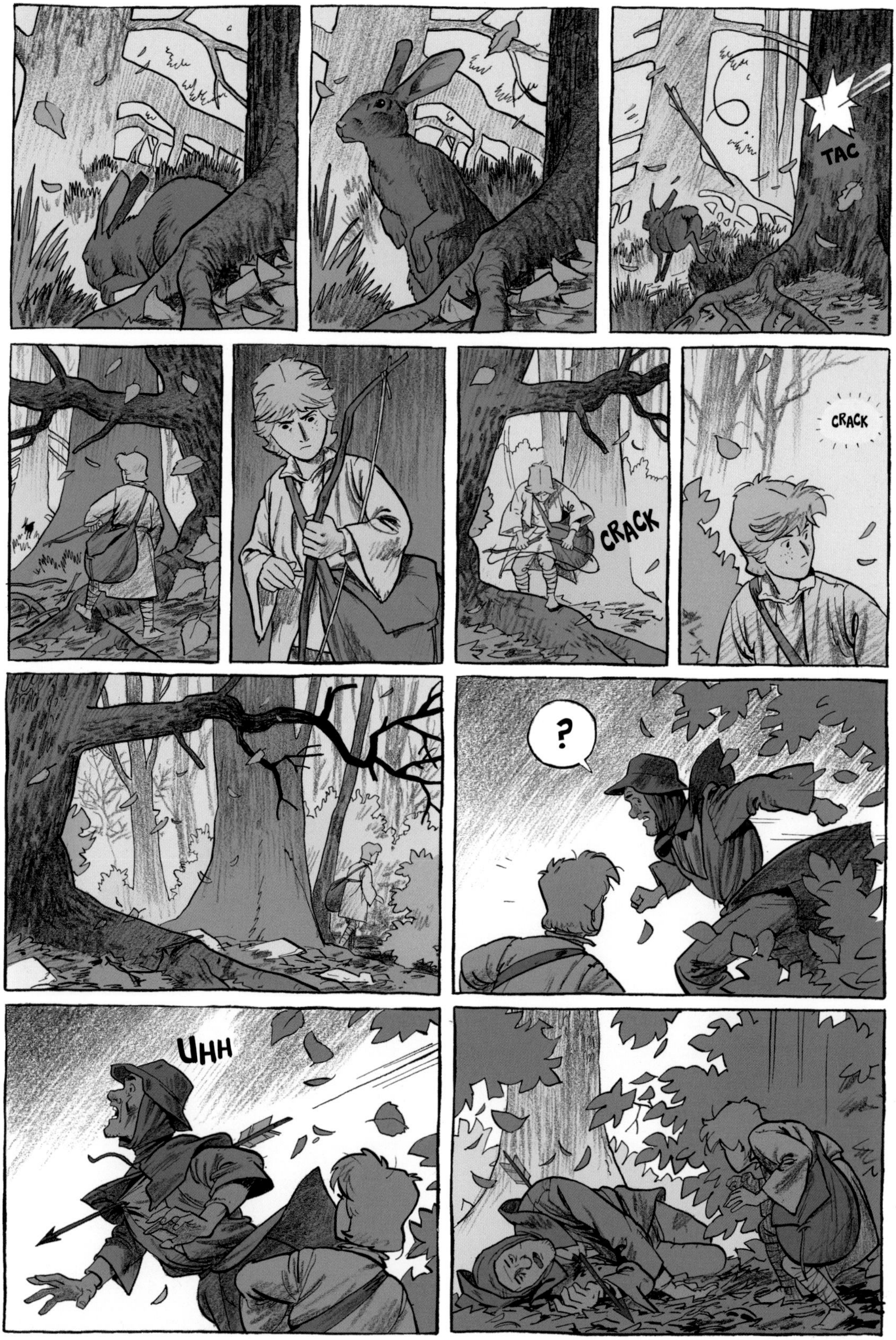
TAC
CRACK
CRACK
?
UHH

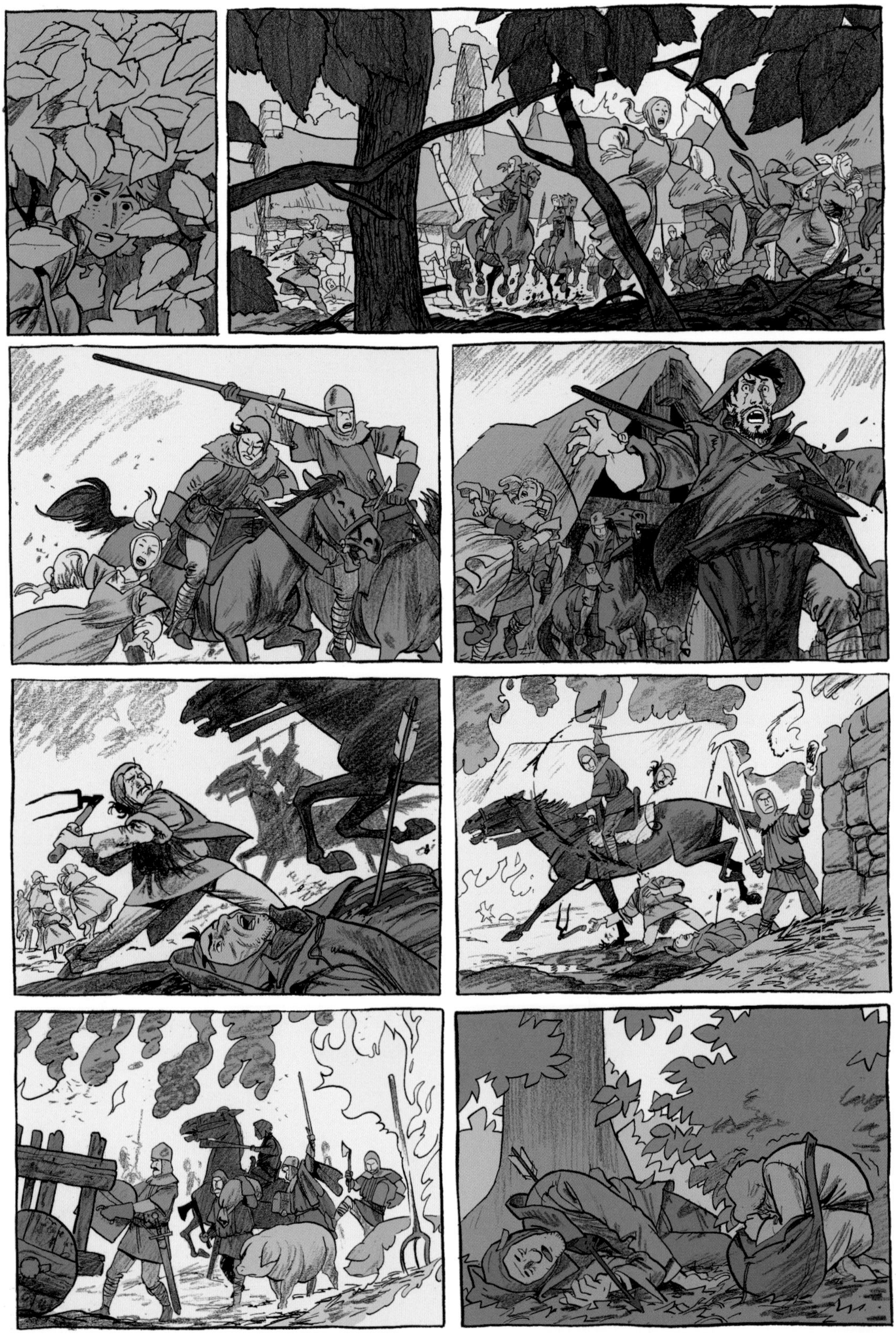

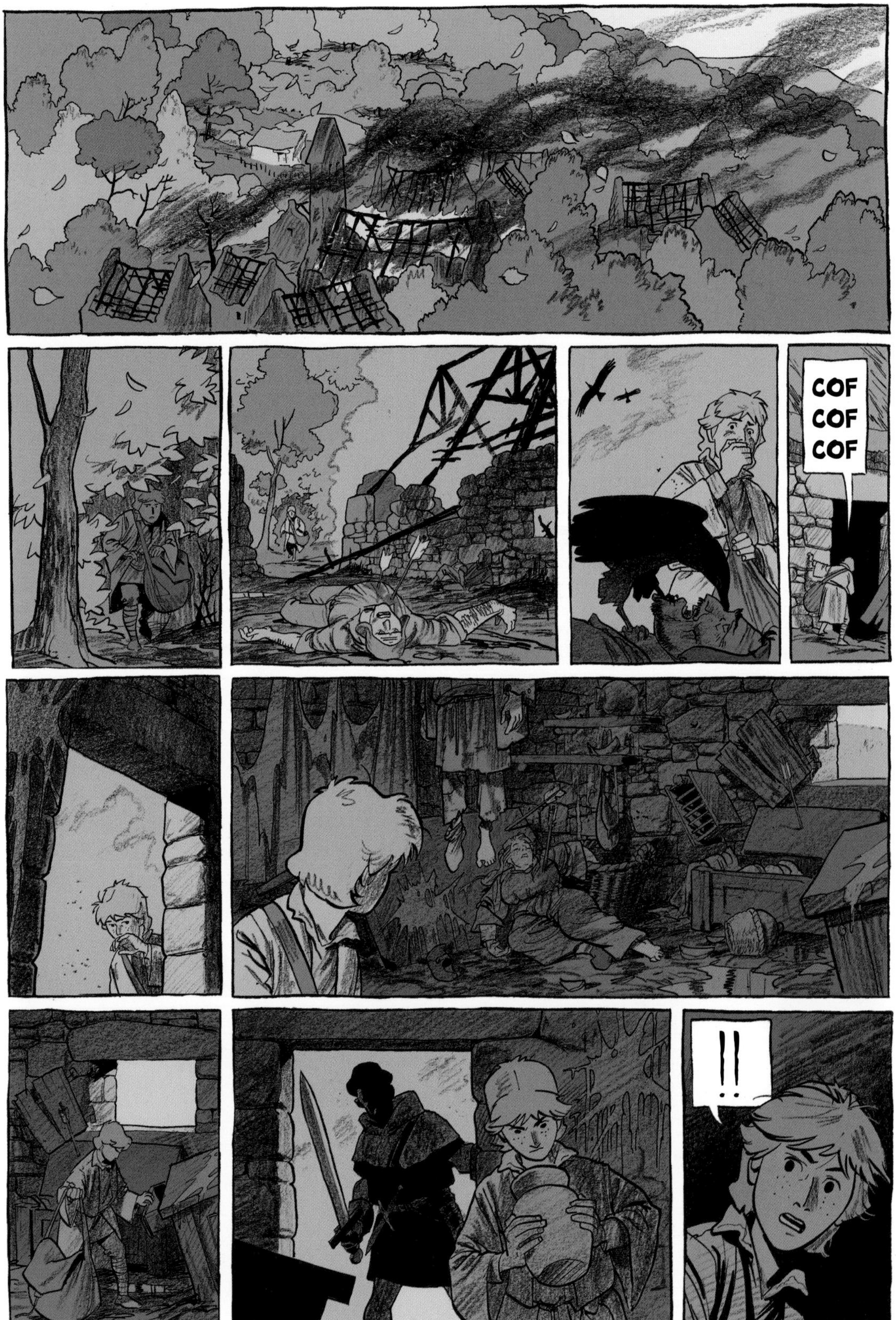
COF
COF
COF
!!

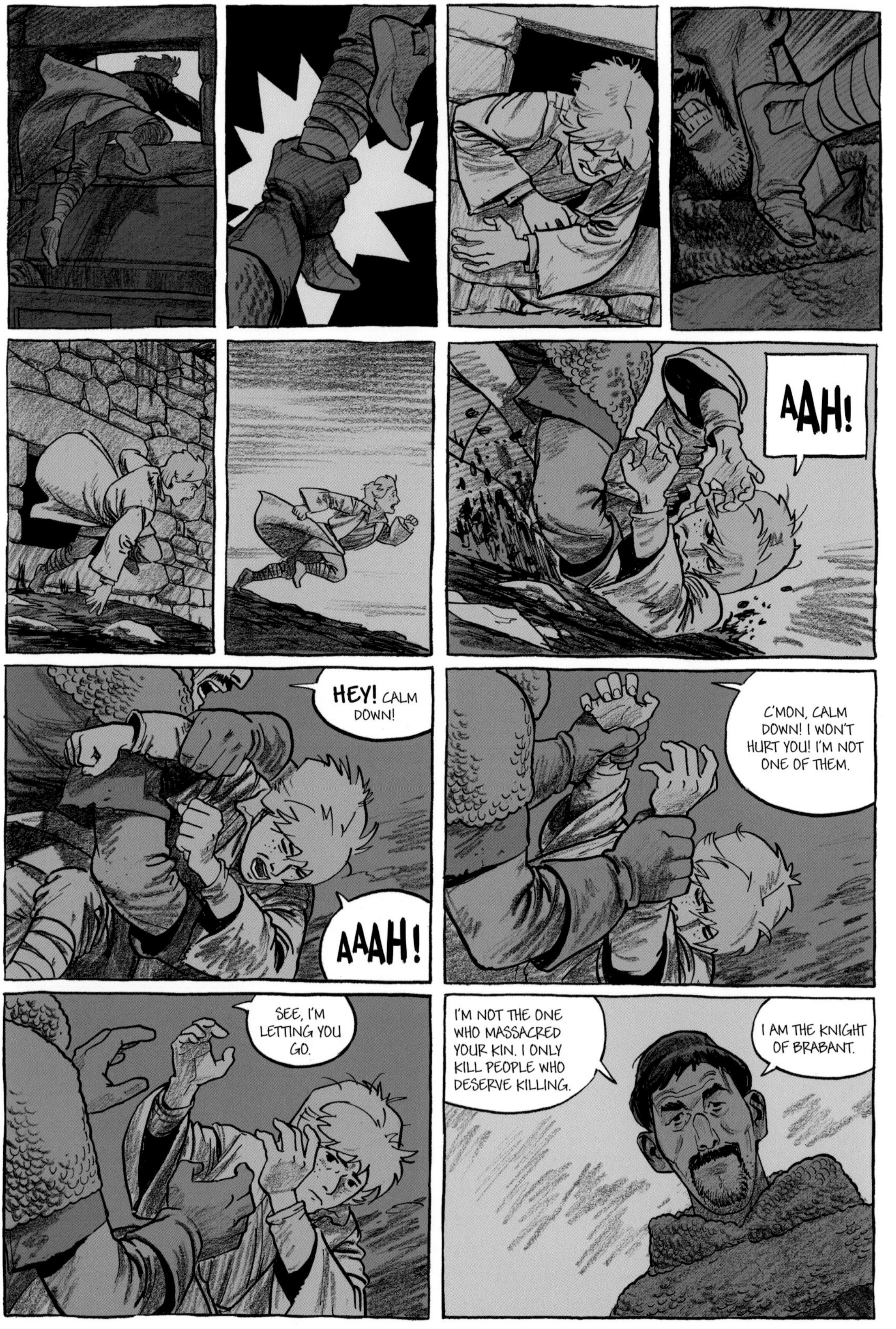
AAH!
HEY! CALM DOWN!
AAAH!
C'MON, CALM DOWN! I WON'T HURT YOU! I'M NOT ONE OF THEM.
SEE, I'M LETTING YOU GO.
I'M NOT THE ONE WHO MASSACRED YOUR KIN. I ONLY KILL PEOPLE WHO DESERVE KILLING.
I AM THE KNIGHT OF BRABANT.

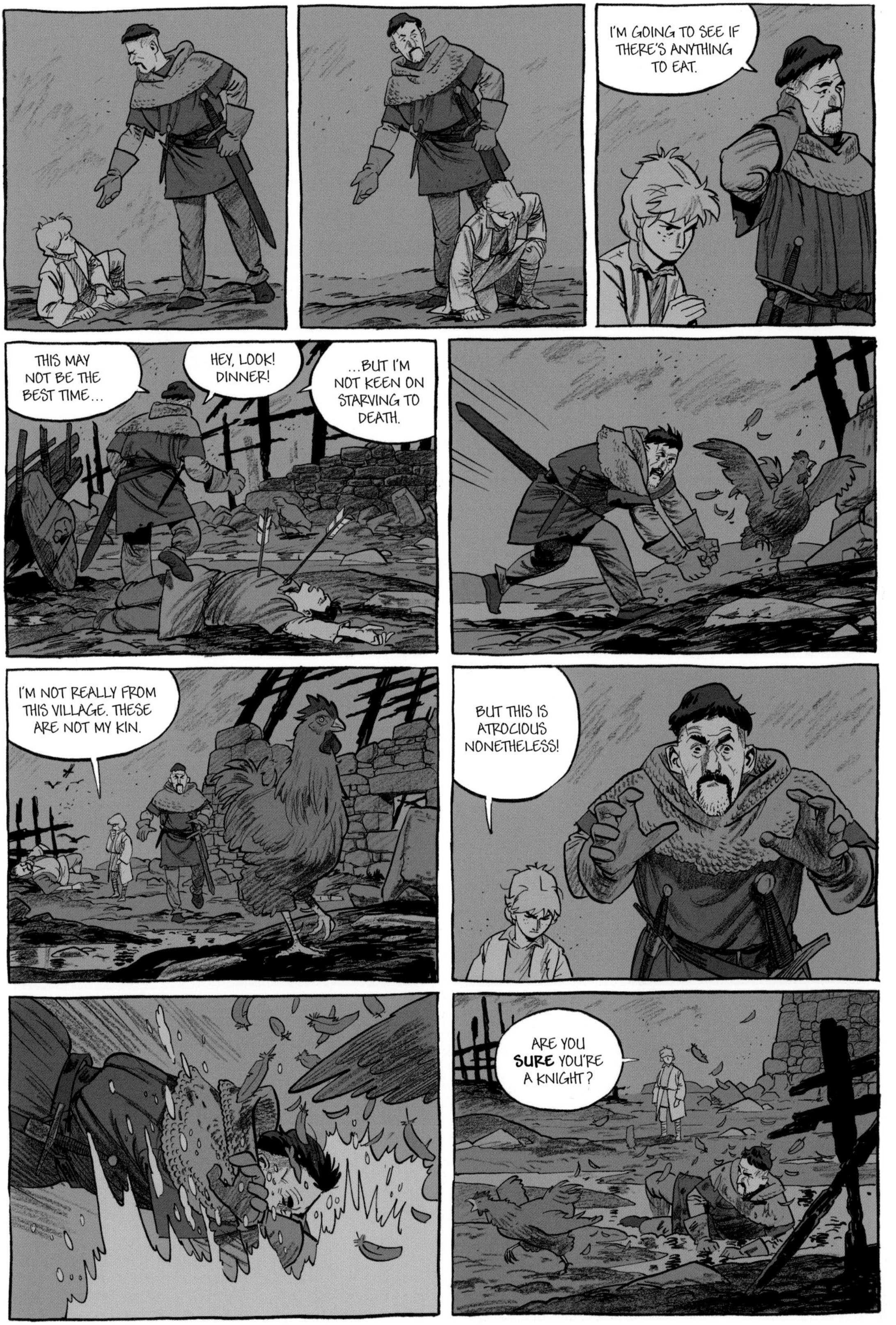
I'M GOING TO SEE IF THERE'S ANYTHING TO EAT.
THIS MAY NOT BE THE BEST TIME…
HEY, LOOK! DINNER!
…BUT I'M NOT KEEN ON STARVING TO DEATH.
I'M NOT REALLY FROM THIS VILLAGE. THESE ARE NOT MY KIN.
BUT THIS IS ATROCIOUS NONETHELESS!
ARE YOU **SURE** YOU'RE A KNIGHT?

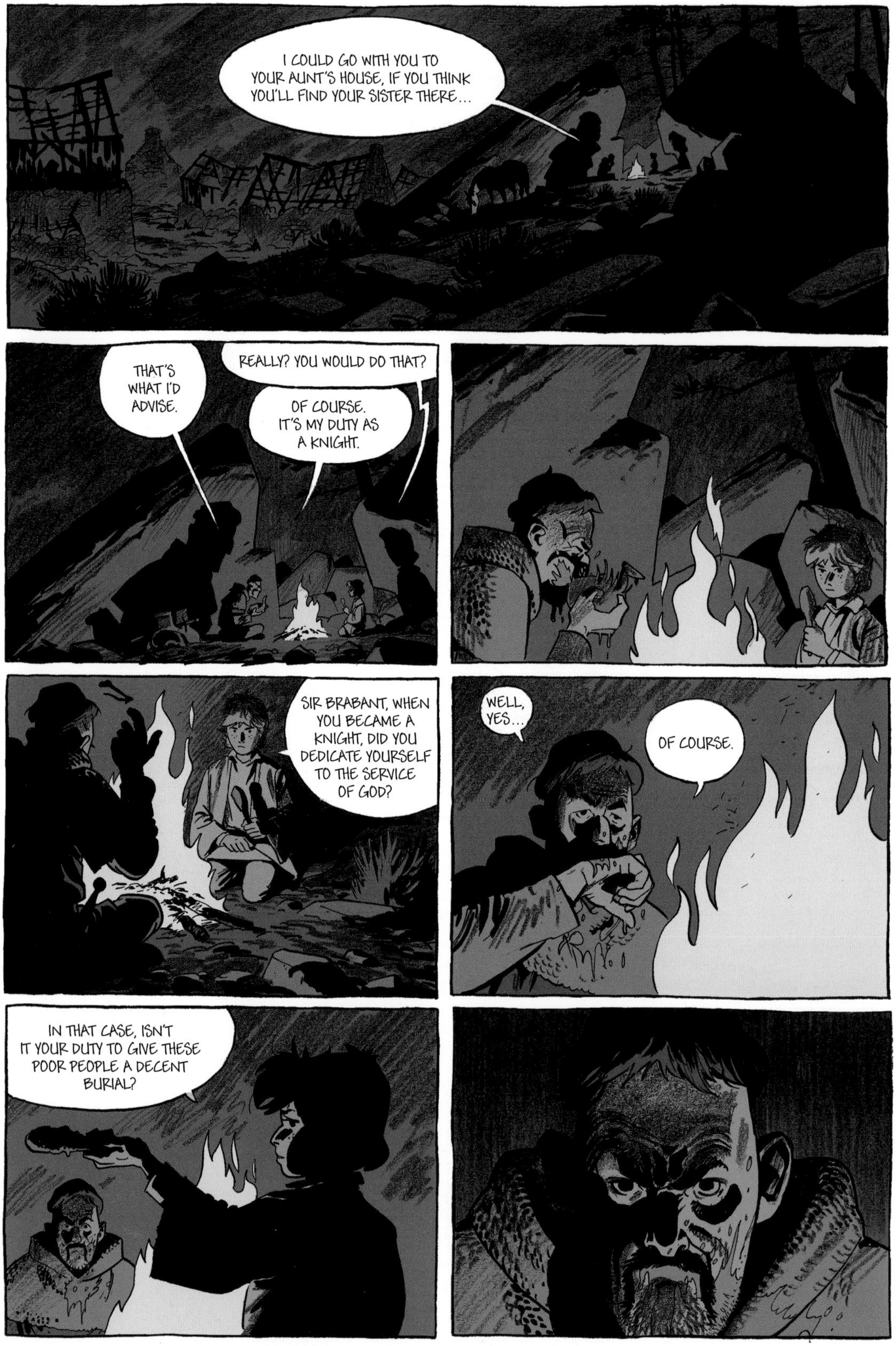
I COULD GO WITH YOU TO YOUR AUNT'S HOUSE, IF YOU THINK YOU'LL FIND YOUR SISTER THERE...
THAT'S WHAT I'D ADVISE.
REALLY? YOU WOULD DO THAT?
OF COURSE. IT'S MY DUTY AS A KNIGHT.
SIR BRABANT, WHEN YOU BECAME A KNIGHT, DID YOU DEDICATE YOURSELF TO THE SERVICE OF GOD?
WELL, YES...
OF COURSE.
IN THAT CASE, ISN'T IT YOUR DUTY TO GIVE THESE POOR PEOPLE A DECENT BURIAL?

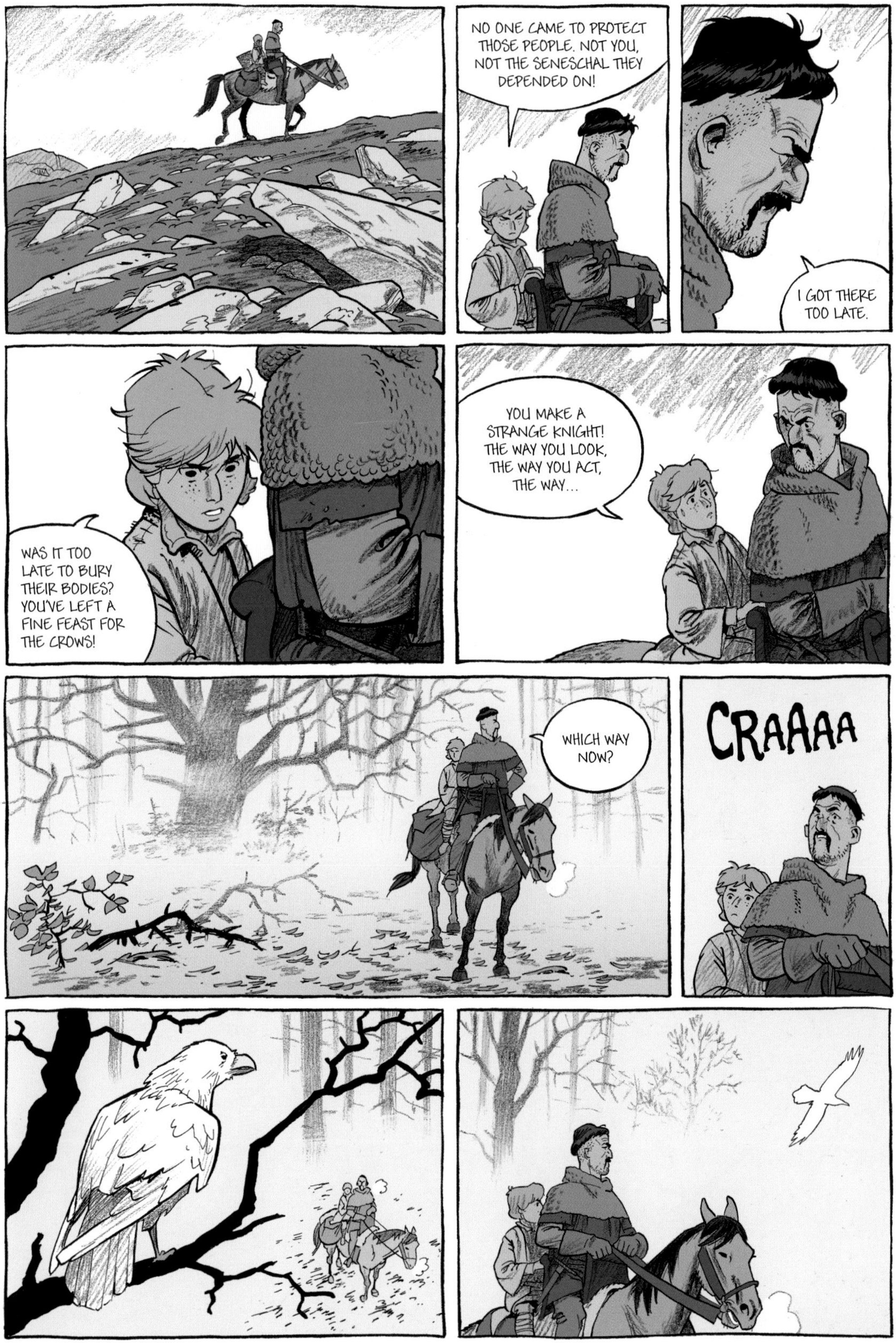
NO ONE CAME TO PROTECT THOSE PEOPLE. NOT YOU, NOT THE SENESCHAL THEY DEPENDED ON!
I GOT THERE TOO LATE.
WAS IT TOO LATE TO BURY THEIR BODIES? YOU'VE LEFT A FINE FEAST FOR THE CROWS!
YOU MAKE A STRANGE KNIGHT! THE WAY YOU LOOK, THE WAY YOU ACT, THE WAY...
WHICH WAY NOW?
CRAAAA

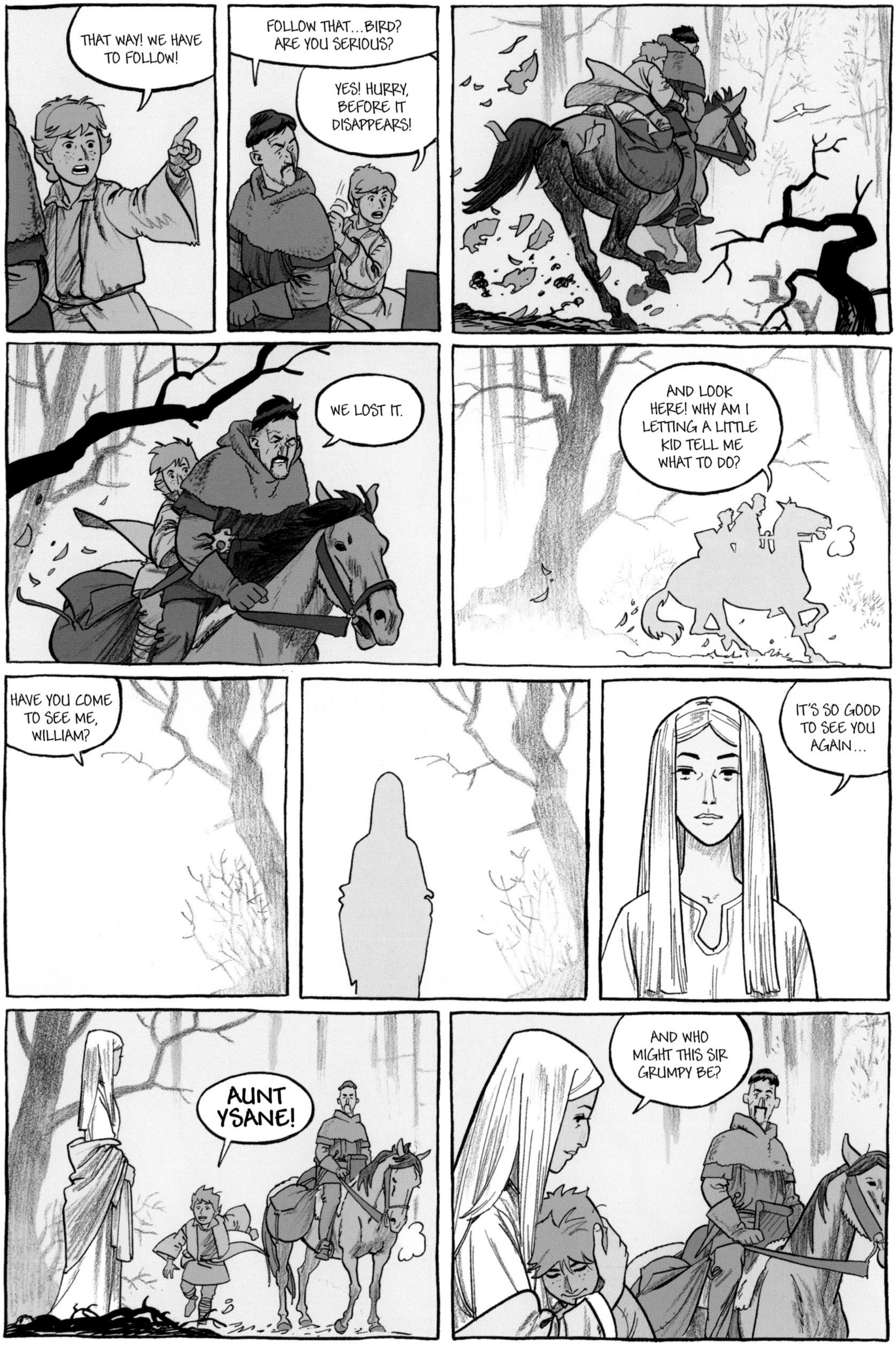

THAT WAY! WE HAVE TO FOLLOW!
FOLLOW THAT...BIRD? ARE YOU SERIOUS?
YES! HURRY, BEFORE IT DISAPPEARS!
WE LOST IT.
AND LOOK HERE! WHY AM I LETTING A LITTLE KID TELL ME WHAT TO DO?
HAVE YOU COME TO SEE ME, WILLIAM?
IT'S SO GOOD TO SEE YOU AGAIN...
AUNT YSANE!
AND WHO MIGHT THIS SIR GRUMPY BE?

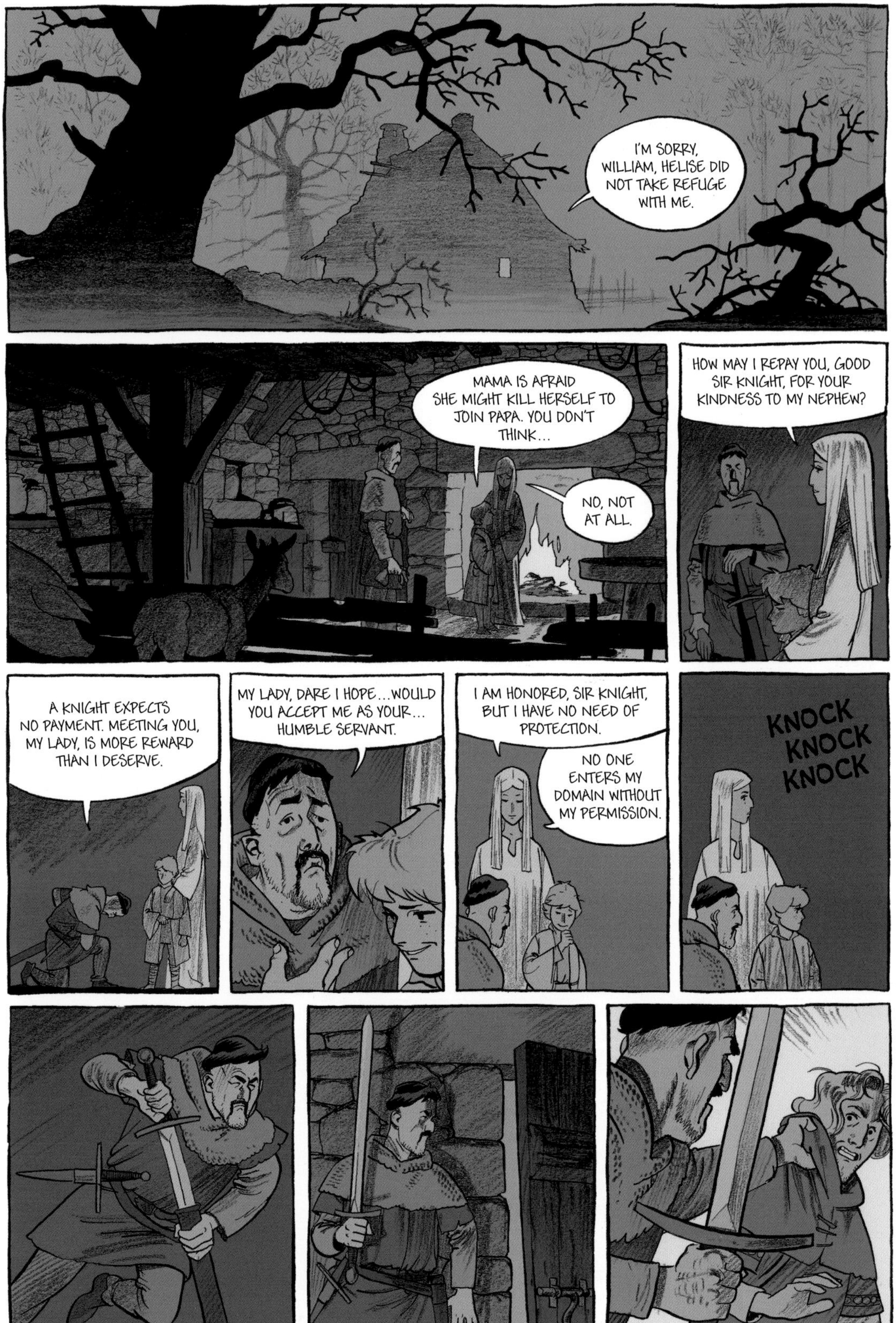
I'M SORRY, WILLIAM, HELISE DID NOT TAKE REFUGE WITH ME.
MAMA IS AFRAID SHE MIGHT KILL HERSELF TO JOIN PAPA. YOU DON'T THINK…
NO, NOT AT ALL.
HOW MAY I REPAY YOU, GOOD SIR KNIGHT, FOR YOUR KINDNESS TO MY NEPHEW?
A KNIGHT EXPECTS NO PAYMENT. MEETING YOU, MY LADY, IS MORE REWARD THAN I DESERVE.
MY LADY, DARE I HOPE…WOULD YOU ACCEPT ME AS YOUR… HUMBLE SERVANT.
I AM HONORED, SIR KNIGHT, BUT I HAVE NO NEED OF PROTECTION.
NO ONE ENTERS MY DOMAIN WITHOUT MY PERMISSION.
KNOCK KNOCK KNOCK

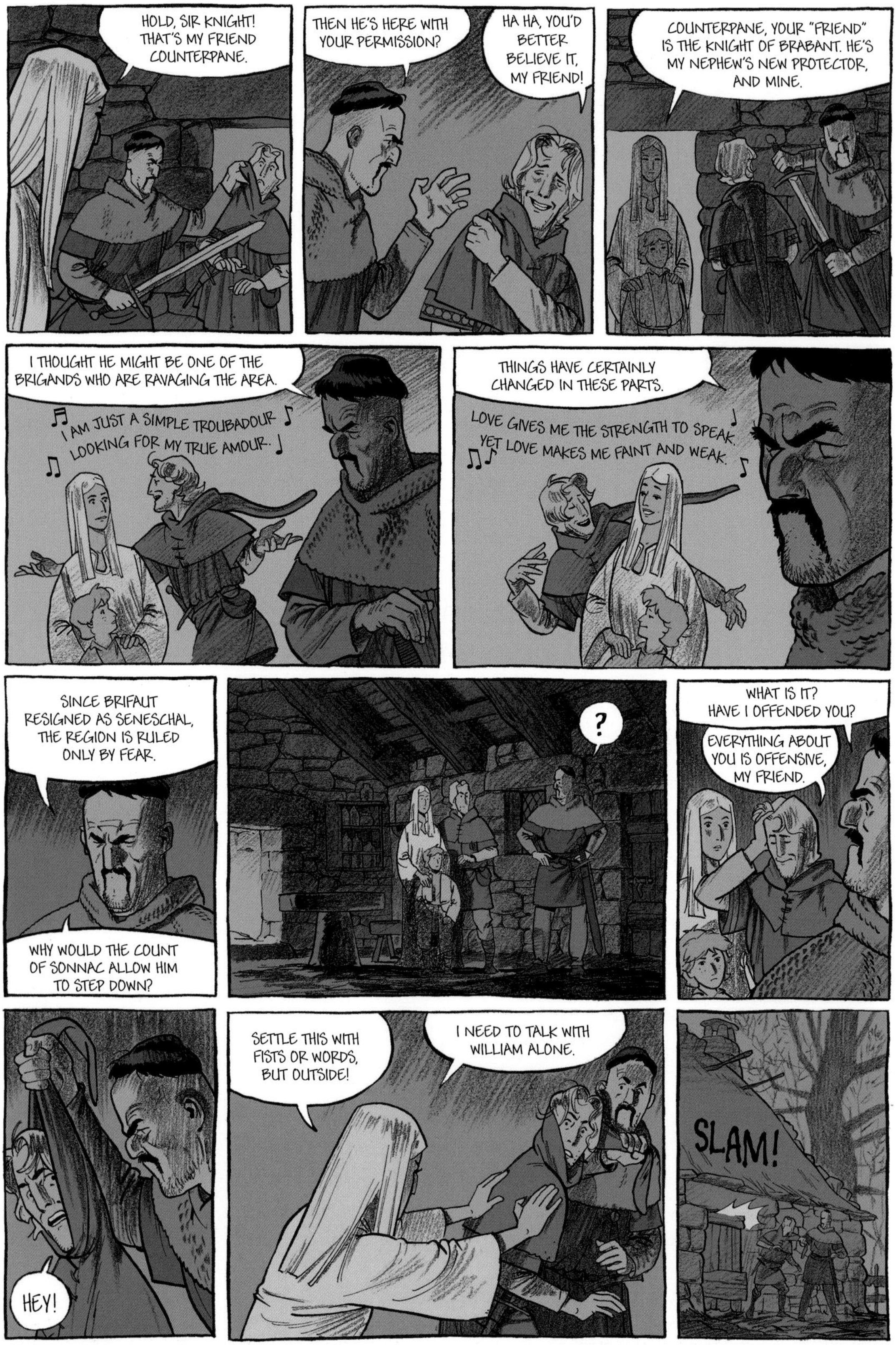
HOLD, SIR KNIGHT! THAT'S MY FRIEND COUNTERPANE.
THEN HE'S HERE WITH YOUR PERMISSION?
HA HA, YOU'D BETTER BELIEVE IT, MY FRIEND!
COUNTERPANE, YOUR "FRIEND" IS THE KNIGHT OF BRABANT. HE'S MY NEPHEW'S NEW PROTECTOR, AND MINE.
I THOUGHT HE MIGHT BE ONE OF THE BRIGANDS WHO ARE RAVAGING THE AREA.
I AM JUST A SIMPLE TROUBADOUR LOOKING FOR MY TRUE AMOUR.
THINGS HAVE CERTAINLY CHANGED IN THESE PARTS.
LOVE GIVES ME THE STRENGTH TO SPEAK, YET LOVE MAKES ME FAINT AND WEAK.
SINCE BRIFAUT RESIGNED AS SENESCHAL, THE REGION IS RULED ONLY BY FEAR.
WHY WOULD THE COUNT OF SONNAC ALLOW HIM TO STEP DOWN?
?
WHAT IS IT? HAVE I OFFENDED YOU?
EVERYTHING ABOUT YOU IS OFFENSIVE, MY FRIEND.
HEY!
SETTLE THIS WITH FISTS OR WORDS, BUT OUTSIDE!
I NEED TO TALK WITH WILLIAM ALONE.
SLAM!

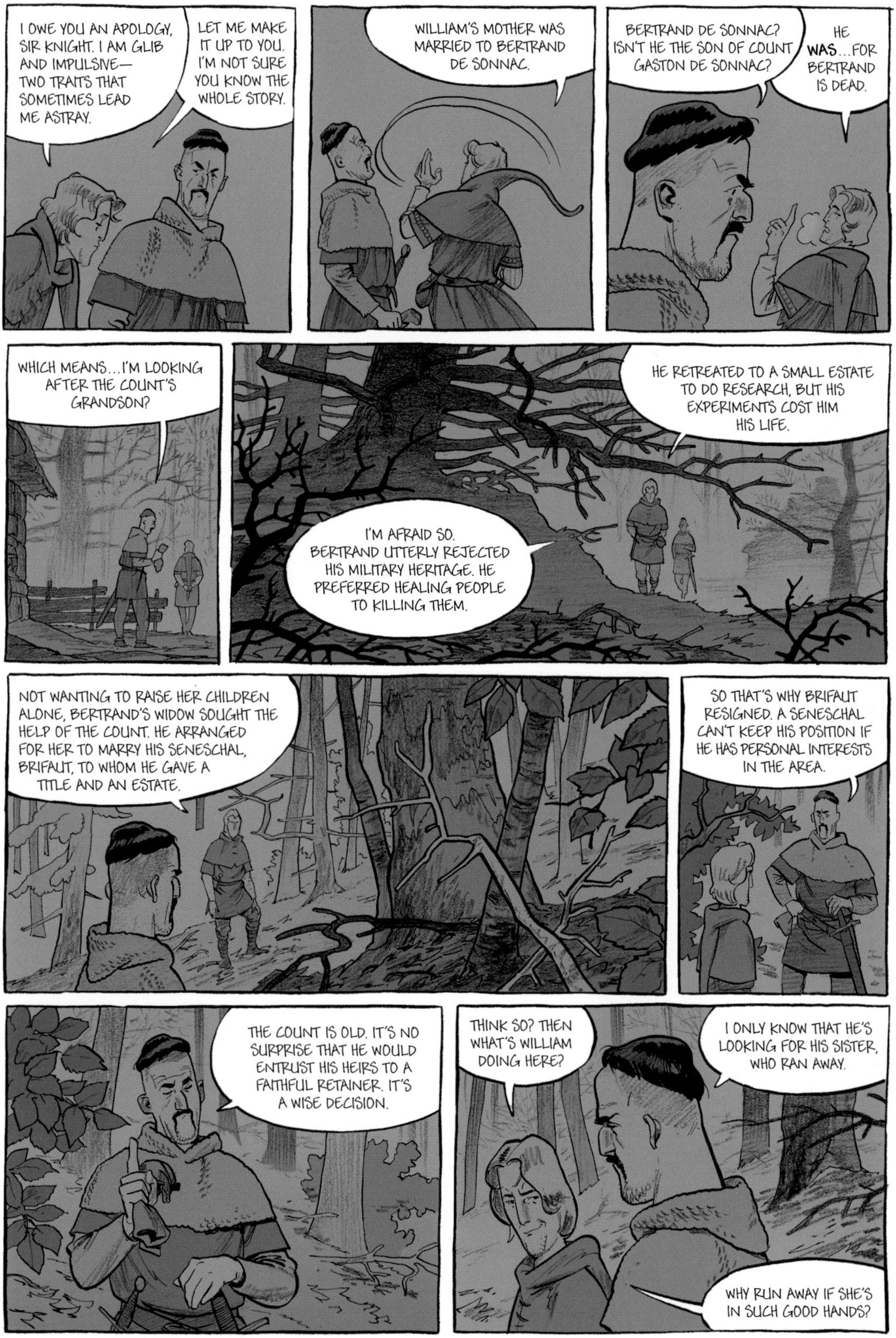
I OWE YOU AN APOLOGY, SIR KNIGHT. I AM GLIB AND IMPULSIVE— TWO TRAITS THAT SOMETIMES LEAD ME ASTRAY.
LET ME MAKE IT UP TO YOU. I'M NOT SURE YOU KNOW THE WHOLE STORY.
WILLIAM'S MOTHER WAS MARRIED TO BERTRAND DE SONNAC.
BERTRAND DE SONNAC? ISN'T HE THE SON OF COUNT GASTON DE SONNAC?
HE **WAS**...FOR BERTRAND IS DEAD.
WHICH MEANS...I'M LOOKING AFTER THE COUNT'S GRANDSON?
I'M AFRAID SO. BERTRAND UTTERLY REJECTED HIS MILITARY HERITAGE. HE PREFERRED HEALING PEOPLE TO KILLING THEM.
HE RETREATED TO A SMALL ESTATE TO DO RESEARCH, BUT HIS EXPERIMENTS COST HIM HIS LIFE.
NOT WANTING TO RAISE HER CHILDREN ALONE, BERTRAND'S WIDOW SOUGHT THE HELP OF THE COUNT. HE ARRANGED FOR HER TO MARRY HIS SENESCHAL, BRIFAUT, TO WHOM HE GAVE A TITLE AND AN ESTATE.
SO THAT'S WHY BRIFAUT RESIGNED. A SENESCHAL CAN'T KEEP HIS POSITION IF HE HAS PERSONAL INTERESTS IN THE AREA.
THE COUNT IS OLD. IT'S NO SURPRISE THAT HE WOULD ENTRUST HIS HEIRS TO A FAITHFUL RETAINER. IT'S A WISE DECISION.
THINK SO? THEN WHAT'S WILLIAM DOING HERE?
I ONLY KNOW THAT HE'S LOOKING FOR HIS SISTER, WHO RAN AWAY.
WHY RUN AWAY IF SHE'S IN SUCH GOOD HANDS?

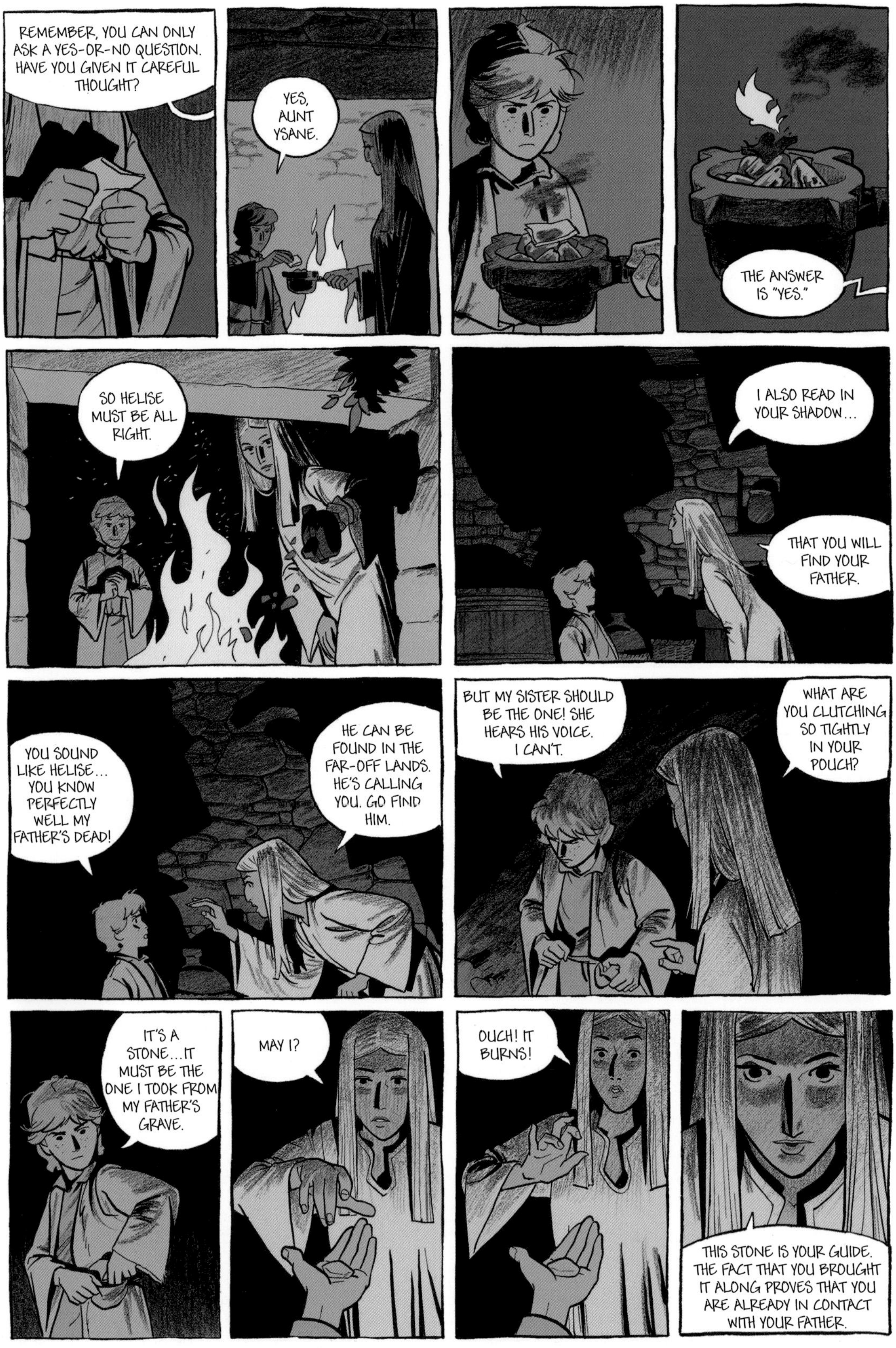
REMEMBER, YOU CAN ONLY ASK A YES-OR-NO QUESTION. HAVE YOU GIVEN IT CAREFUL THOUGHT?
YES, AUNT YSANE.
THE ANSWER IS "YES."
SO HELISE MUST BE ALL RIGHT.
I ALSO READ IN YOUR SHADOW...
THAT YOU WILL FIND YOUR FATHER.
YOU SOUND LIKE HELISE... YOU KNOW PERFECTLY WELL MY FATHER'S DEAD!
HE CAN BE FOUND IN THE FAR-OFF LANDS. HE'S CALLING YOU. GO FIND HIM.
BUT MY SISTER SHOULD BE THE ONE! SHE HEARS HIS VOICE. I CAN'T.
WHAT ARE YOU CLUTCHING SO TIGHTLY IN YOUR POUCH?
IT'S A STONE... IT MUST BE THE ONE I TOOK FROM MY FATHER'S GRAVE.
MAY I?
OUCH! IT BURNS!
THIS STONE IS YOUR GUIDE. THE FACT THAT YOU BROUGHT IT ALONG PROVES THAT YOU ARE ALREADY IN CONTACT WITH YOUR FATHER.

YOU'VE GOT QUITE A MIX OF THINGS HERE. SOME USEFUL, SOME NOT. SOME OF IT'S GONE BAD.

HOW DID YOU CHOOSE WHAT TO TAKE?

I JUST TOOK WHATEVER I COULD.

DID YOUR FATHER SHARE ANY OF HIS SECRETS WITH YOU?

NONE.

LET ME HELP YOU LIGHTEN YOUR BAG. IT'S USELESS TO CARRY ALL THIS WITH YOU.

WHAT A FRIENDLY GOAT YOU HAVE! WHAT'S HER NAME?

SHE'S NOT MY GOAT. SHE JUST SHOWED UP YESTERDAY. YOU CAN GIVE HER ANY NAME YOU LIKE.

SKRITCH SKRITCH

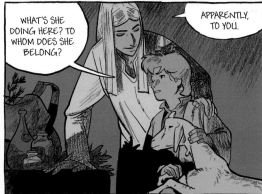

WHAT'S SHE DOING HERE? TO WHOM DOES SHE BELONG?

APPARENTLY, TO YOU.

TAP TAP TAP

IT'S FREEZING OUT HERE!

CAN WE COME IN NOW?

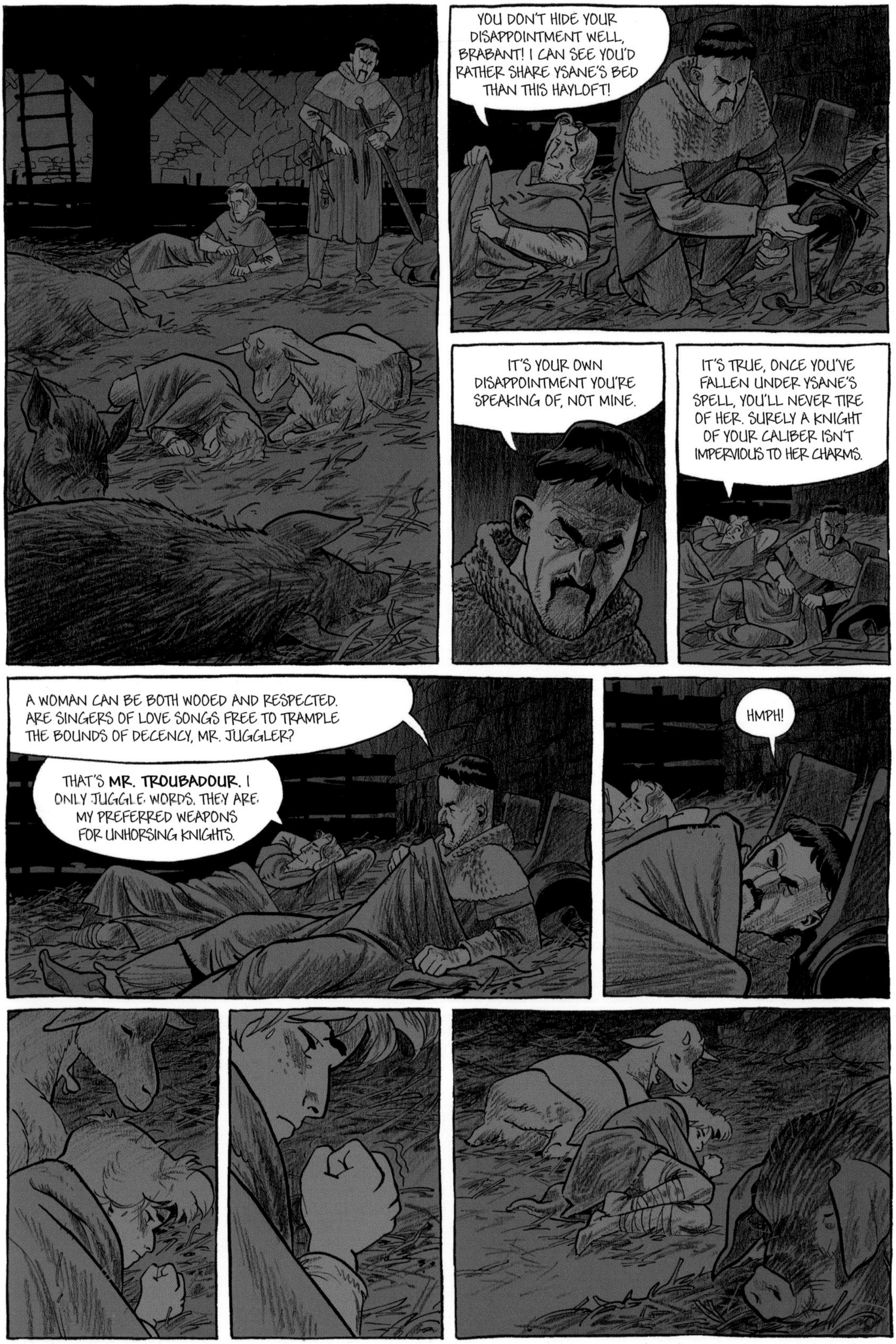
YOU DON'T HIDE YOUR DISAPPOINTMENT WELL, BRABANT! I CAN SEE YOU'D RATHER SHARE YSANE'S BED THAN THIS HAYLOFT!
IT'S YOUR OWN DISAPPOINTMENT YOU'RE SPEAKING OF, NOT MINE.
IT'S TRUE, ONCE YOU'VE FALLEN UNDER YSANE'S SPELL, YOU'LL NEVER TIRE OF HER. SURELY A KNIGHT OF YOUR CALIBER ISN'T IMPERVIOUS TO HER CHARMS.
A WOMAN CAN BE BOTH WOOED AND RESPECTED. ARE SINGERS OF LOVE SONGS FREE TO TRAMPLE THE BOUNDS OF DECENCY, MR. JUGGLER?
THAT'S MR. TROUBADOUR. I ONLY JUGGLE WORDS. THEY ARE MY PREFERRED WEAPONS FOR UNHORSING KNIGHTS.
HMPH!

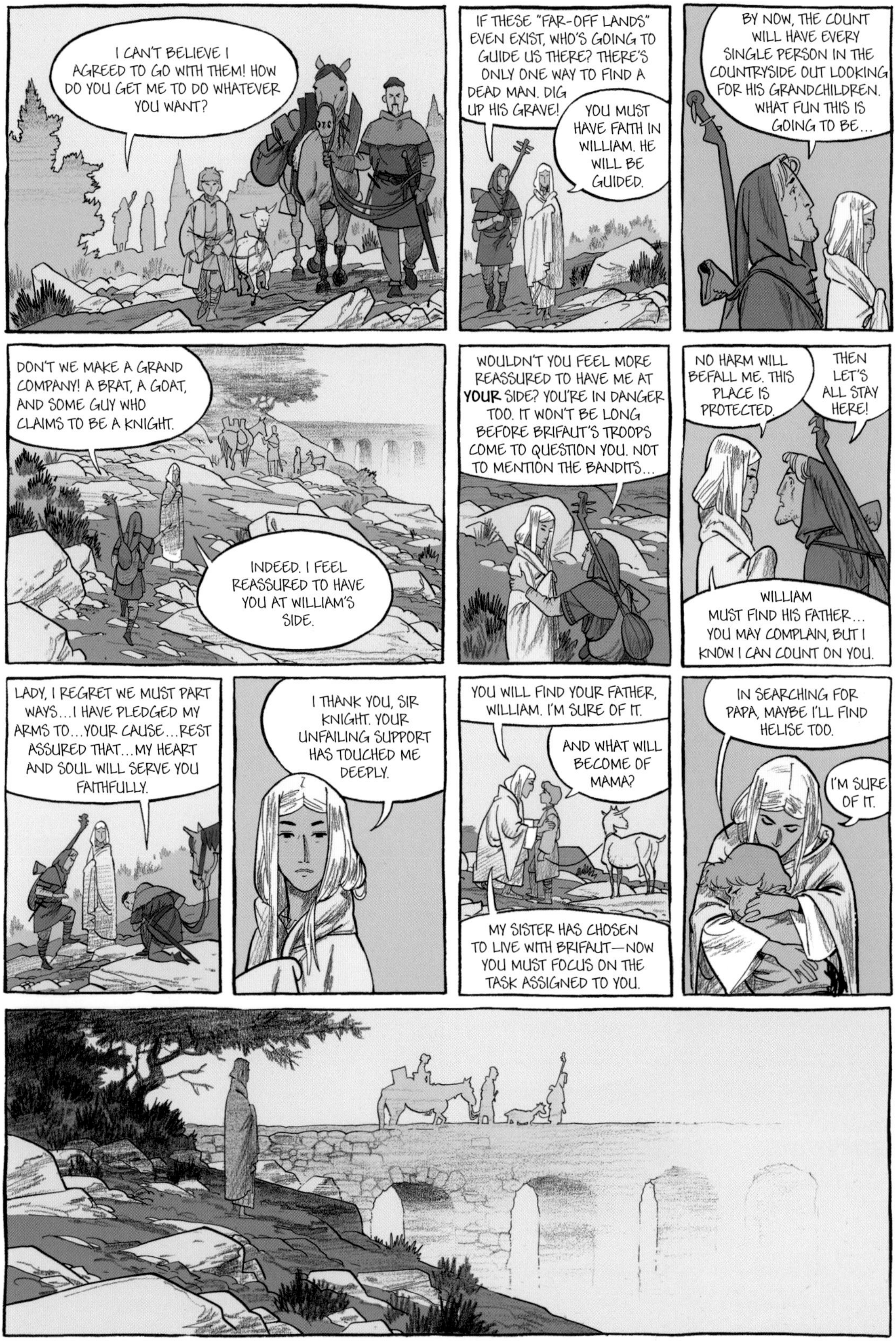

I CAN'T BELIEVE I AGREED TO GO WITH THEM! HOW DO YOU GET ME TO DO WHATEVER YOU WANT?
IF THESE "FAR-OFF LANDS" EVEN EXIST, WHO'S GOING TO GUIDE US THERE? THERE'S ONLY ONE WAY TO FIND A DEAD MAN. DIG UP HIS GRAVE!
YOU MUST HAVE FAITH IN WILLIAM. HE WILL BE GUIDED.
BY NOW, THE COUNT WILL HAVE EVERY SINGLE PERSON IN THE COUNTRYSIDE OUT LOOKING FOR HIS GRANDCHILDREN. WHAT FUN THIS IS GOING TO BE...
DON'T WE MAKE A GRAND COMPANY! A BRAT, A GOAT, AND SOME GUY WHO CLAIMS TO BE A KNIGHT.
INDEED. I FEEL REASSURED TO HAVE YOU AT WILLIAM'S SIDE.
WOULDN'T YOU FEEL MORE REASSURED TO HAVE ME AT **YOUR** SIDE? YOU'RE IN DANGER TOO. IT WON'T BE LONG BEFORE BRIFAUT'S TROOPS COME TO QUESTION YOU. NOT TO MENTION THE BANDITS...
NO HARM WILL BEFALL ME. THIS PLACE IS PROTECTED.
THEN LET'S ALL STAY HERE!
WILLIAM MUST FIND HIS FATHER... YOU MAY COMPLAIN, BUT I KNOW I CAN COUNT ON YOU.
LADY, I REGRET WE MUST PART WAYS... I HAVE PLEDGED MY ARMS TO... YOUR CAUSE... REST ASSURED THAT... MY HEART AND SOUL WILL SERVE YOU FAITHFULLY.
I THANK YOU, SIR KNIGHT. YOUR UNFAILING SUPPORT HAS TOUCHED ME DEEPLY.
YOU WILL FIND YOUR FATHER, WILLIAM. I'M SURE OF IT.
AND WHAT WILL BECOME OF MAMA?
MY SISTER HAS CHOSEN TO LIVE WITH BRIFAUT—NOW YOU MUST FOCUS ON THE TASK ASSIGNED TO YOU.
IN SEARCHING FOR PAPA, MAYBE I'LL FIND HELISE TOO.
I'M SURE OF IT.

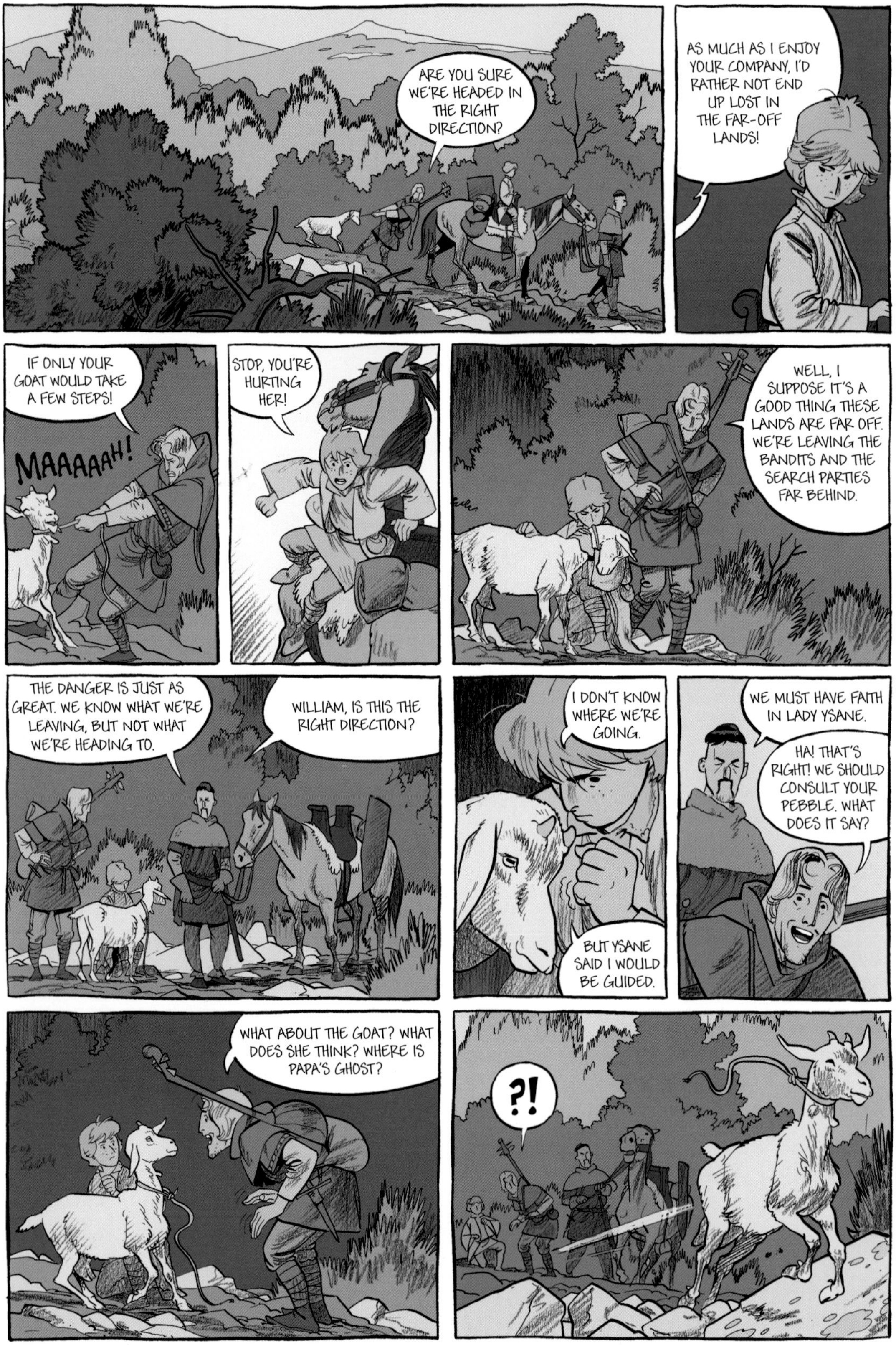
ARE YOU SURE WE'RE HEADED IN THE RIGHT DIRECTION?
AS MUCH AS I ENJOY YOUR COMPANY, I'D RATHER NOT END UP LOST IN THE FAR-OFF LANDS!
IF ONLY YOUR GOAT WOULD TAKE A FEW STEPS!
MAAAAAH!
STOP, YOU'RE HURTING HER!
WELL, I SUPPOSE IT'S A GOOD THING THESE LANDS ARE FAR OFF. WE'RE LEAVING THE BANDITS AND THE SEARCH PARTIES FAR BEHIND.
THE DANGER IS JUST AS GREAT. WE KNOW WHAT WE'RE LEAVING, BUT NOT WHAT WE'RE HEADING TO.
WILLIAM, IS THIS THE RIGHT DIRECTION?
I DON'T KNOW WHERE WE'RE GOING.
BUT YSANE SAID I WOULD BE GUIDED.
WE MUST HAVE FAITH IN LADY YSANE.
HA! THAT'S RIGHT! WE SHOULD CONSULT YOUR PEBBLE. WHAT DOES IT SAY?
WHAT ABOUT THE GOAT? WHAT DOES SHE THINK? WHERE IS PAPA'S GHOST?
?!

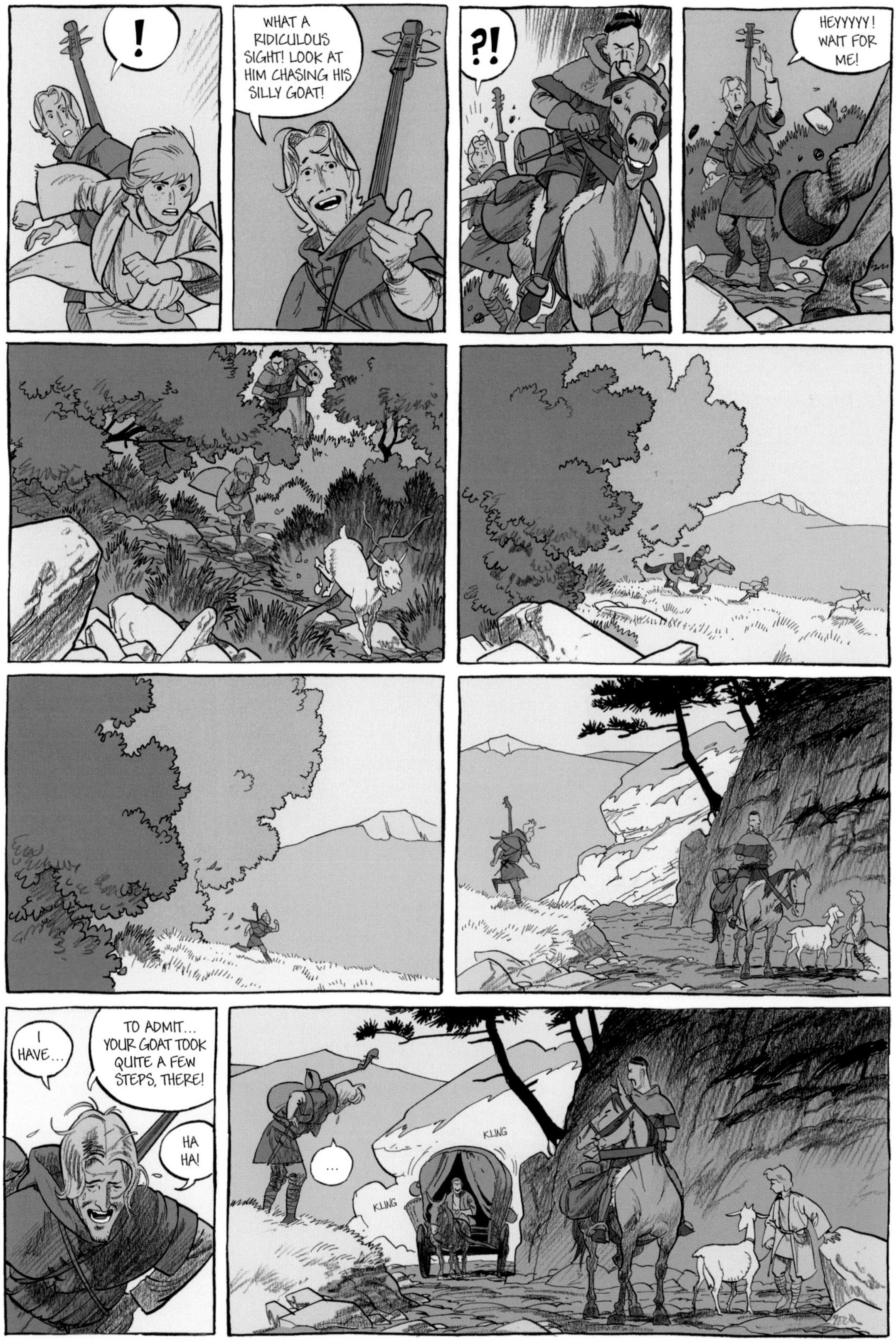
!
WHAT A RIDICULOUS SIGHT! LOOK AT HIM CHASING HIS SILLY GOAT!
?!
HEYYYYY! WAIT FOR ME!
I HAVE...
TO ADMIT... YOUR GOAT TOOK QUITE A FEW STEPS, THERE!
HA HA!
...
KLING
KLING

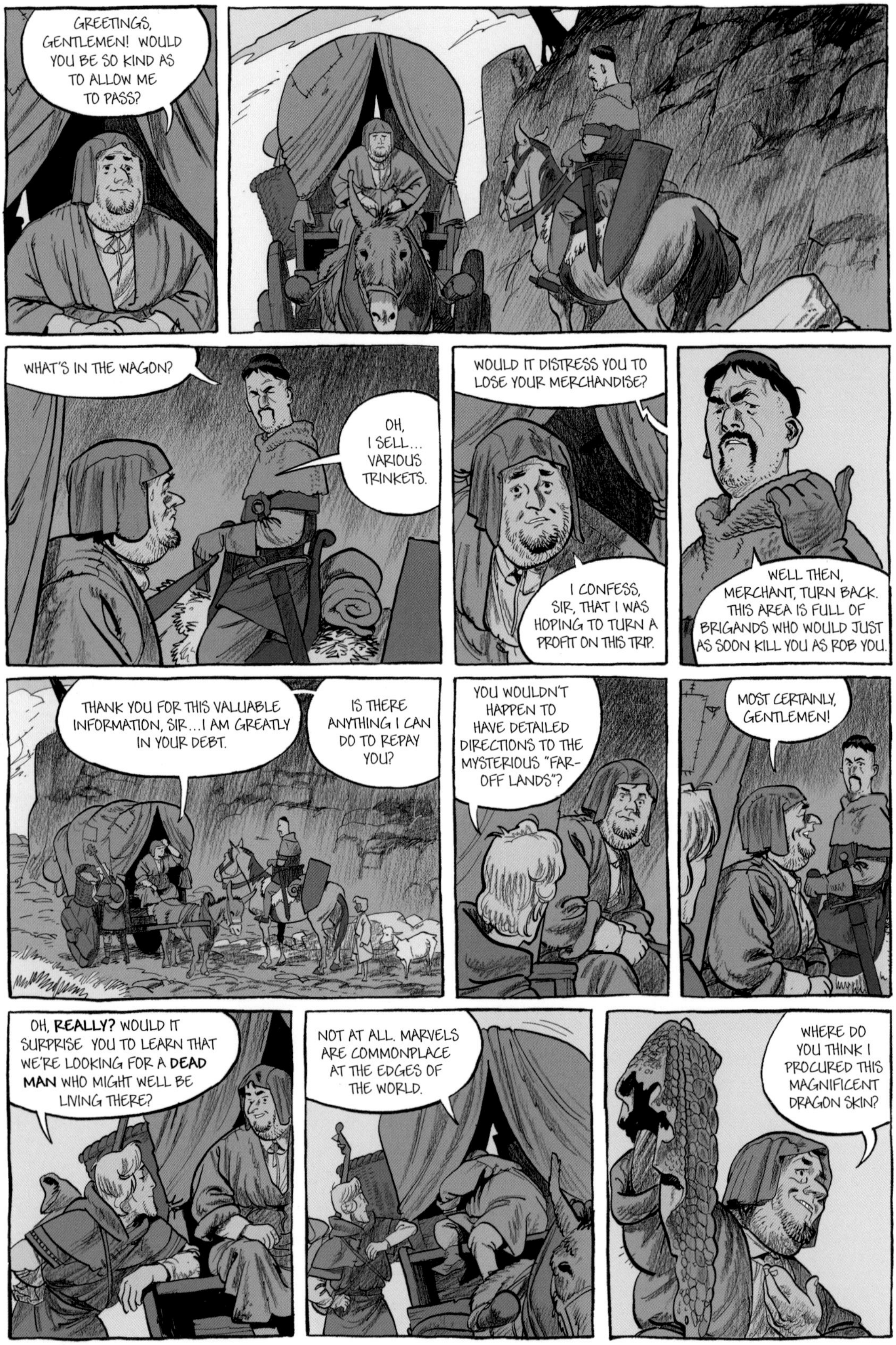
GREETINGS, GENTLEMEN! WOULD YOU BE SO KIND AS TO ALLOW ME TO PASS?
WHAT'S IN THE WAGON?
OH, I SELL... VARIOUS TRINKETS.
WOULD IT DISTRESS YOU TO LOSE YOUR MERCHANDISE?
I CONFESS, SIR, THAT I WAS HOPING TO TURN A PROFIT ON THIS TRIP.
WELL THEN, MERCHANT, TURN BACK. THIS AREA IS FULL OF BRIGANDS WHO WOULD JUST AS SOON KILL YOU AS ROB YOU.
THANK YOU FOR THIS VALUABLE INFORMATION, SIR...I AM GREATLY IN YOUR DEBT.
IS THERE ANYTHING I CAN DO TO REPAY YOU?
YOU WOULDN'T HAPPEN TO HAVE DETAILED DIRECTIONS TO THE MYSTERIOUS "FAR-OFF LANDS"?
MOST CERTAINLY, GENTLEMEN!
OH, **REALLY?** WOULD IT SURPRISE YOU TO LEARN THAT WE'RE LOOKING FOR A **DEAD MAN** WHO MIGHT WELL BE LIVING THERE?
NOT AT ALL. MARVELS ARE COMMONPLACE AT THE EDGES OF THE WORLD.
WHERE DO YOU THINK I PROCURED THIS MAGNIFICENT DRAGON SKIN?

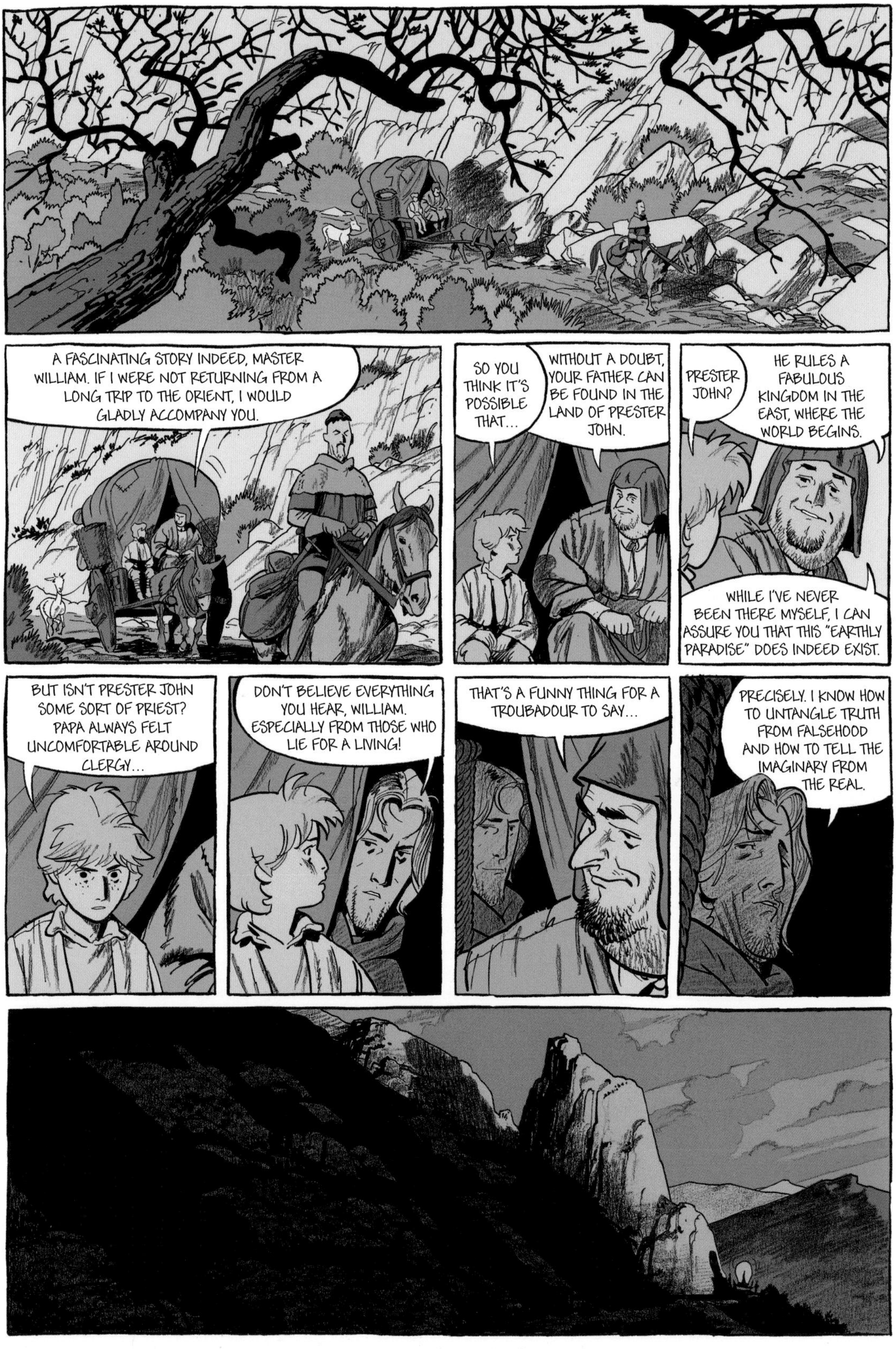
A FASCINATING STORY INDEED, MASTER WILLIAM. IF I WERE NOT RETURNING FROM A LONG TRIP TO THE ORIENT, I WOULD GLADLY ACCOMPANY YOU.
SO YOU THINK IT'S POSSIBLE THAT...
WITHOUT A DOUBT, YOUR FATHER CAN BE FOUND IN THE LAND OF PRESTER JOHN.
PRESTER JOHN?
HE RULES A FABULOUS KINGDOM IN THE EAST, WHERE THE WORLD BEGINS.
WHILE I'VE NEVER BEEN THERE MYSELF, I CAN ASSURE YOU THAT THIS "EARTHLY PARADISE" DOES INDEED EXIST.
BUT ISN'T PRESTER JOHN SOME SORT OF PRIEST? PAPA ALWAYS FELT UNCOMFORTABLE AROUND CLERGY...
DON'T BELIEVE EVERYTHING YOU HEAR, WILLIAM. ESPECIALLY FROM THOSE WHO LIE FOR A LIVING!
THAT'S A FUNNY THING FOR A TROUBADOUR TO SAY...
PRECISELY. I KNOW HOW TO UNTANGLE TRUTH FROM FALSEHOOD AND HOW TO TELL THE IMAGINARY FROM THE REAL.

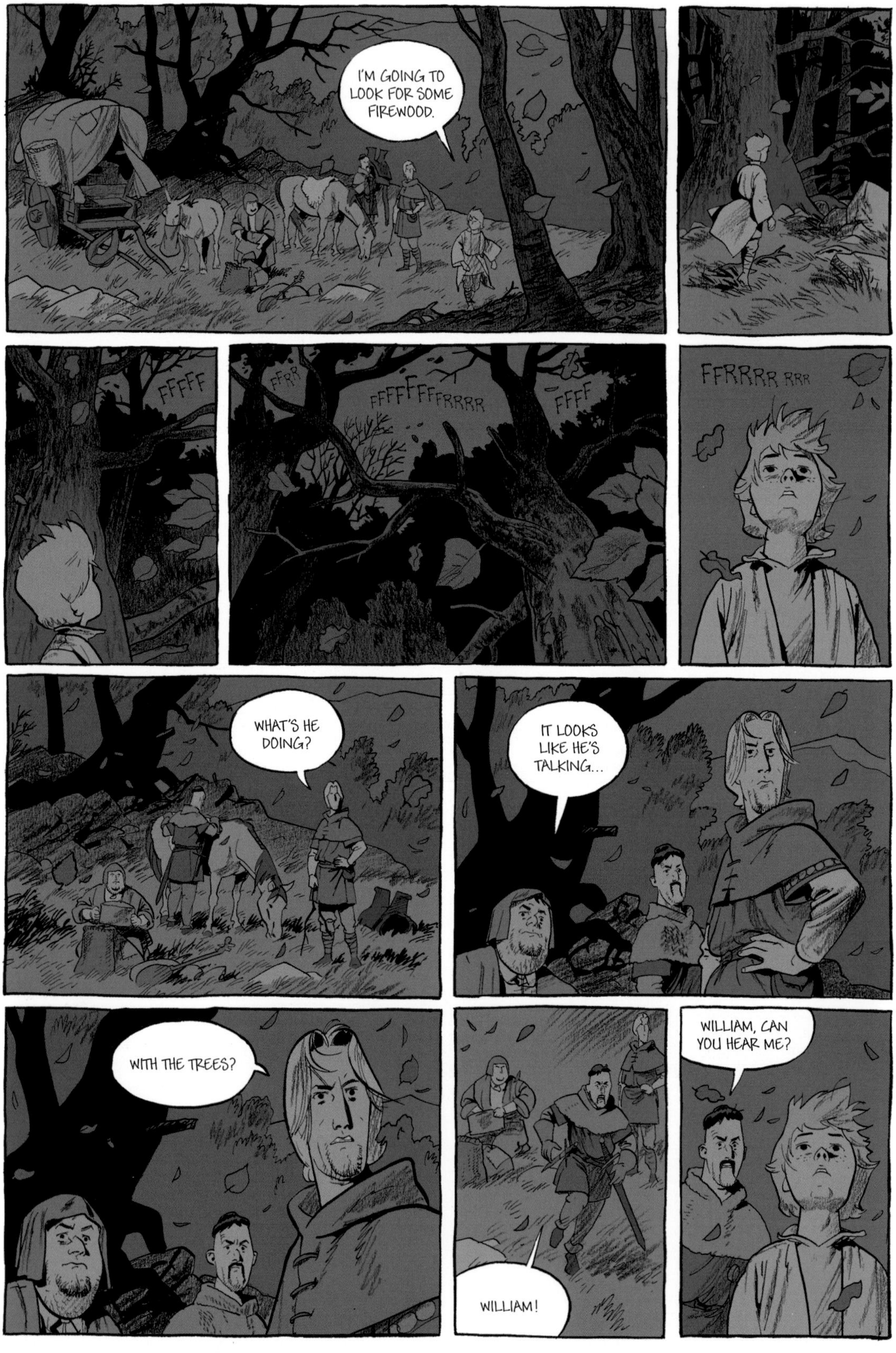

I'M GOING TO LOOK FOR SOME FIREWOOD.
FFFFF
FFRR
FFFFFFFRRRRR
FFFF
FFRRRR RRR
WHAT'S HE DOING?
IT LOOKS LIKE HE'S TALKING...
WITH THE TREES?
WILLIAM!
WILLIAM, CAN YOU HEAR ME?

FFFF FFFFF

FFFB FFFFFFFFFFFFFBRRRR RRFFF

HEY! WHAT'S GOING ON? SNAP OUT OF IT, WILLIAM!

WERE YOU TALKING WITH SOMEONE?

HUH? NO, I WAS JUST LOOKING FOR FIREWOOD.

ARE YOU COMING WITH ME?

GIVE ME SOME MORE PEAS AND BACON! I DIDN'T EXPECT SUCH DECENT GRUB FROM A TRAVELING PEDDLER!

YOU'RE TOO KIND, SIR KNIGHT.

AND YOUR WINE IS EXCELLENT!

COME ON, WILLIAM. HAVE A TASTE!

NO, THANK YOU.

WHAT? ARE YOU TOO GOOD TO DRINK WITH US?

ARE WE YOUR FRIENDS OR NOT?

C'MON, LIVE A LITTLE!

HA HA HA!

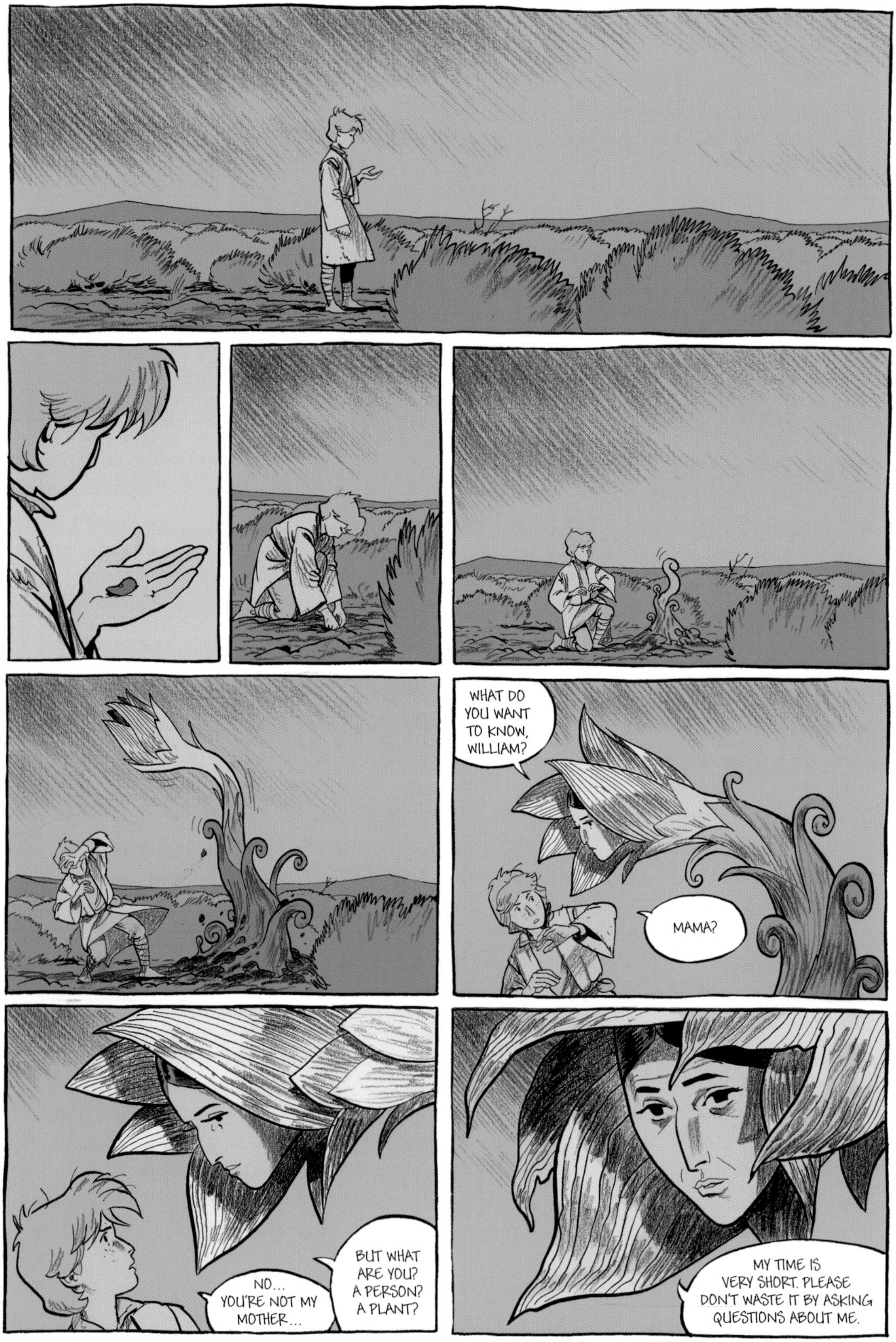
WHAT DO YOU WANT TO KNOW, WILLIAM?
MAMA?
NO… YOU'RE NOT MY MOTHER…
BUT WHAT ARE YOU? A PERSON? A PLANT?
MY TIME IS VERY SHORT. PLEASE DON'T WASTE IT BY ASKING QUESTIONS ABOUT ME.

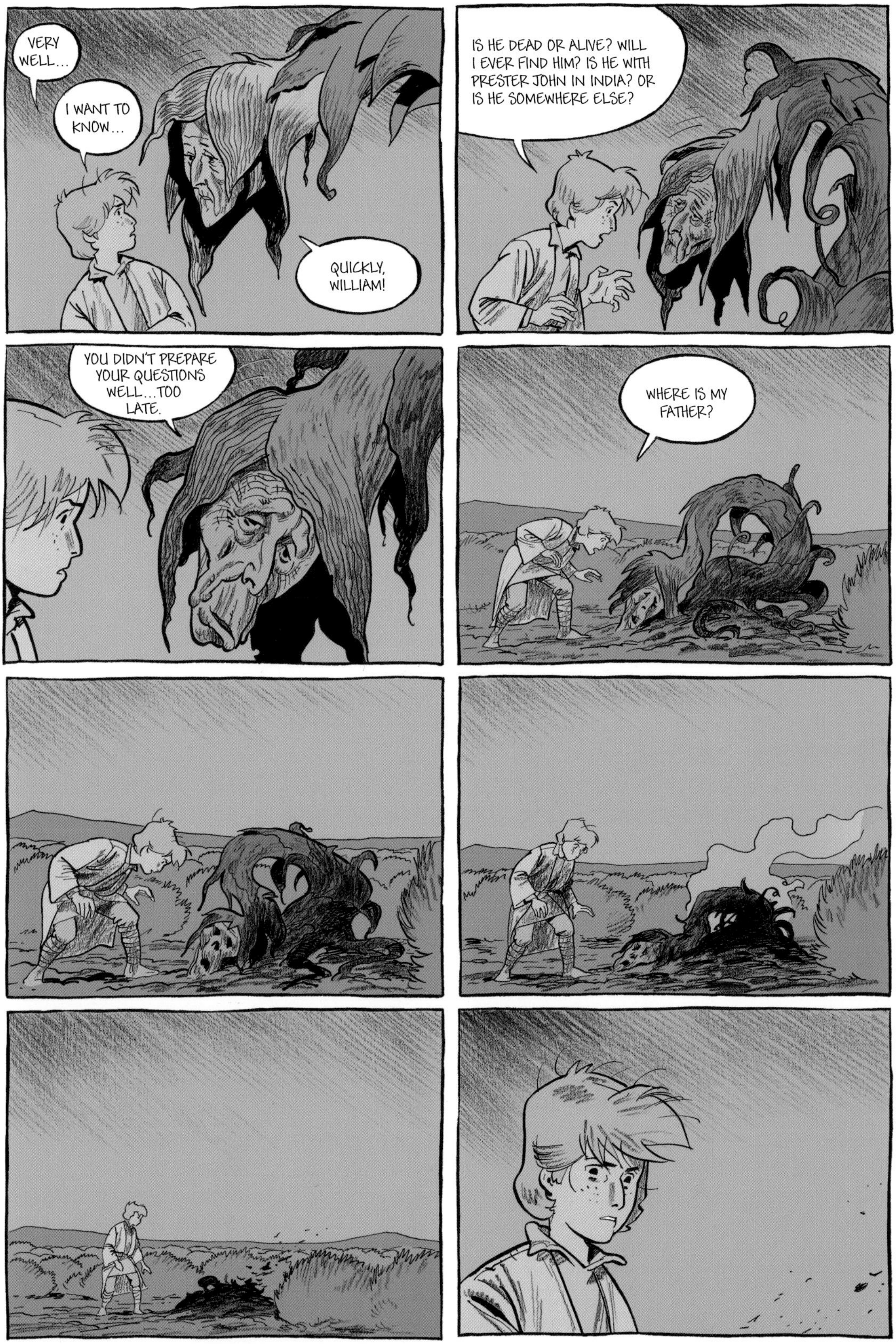
VERY WELL…
I WANT TO KNOW…
QUICKLY, WILLIAM!
IS HE DEAD OR ALIVE? WILL I EVER FIND HIM? IS HE WITH PRESTER JOHN IN INDIA? OR IS HE SOMEWHERE ELSE?
YOU DIDN'T PREPARE YOUR QUESTIONS WELL…TOO LATE.
WHERE IS MY FATHER?

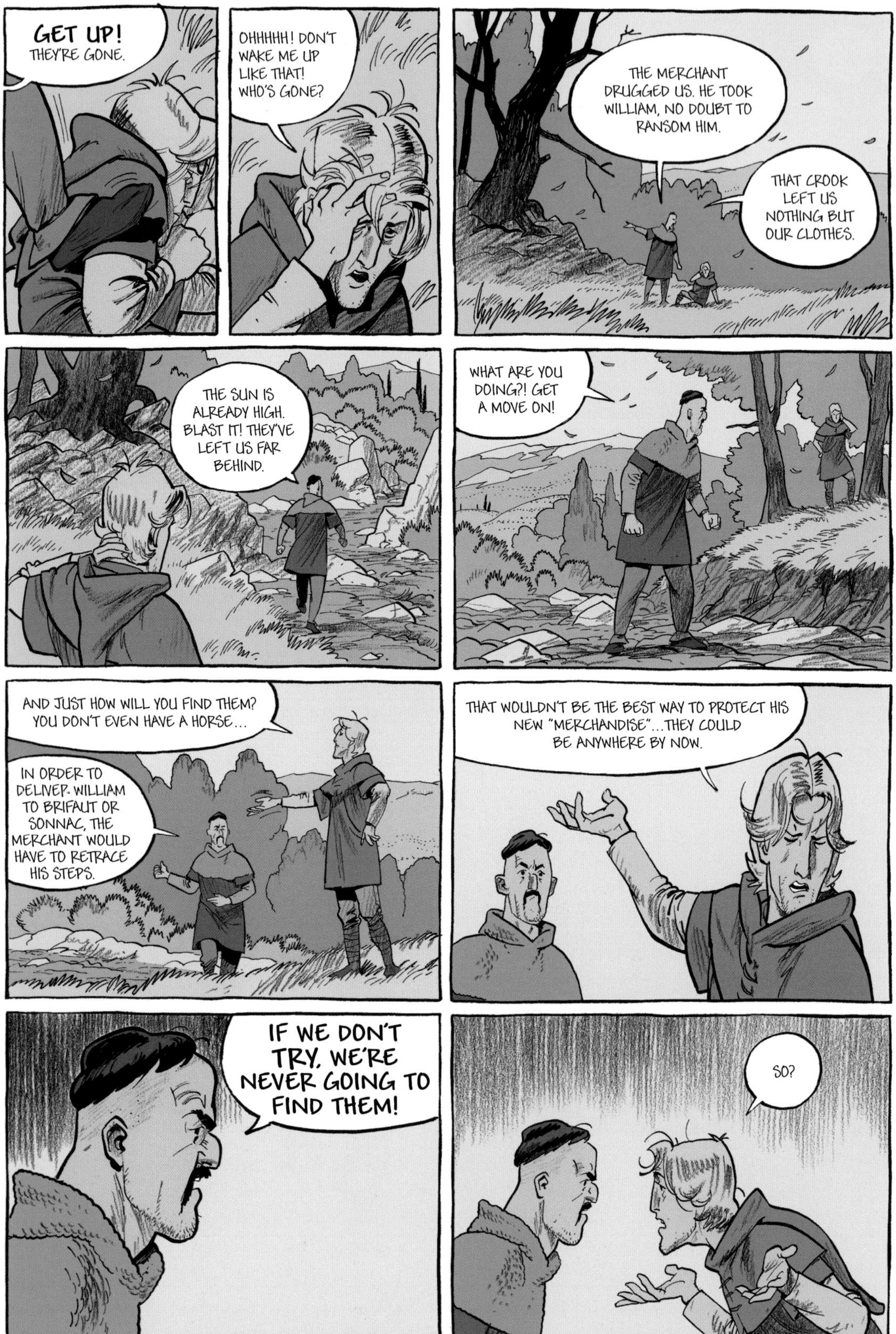
GET UP! THEY'RE GONE.
OHHHHH! DON'T WAKE ME UP LIKE THAT! WHO'S GONE?
THE MERCHANT DRUGGED US. HE TOOK WILLIAM, NO DOUBT TO RANSOM HIM.
THAT CROOK LEFT US NOTHING BUT OUR CLOTHES.
THE SUN IS ALREADY HIGH. BLAST IT! THEY'VE LEFT US FAR BEHIND.
WHAT ARE YOU DOING?! GET A MOVE ON!
AND JUST HOW WILL YOU FIND THEM? YOU DON'T EVEN HAVE A HORSE...
IN ORDER TO DELIVER WILLIAM TO BRIFAUT OR SONNAC, THE MERCHANT WOULD HAVE TO RETRACE HIS STEPS.
THAT WOULDN'T BE THE BEST WAY TO PROTECT HIS NEW "MERCHANDISE"...THEY COULD BE ANYWHERE BY NOW.
IF WE DON'T TRY, WE'RE NEVER GOING TO FIND THEM!
SO?

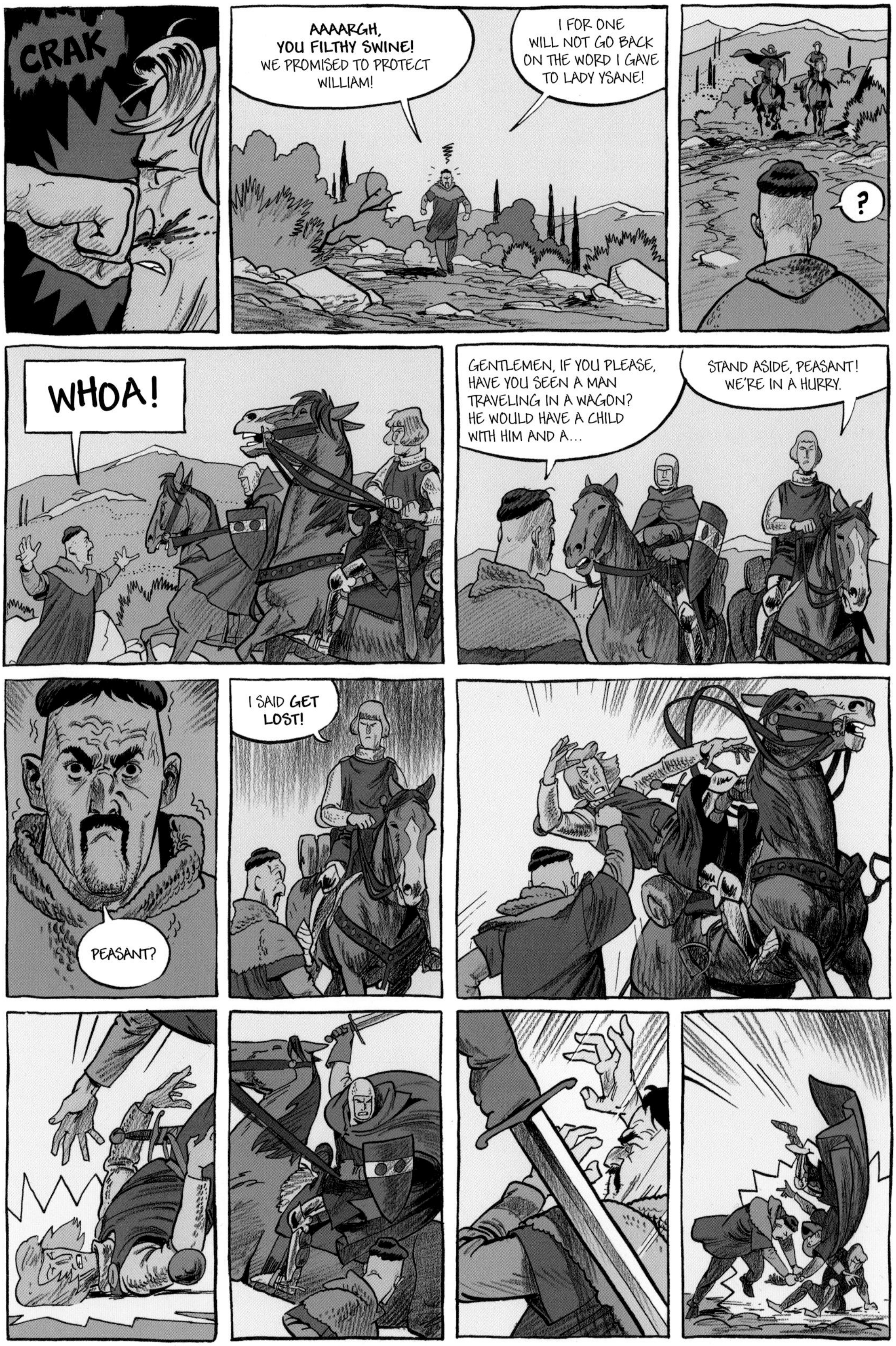
CRAK
AAAARGH, YOU FILTHY SWINE! WE PROMISED TO PROTECT WILLIAM!
I FOR ONE WILL NOT GO BACK ON THE WORD I GAVE TO LADY YSANE!
?
WHOA!
GENTLEMEN, IF YOU PLEASE, HAVE YOU SEEN A MAN TRAVELING IN A WAGON? HE WOULD HAVE A CHILD WITH HIM AND A...
STAND ASIDE, PEASANT! WE'RE IN A HURRY.
PEASANT?
I SAID GET LOST!

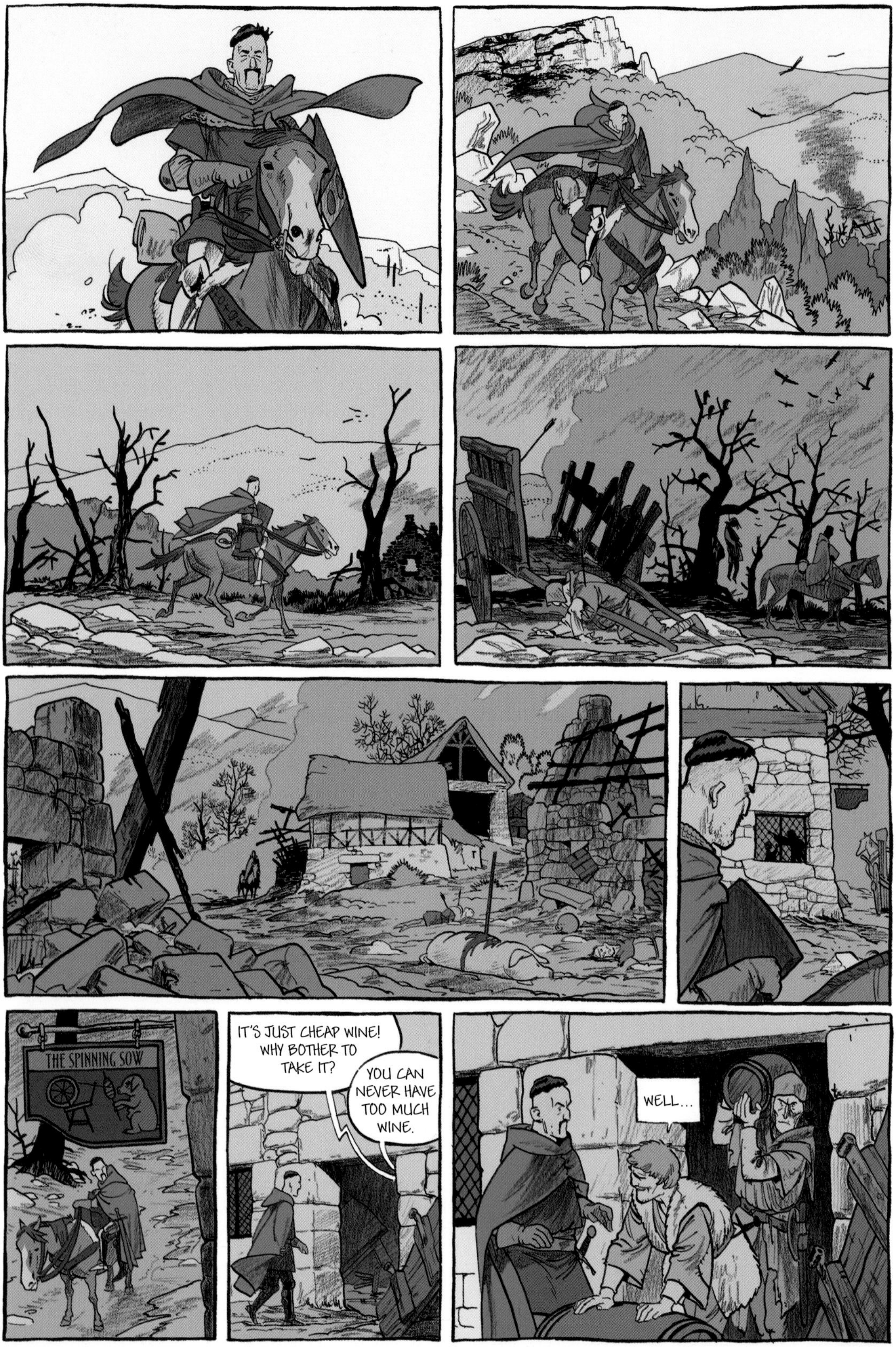
THE SPINNING SOW
IT'S JUST CHEAP WINE! WHY BOTHER TO TAKE IT?
YOU CAN NEVER HAVE TOO MUCH WINE.
WELL...

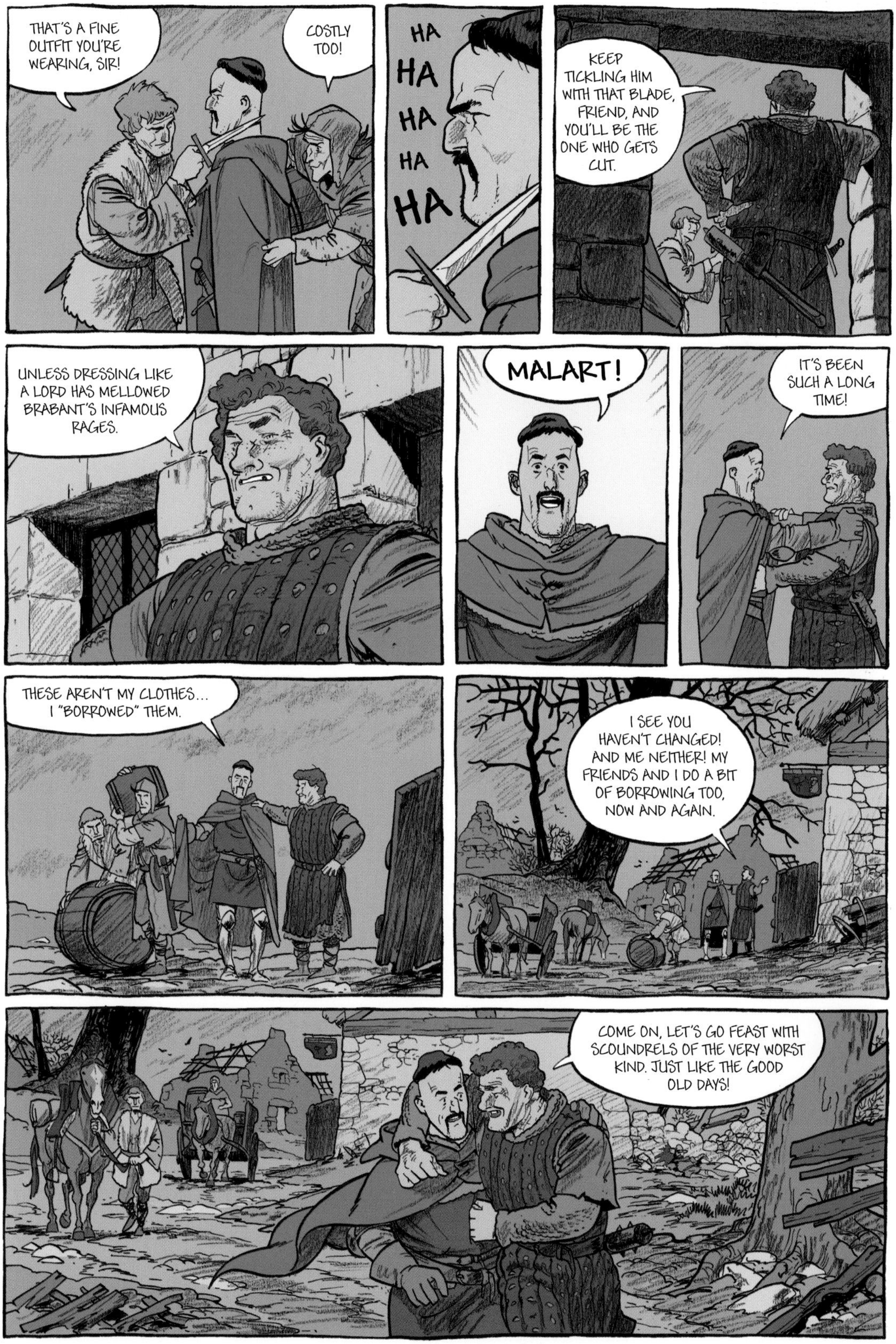
THAT'S A FINE OUTFIT YOU'RE WEARING, SIR!
COSTLY TOO!
HA HA HA HA HA
KEEP TICKLING HIM WITH THAT BLADE, FRIEND, AND YOU'LL BE THE ONE WHO GETS CUT.
UNLESS DRESSING LIKE A LORD HAS MELLOWED BRABANT'S INFAMOUS RAGES.
MALART!
IT'S BEEN SUCH A LONG TIME!
THESE AREN'T MY CLOTHES... I "BORROWED" THEM.
I SEE YOU HAVEN'T CHANGED! AND ME NEITHER! MY FRIENDS AND I DO A BIT OF BORROWING TOO, NOW AND AGAIN.
COME ON, LET'S GO FEAST WITH SCOUNDRELS OF THE VERY WORST KIND. JUST LIKE THE GOOD OLD DAYS!

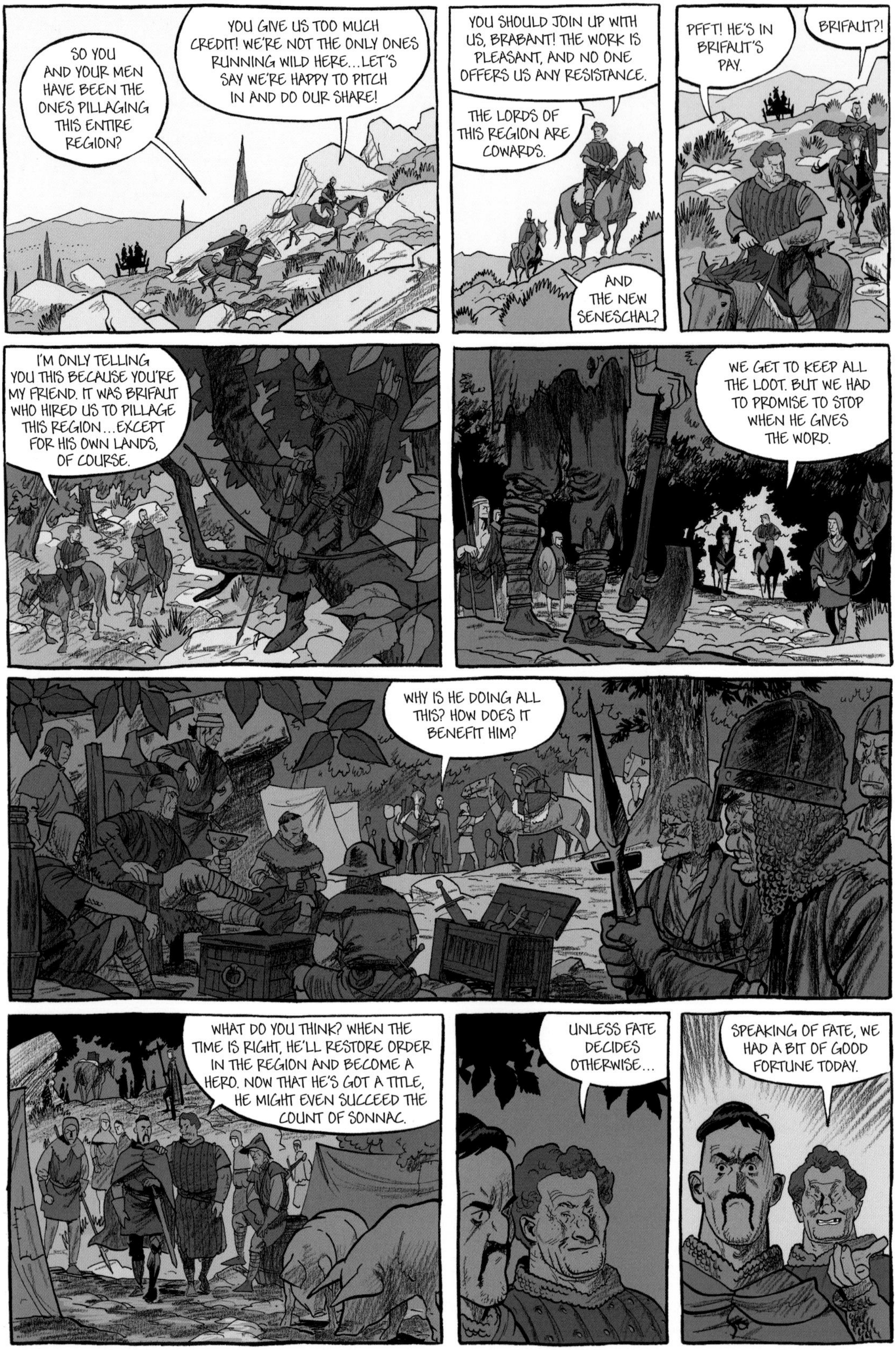
SO YOU AND YOUR MEN HAVE BEEN THE ONES PILLAGING THIS ENTIRE REGION?
YOU GIVE US TOO MUCH CREDIT! WE'RE NOT THE ONLY ONES RUNNING WILD HERE... LET'S SAY WE'RE HAPPY TO PITCH IN AND DO OUR SHARE!
YOU SHOULD JOIN UP WITH US, BRABANT! THE WORK IS PLEASANT, AND NO ONE OFFERS US ANY RESISTANCE.
THE LORDS OF THIS REGION ARE COWARDS.
AND THE NEW SENESCHAL?
PFFT! HE'S IN BRIFAUT'S PAY.
BRIFAUT?!
I'M ONLY TELLING YOU THIS BECAUSE YOU'RE MY FRIEND. IT WAS BRIFAUT WHO HIRED US TO PILLAGE THIS REGION... EXCEPT FOR HIS OWN LANDS, OF COURSE.
WE GET TO KEEP ALL THE LOOT. BUT WE HAD TO PROMISE TO STOP WHEN HE GIVES THE WORD.
WHY IS HE DOING ALL THIS? HOW DOES IT BENEFIT HIM?
WHAT DO YOU THINK? WHEN THE TIME IS RIGHT, HE'LL RESTORE ORDER IN THE REGION AND BECOME A HERO. NOW THAT HE'S GOT A TITLE, HE MIGHT EVEN SUCCEED THE COUNT OF SONNAC.
UNLESS FATE DECIDES OTHERWISE...
SPEAKING OF FATE, WE HAD A BIT OF GOOD FORTUNE TODAY.

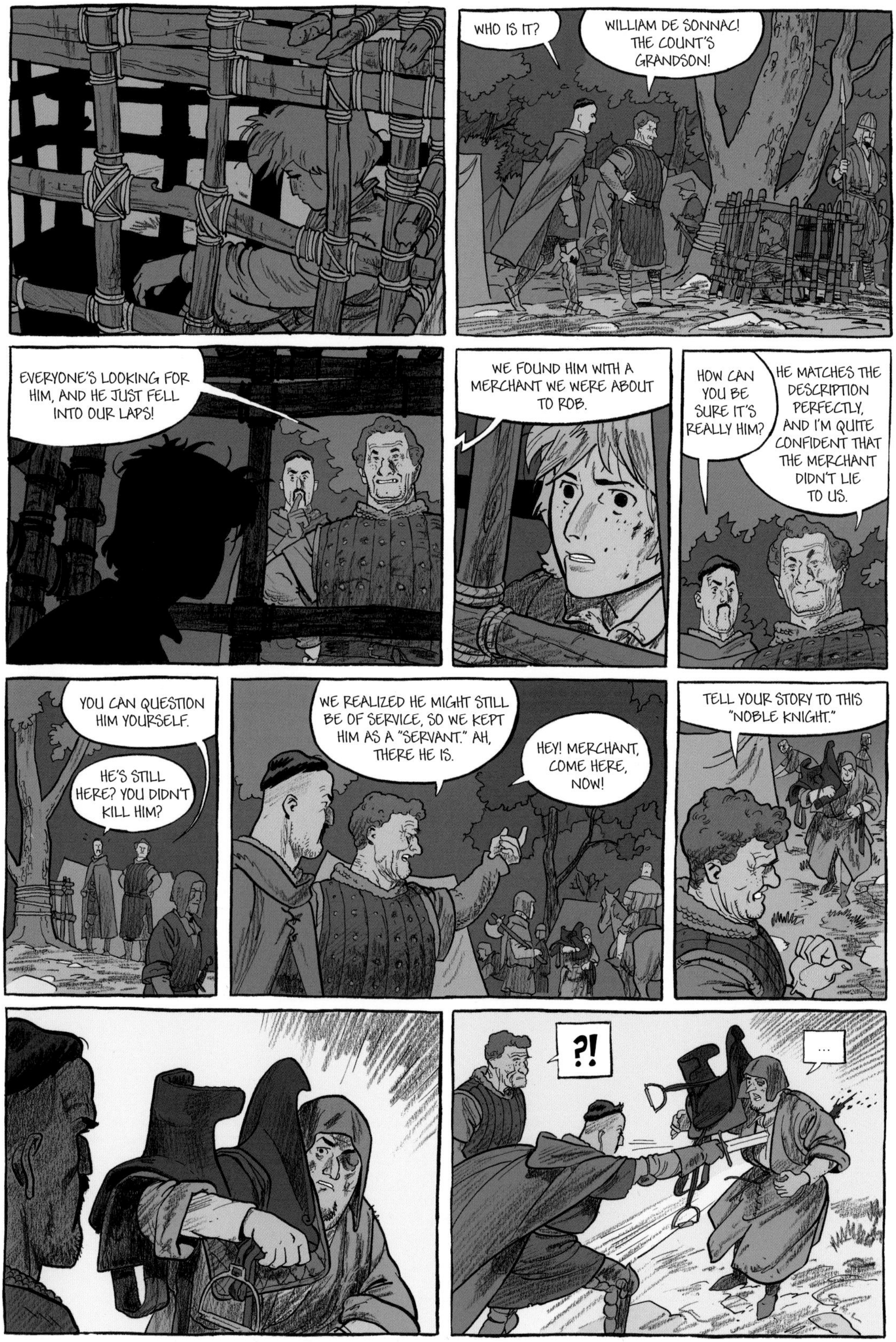
WHO IS IT?
WILLIAM DE SONNAC! THE COUNT'S GRANDSON!
EVERYONE'S LOOKING FOR HIM, AND HE JUST FELL INTO OUR LAPS!
WE FOUND HIM WITH A MERCHANT WE WERE ABOUT TO ROB.
HOW CAN YOU BE SURE IT'S REALLY HIM?
HE MATCHES THE DESCRIPTION PERFECTLY, AND I'M QUITE CONFIDENT THAT THE MERCHANT DIDN'T LIE TO US.
YOU CAN QUESTION HIM YOURSELF.
HE'S STILL HERE? YOU DIDN'T KILL HIM?
WE REALIZED HE MIGHT STILL BE OF SERVICE, SO WE KEPT HIM AS A "SERVANT." AH, THERE HE IS.
HEY! MERCHANT, COME HERE, NOW!
TELL YOUR STORY TO THIS "NOBLE KNIGHT."
?!
...

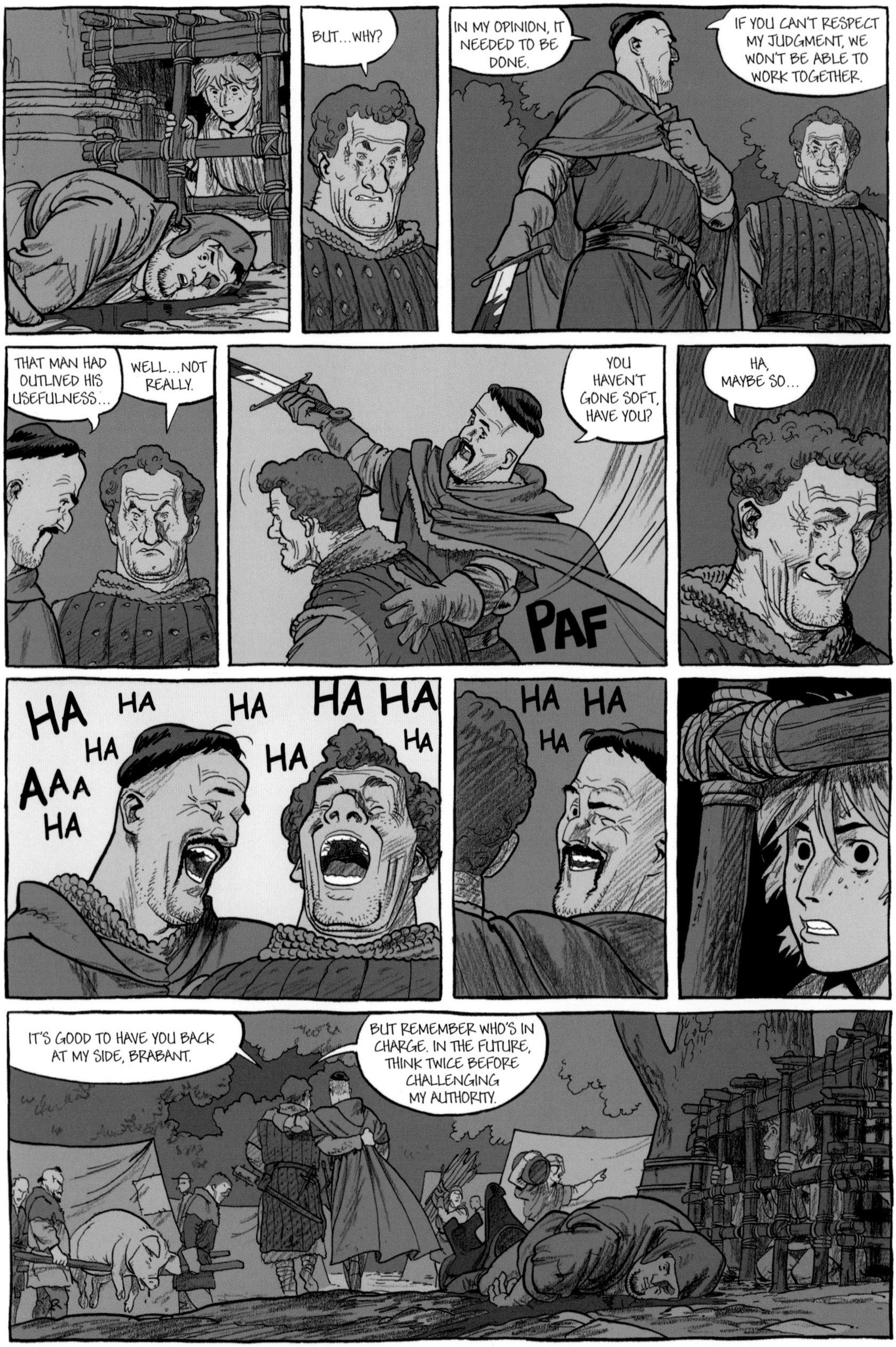
BUT...WHY?
IN MY OPINION, IT NEEDED TO BE DONE.
IF YOU CAN'T RESPECT MY JUDGMENT, WE WON'T BE ABLE TO WORK TOGETHER.
THAT MAN HAD OUTLIVED HIS USEFULNESS...
WELL...NOT REALLY.
YOU HAVEN'T GONE SOFT, HAVE YOU?
PAF
HA, MAYBE SO...
HA HA HA HA HA HA HA HA AAA HA
HA HA HA
IT'S GOOD TO HAVE YOU BACK AT MY SIDE, BRABANT.
BUT REMEMBER WHO'S IN CHARGE. IN THE FUTURE, THINK TWICE BEFORE CHALLENGING MY AUTHORITY.

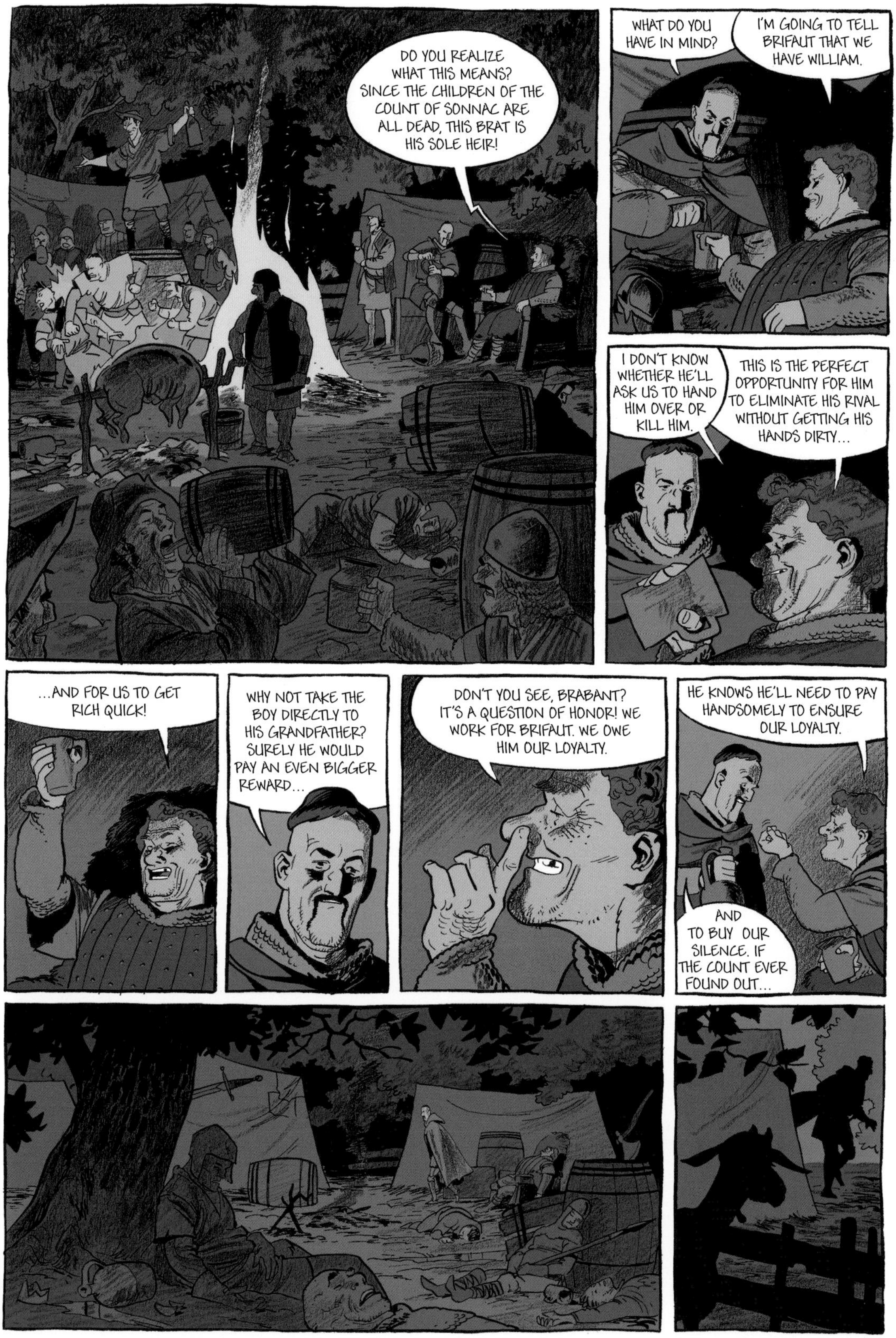
DO YOU REALIZE WHAT THIS MEANS? SINCE THE CHILDREN OF THE COUNT OF SONNAC ARE ALL DEAD, THIS BRAT IS HIS SOLE HEIR!
WHAT DO YOU HAVE IN MIND?
I'M GOING TO TELL BRIFAUT THAT WE HAVE WILLIAM.
I DON'T KNOW WHETHER HE'LL ASK US TO HAND HIM OVER OR KILL HIM.
THIS IS THE PERFECT OPPORTUNITY FOR HIM TO ELIMINATE HIS RIVAL WITHOUT GETTING HIS HANDS DIRTY...
...AND FOR US TO GET RICH QUICK!
WHY NOT TAKE THE BOY DIRECTLY TO HIS GRANDFATHER? SURELY HE WOULD PAY AN EVEN BIGGER REWARD...
DON'T YOU SEE, BRABANT? IT'S A QUESTION OF HONOR! WE WORK FOR BRIFAUT. WE OWE HIM OUR LOYALTY.
HE KNOWS HE'LL NEED TO PAY HANDSOMELY TO ENSURE OUR LOYALTY.
AND TO BUY OUR SILENCE. IF THE COUNT EVER FOUND OUT...

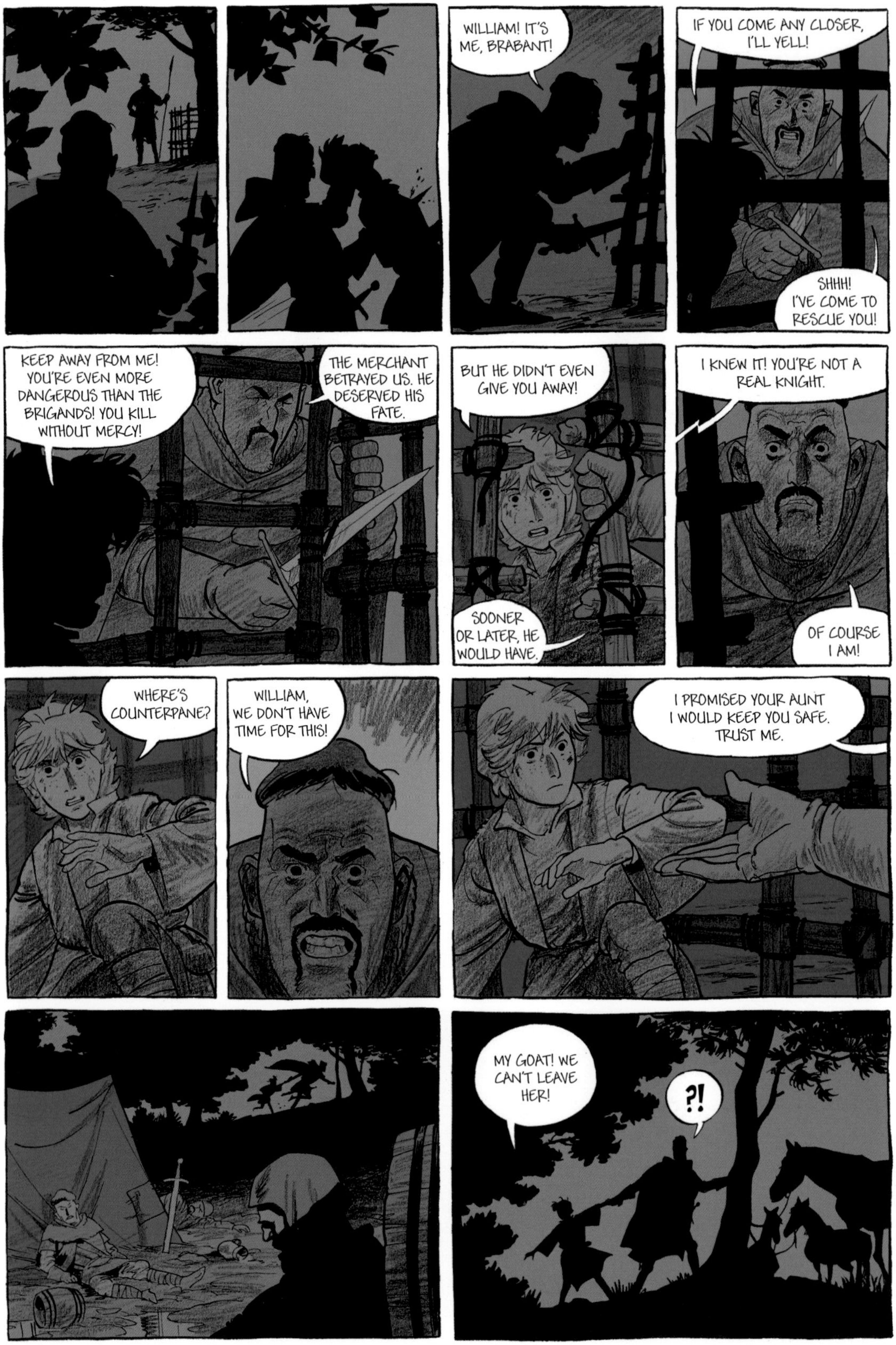

WILLIAM! IT'S ME, BRABANT!
IF YOU COME ANY CLOSER, I'LL YELL!
SHHH! I'VE COME TO RESCUE YOU!
KEEP AWAY FROM ME! YOU'RE EVEN MORE DANGEROUS THAN THE BRIGANDS! YOU KILL WITHOUT MERCY!
THE MERCHANT BETRAYED US. HE DESERVED HIS FATE.
BUT HE DIDN'T EVEN GIVE YOU AWAY!
SOONER OR LATER, HE WOULD HAVE.
I KNEW IT! YOU'RE NOT A REAL KNIGHT.
OF COURSE I AM!
WHERE'S COUNTERPANE?
WILLIAM, WE DON'T HAVE TIME FOR THIS!
I PROMISED YOUR AUNT I WOULD KEEP YOU SAFE. TRUST ME.
MY GOAT! WE CAN'T LEAVE HER!
?!

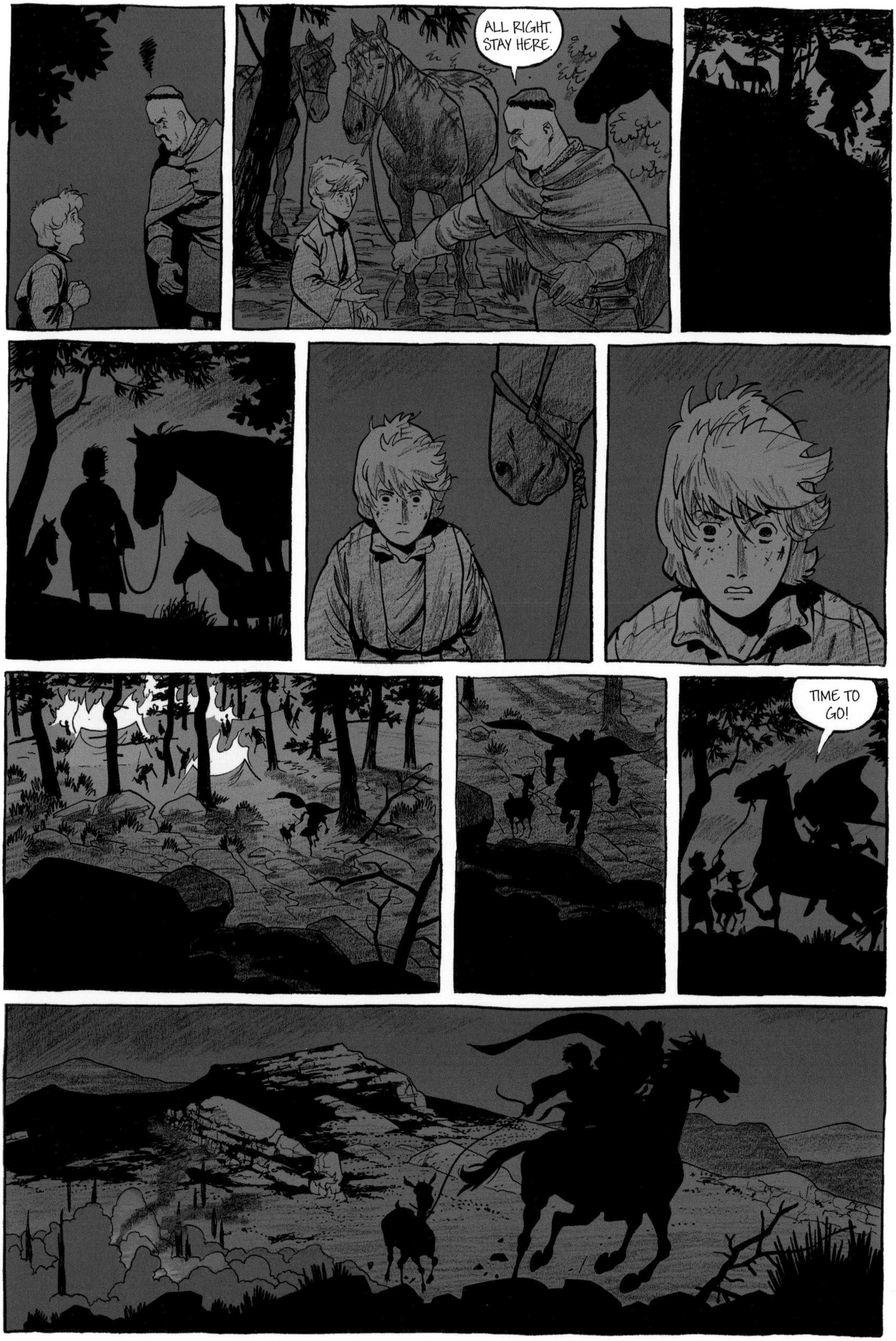
ALL RIGHT. STAY HERE.
TIME TO GO!

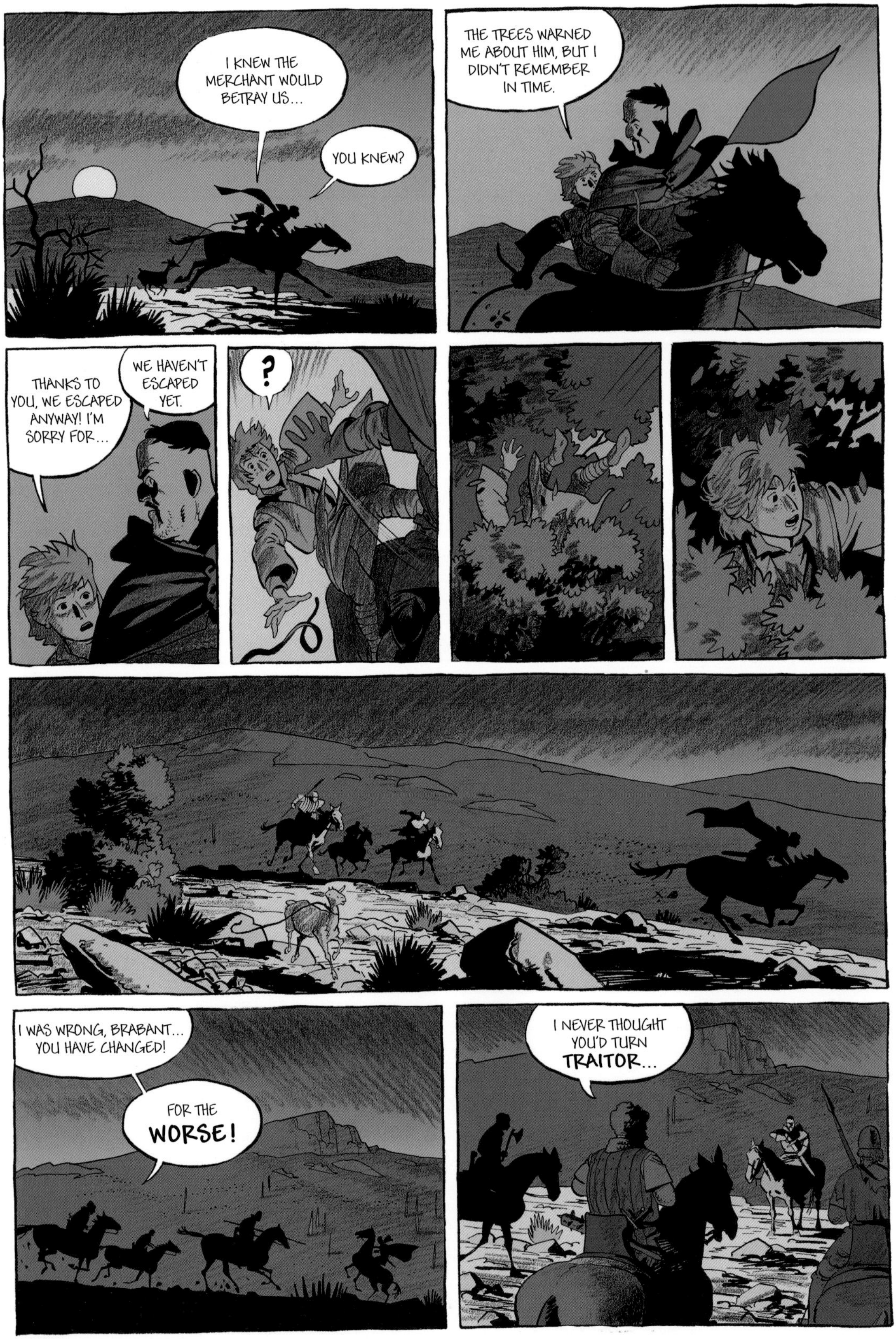

I KNEW THE MERCHANT WOULD BETRAY US...
YOU KNEW?
THE TREES WARNED ME ABOUT HIM, BUT I DIDN'T REMEMBER IN TIME.
THANKS TO YOU, WE ESCAPED ANYWAY! I'M SORRY FOR...
WE HAVEN'T ESCAPED YET.
?
I WAS WRONG, BRABANT... YOU HAVE CHANGED!
FOR THE WORSE!
I NEVER THOUGHT YOU'D TURN TRAITOR...

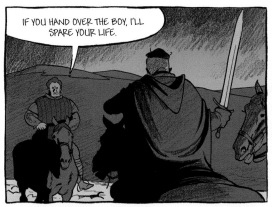

IF YOU HAND OVER THE BOY, I'LL SPARE YOUR LIFE.

DON'T KILL HIM!

WHAT A NOBLE GESTURE, YOUNG MASTER!

!!

IN A FAIR FIGHT, I KNOW YOU'D WIN, BRABANT.

BUT THIS ISN'T A FAIR FIGHT!

NoooOOOoooooo!

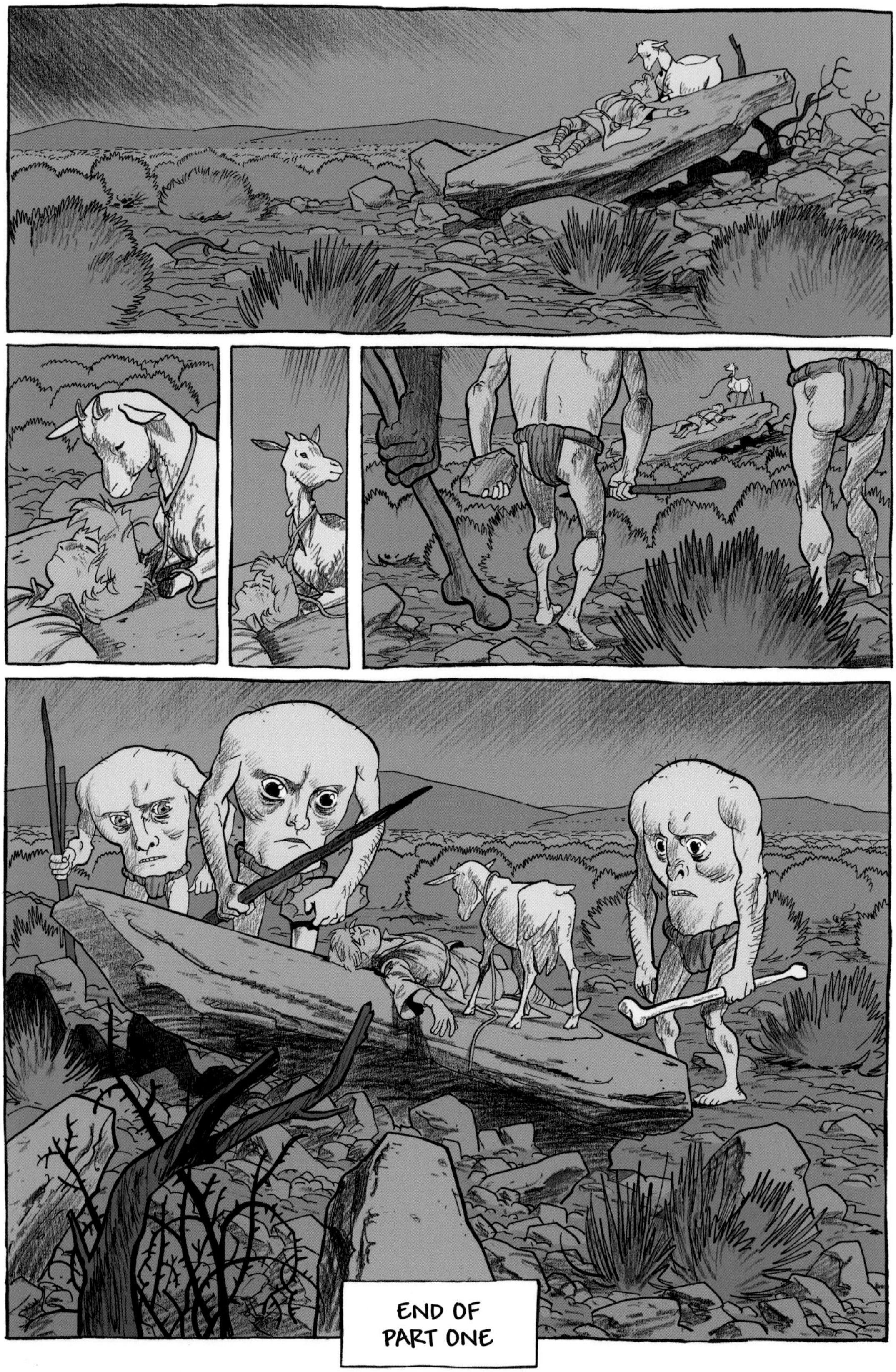
END OF PART ONE

PART 2:
THE LAND OF TRUTH

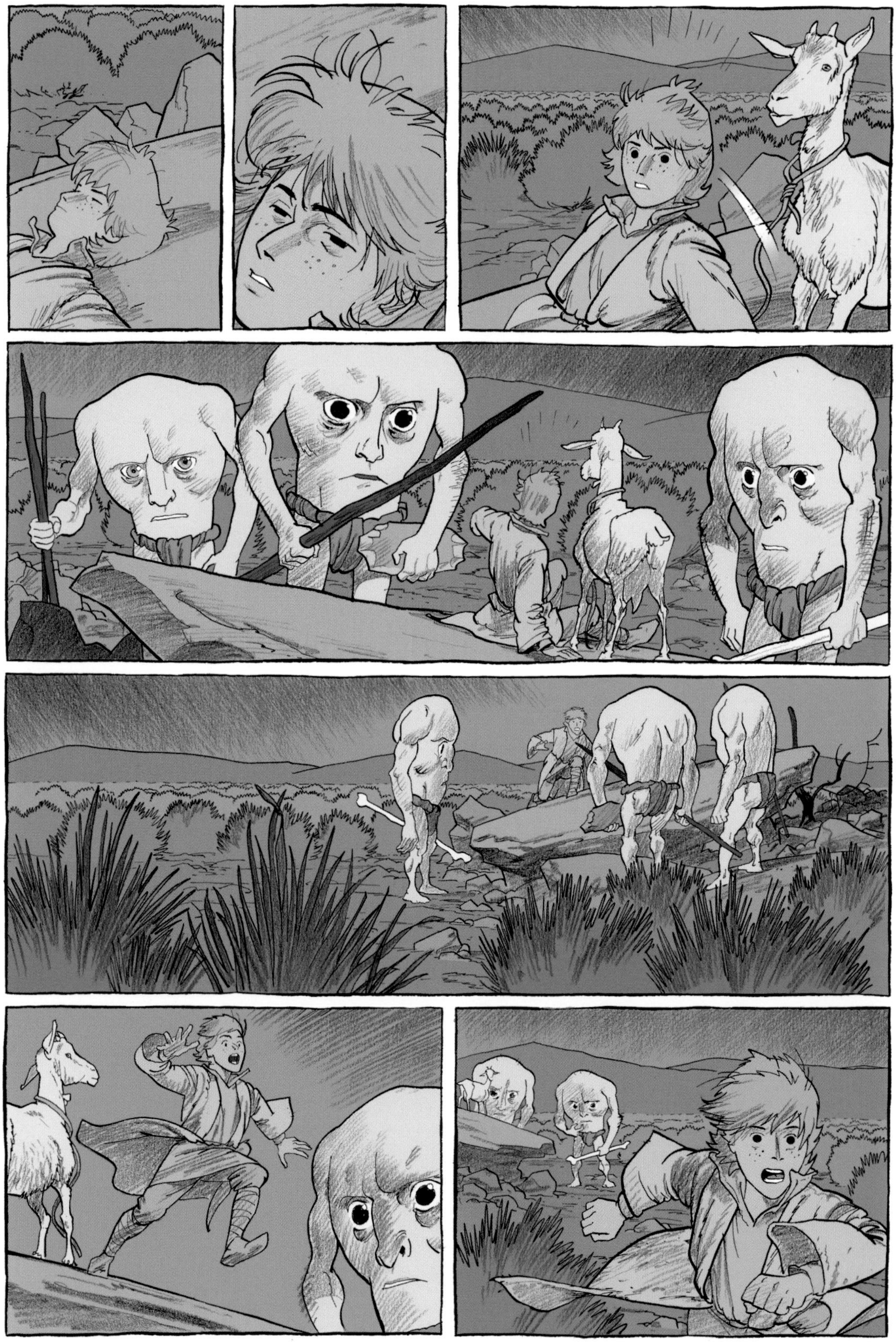

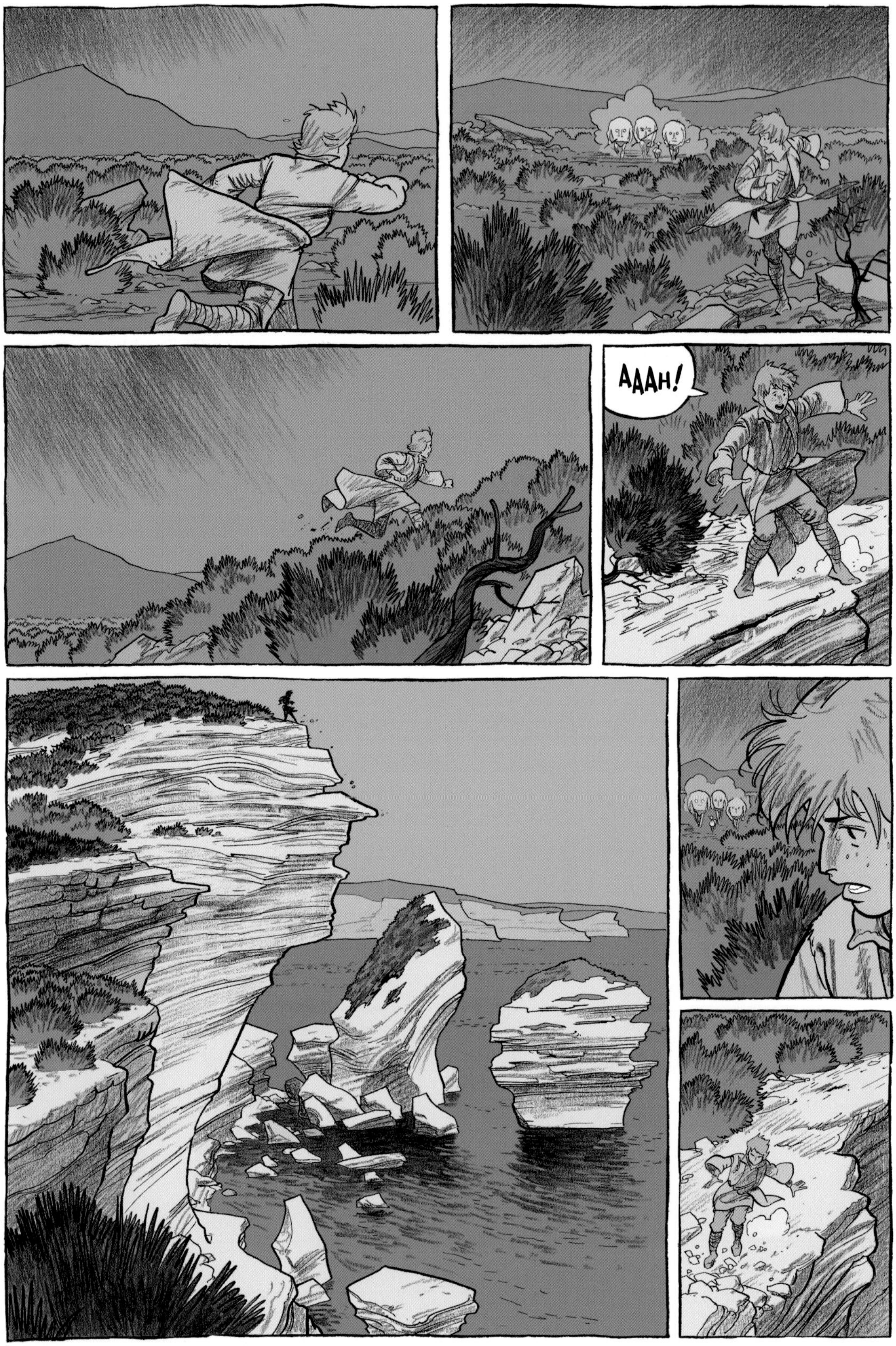
AAAH!

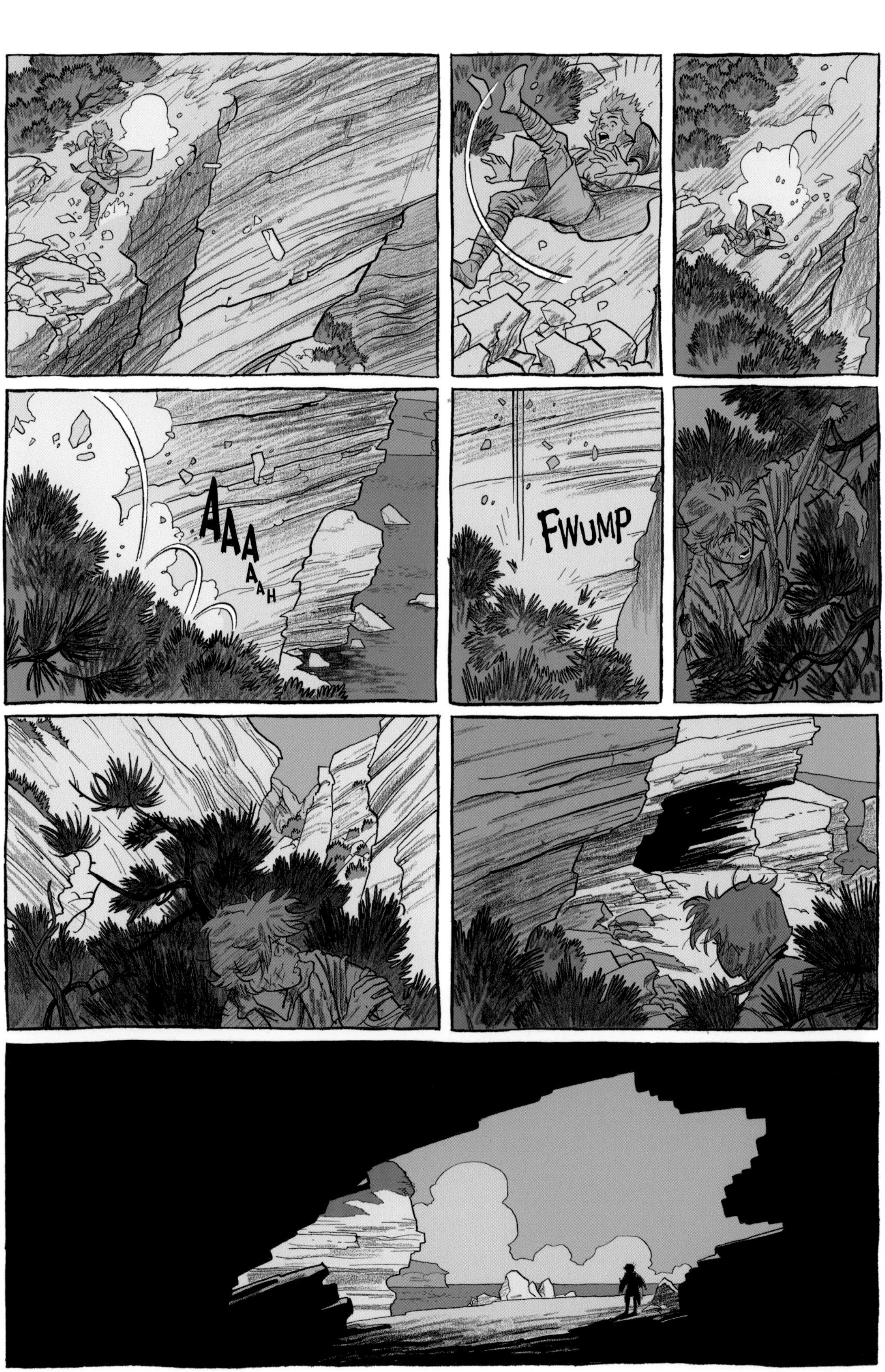
AAAAAAH
FWUMP

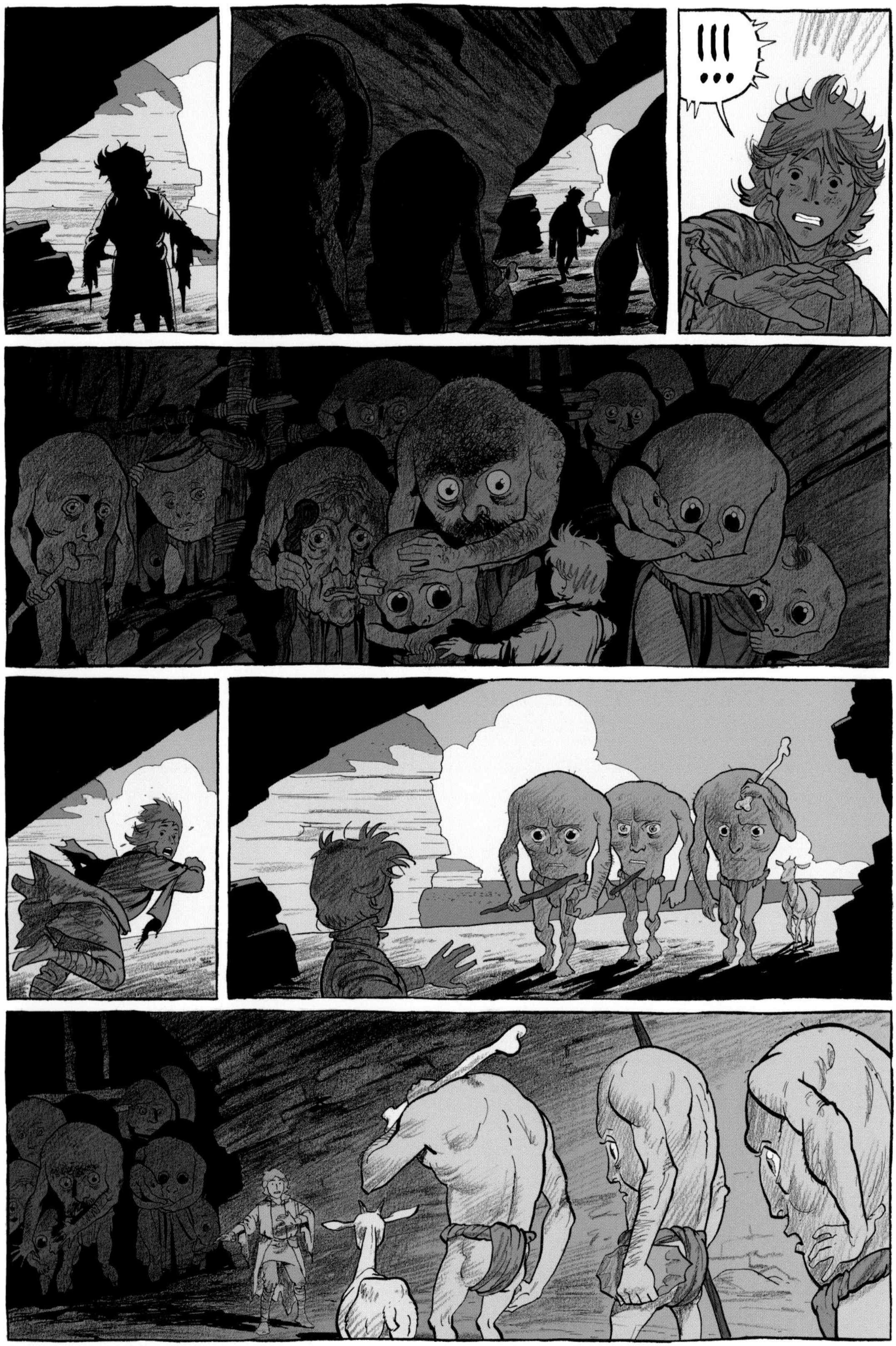
!!!
...

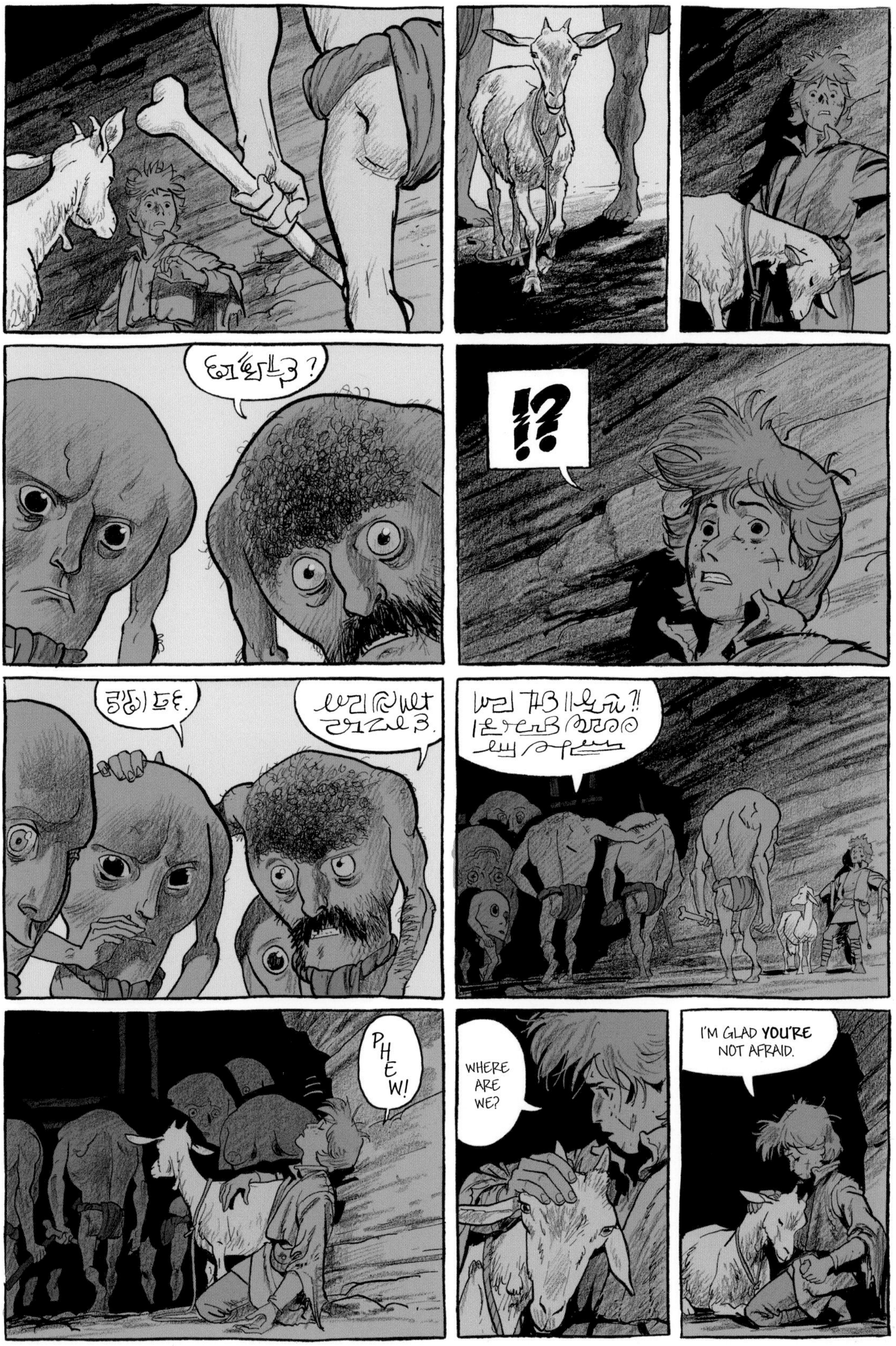
!?
PHEW!
WHERE ARE WE?
I'M GLAD **YOU'RE** NOT AFRAID.

THEY MAY LOOK HIDEOUS, BUT THEY SEEM HARMLESS.

?

ESPECIALLY THE WHITE FOUR-LEGGED ONE.

THE OTHER ONE DOESN'T SEEM TOO SCARY EITHER.

I CAN UNDERSTAND WHAT THEY'RE SAYING...

I UNDERSTAND EVERYTHING!

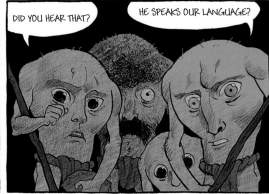

DID YOU HEAR THAT?

HE SPEAKS OUR LANGUAGE?

WHY DIDN'T HE ANSWER US RIGHT AWAY?

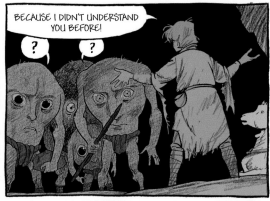

BECAUSE I DIDN'T UNDERSTAND YOU BEFORE!

?   ?

OH, NO! WHAT HAPPENED?

DOES THIS STRANGE CREATURE SPEAK OUR LANGUAGE OR NOT?

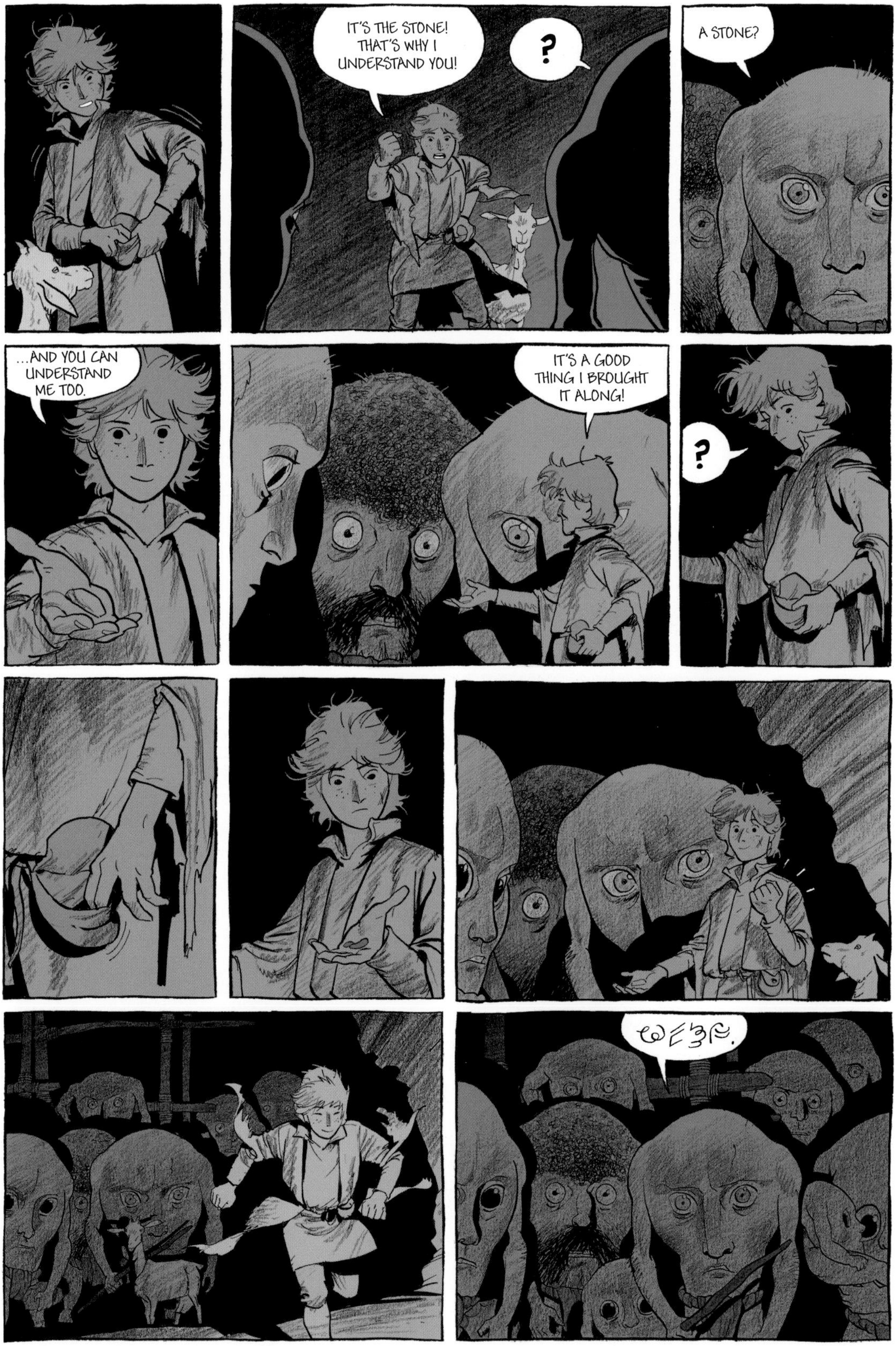
IT'S THE STONE! THAT'S WHY I UNDERSTAND YOU!
?
A STONE?
...AND YOU CAN UNDERSTAND ME TOO.
IT'S A GOOD THING I BROUGHT IT ALONG!
?

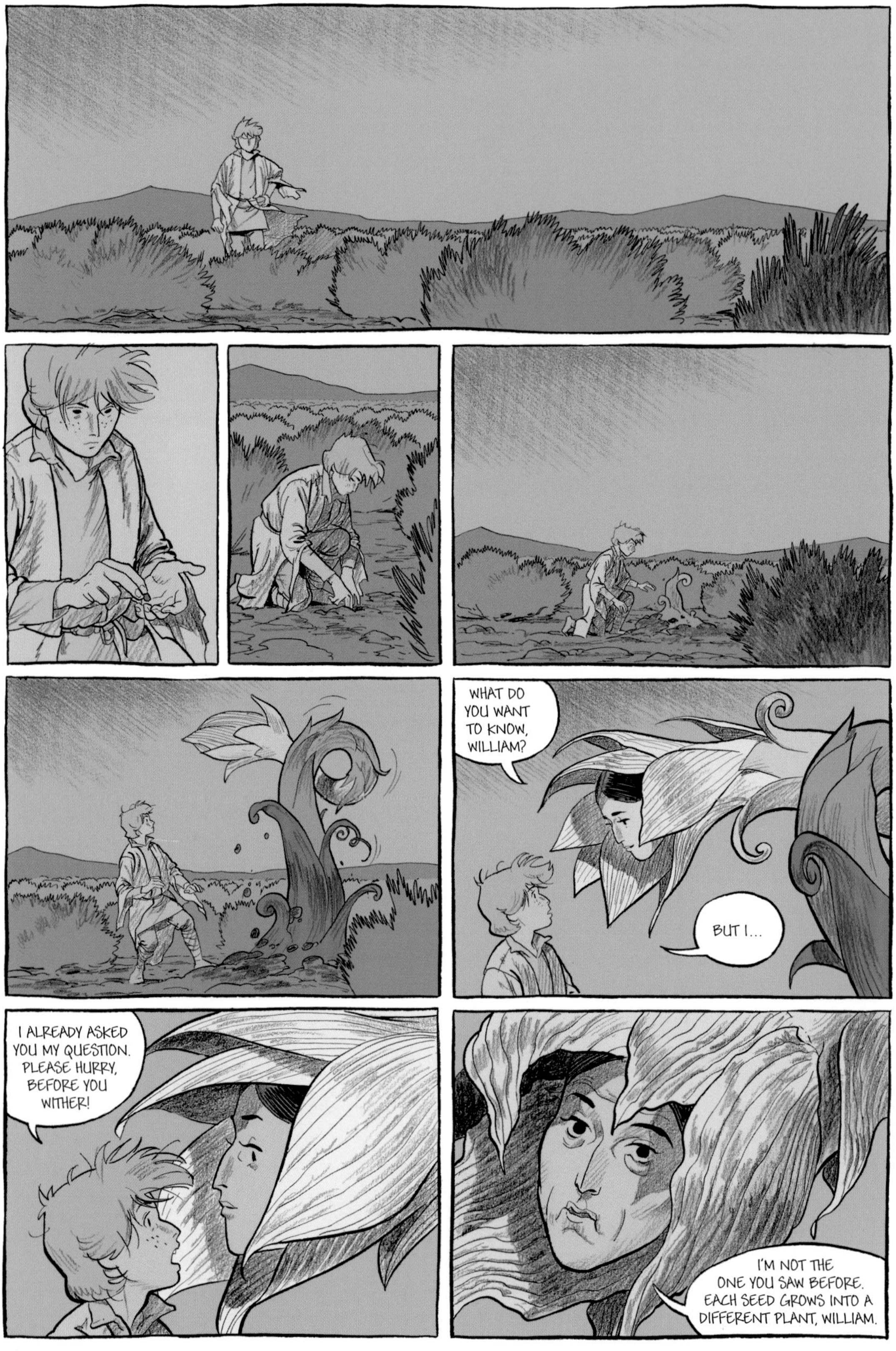
WHAT DO YOU WANT TO KNOW, WILLIAM?
BUT I...
I ALREADY ASKED YOU MY QUESTION. PLEASE HURRY, BEFORE YOU WITHER!
I'M NOT THE ONE YOU SAW BEFORE. EACH SEED GROWS INTO A DIFFERENT PLANT, WILLIAM.

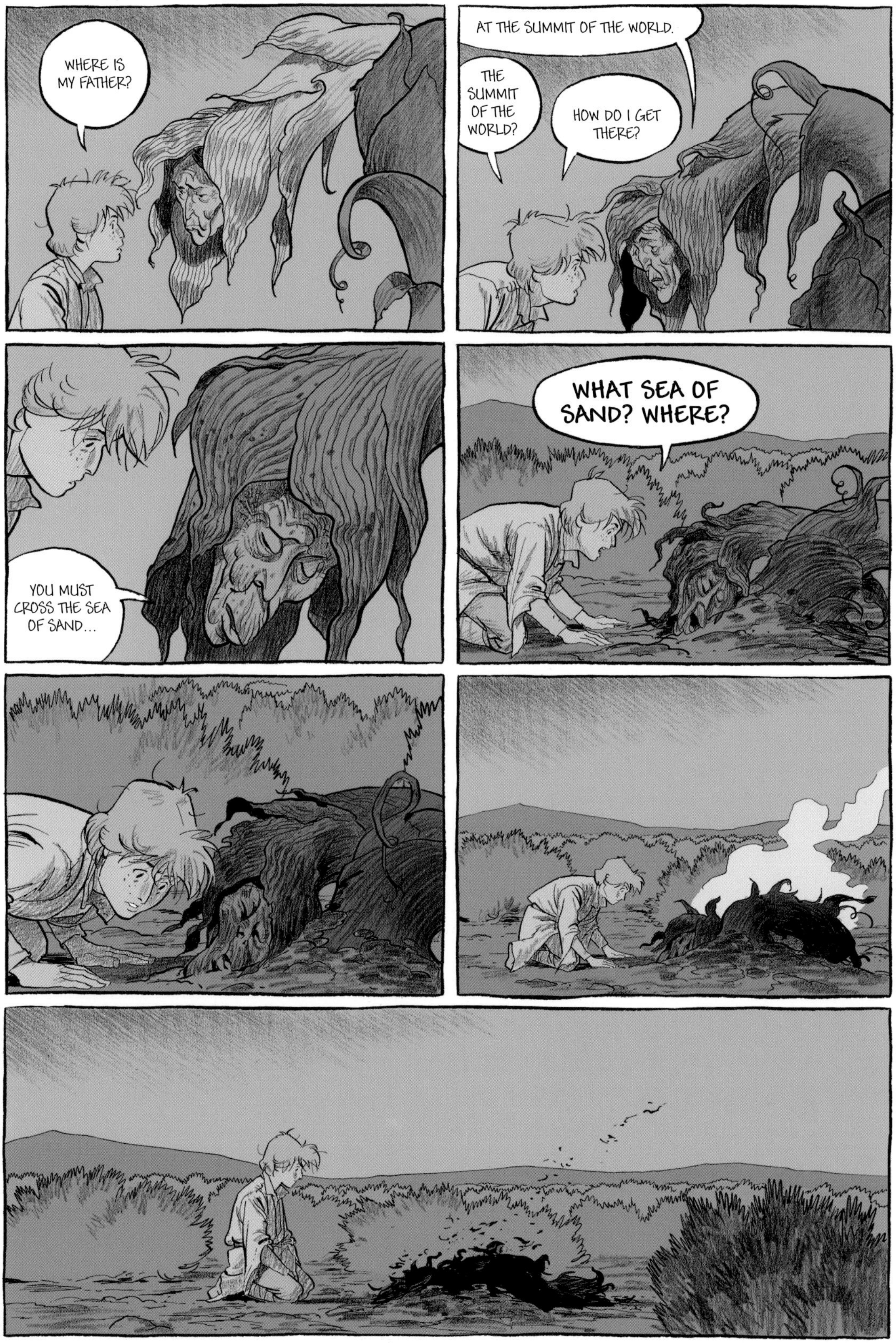
WHERE IS MY FATHER?
AT THE SUMMIT OF THE WORLD.
THE SUMMIT OF THE WORLD?
HOW DO I GET THERE?
YOU MUST CROSS THE SEA OF SAND...
WHAT SEA OF SAND? WHERE?

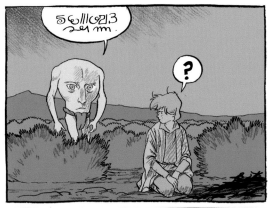

WHY DID YOU RUN OFF LIKE THAT?

WHO ARE YOU?

WHERE DO YOU COME FROM?

I DON'T KNOW HOW I GOT HERE...

I'M LOOKING FOR MY FATHER.

HAVE YOU HEARD OF THE SEA OF SAND? HOW CAN I GET THERE?

A SEA OF SAND? NO...

I ONLY KNOW THE SEA THAT ENCIRCLES THE WORLD.

WELL, AT LEAST **OUR** WORLD, SINCE YOU ARE PROOF THAT OTHER WORLDS EXIST!

I'VE HEARD LEGENDS ABOUT PEOPLE WHO CAME FROM ELSEWHERE, PEOPLE LIKE... LIKE YOU.

PEOPLE WITH THEIR EYES AND MOUTHS ABOVE THEIR...BODIES... I MEAN...IT DOESN'T BOTHER ME AT ALL...

BUT UNLIKE THE OTHERS, I ALWAYS KNEW THE LEGENDS WERE TRUE!

HOW AM I GOING TO FIND THIS SEA OF SAND? SHOULD I USE MY LAST SEED TO FIND OUT?

I DON'T REALLY UNDERSTAND WHAT YOU'RE SAYING, BUT I KNOW THERE'S NO SEA OF SAND IN THE WORLD I LIVE IN.

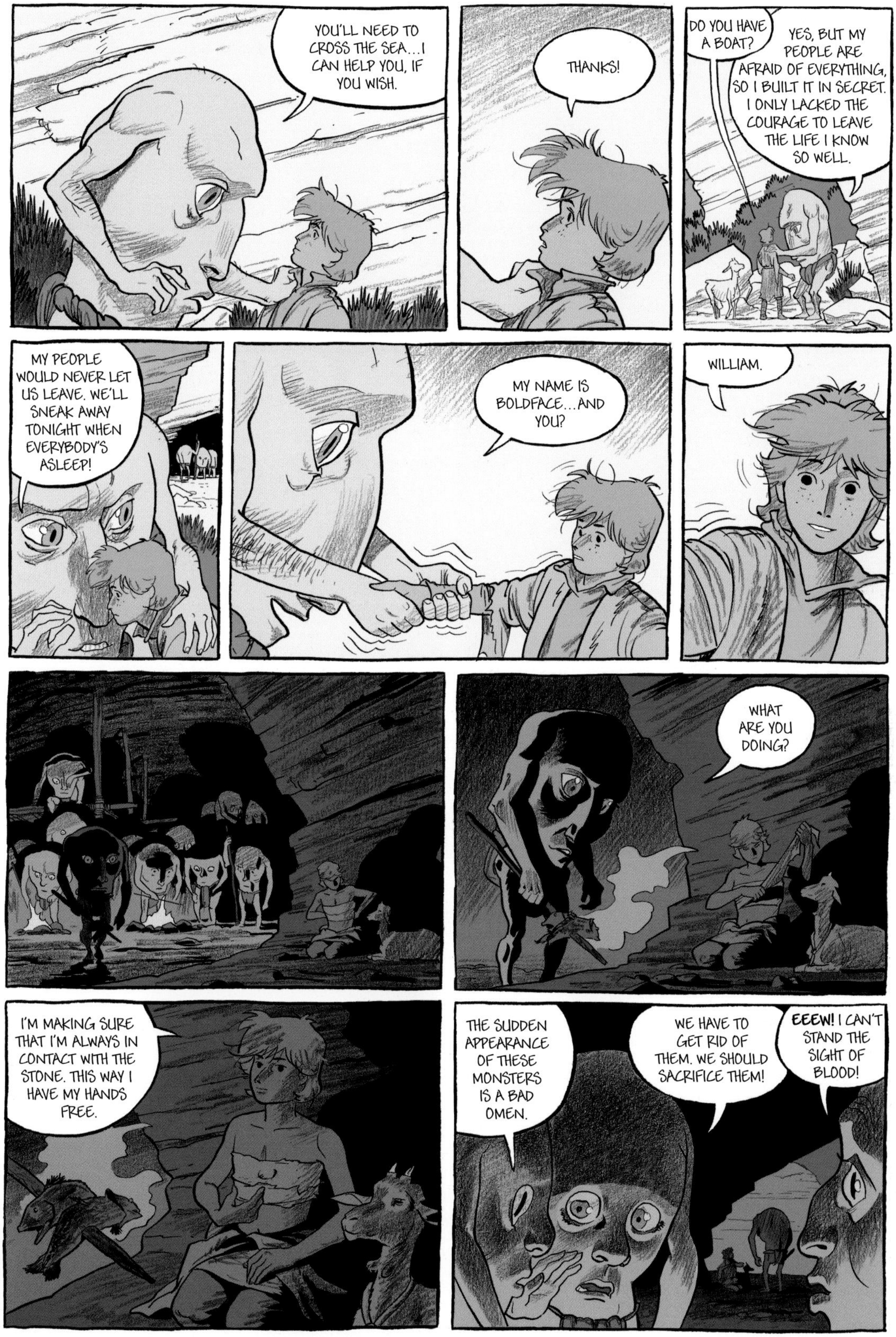
YOU'LL NEED TO CROSS THE SEA…I CAN HELP YOU, IF YOU WISH.
THANKS!
DO YOU HAVE A BOAT?
YES, BUT MY PEOPLE ARE AFRAID OF EVERYTHING, SO I BUILT IT IN SECRET. I ONLY LACKED THE COURAGE TO LEAVE THE LIFE I KNOW SO WELL.
MY PEOPLE WOULD NEVER LET US LEAVE. WE'LL SNEAK AWAY TONIGHT WHEN EVERYBODY'S ASLEEP!
MY NAME IS BOLDFACE…AND YOU?
WILLIAM.
WHAT ARE YOU DOING?
I'M MAKING SURE THAT I'M ALWAYS IN CONTACT WITH THE STONE. THIS WAY I HAVE MY HANDS FREE.
THE SUDDEN APPEARANCE OF THESE MONSTERS IS A BAD OMEN.
WE HAVE TO GET RID OF THEM. WE SHOULD SACRIFICE THEM!
EEEW! I CAN'T STAND THE SIGHT OF BLOOD!

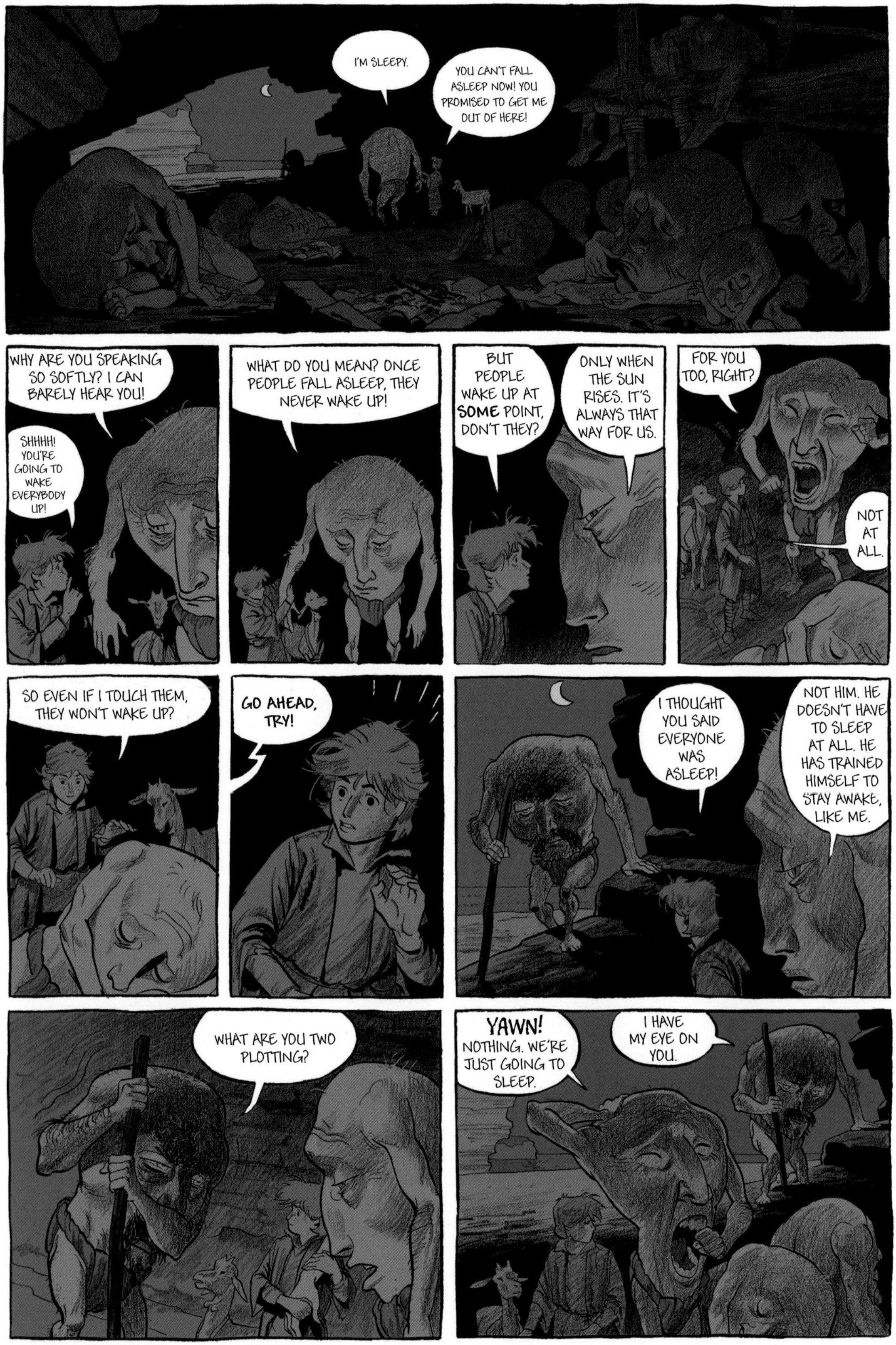

I'M SLEEPY.
YOU CAN'T FALL ASLEEP NOW! YOU PROMISED TO GET ME OUT OF HERE!
WHY ARE YOU SPEAKING SO SOFTLY? I CAN BARELY HEAR YOU!
SHHHH! YOU'RE GOING TO WAKE EVERYBODY UP!
WHAT DO YOU MEAN? ONCE PEOPLE FALL ASLEEP, THEY NEVER WAKE UP!
BUT PEOPLE WAKE UP AT SOME POINT, DON'T THEY?
ONLY WHEN THE SUN RISES. IT'S ALWAYS THAT WAY FOR US.
FOR YOU TOO, RIGHT?
NOT AT ALL.
SO EVEN IF I TOUCH THEM, THEY WON'T WAKE UP?
GO AHEAD, TRY!
I THOUGHT YOU SAID EVERYONE WAS ASLEEP!
NOT HIM. HE DOESN'T HAVE TO SLEEP AT ALL. HE HAS TRAINED HIMSELF TO STAY AWAKE, LIKE ME.
WHAT ARE YOU TWO PLOTTING?
YAWN! NOTHING. WE'RE JUST GOING TO SLEEP.
I HAVE MY EYE ON YOU.

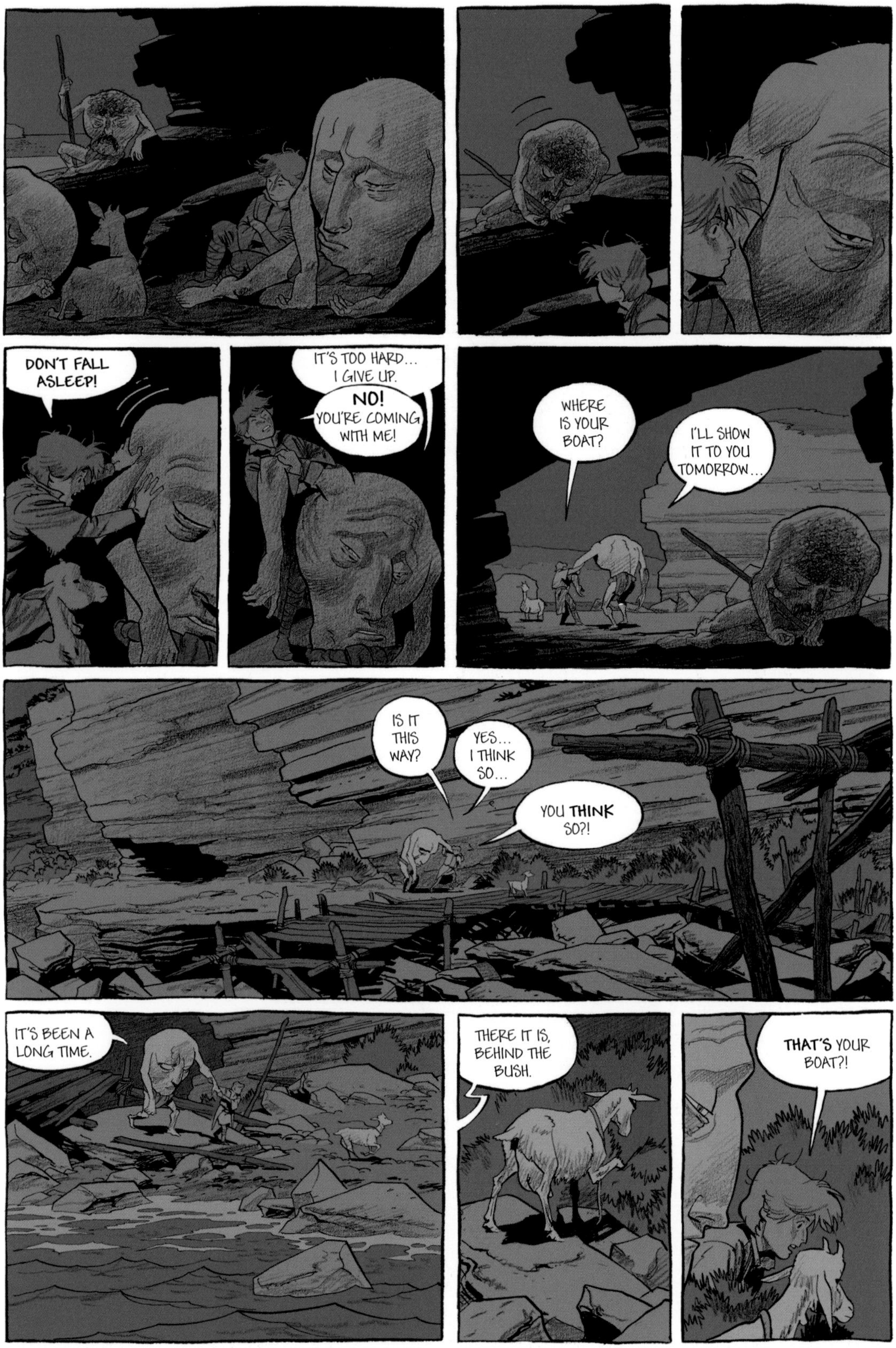
DON'T FALL ASLEEP!
IT'S TOO HARD… I GIVE UP.
NO! YOU'RE COMING WITH ME!
WHERE IS YOUR BOAT?
I'LL SHOW IT TO YOU TOMORROW…
IS IT THIS WAY?
YES… I THINK SO…
YOU THINK SO?!
IT'S BEEN A LONG TIME.
THERE IT IS, BEHIND THE BUSH.
THAT'S YOUR BOAT?!

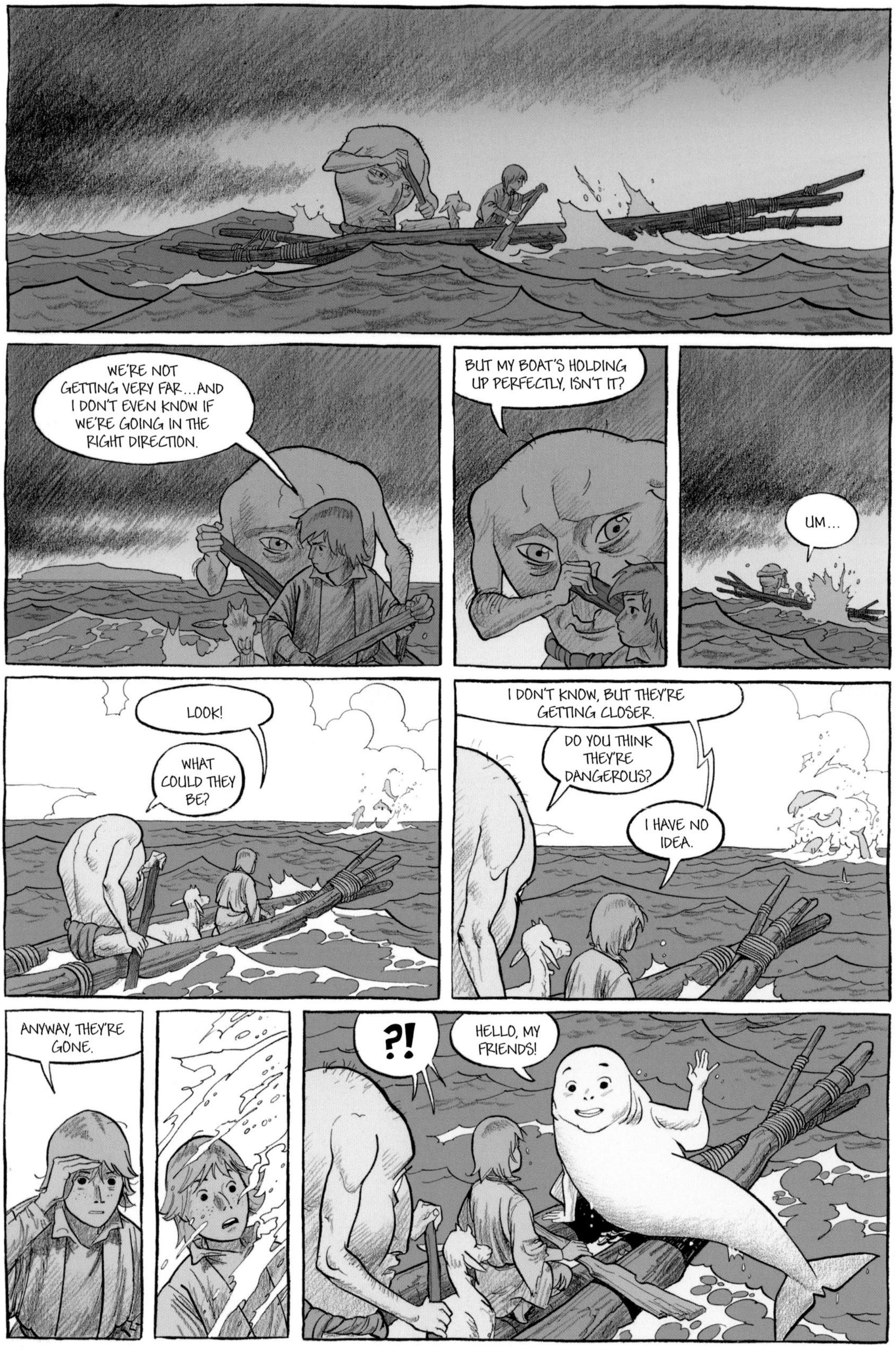
WE'RE NOT GETTING VERY FAR…AND I DON'T EVEN KNOW IF WE'RE GOING IN THE RIGHT DIRECTION.
BUT MY BOAT'S HOLDING UP PERFECTLY, ISN'T IT?
UM…
LOOK!
WHAT COULD THEY BE?
I DON'T KNOW, BUT THEY'RE GETTING CLOSER.
DO YOU THINK THEY'RE DANGEROUS?
I HAVE NO IDEA.
ANYWAY, THEY'RE GONE.
?!
HELLO, MY FRIENDS!

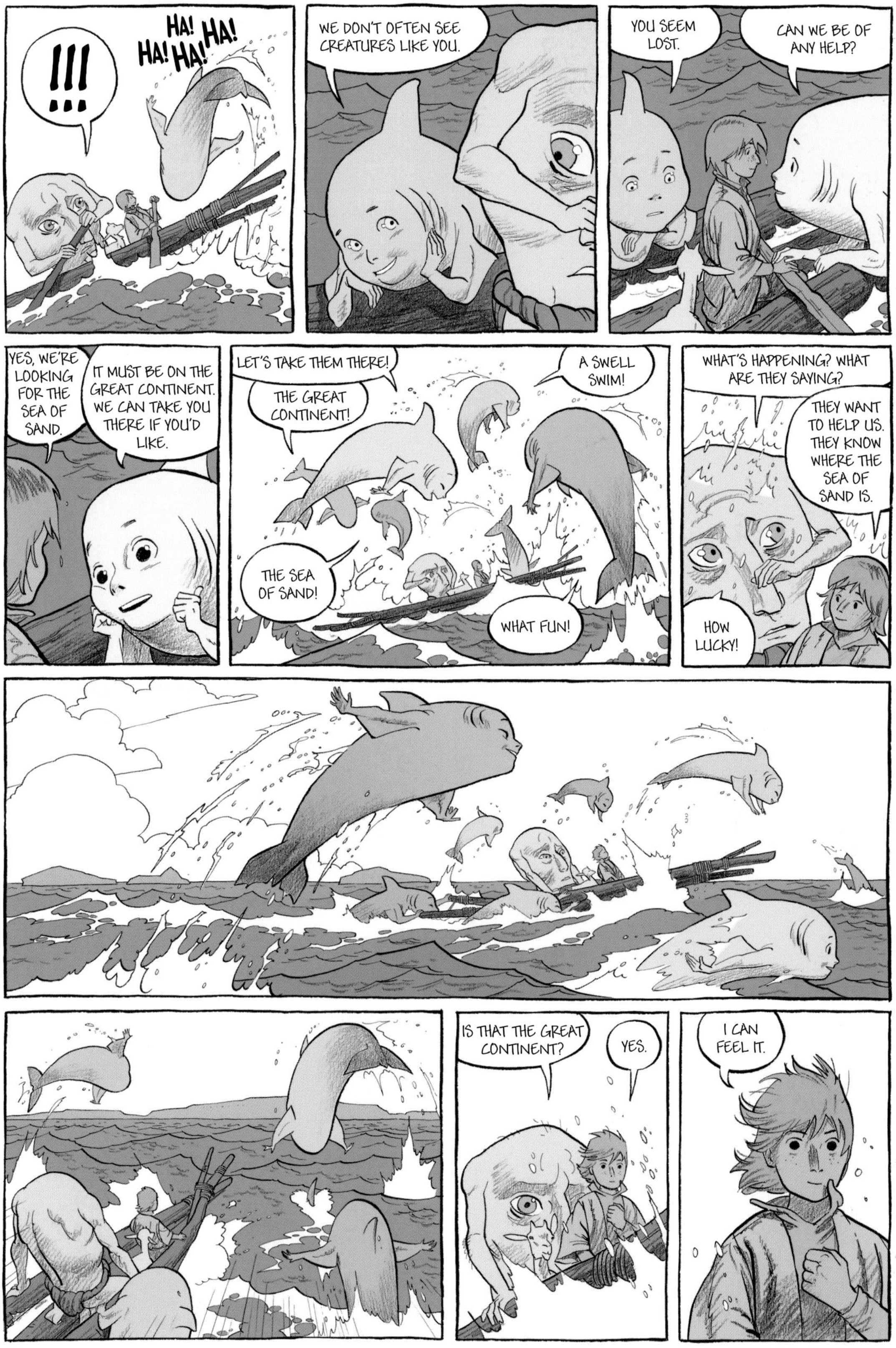
!!!
HA! HA! HA! HA!
WE DON'T OFTEN SEE CREATURES LIKE YOU.
YOU SEEM LOST.
CAN WE BE OF ANY HELP?
YES, WE'RE LOOKING FOR THE SEA OF SAND.
IT MUST BE ON THE GREAT CONTINENT. WE CAN TAKE YOU THERE IF YOU'D LIKE.
LET'S TAKE THEM THERE!
A SWELL SWIM!
THE GREAT CONTINENT!
THE SEA OF SAND!
WHAT FUN!
WHAT'S HAPPENING? WHAT ARE THEY SAYING?
THEY WANT TO HELP US. THEY KNOW WHERE THE SEA OF SAND IS.
HOW LUCKY!
IS THAT THE GREAT CONTINENT?
YES.
I CAN FEEL IT.

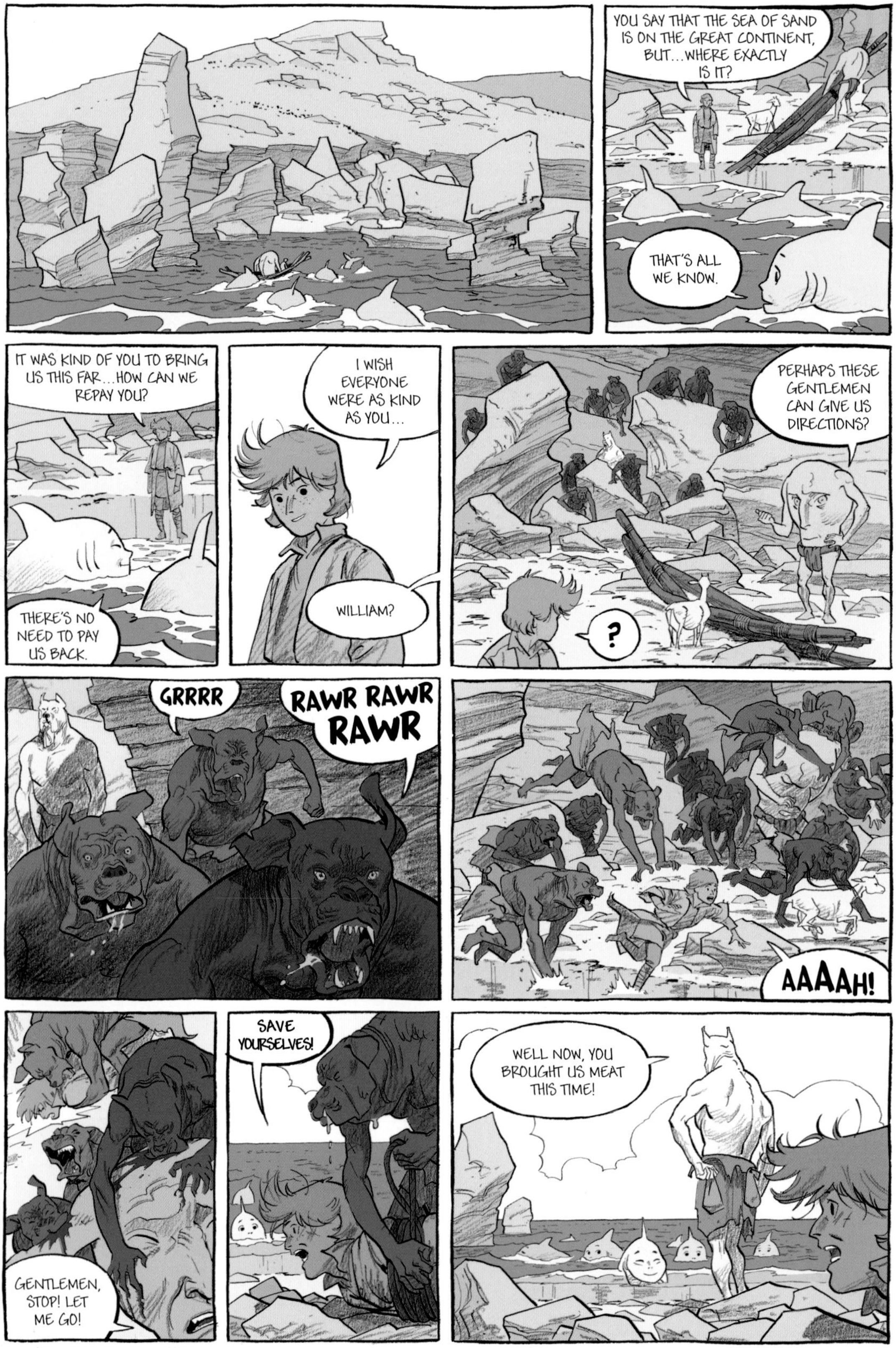
YOU SAY THAT THE SEA OF SAND IS ON THE GREAT CONTINENT, BUT...WHERE EXACTLY IS IT?
THAT'S ALL WE KNOW.
IT WAS KIND OF YOU TO BRING US THIS FAR...HOW CAN WE REPAY YOU?
THERE'S NO NEED TO PAY US BACK.
I WISH EVERYONE WERE AS KIND AS YOU...
WILLIAM?
PERHAPS THESE GENTLEMEN CAN GIVE US DIRECTIONS?
?
GRRRR
RAWR RAWR RAWR
AAAAH!
GENTLEMEN, STOP! LET ME GO!
SAVE YOURSELVES!
WELL NOW, YOU BROUGHT US MEAT THIS TIME!

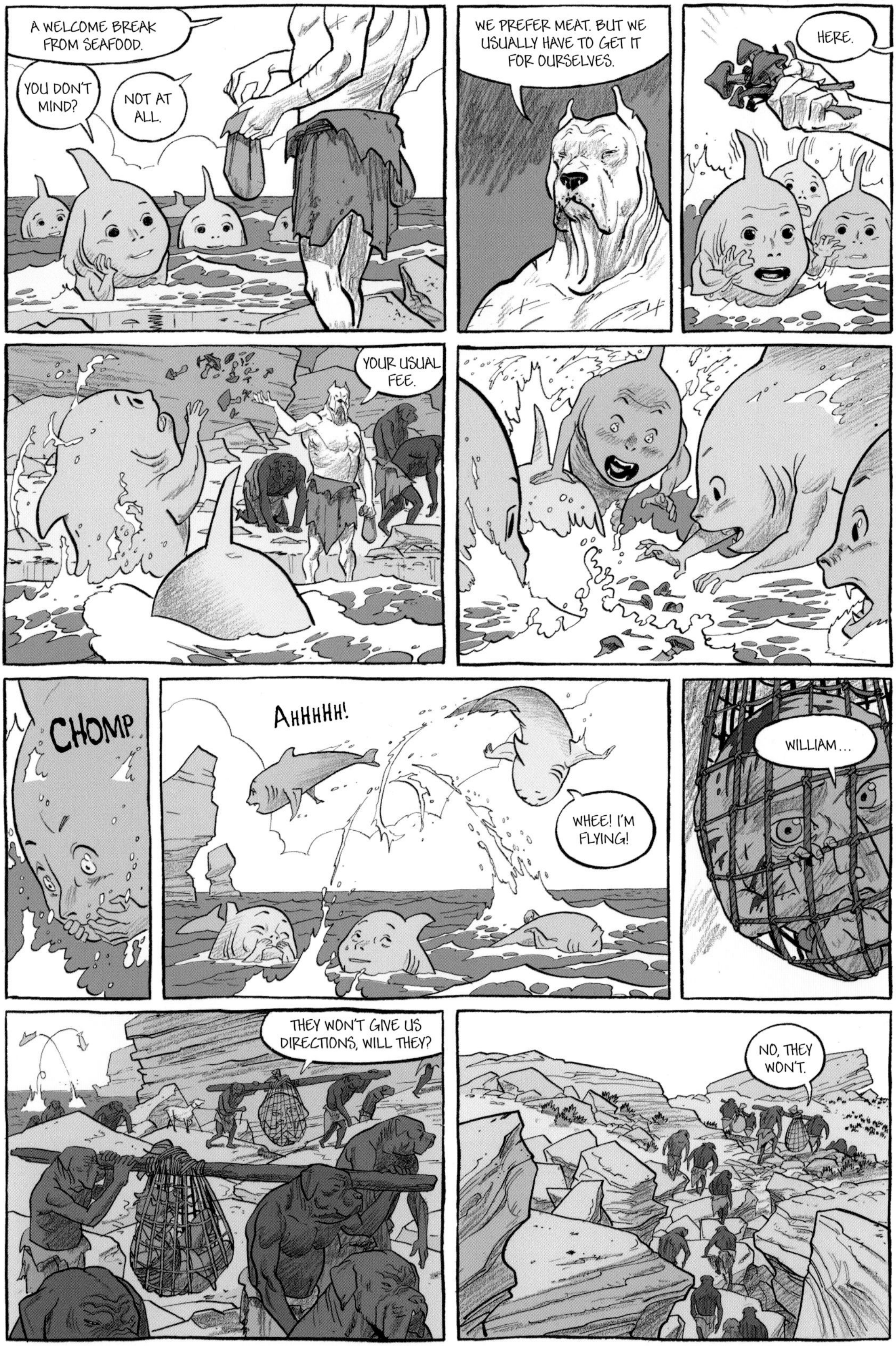
A WELCOME BREAK FROM SEAFOOD.
YOU DON'T MIND?
NOT AT ALL.
WE PREFER MEAT. BUT WE USUALLY HAVE TO GET IT FOR OURSELVES.
HERE.
YOUR USUAL FEE.
CHOMP
AHHHHH!
WHEE! I'M FLYING!
WILLIAM...
THEY WON'T GIVE US DIRECTIONS, WILL THEY?
NO, THEY WON'T.

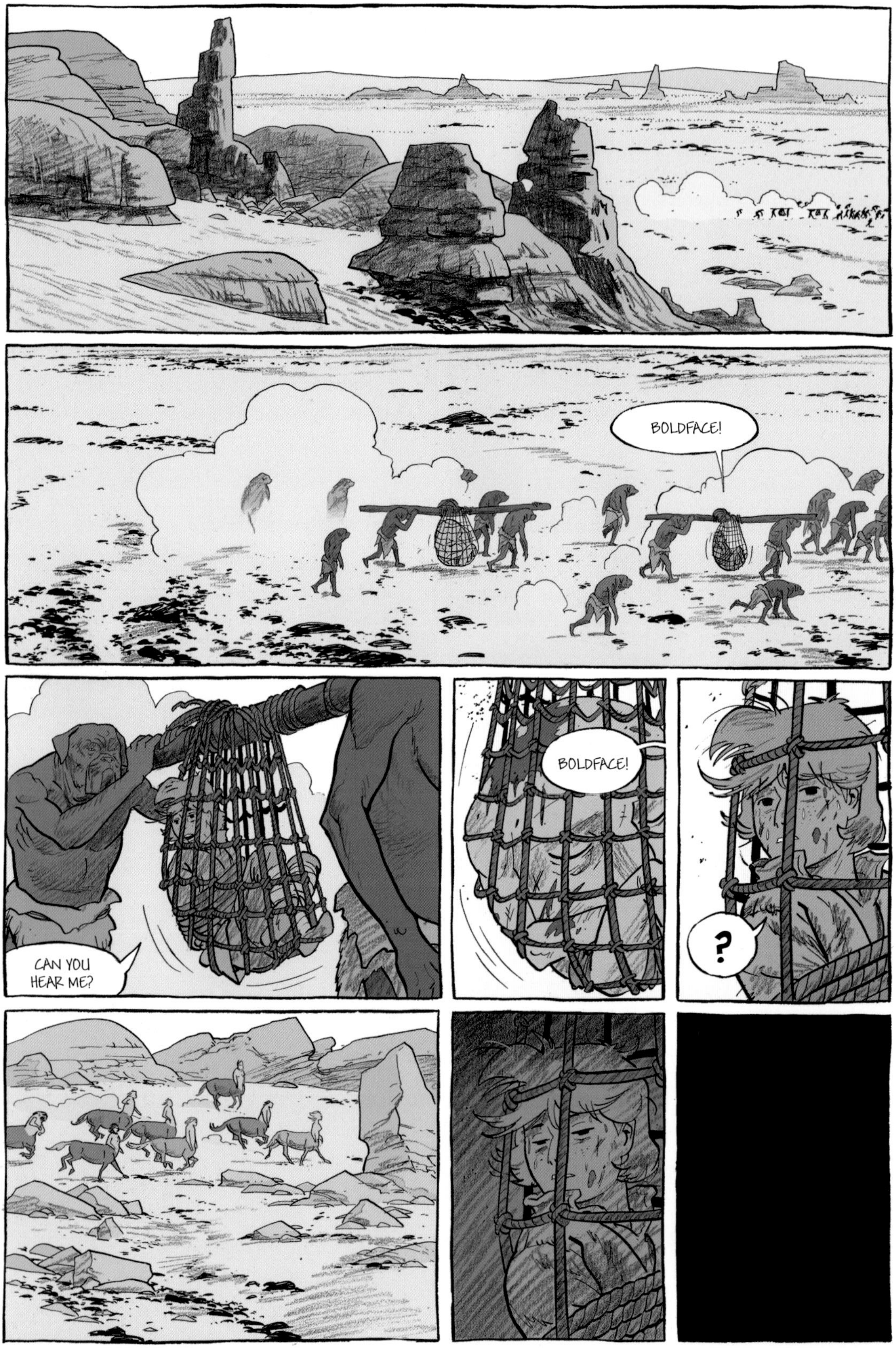
BOLDFACE!
CAN YOU HEAR ME?
BOLDFACE!
?

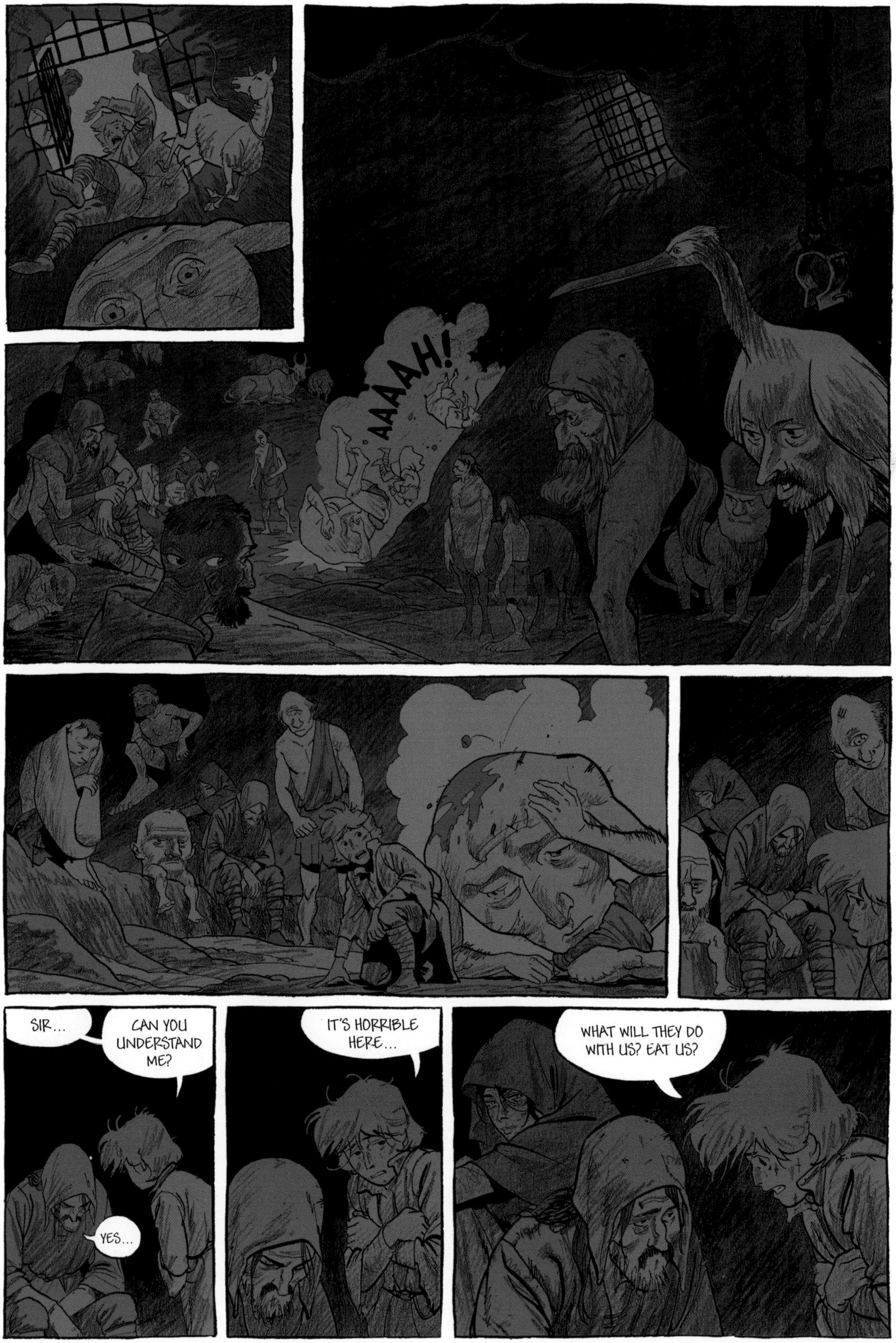
AAAAH!
SIR…
CAN YOU UNDERSTAND ME?
YES…
IT'S HORRIBLE HERE…
WHAT WILL THEY DO WITH US? EAT US?

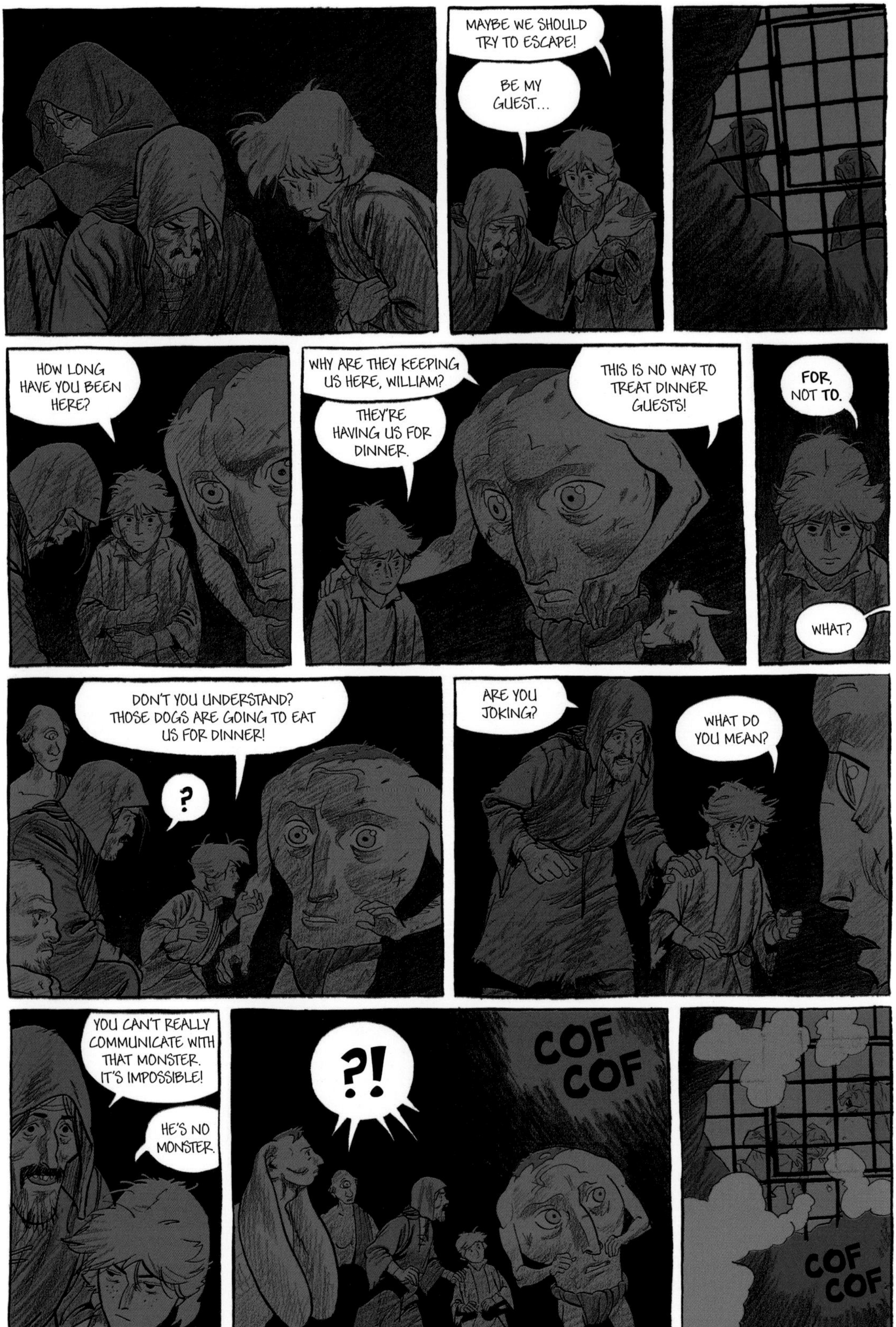

MAYBE WE SHOULD TRY TO ESCAPE!
BE MY GUEST...
HOW LONG HAVE YOU BEEN HERE?
WHY ARE THEY KEEPING US HERE, WILLIAM?
THEY'RE HAVING US FOR DINNER.
THIS IS NO WAY TO TREAT DINNER GUESTS!
FOR, NOT TO.
WHAT?
DON'T YOU UNDERSTAND? THOSE DOGS ARE GOING TO EAT US FOR DINNER!
?
ARE YOU JOKING?
WHAT DO YOU MEAN?
YOU CAN'T REALLY COMMUNICATE WITH THAT MONSTER. IT'S IMPOSSIBLE!
HE'S NO MONSTER.
?!
COF COF
COF COF

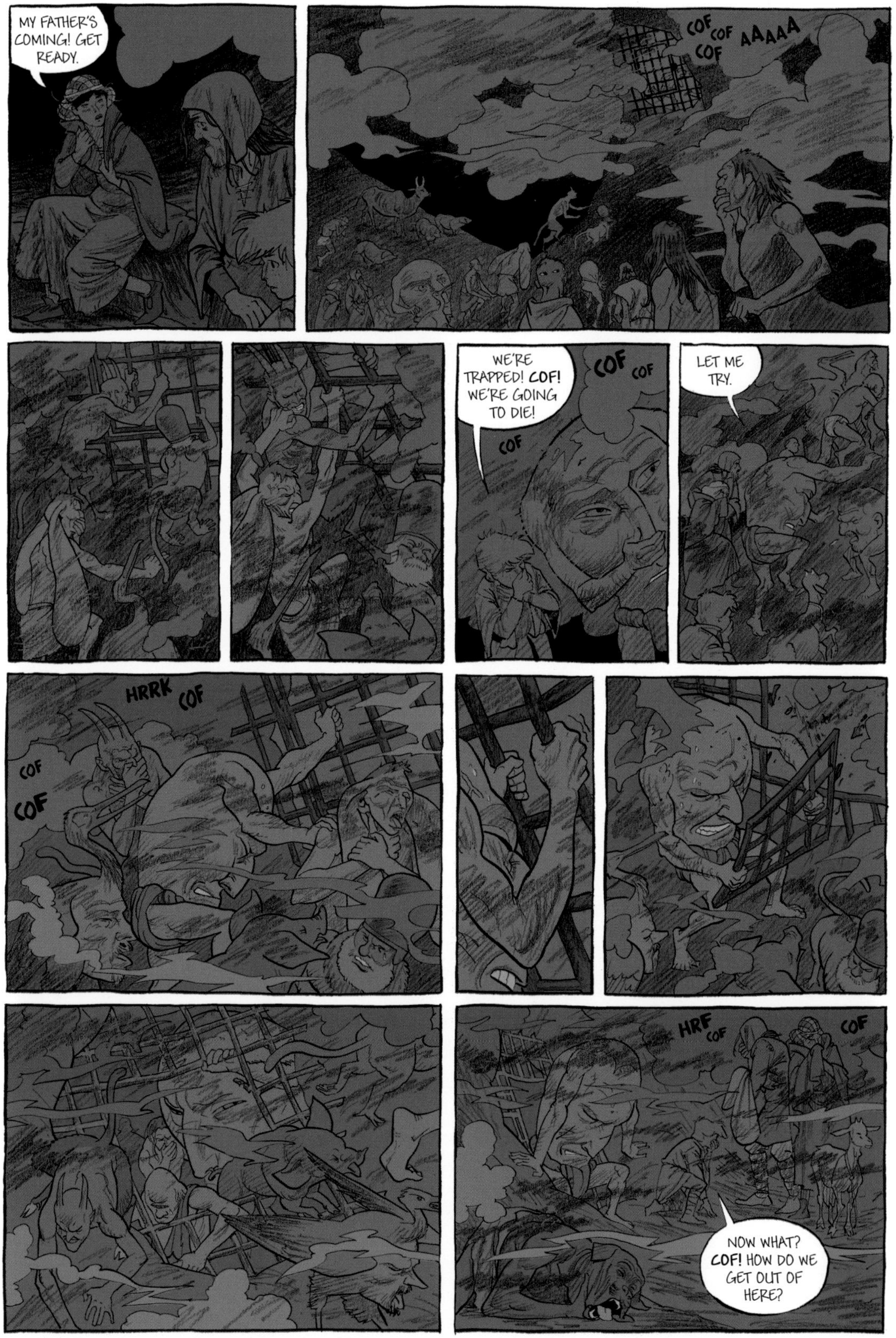

MY FATHER'S COMING! GET READY.
COF COF COF AAAAA
WE'RE TRAPPED! COF! WE'RE GOING TO DIE!
COF COF
COF
LET ME TRY.
HRRK COF
COF
COF
HRF COF
COF
NOW WHAT? COF! HOW DO WE GET OUT OF HERE?

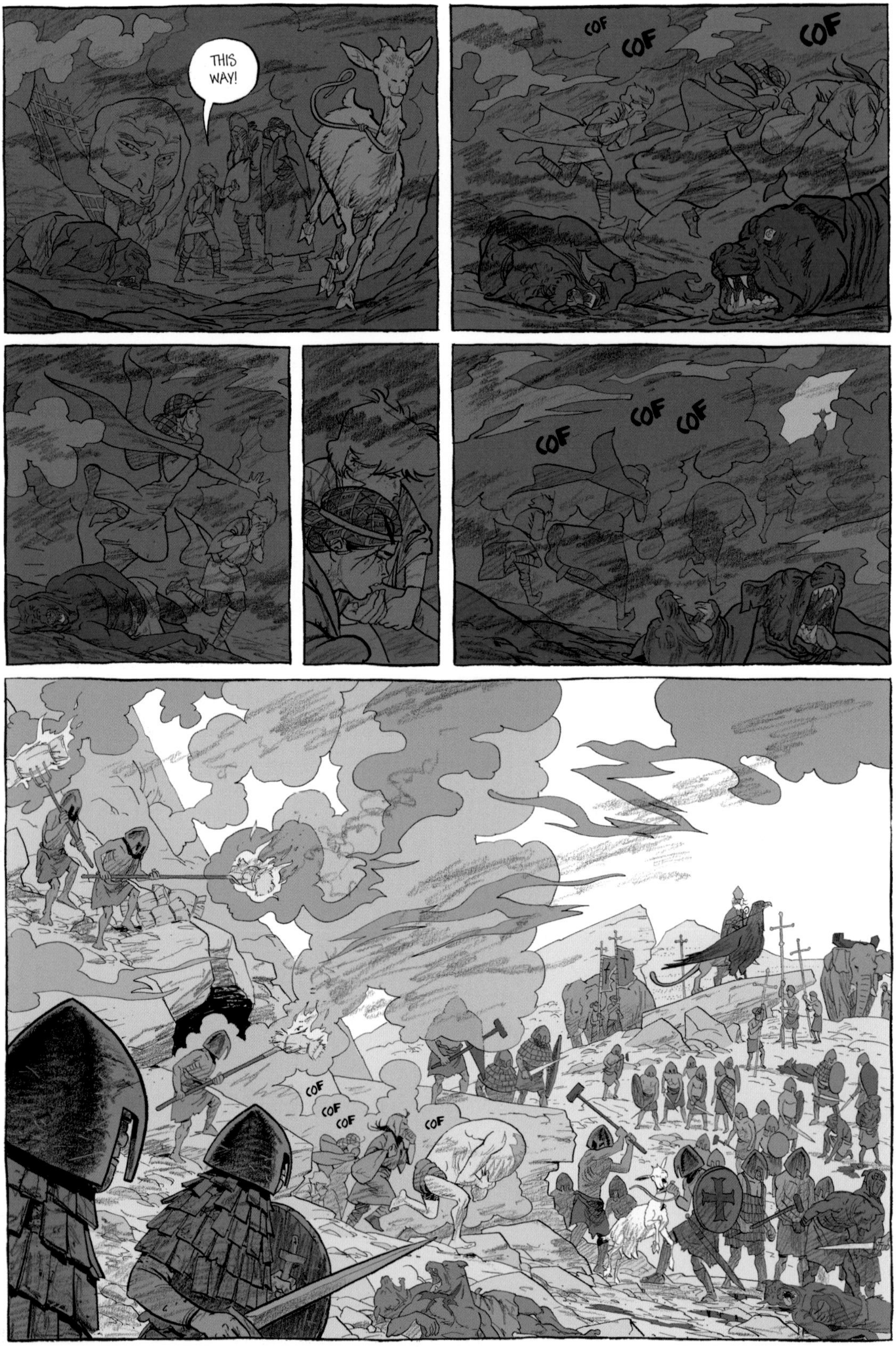
THIS WAY!
COF
COF
COF
COF
COF
COF
COF
COF
COF
COF

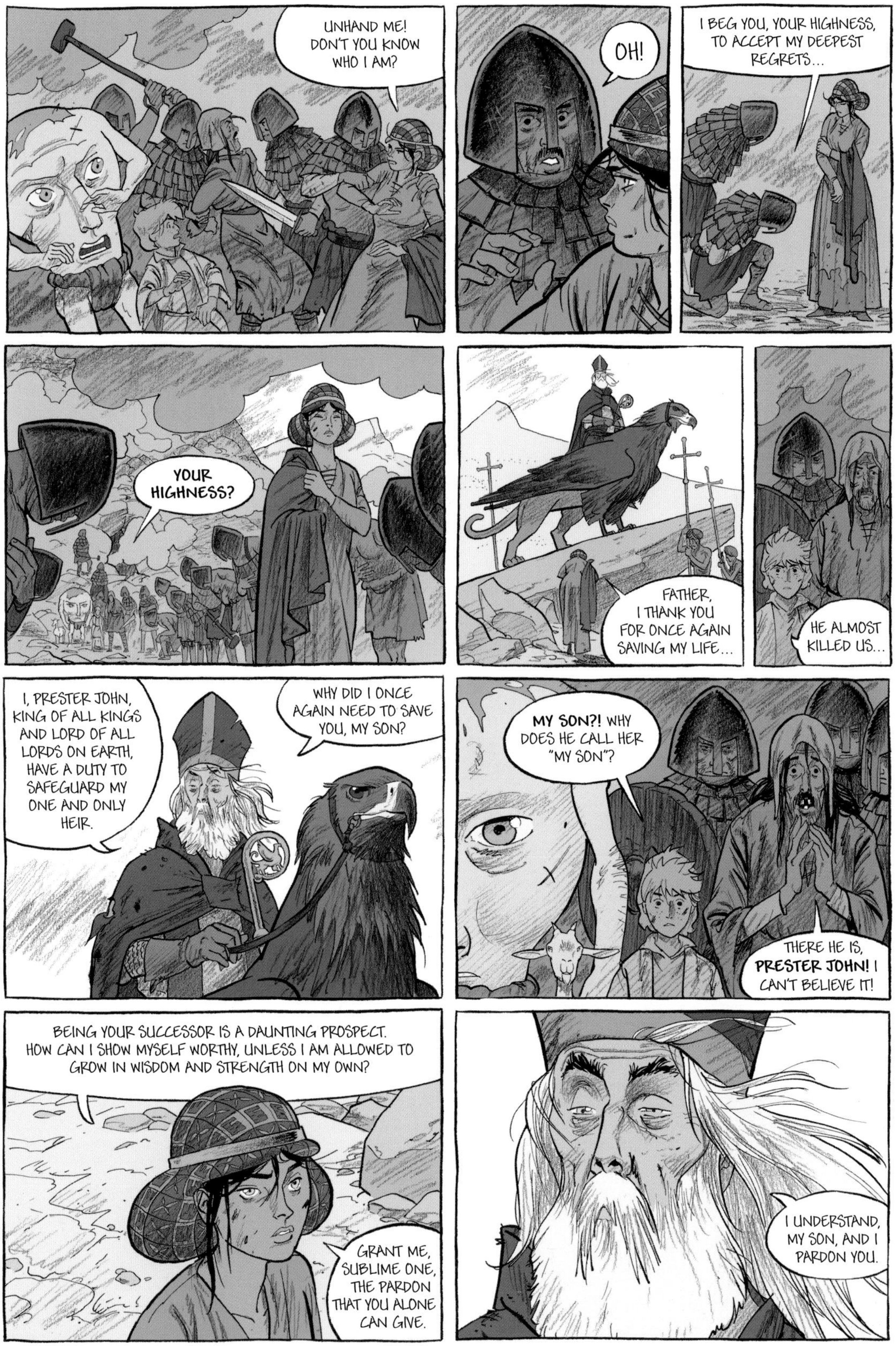
UNHAND ME! DON'T YOU KNOW WHO I AM?
OH!
I BEG YOU, YOUR HIGHNESS, TO ACCEPT MY DEEPEST REGRETS...
YOUR HIGHNESS?
FATHER, I THANK YOU FOR ONCE AGAIN SAVING MY LIFE...
HE ALMOST KILLED US...
I, PRESTER JOHN, KING OF ALL KINGS AND LORD OF ALL LORDS ON EARTH, HAVE A DUTY TO SAFEGUARD MY ONE AND ONLY HEIR.
WHY DID I ONCE AGAIN NEED TO SAVE YOU, MY SON?
MY SON?! WHY DOES HE CALL HER "MY SON"?
THERE HE IS, PRESTER JOHN! I CAN'T BELIEVE IT!
BEING YOUR SUCCESSOR IS A DAUNTING PROSPECT. HOW CAN I SHOW MYSELF WORTHY, UNLESS I AM ALLOWED TO GROW IN WISDOM AND STRENGTH ON MY OWN?
GRANT ME, SUBLIME ONE, THE PARDON THAT YOU ALONE CAN GIVE.
I UNDERSTAND, MY SON, AND I PARDON YOU.

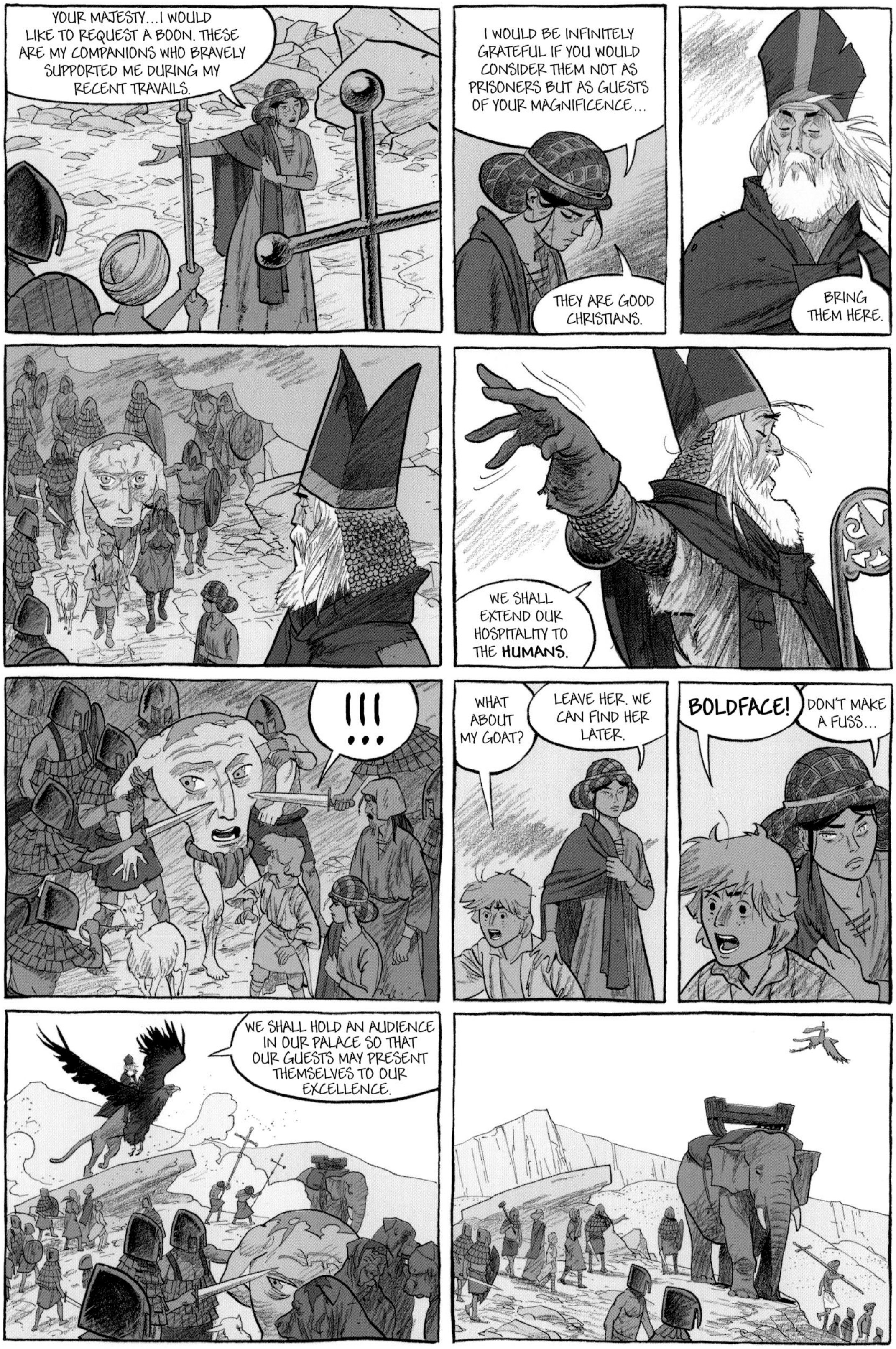
YOUR MAJESTY...I WOULD LIKE TO REQUEST A BOON. THESE ARE MY COMPANIONS WHO BRAVELY SUPPORTED ME DURING MY RECENT TRAVAILS.
I WOULD BE INFINITELY GRATEFUL IF YOU WOULD CONSIDER THEM NOT AS PRISONERS BUT AS GUESTS OF YOUR MAGNIFICENCE...
THEY ARE GOOD CHRISTIANS.
BRING THEM HERE.
WE SHALL EXTEND OUR HOSPITALITY TO THE **HUMANS.**
!!!...
WHAT ABOUT MY GOAT?
LEAVE HER. WE CAN FIND HER LATER.
BOLDFACE!
DON'T MAKE A FUSS...
WE SHALL HOLD AN AUDIENCE IN OUR PALACE SO THAT OUR GUESTS MAY PRESENT THEMSELVES TO OUR EXCELLENCE.

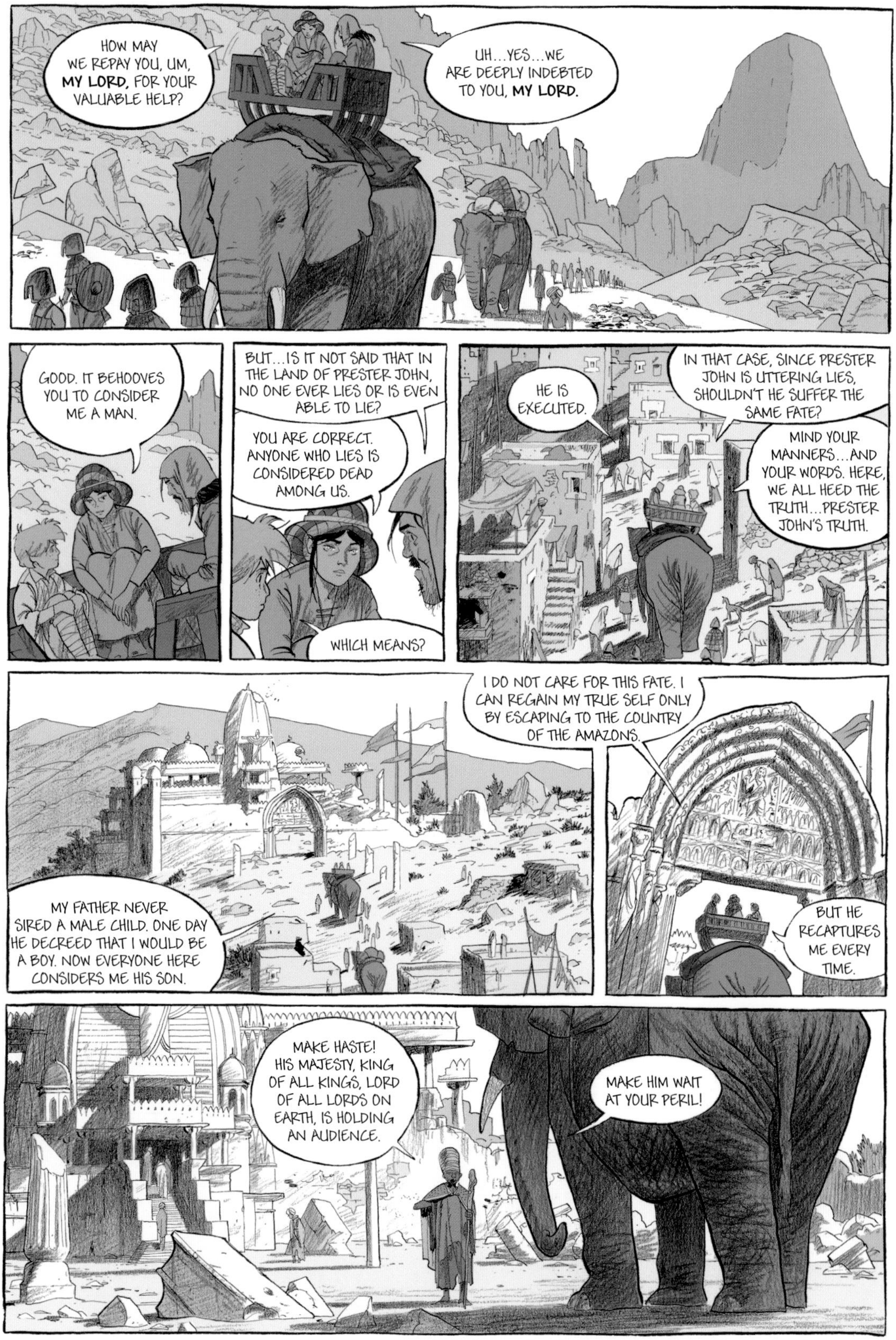

HOW MAY WE REPAY YOU, UM, **MY LORD,** FOR YOUR VALUABLE HELP?
UH...YES...WE ARE DEEPLY INDEBTED TO YOU, **MY LORD.**
GOOD. IT BEHOOVES YOU TO CONSIDER ME A MAN.
BUT...IS IT NOT SAID THAT IN THE LAND OF PRESTER JOHN, NO ONE EVER LIES OR IS EVEN ABLE TO LIE?
YOU ARE CORRECT. ANYONE WHO LIES IS CONSIDERED DEAD AMONG US.
WHICH MEANS?
HE IS EXECUTED.
IN THAT CASE, SINCE PRESTER JOHN IS UTTERING LIES, SHOULDN'T HE SUFFER THE SAME FATE?
MIND YOUR MANNERS...AND YOUR WORDS. HERE, WE ALL HEED THE TRUTH...PRESTER JOHN'S TRUTH.
MY FATHER NEVER SIRED A MALE CHILD. ONE DAY HE DECREED THAT I WOULD BE A BOY. NOW EVERYONE HERE CONSIDERS ME HIS SON.
I DO NOT CARE FOR THIS FATE. I CAN REGAIN MY TRUE SELF ONLY BY ESCAPING TO THE COUNTRY OF THE AMAZONS.
BUT HE RECAPTURES ME EVERY TIME.
MAKE HASTE! HIS MAJESTY, KING OF ALL KINGS, LORD OF ALL LORDS ON EARTH, IS HOLDING AN AUDIENCE.
MAKE HIM WAIT AT YOUR PERIL!

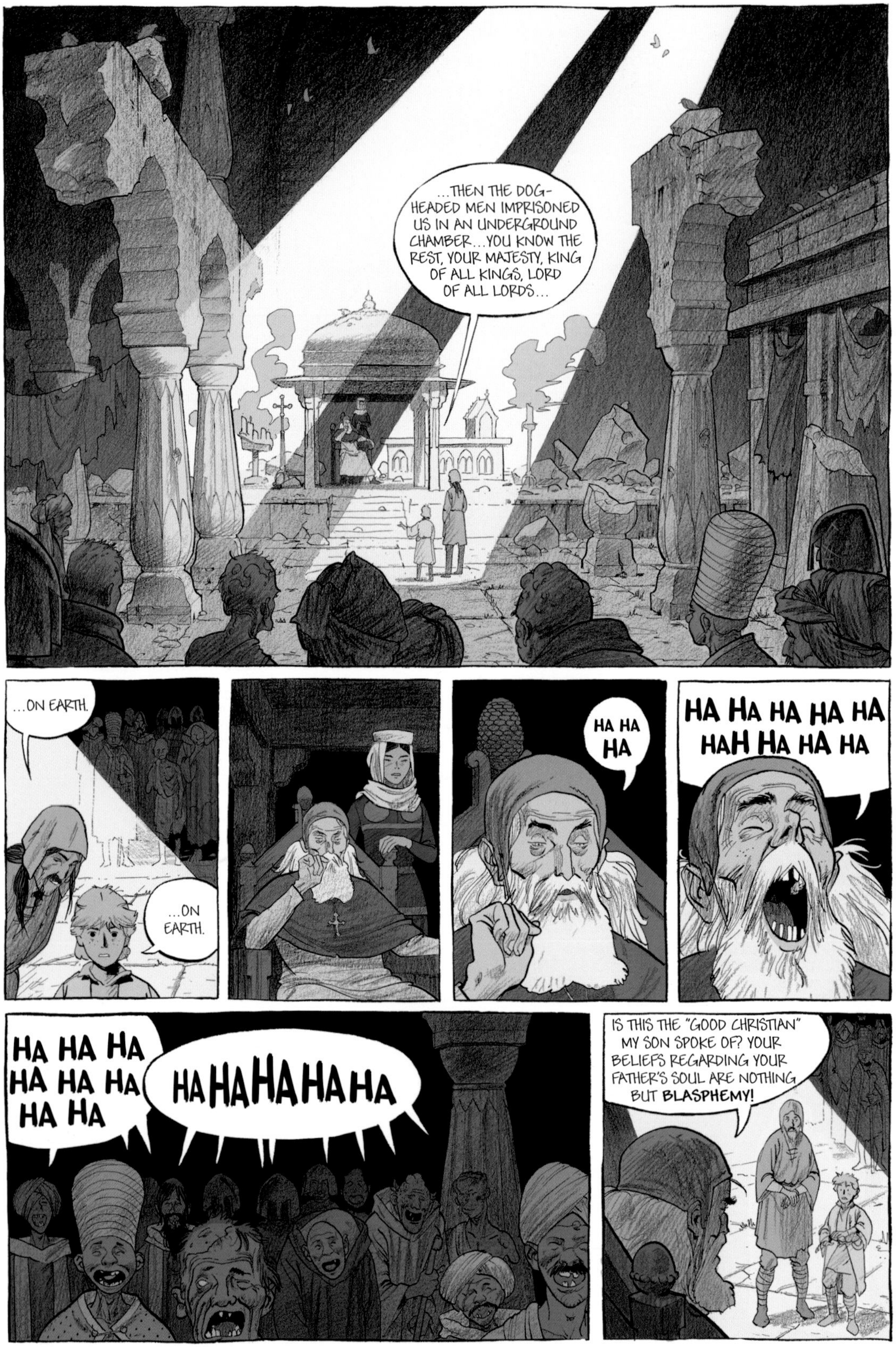
...THEN THE DOG-HEADED MEN IMPRISONED US IN AN UNDERGROUND CHAMBER... YOU KNOW THE REST, YOUR MAJESTY, KING OF ALL KINGS, LORD OF ALL LORDS...
...ON EARTH.
...ON EARTH.
HA HA HA
HA HA HA HA HA HAH HA HA HA HA
HA HA HA HA HA HA HA HA
HA HA HA HA HA HA
IS THIS THE "GOOD CHRISTIAN" MY SON SPOKE OF? YOUR BELIEFS REGARDING YOUR FATHER'S SOUL ARE NOTHING BUT **BLASPHEMY!**

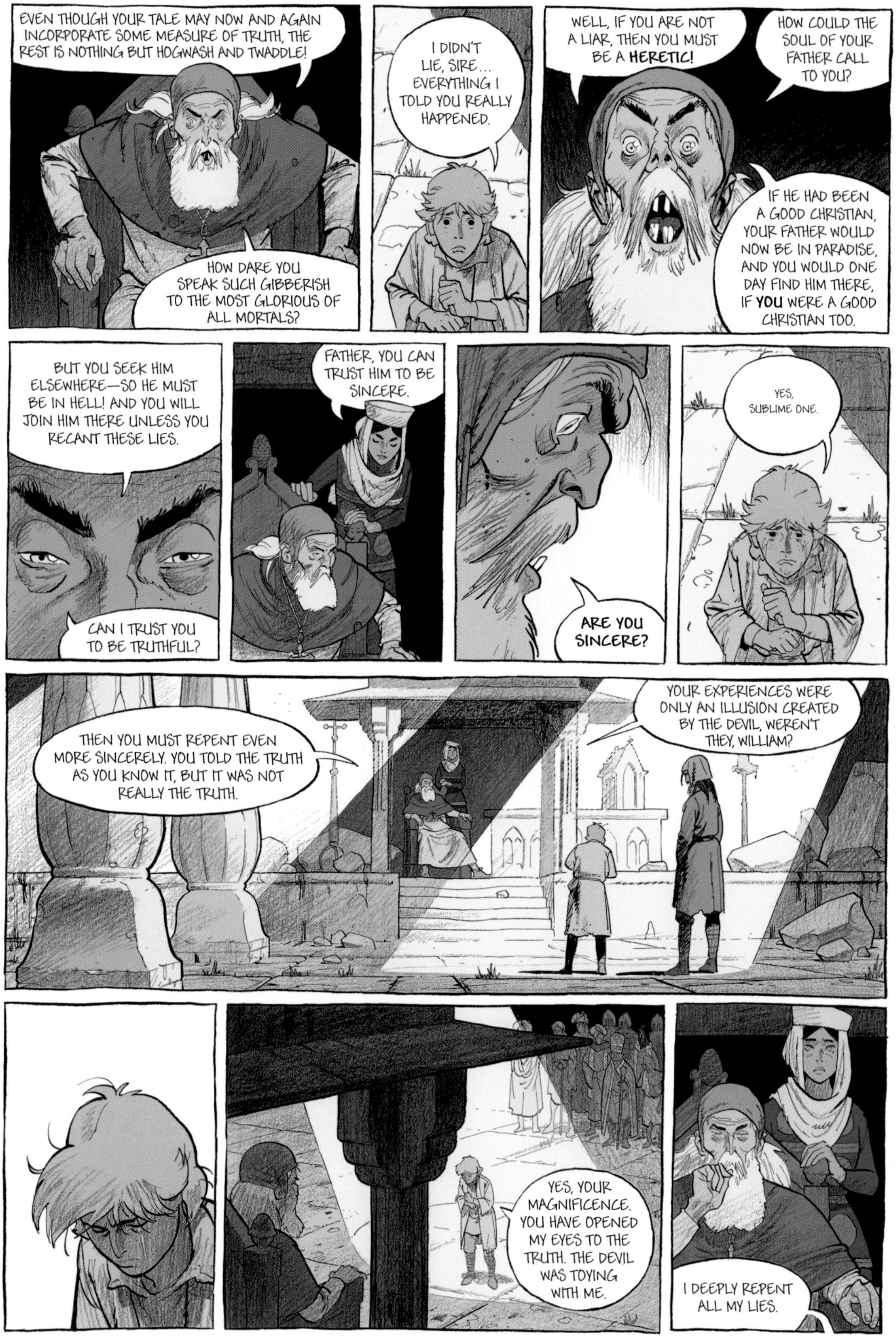

EVEN THOUGH YOUR TALE MAY NOW AND AGAIN INCORPORATE SOME MEASURE OF TRUTH, THE REST IS NOTHING BUT HOGWASH AND TWADDLE!
HOW DARE YOU SPEAK SUCH GIBBERISH TO THE MOST GLORIOUS OF ALL MORTALS?
I DIDN'T LIE, SIRE… EVERYTHING I TOLD YOU REALLY HAPPENED.
WELL, IF YOU ARE NOT A LIAR, THEN YOU MUST BE A **HERETIC!**
HOW COULD THE SOUL OF YOUR FATHER CALL TO YOU?
IF HE HAD BEEN A GOOD CHRISTIAN, YOUR FATHER WOULD NOW BE IN PARADISE, AND YOU WOULD ONE DAY FIND HIM THERE, IF **YOU** WERE A GOOD CHRISTIAN TOO.
BUT YOU SEEK HIM ELSEWHERE—SO HE MUST BE IN HELL! AND YOU WILL JOIN HIM THERE UNLESS YOU RECANT THESE LIES.
CAN I TRUST YOU TO BE TRUTHFUL?
FATHER, YOU CAN TRUST HIM TO BE SINCERE.
ARE YOU SINCERE?
YES, SUBLIME ONE.
THEN YOU MUST REPENT EVEN MORE SINCERELY. YOU TOLD THE TRUTH AS YOU KNOW IT, BUT IT WAS NOT REALLY THE TRUTH.
YOUR EXPERIENCES WERE ONLY AN ILLUSION CREATED BY THE DEVIL, WEREN'T THEY, WILLIAM?
YES, YOUR MAGNIFICENCE. YOU HAVE OPENED MY EYES TO THE TRUTH. THE DEVIL WAS TOYING WITH ME.
I DEEPLY REPENT ALL MY LIES.

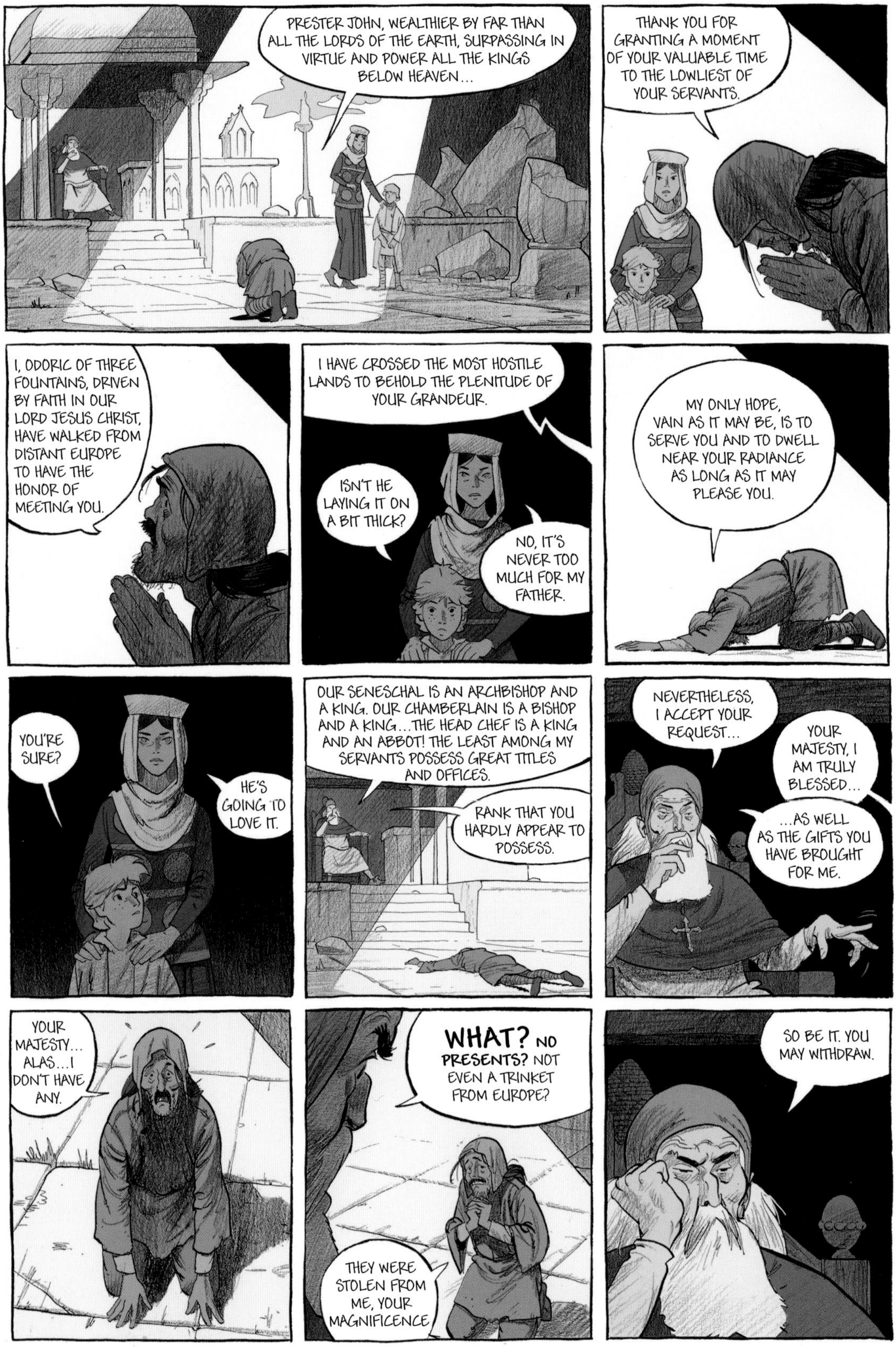

PRESTER JOHN, WEALTHIER BY FAR THAN ALL THE LORDS OF THE EARTH, SURPASSING IN VIRTUE AND POWER ALL THE KINGS BELOW HEAVEN…
THANK YOU FOR GRANTING A MOMENT OF YOUR VALUABLE TIME TO THE LOWLIEST OF YOUR SERVANTS.
I, ODORIC OF THREE FOUNTAINS, DRIVEN BY FAITH IN OUR LORD JESUS CHRIST, HAVE WALKED FROM DISTANT EUROPE TO HAVE THE HONOR OF MEETING YOU.
I HAVE CROSSED THE MOST HOSTILE LANDS TO BEHOLD THE PLENITUDE OF YOUR GRANDEUR.
ISN'T HE LAYING IT ON A BIT THICK?
NO, IT'S NEVER TOO MUCH FOR MY FATHER.
MY ONLY HOPE, VAIN AS IT MAY BE, IS TO SERVE YOU AND TO DWELL NEAR YOUR RADIANCE AS LONG AS IT MAY PLEASE YOU.
YOU'RE SURE?
HE'S GOING TO LOVE IT.
OUR SENESCHAL IS AN ARCHBISHOP AND A KING. OUR CHAMBERLAIN IS A BISHOP AND A KING…THE HEAD CHEF IS A KING AND AN ABBOT! THE LEAST AMONG MY SERVANTS POSSESS GREAT TITLES AND OFFICES.
RANK THAT YOU HARDLY APPEAR TO POSSESS.
NEVERTHELESS, I ACCEPT YOUR REQUEST…
YOUR MAJESTY, I AM TRULY BLESSED…
…AS WELL AS THE GIFTS YOU HAVE BROUGHT FOR ME.
YOUR MAJESTY… ALAS…I DON'T HAVE ANY.
WHAT? NO PRESENTS? NOT EVEN A TRINKET FROM EUROPE?
THEY WERE STOLEN FROM ME, YOUR MAGNIFICENCE.
SO BE IT. YOU MAY WITHDRAW.

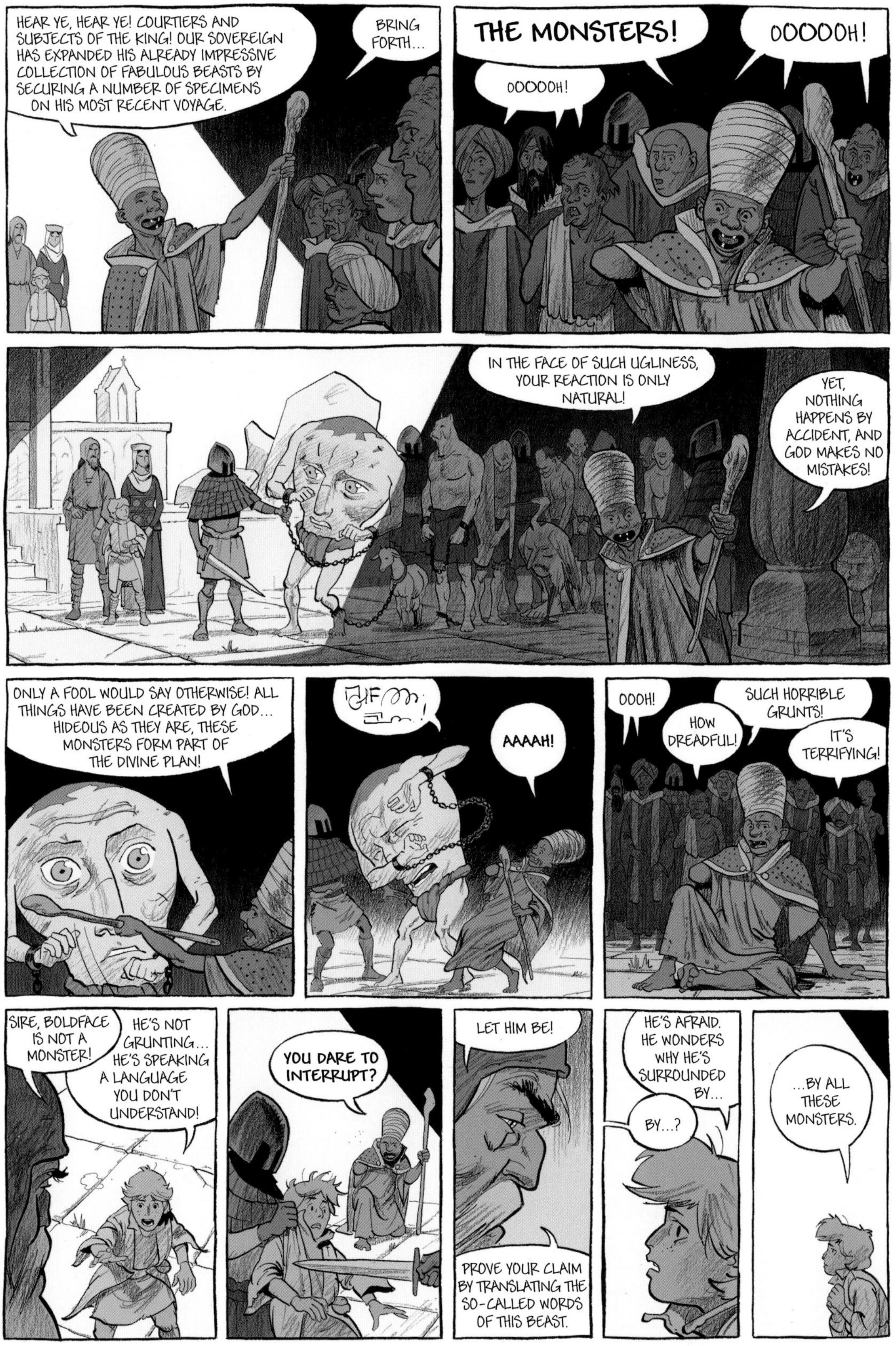
HEAR YE, HEAR YE! COURTIERS AND SUBJECTS OF THE KING! OUR SOVEREIGN HAS EXPANDED HIS ALREADY IMPRESSIVE COLLECTION OF FABULOUS BEASTS BY SECURING A NUMBER OF SPECIMENS ON HIS MOST RECENT VOYAGE.
BRING FORTH…
THE MONSTERS!
OOOOOH!
OOOOOH!
IN THE FACE OF SUCH UGLINESS, YOUR REACTION IS ONLY NATURAL!
YET, NOTHING HAPPENS BY ACCIDENT, AND GOD MAKES NO MISTAKES!
ONLY A FOOL WOULD SAY OTHERWISE! ALL THINGS HAVE BEEN CREATED BY GOD… HIDEOUS AS THEY ARE, THESE MONSTERS FORM PART OF THE DIVINE PLAN!
AAAAH!
OOOH!
SUCH HORRIBLE GRUNTS!
HOW DREADFUL!
IT'S TERRIFYING!
SIRE, BOLDFACE IS NOT A MONSTER!
HE'S NOT GRUNTING… HE'S SPEAKING A LANGUAGE YOU DON'T UNDERSTAND!
YOU DARE TO INTERRUPT?
LET HIM BE!
PROVE YOUR CLAIM BY TRANSLATING THE SO-CALLED WORDS OF THIS BEAST.
HE'S AFRAID. HE WONDERS WHY HE'S SURROUNDED BY…
BY…?
…BY ALL THESE MONSTERS.

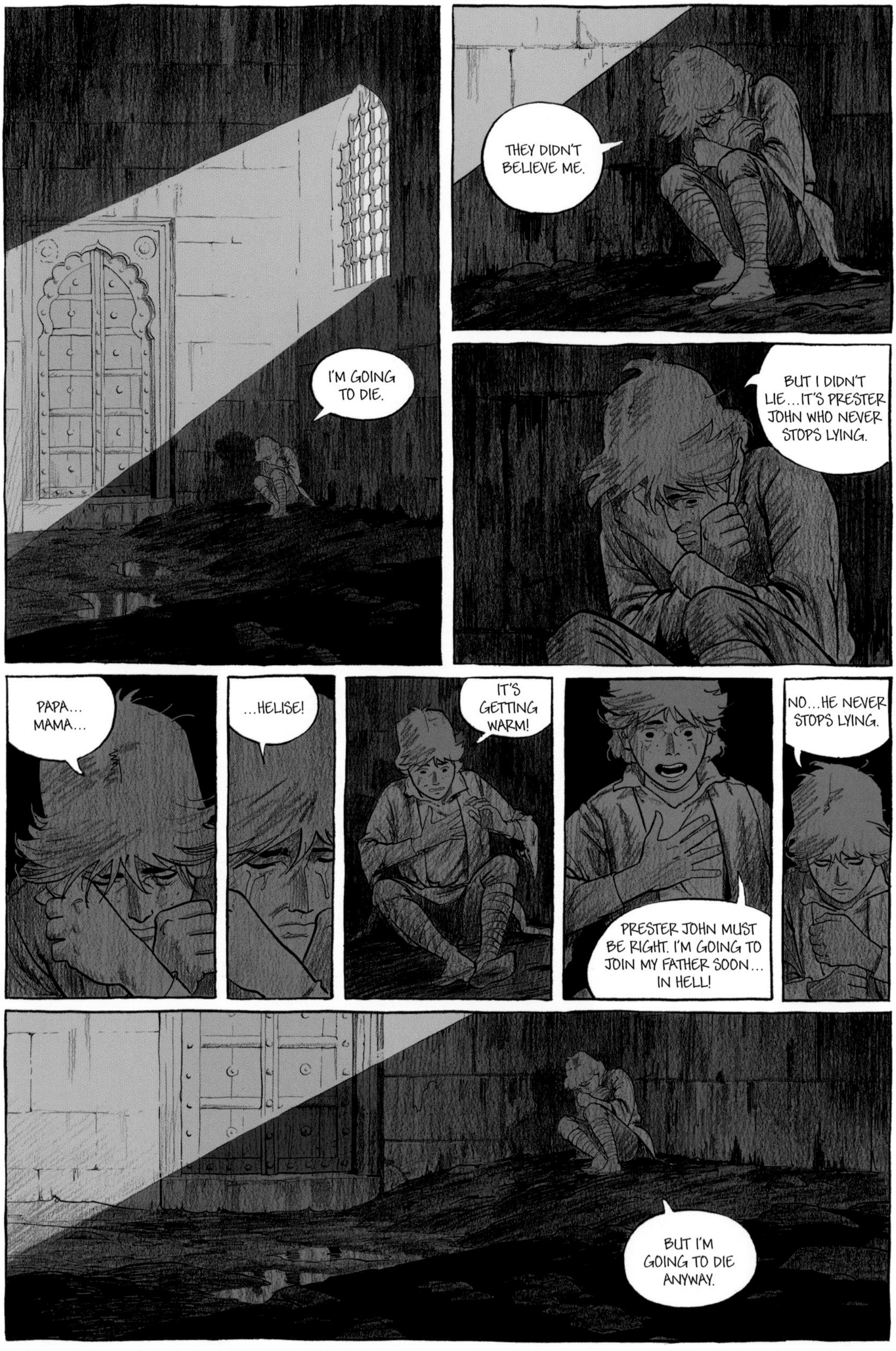
I'M GOING TO DIE.
THEY DIDN'T BELIEVE ME.
BUT I DIDN'T LIE... IT'S PRESTER JOHN WHO NEVER STOPS LYING.
PAPA... MAMA...
...HELISE!
IT'S GETTING WARM!
PRESTER JOHN MUST BE RIGHT. I'M GOING TO JOIN MY FATHER SOON... IN HELL!
NO... HE NEVER STOPS LYING.
BUT I'M GOING TO DIE ANYWAY.

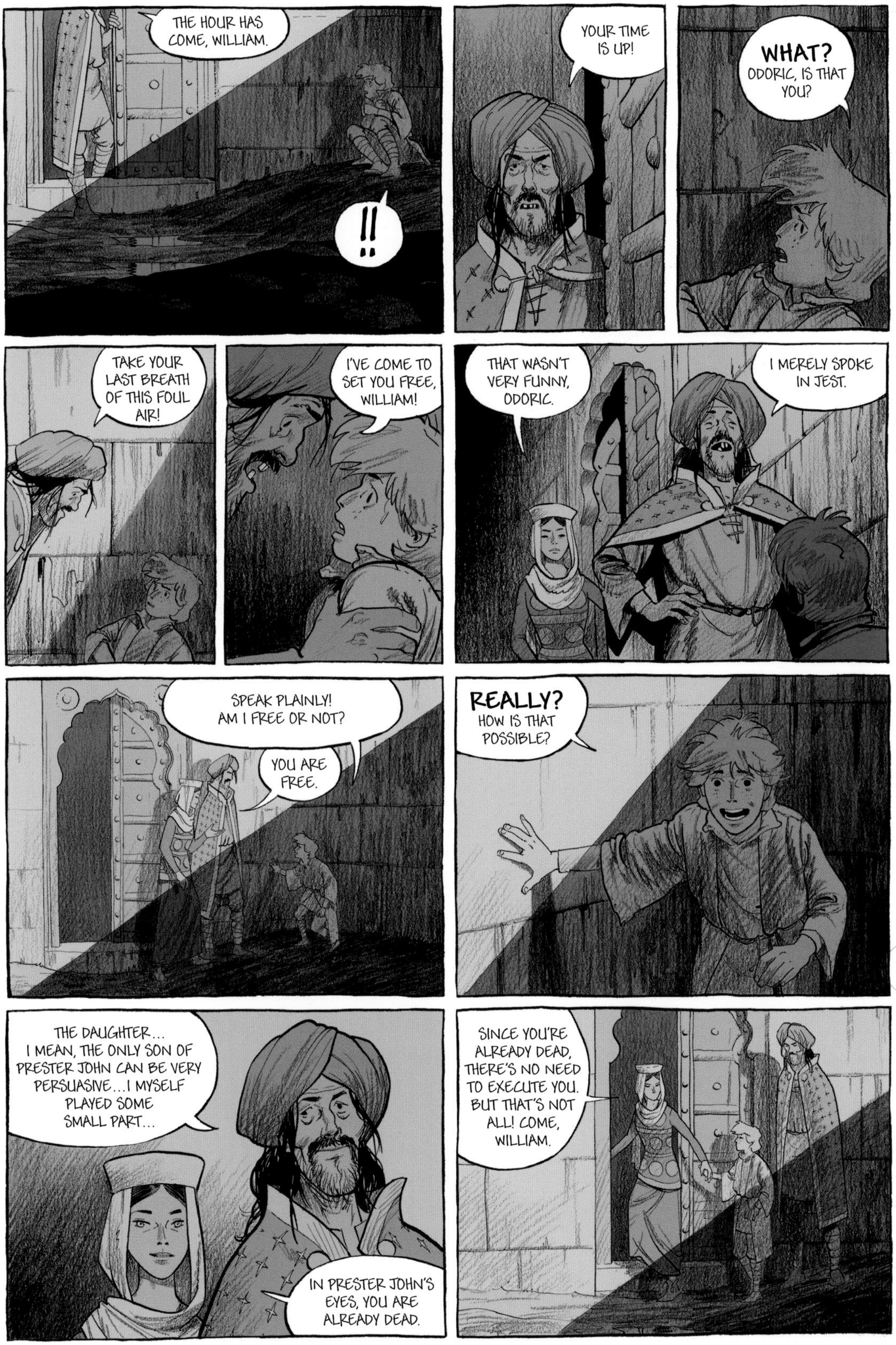
THE HOUR HAS COME, WILLIAM.
!!
YOUR TIME IS UP!
WHAT? ODORIC, IS THAT YOU?
TAKE YOUR LAST BREATH OF THIS FOUL AIR!
I'VE COME TO SET YOU FREE, WILLIAM!
THAT WASN'T VERY FUNNY, ODORIC.
I MERELY SPOKE IN JEST.
SPEAK PLAINLY! AM I FREE OR NOT?
YOU ARE FREE.
REALLY? HOW IS THAT POSSIBLE?
THE DAUGHTER… I MEAN, THE ONLY SON OF PRESTER JOHN CAN BE VERY PERSUASIVE…I MYSELF PLAYED SOME SMALL PART…
IN PRESTER JOHN'S EYES, YOU ARE ALREADY DEAD.
SINCE YOU'RE ALREADY DEAD, THERE'S NO NEED TO EXECUTE YOU. BUT THAT'S NOT ALL! COME, WILLIAM.

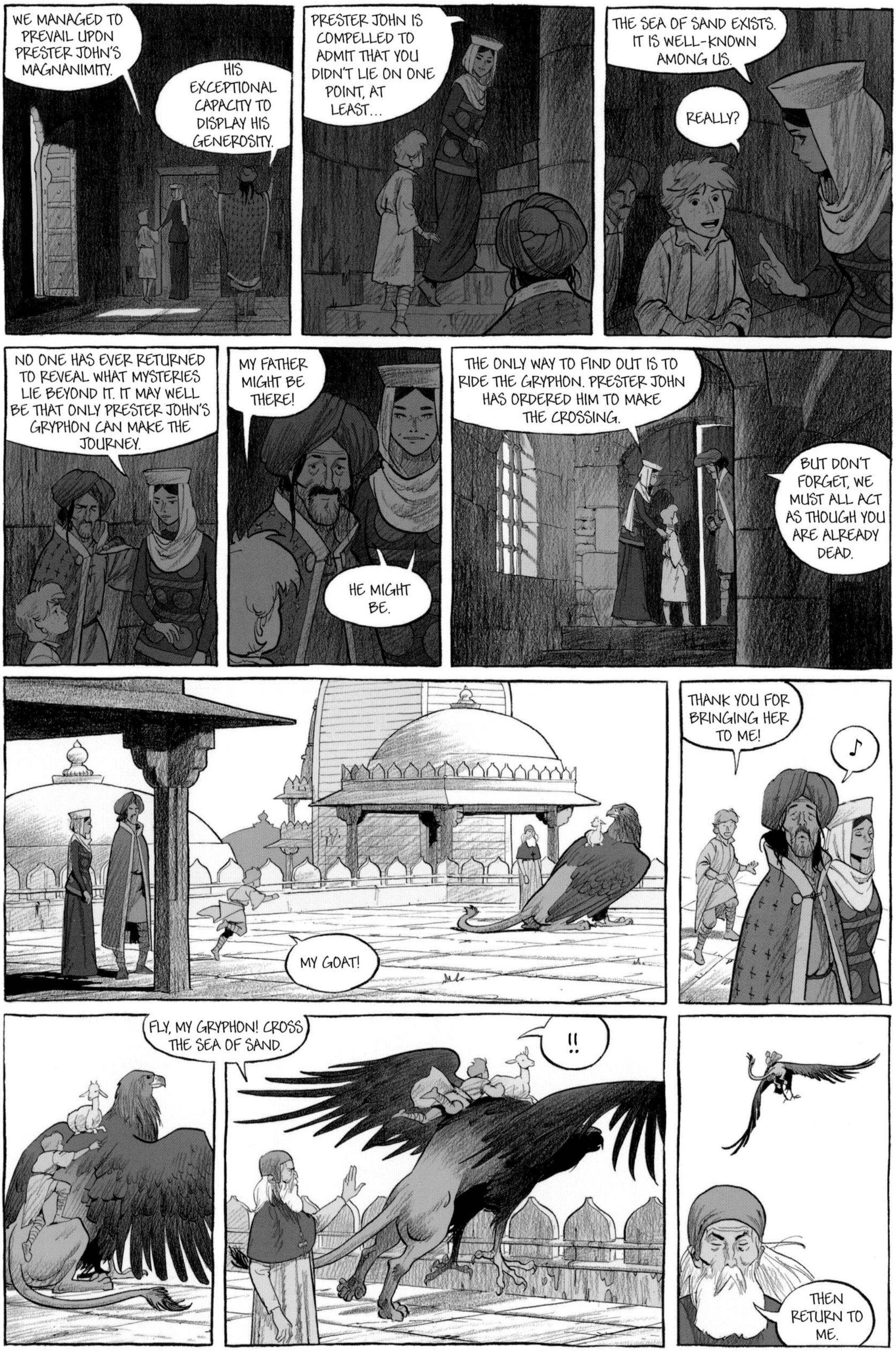

WE MANAGED TO PREVAIL UPON PRESTER JOHN'S MAGNANIMITY.
HIS EXCEPTIONAL CAPACITY TO DISPLAY HIS GENEROSITY.
PRESTER JOHN IS COMPELLED TO ADMIT THAT YOU DIDN'T LIE ON ONE POINT, AT LEAST...
THE SEA OF SAND EXISTS. IT IS WELL-KNOWN AMONG US.
REALLY?
NO ONE HAS EVER RETURNED TO REVEAL WHAT MYSTERIES LIE BEYOND IT. IT MAY WELL BE THAT ONLY PRESTER JOHN'S GRYPHON CAN MAKE THE JOURNEY.
MY FATHER MIGHT BE THERE!
HE MIGHT BE.
THE ONLY WAY TO FIND OUT IS TO RIDE THE GRYPHON. PRESTER JOHN HAS ORDERED HIM TO MAKE THE CROSSING.
BUT DON'T FORGET, WE MUST ALL ACT AS THOUGH YOU ARE ALREADY DEAD.
MY GOAT!
THANK YOU FOR BRINGING HER TO ME!
♪
FLY, MY GRYPHON! CROSS THE SEA OF SAND.
!!
THEN RETURN TO ME.

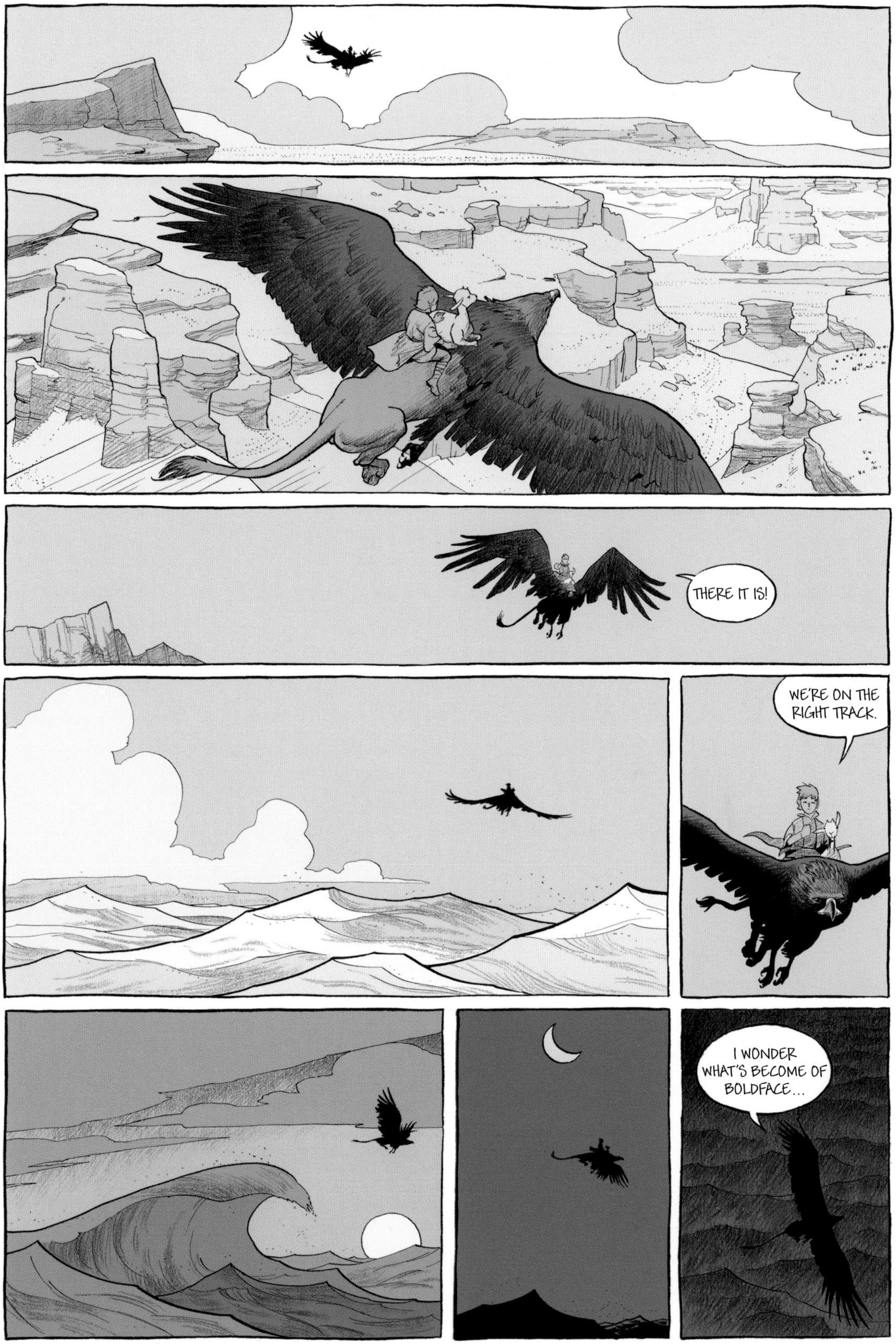
THERE IT IS!
WE'RE ON THE RIGHT TRACK.
I WONDER WHAT'S BECOME OF BOLDFACE...

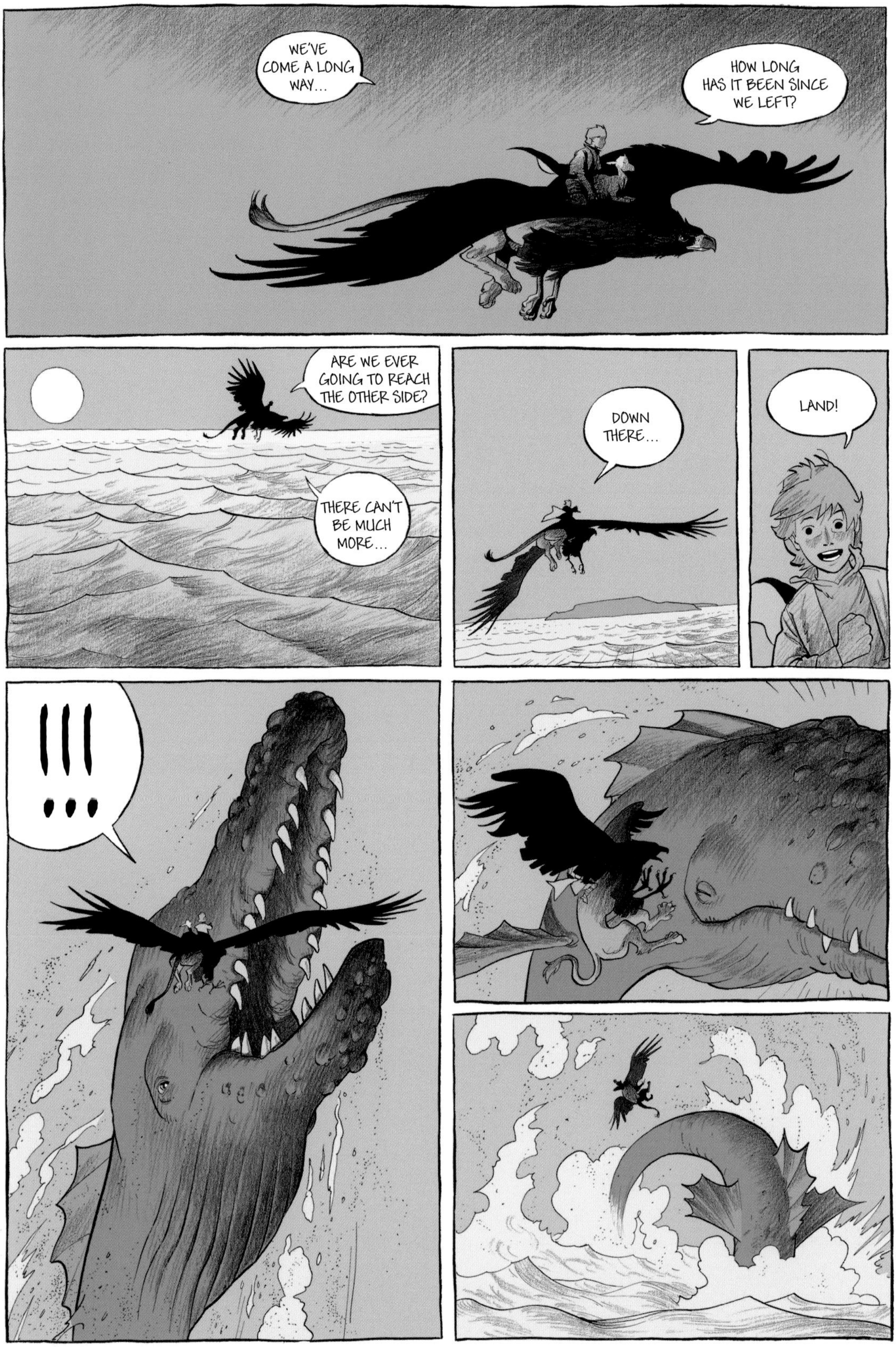
WE'VE COME A LONG WAY...
HOW LONG HAS IT BEEN SINCE WE LEFT?
ARE WE EVER GOING TO REACH THE OTHER SIDE?
THERE CAN'T BE MUCH MORE...
DOWN THERE...
LAND!
!!!
...

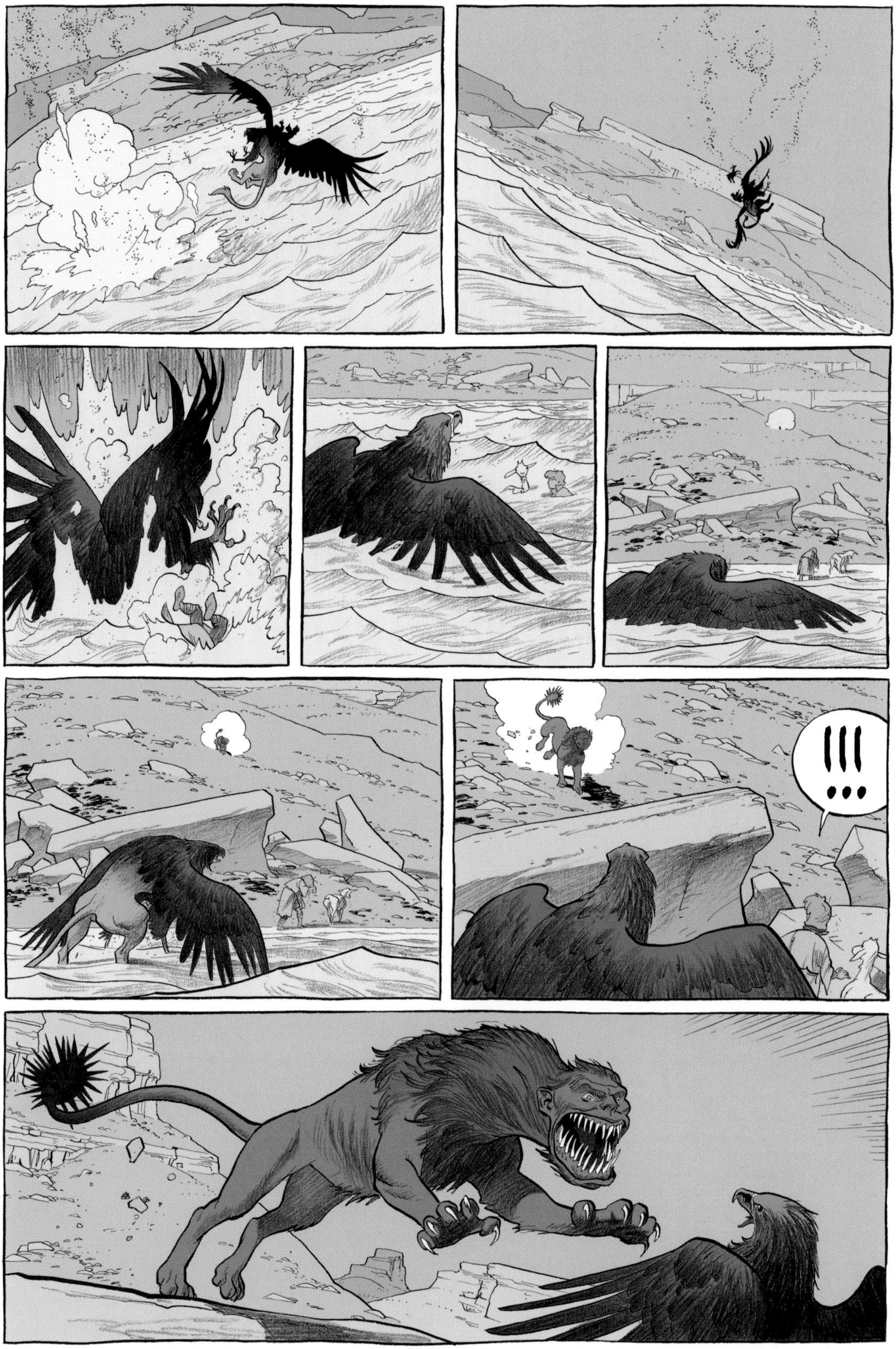
!!!
...

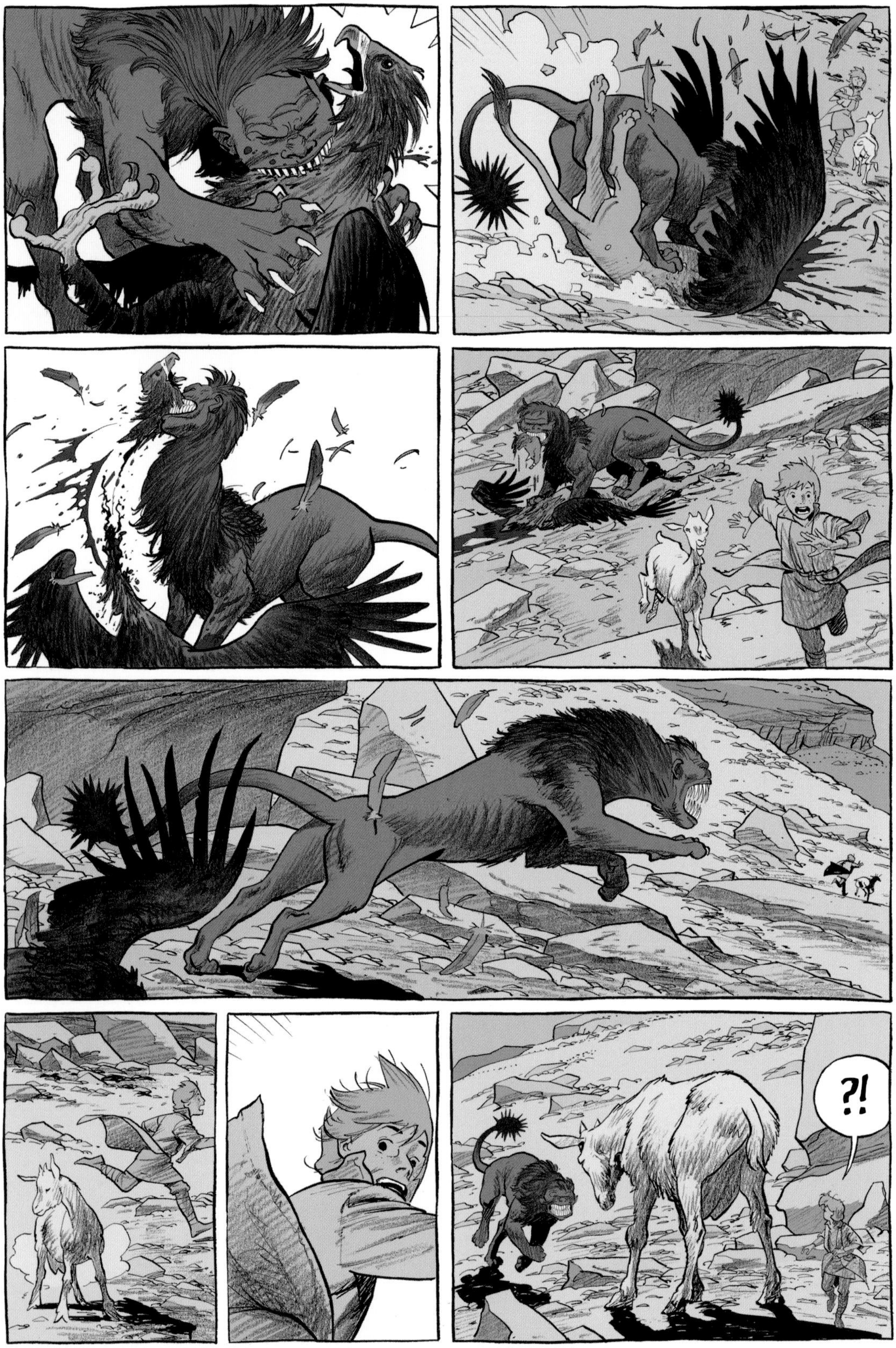
?!

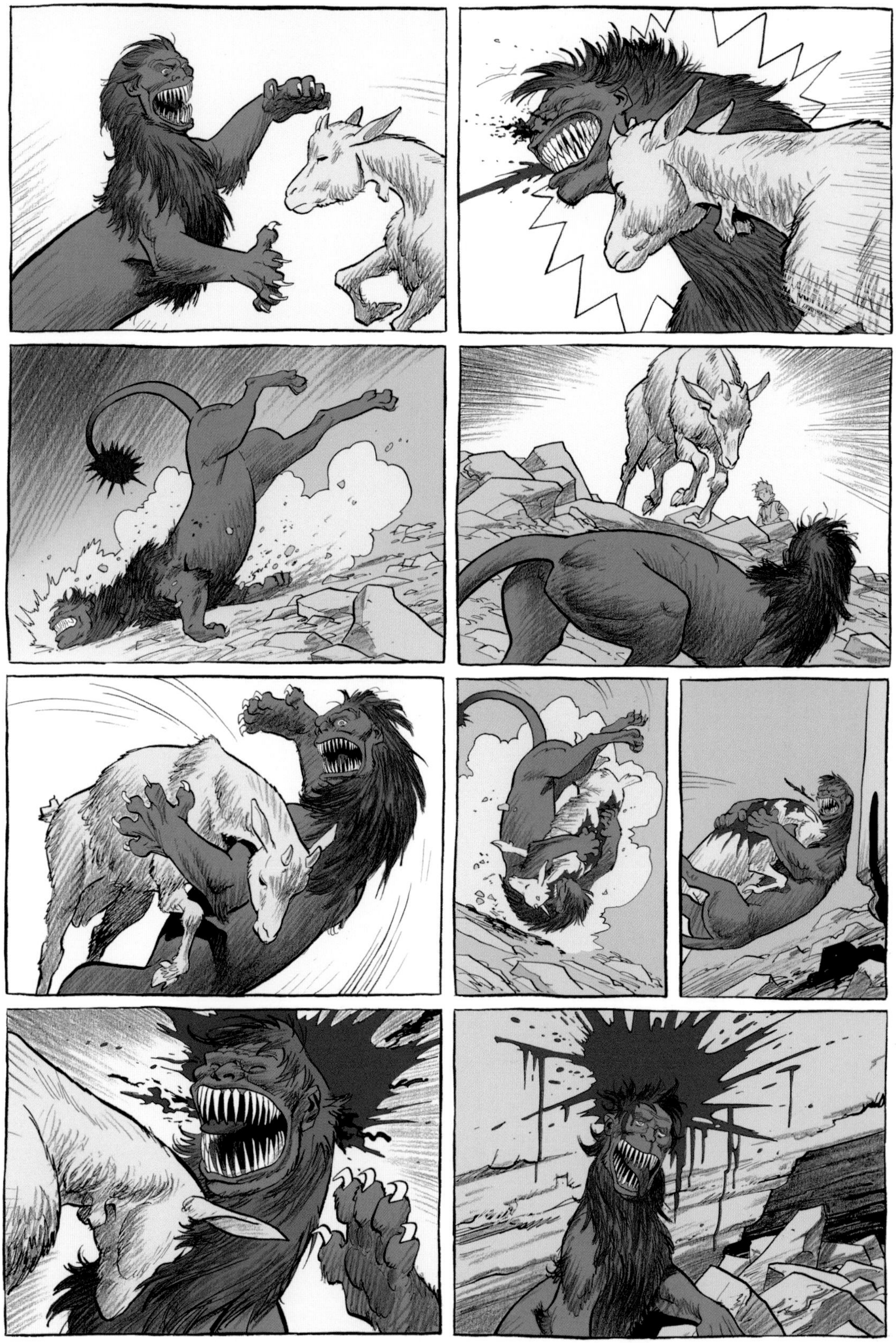

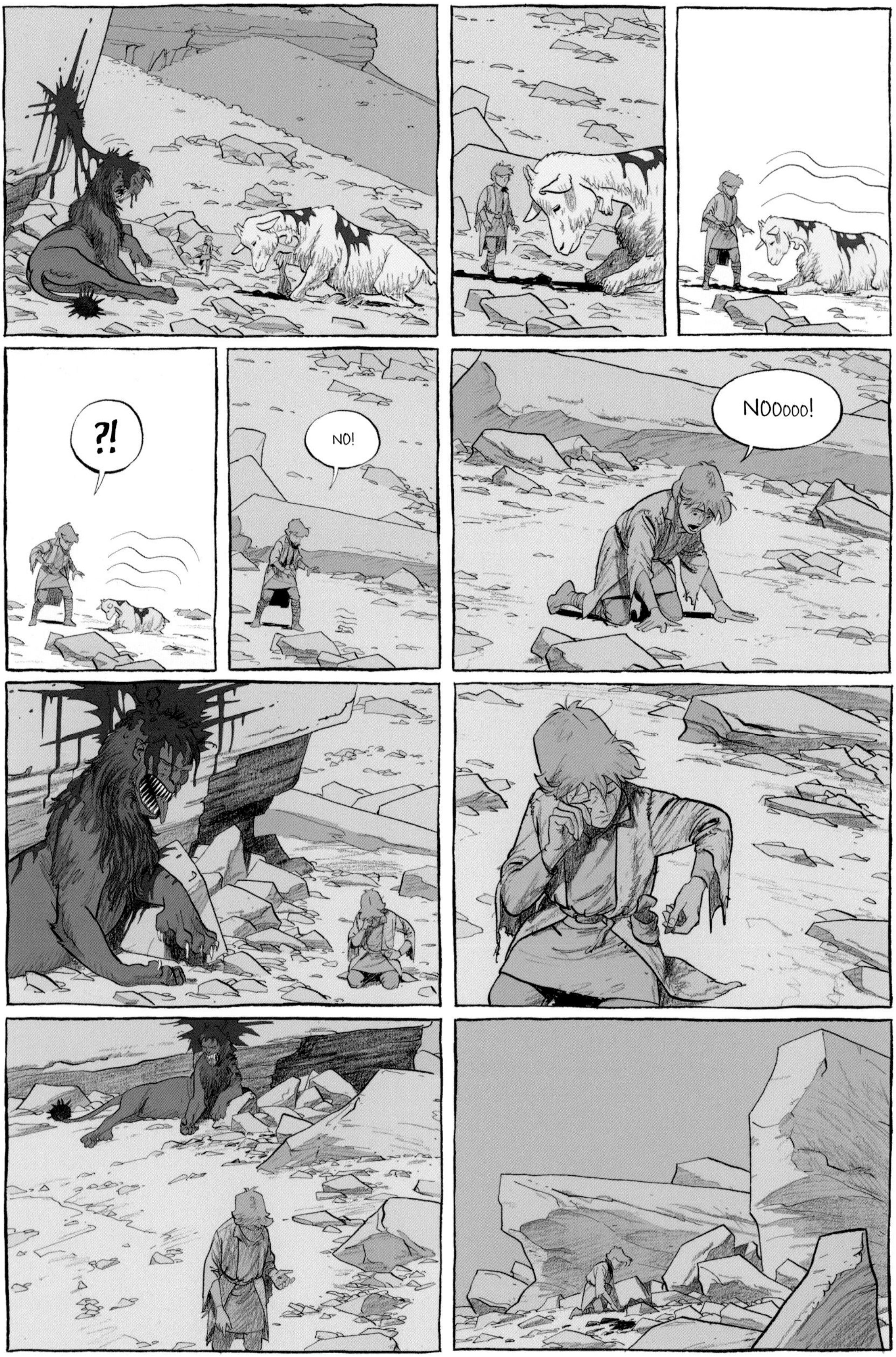
?!
NO!
NOOOOO!

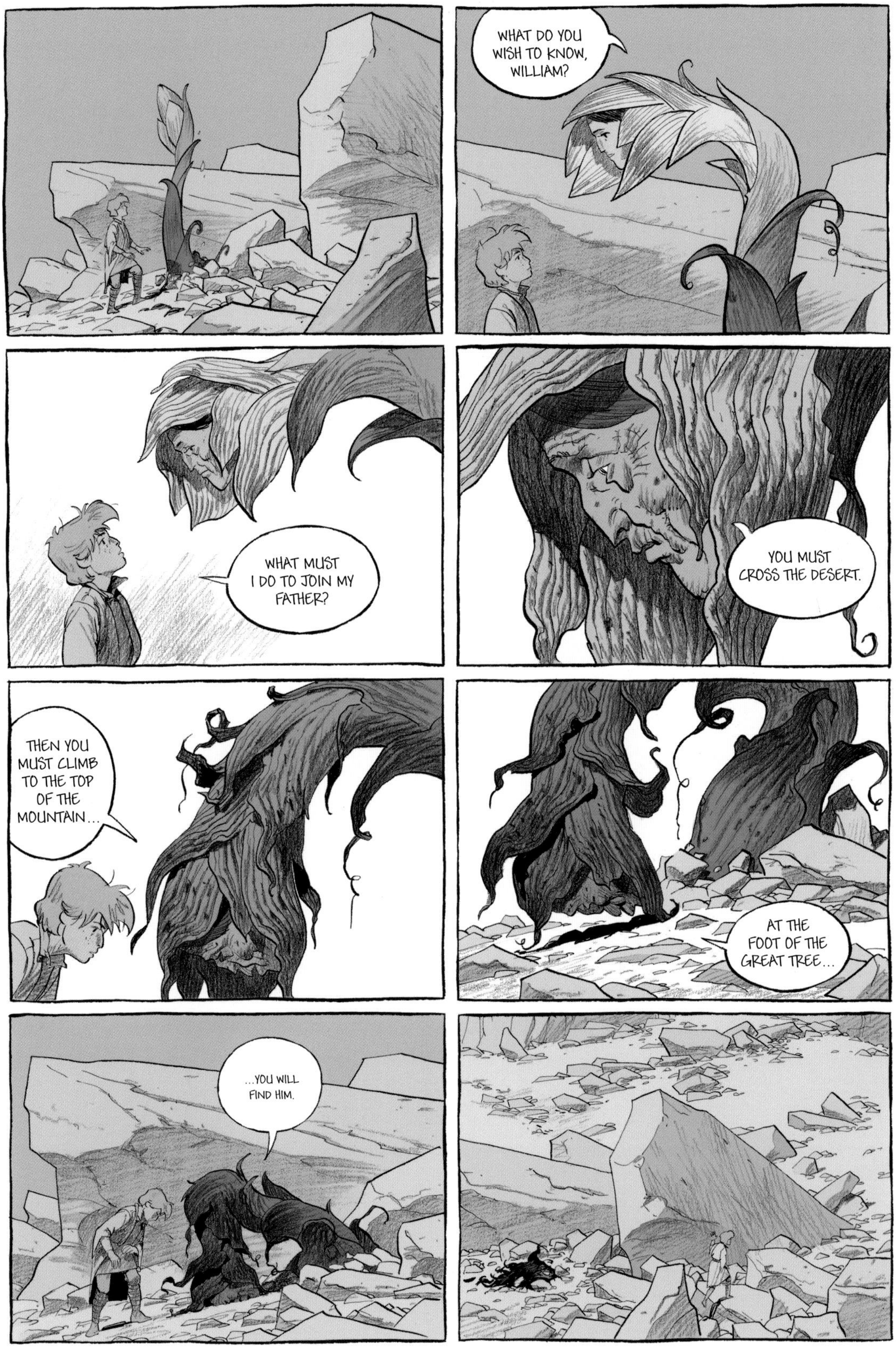
WHAT DO YOU WISH TO KNOW, WILLIAM?
WHAT MUST I DO TO JOIN MY FATHER?
YOU MUST CROSS THE DESERT.
THEN YOU MUST CLIMB TO THE TOP OF THE MOUNTAIN…
AT THE FOOT OF THE GREAT TREE…
…YOU WILL FIND HIM.

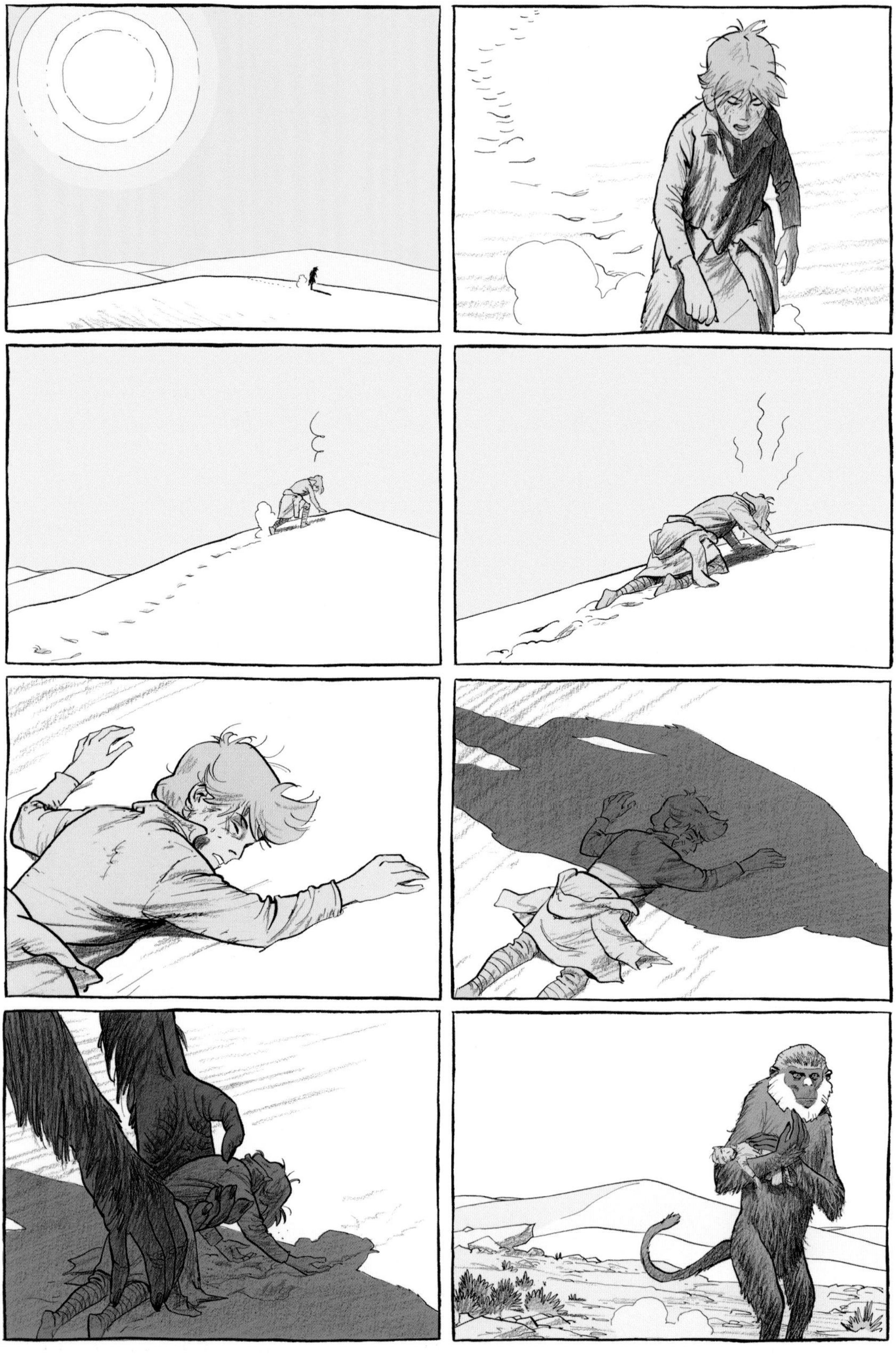

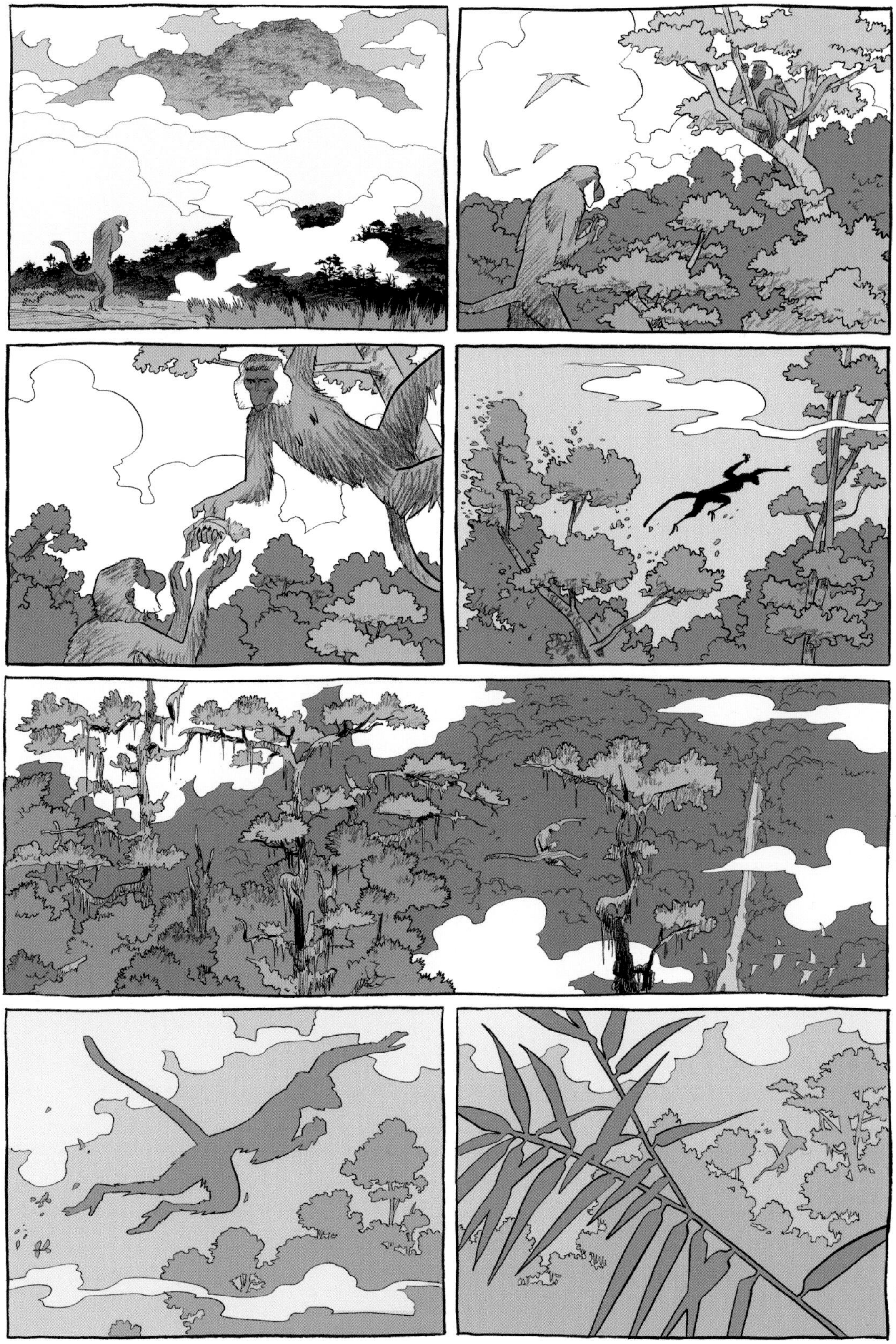

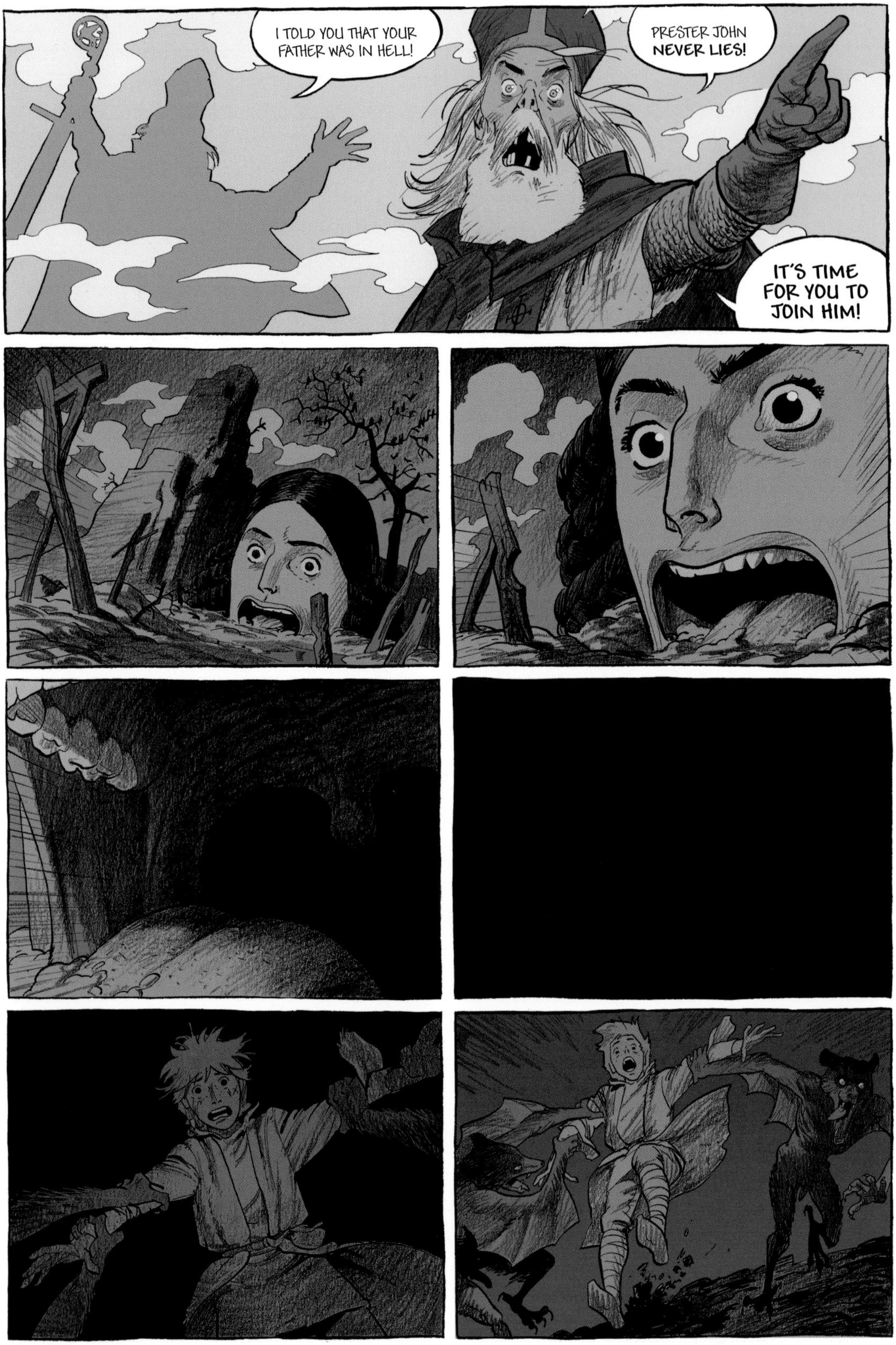
I TOLD YOU THAT YOUR FATHER WAS IN HELL!
PRESTER JOHN NEVER LIES!
IT'S TIME FOR YOU TO JOIN HIM!

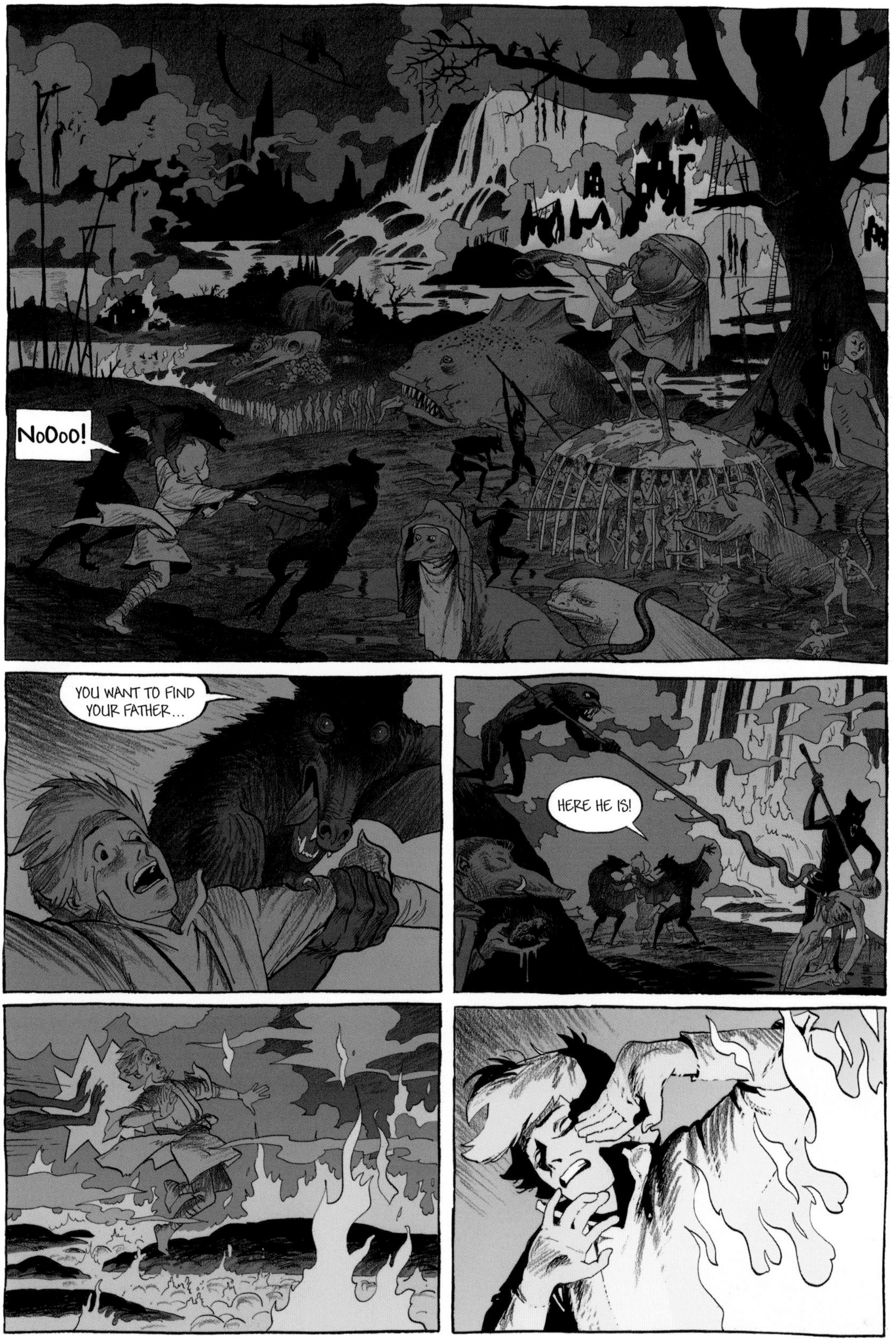
NoOoo!
YOU WANT TO FIND YOUR FATHER...
HERE HE IS!

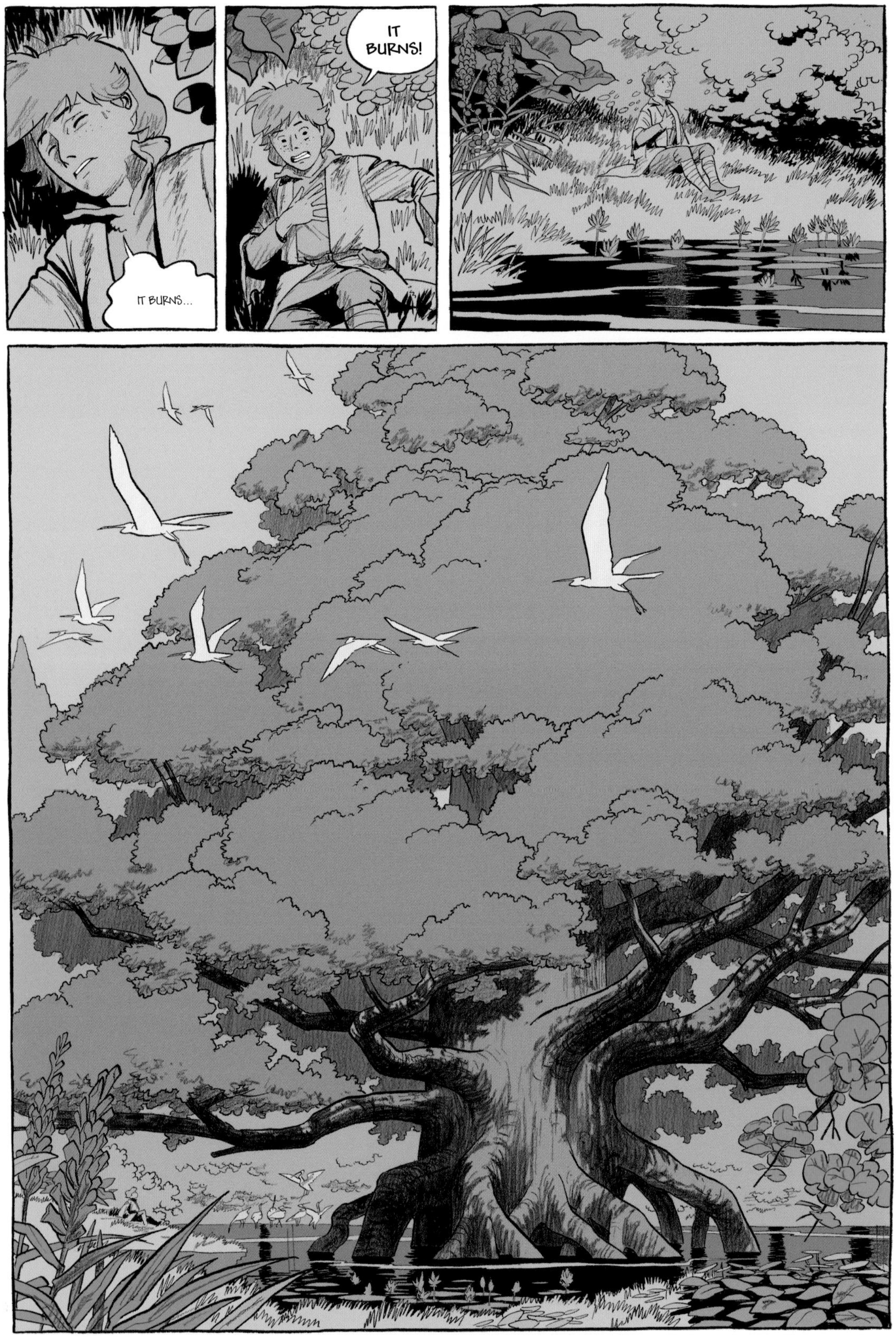
IT BURNS...
IT BURNS!

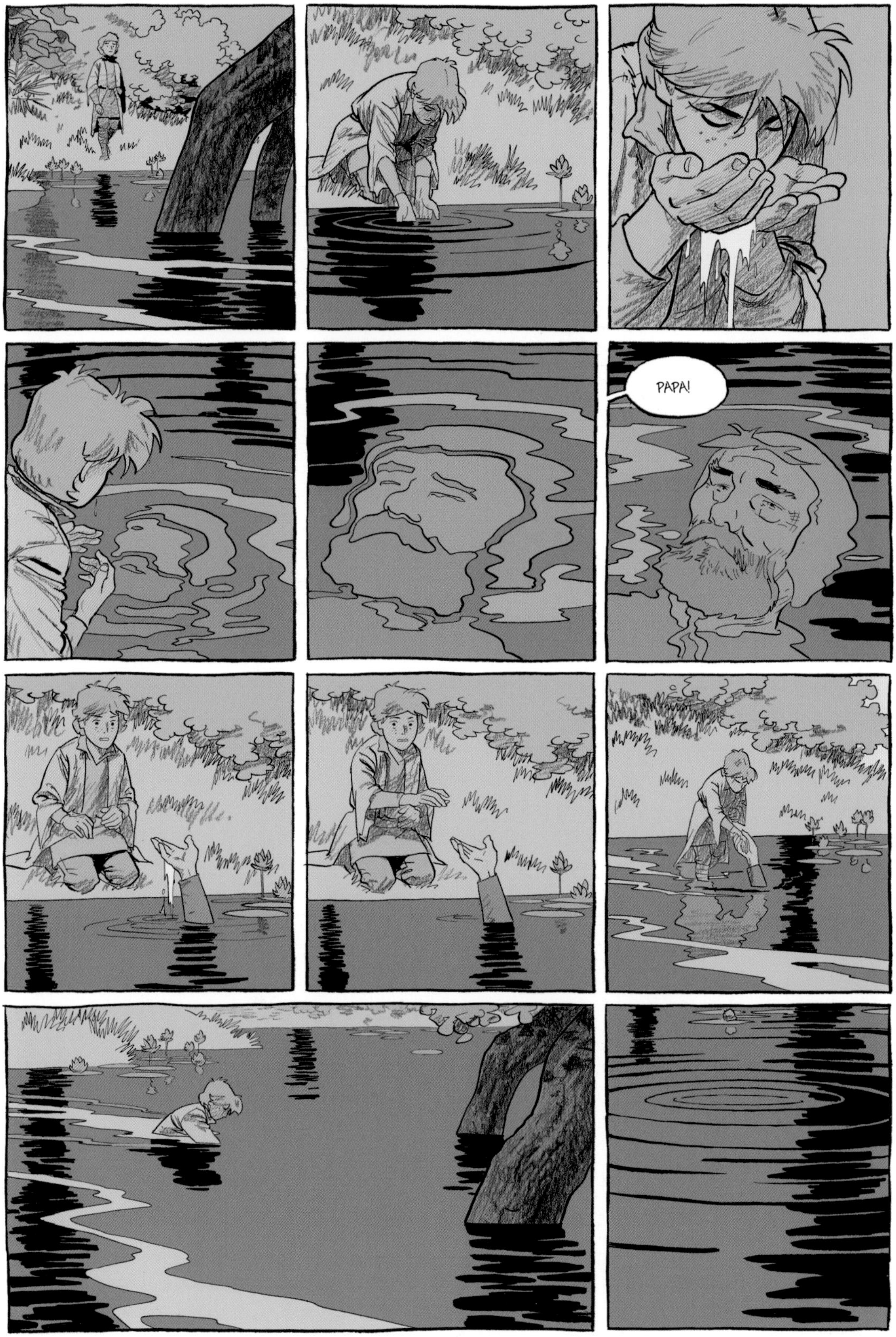
PAPA!

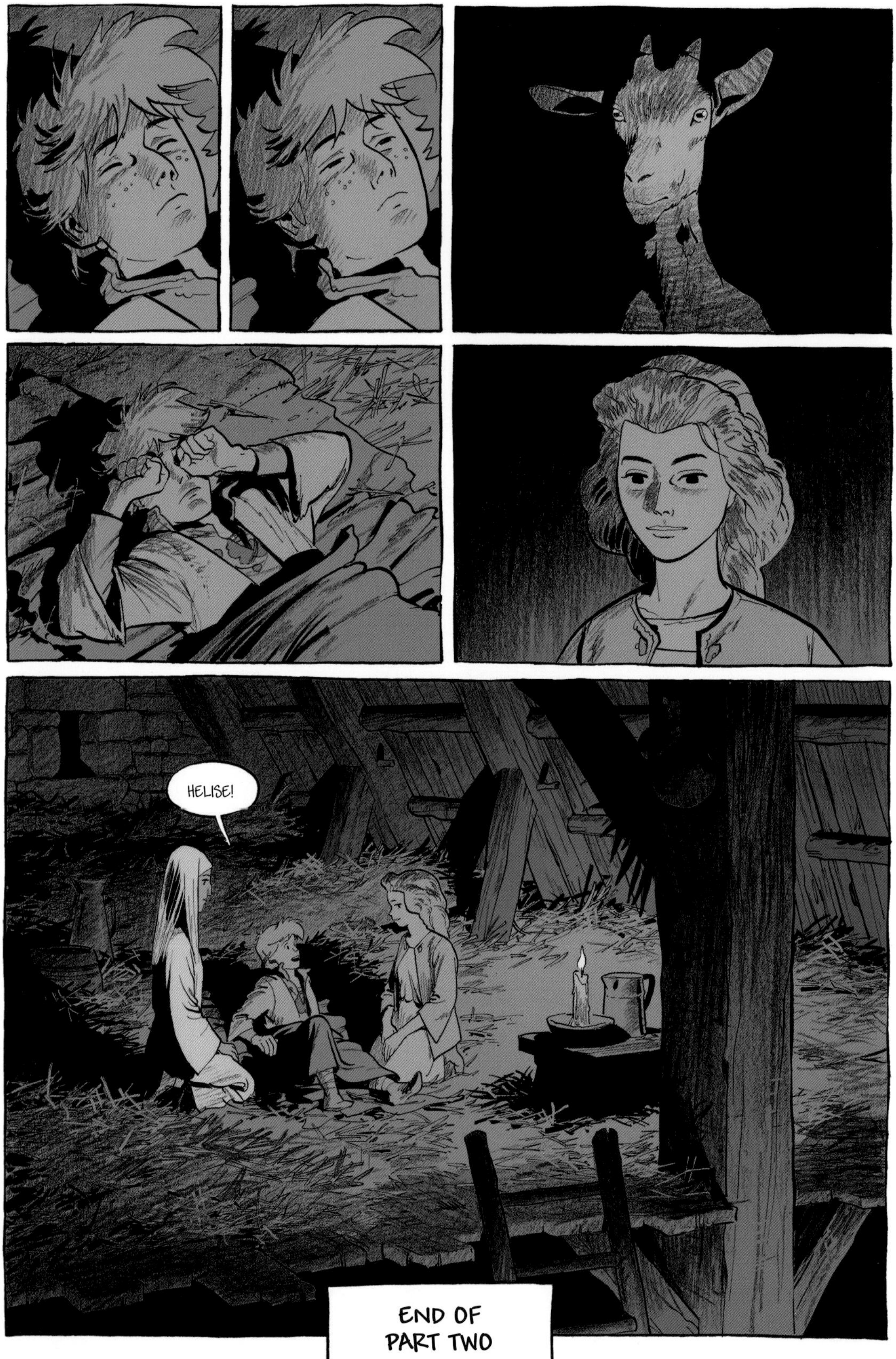
HELISE!
END OF
PART TWO

PART 3:
MOTHER, LAND

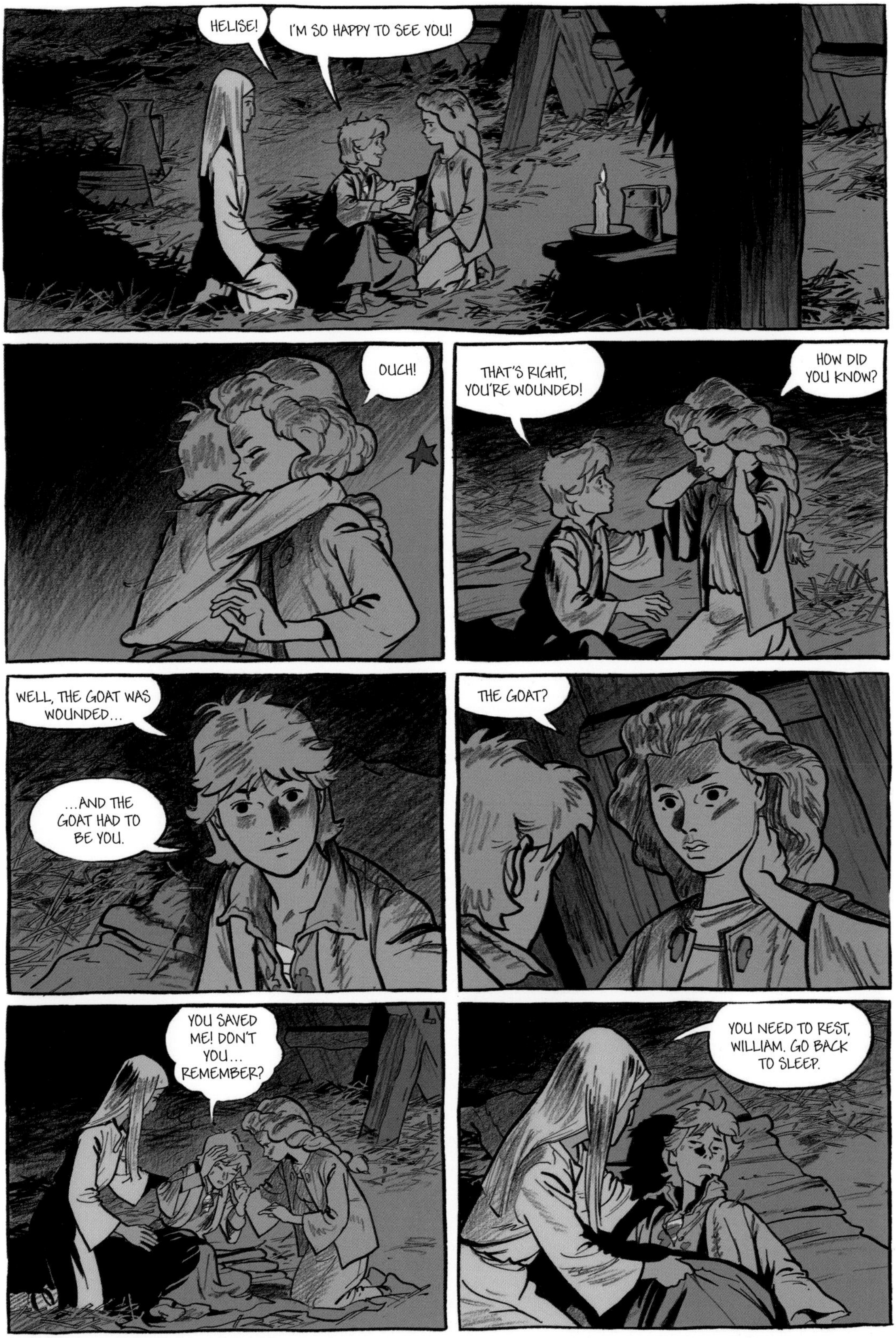
HELISE!
I'M SO HAPPY TO SEE YOU!
OUCH!
THAT'S RIGHT, YOU'RE WOUNDED!
HOW DID YOU KNOW?
WELL, THE GOAT WAS WOUNDED...
...AND THE GOAT HAD TO BE YOU.
THE GOAT?
YOU SAVED ME! DON'T YOU... REMEMBER?
YOU NEED TO REST, WILLIAM. GO BACK TO SLEEP.

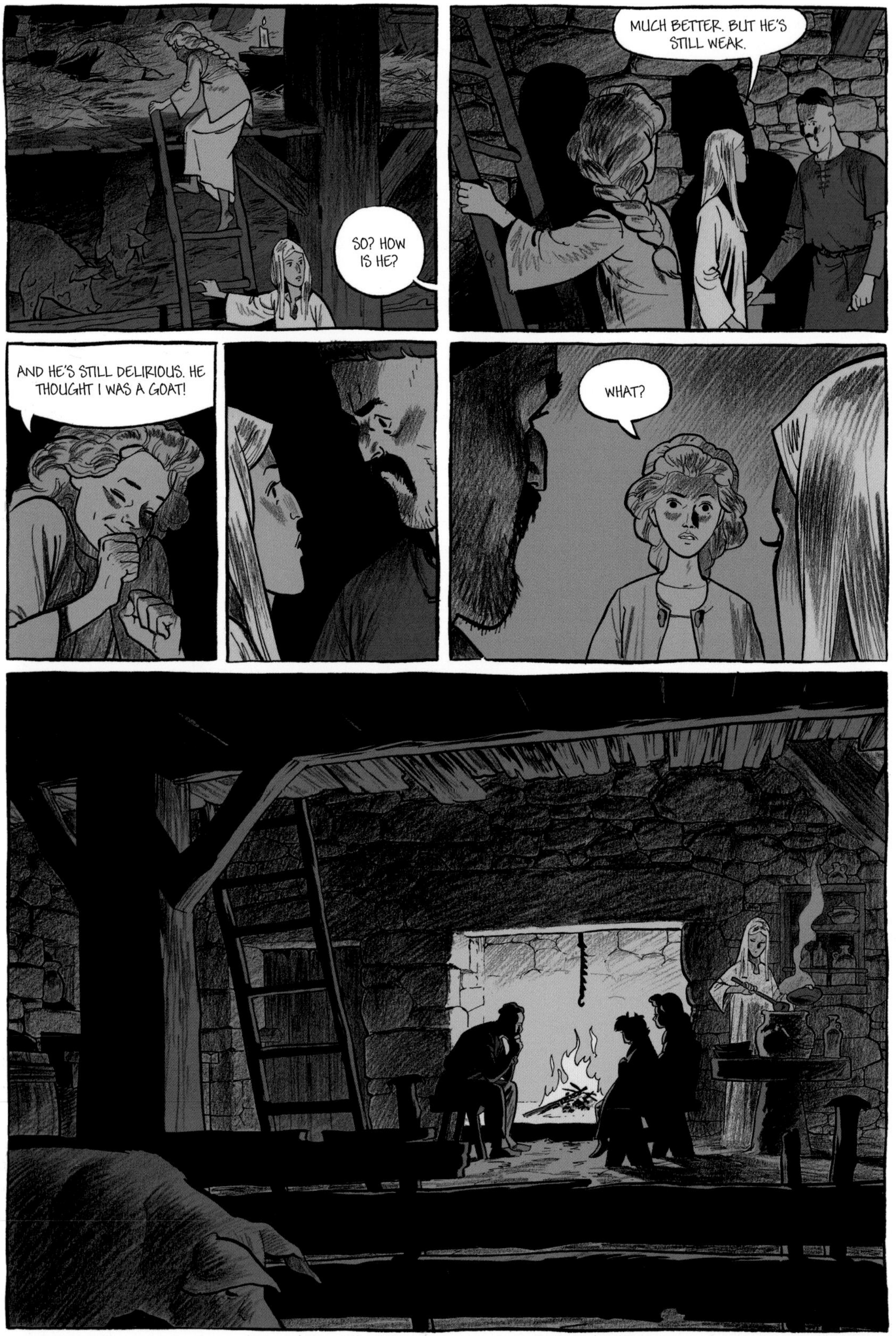
SO? HOW IS HE?
MUCH BETTER. BUT HE'S STILL WEAK.
AND HE'S STILL DELIRIOUS. HE THOUGHT I WAS A GOAT!
WHAT?

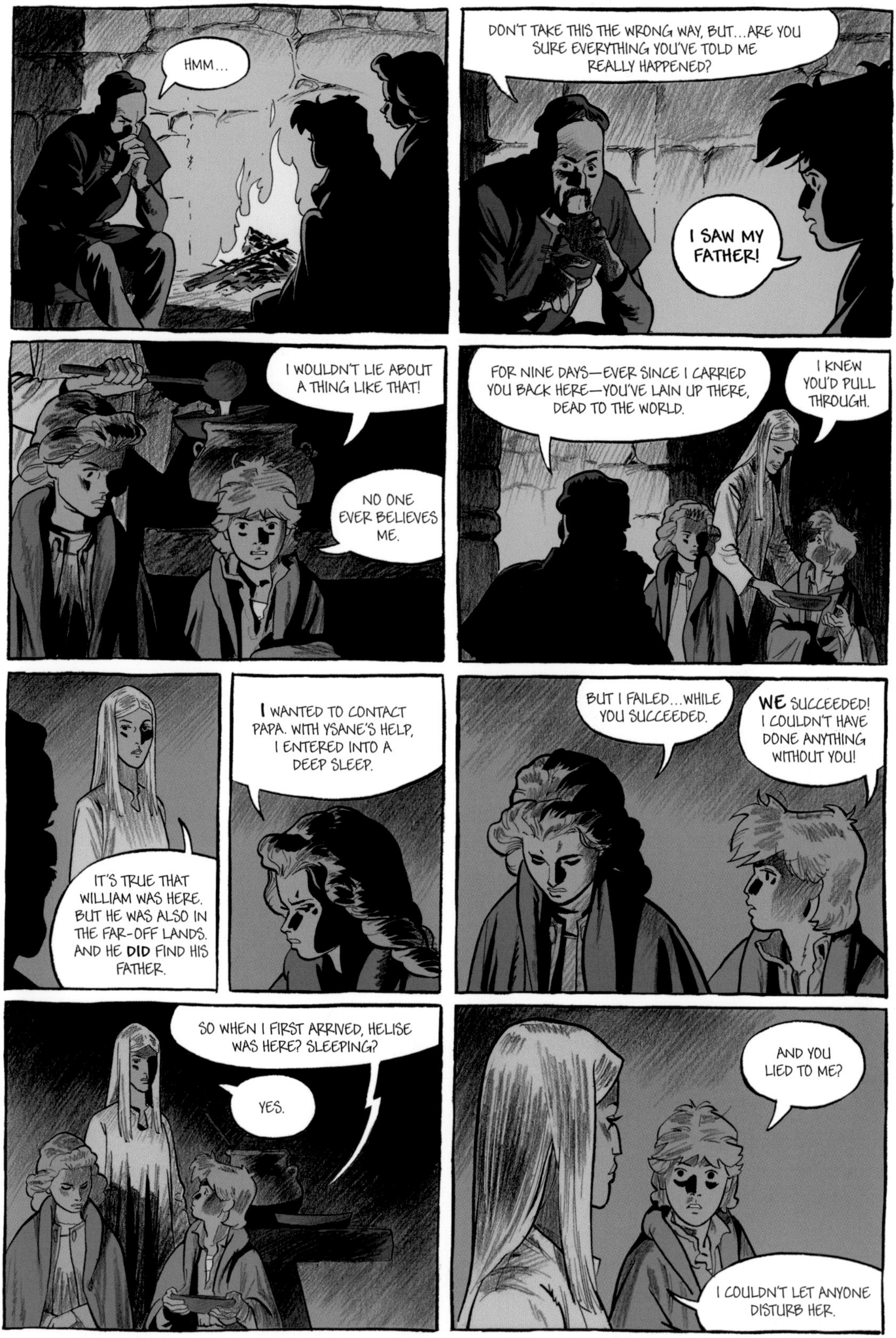
HMM...
DON'T TAKE THIS THE WRONG WAY, BUT...ARE YOU SURE EVERYTHING YOU'VE TOLD ME REALLY HAPPENED?
I SAW MY FATHER!
I WOULDN'T LIE ABOUT A THING LIKE THAT!
NO ONE EVER BELIEVES ME.
FOR NINE DAYS—EVER SINCE I CARRIED YOU BACK HERE—YOU'VE LAIN UP THERE, DEAD TO THE WORLD.
I KNEW YOU'D PULL THROUGH.
IT'S TRUE THAT WILLIAM WAS HERE. BUT HE WAS ALSO IN THE FAR-OFF LANDS. AND HE DID FIND HIS FATHER.
I WANTED TO CONTACT PAPA. WITH YSANE'S HELP, I ENTERED INTO A DEEP SLEEP.
BUT I FAILED...WHILE YOU SUCCEEDED.
WE SUCCEEDED! I COULDN'T HAVE DONE ANYTHING WITHOUT YOU!
SO WHEN I FIRST ARRIVED, HELISE WAS HERE? SLEEPING?
YES.
AND YOU LIED TO ME?
I COULDN'T LET ANYONE DISTURB HER.

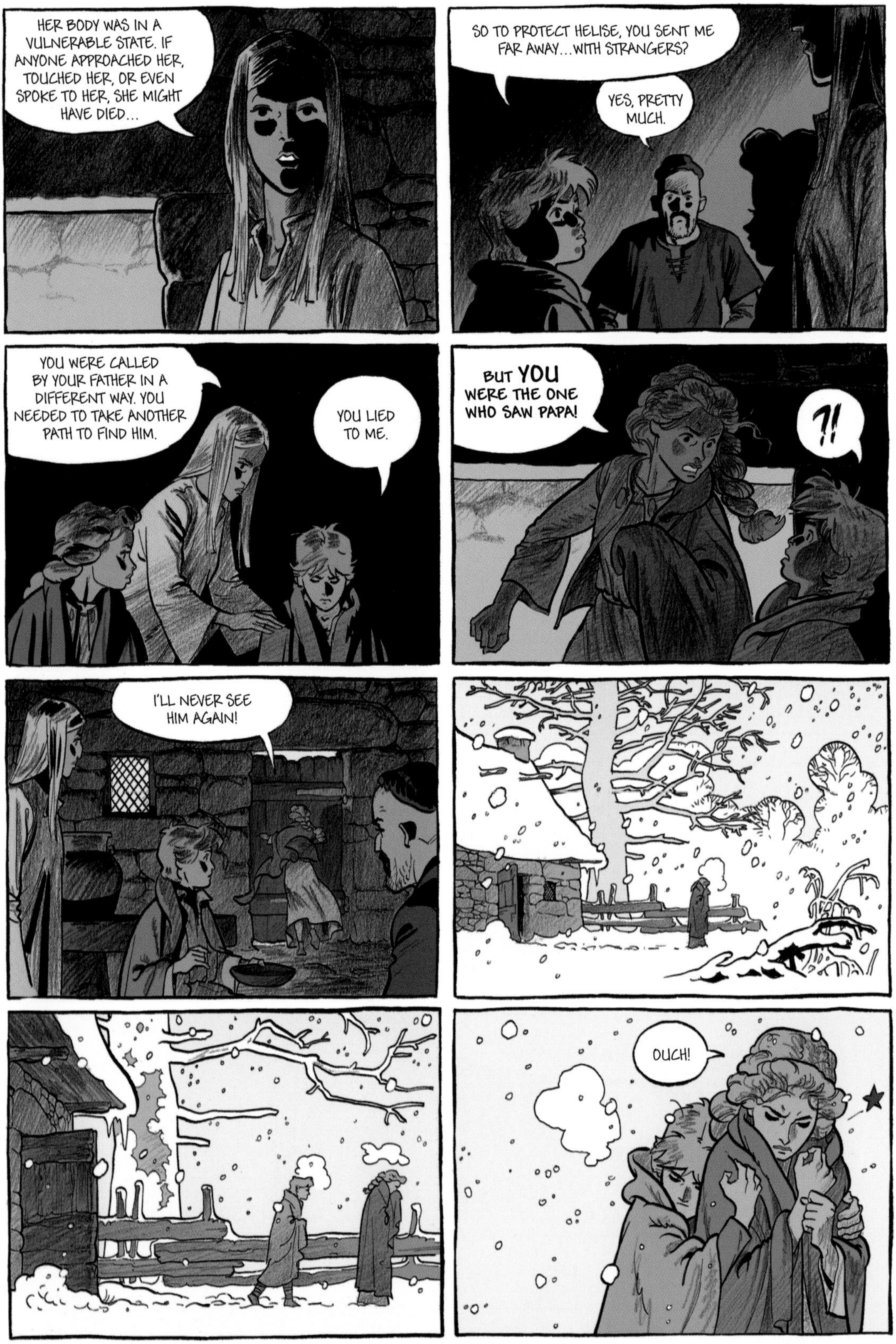
HER BODY WAS IN A VULNERABLE STATE. IF ANYONE APPROACHED HER, TOUCHED HER, OR EVEN SPOKE TO HER, SHE MIGHT HAVE DIED…
SO TO PROTECT HELISE, YOU SENT ME FAR AWAY… WITH STRANGERS?
YES, PRETTY MUCH.
YOU WERE CALLED BY YOUR FATHER IN A DIFFERENT WAY. YOU NEEDED TO TAKE ANOTHER PATH TO FIND HIM.
YOU LIED TO ME.
BUT YOU WERE THE ONE WHO SAW PAPA!
?!
I'LL NEVER SEE HIM AGAIN!
OUCH!

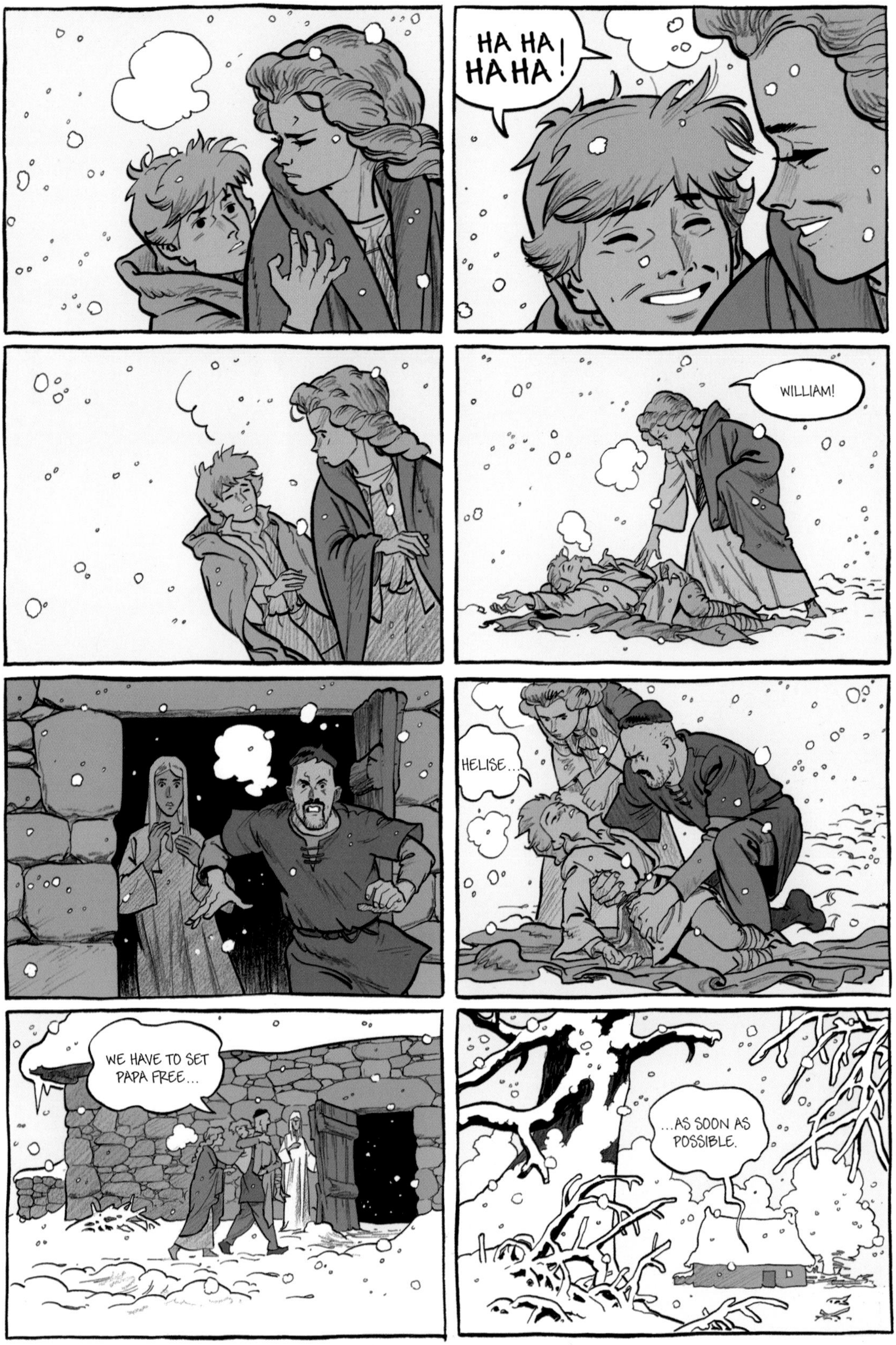
HA HA
HA HA!
WILLIAM!
HELISE...
WE HAVE TO SET PAPA FREE...
...AS SOON AS POSSIBLE.

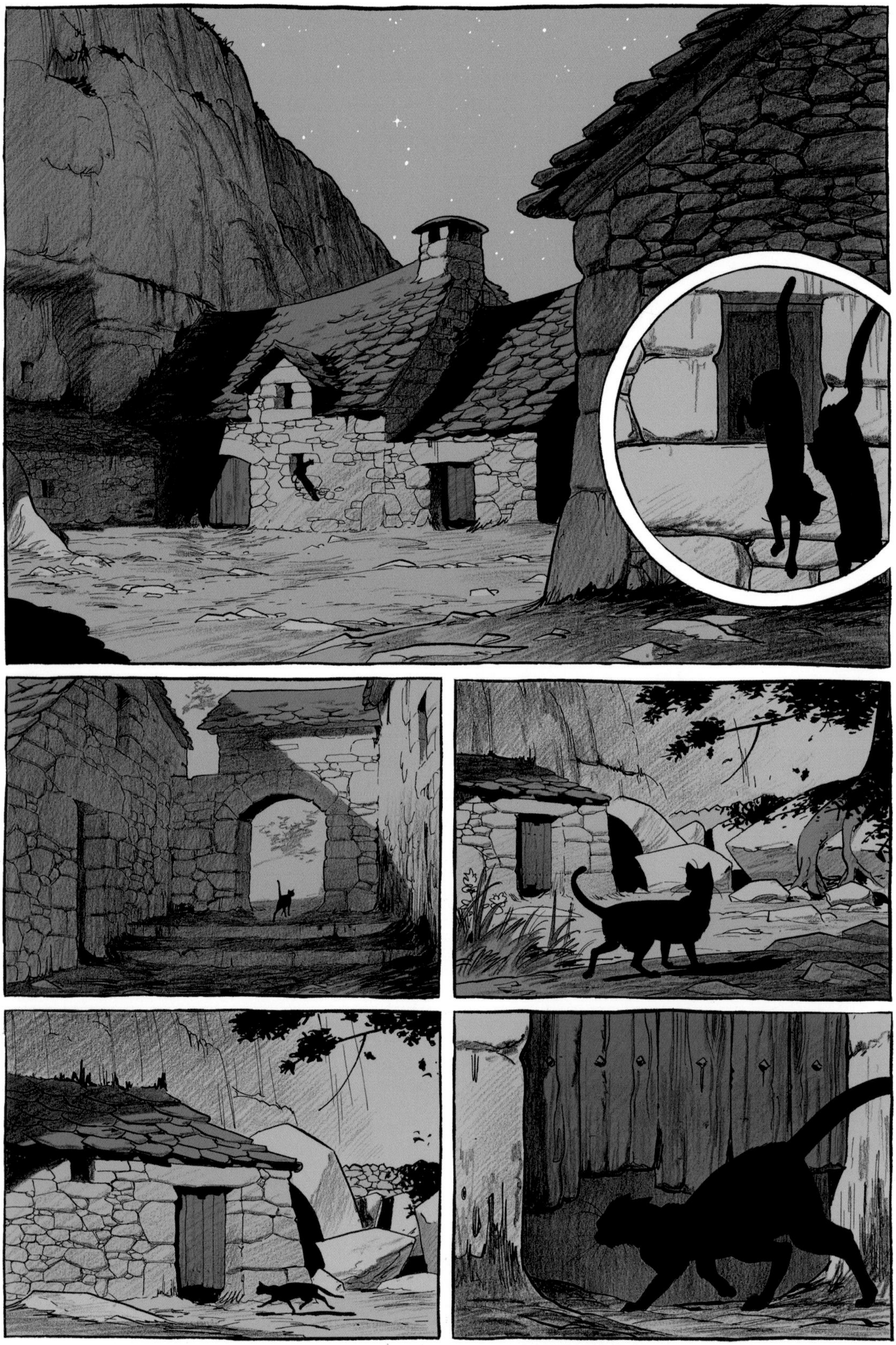

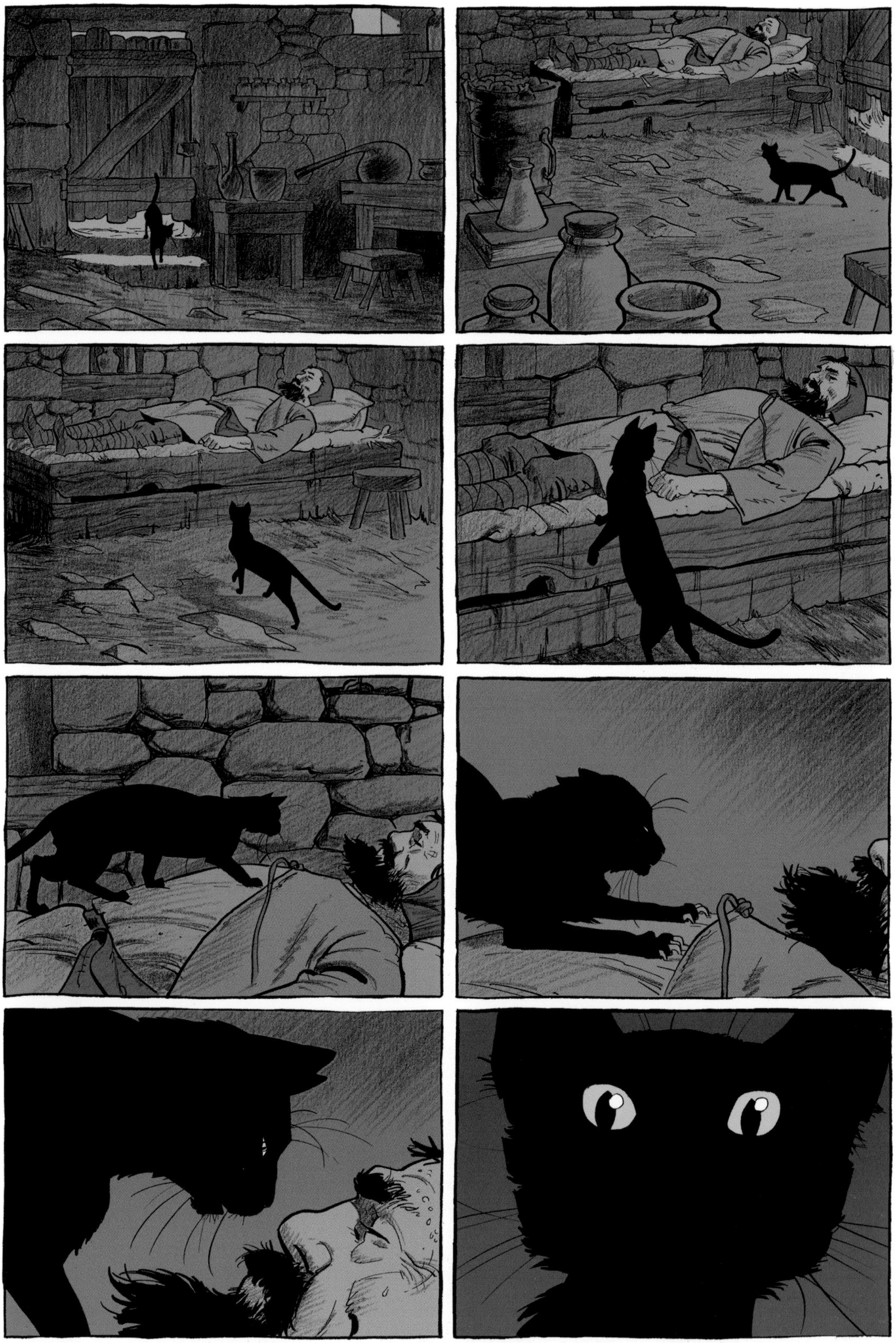

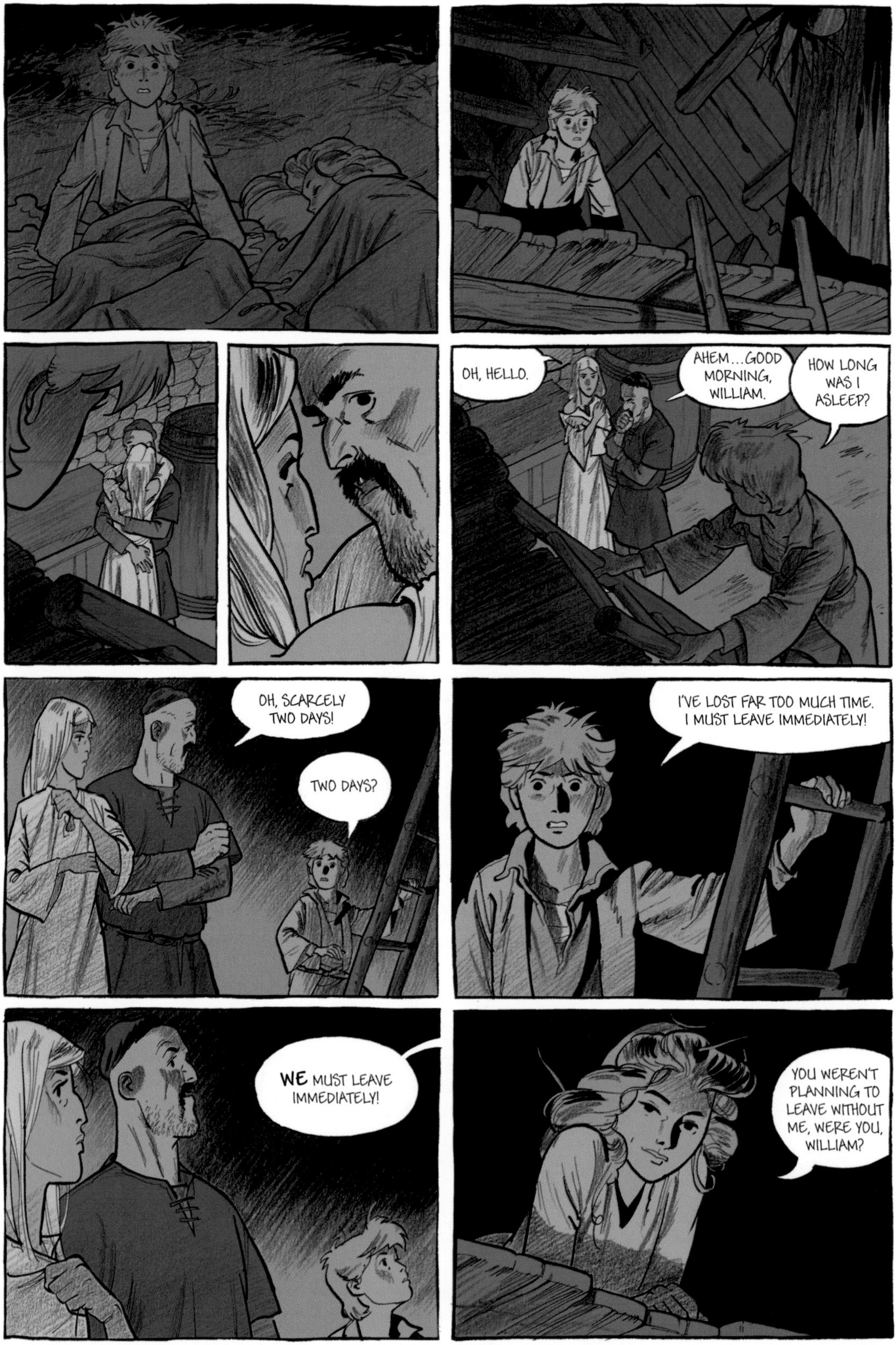
OH, HELLO.
AHEM...GOOD MORNING, WILLIAM.
HOW LONG WAS I ASLEEP?
OH, SCARCELY TWO DAYS!
TWO DAYS?
I'VE LOST FAR TOO MUCH TIME. I MUST LEAVE IMMEDIATELY!
WE MUST LEAVE IMMEDIATELY!
YOU WEREN'T PLANNING TO LEAVE WITHOUT ME, WERE YOU, WILLIAM?

YOU'RE NOT YET HEALED, AND IT'S THE DEAD OF WINTER.

I KNOW PAPA WILL NEVER RETURN. BUT HIS SOUL IS TRAPPED BETWEEN TWO WORLDS, AND WE MUST FREE HIM.

HE'S COUNTING ON US.

YOU ARE FAR FROM HOME. THE ROADS ARE IMPASSABLE. YOU DON'T HAVE THE STRENGTH TO ACCOMPLISH THE MISSION YOUR FATHER ENTRUSTED TO YOU.

THE BEST WAY TO FAIL WOULD BE TO LEAVE NOW.

WHEN YOU'RE WELL, I'LL GO WITH YOU. WE'LL MAKE IT, I PROMISE.

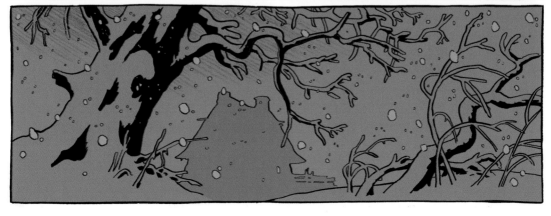

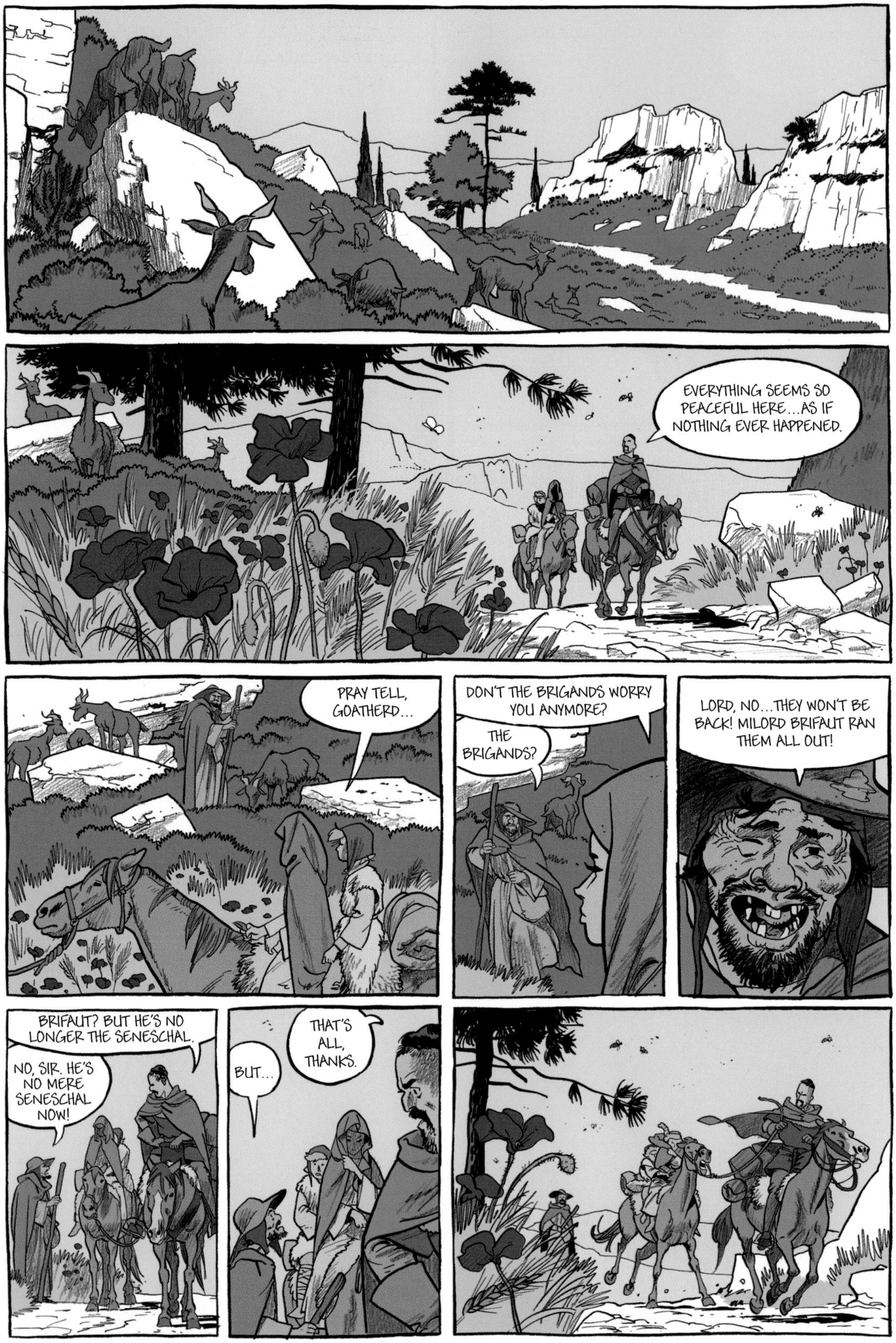
EVERYTHING SEEMS SO PEACEFUL HERE…AS IF NOTHING EVER HAPPENED.
PRAY TELL, GOATHERD…
DON'T THE BRIGANDS WORRY YOU ANYMORE?
THE BRIGANDS?
LORD, NO…THEY WON'T BE BACK! MILORD BRIFAUT RAN THEM ALL OUT!
BRIFAUT? BUT HE'S NO LONGER THE SENESCHAL.
NO, SIR. HE'S NO MERE SENESCHAL NOW!
BUT…
THAT'S ALL, THANKS.

WE'RE ALMOST THERE. WE'LL CROSS A STREAM SOON.

FROM ATOP THAT HILL, WE CAN SEE THE HOUSE.

IT LOOKS LIKE SOMEONE'S HOME!

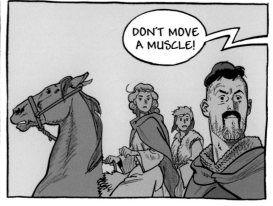
DON'T MOVE A MUSCLE!

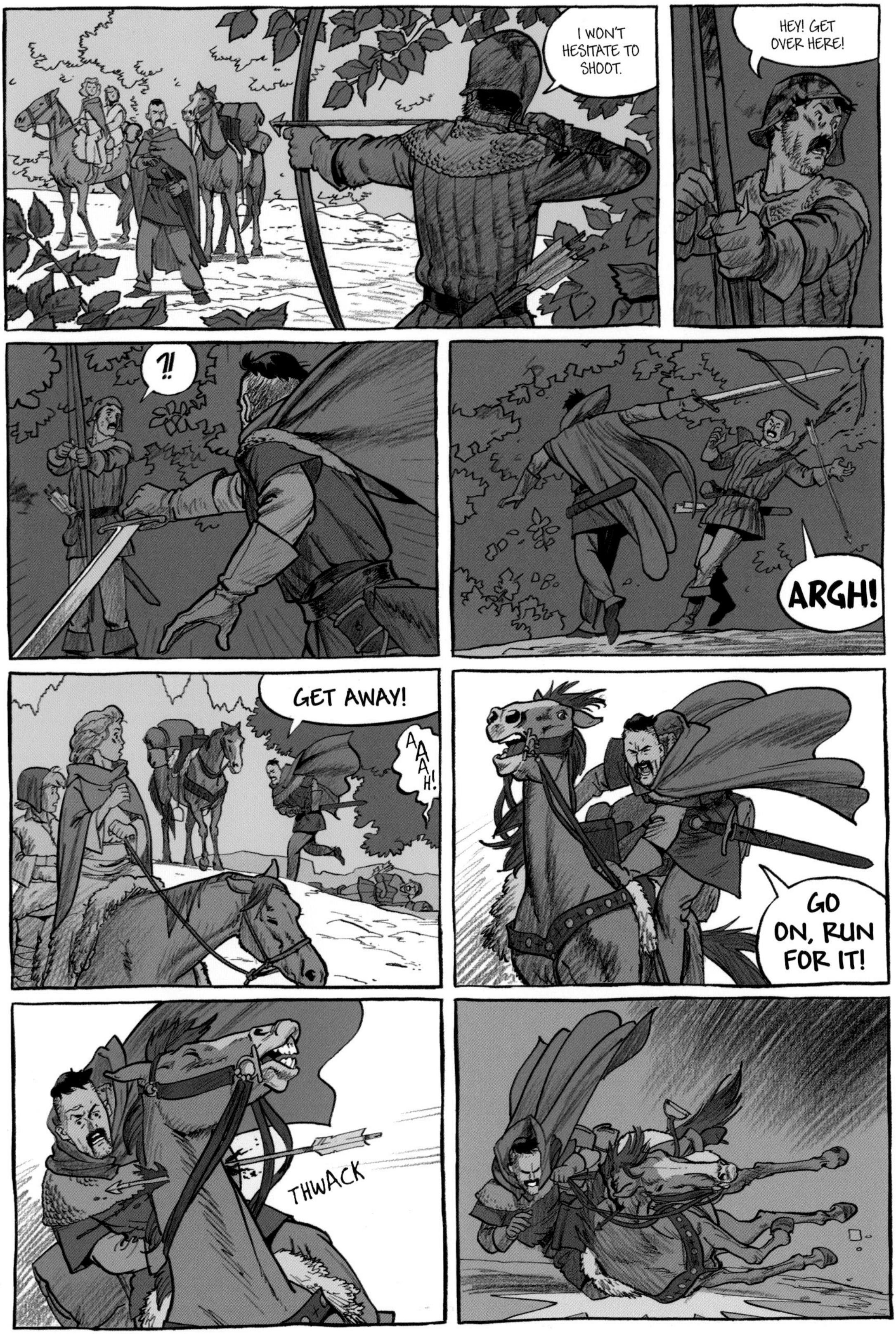
I WON'T HESITATE TO SHOOT.
HEY! GET OVER HERE!
?!
ARGH!
GET AWAY!
AAAH!
GO ON, RUN FOR IT!
THWACK

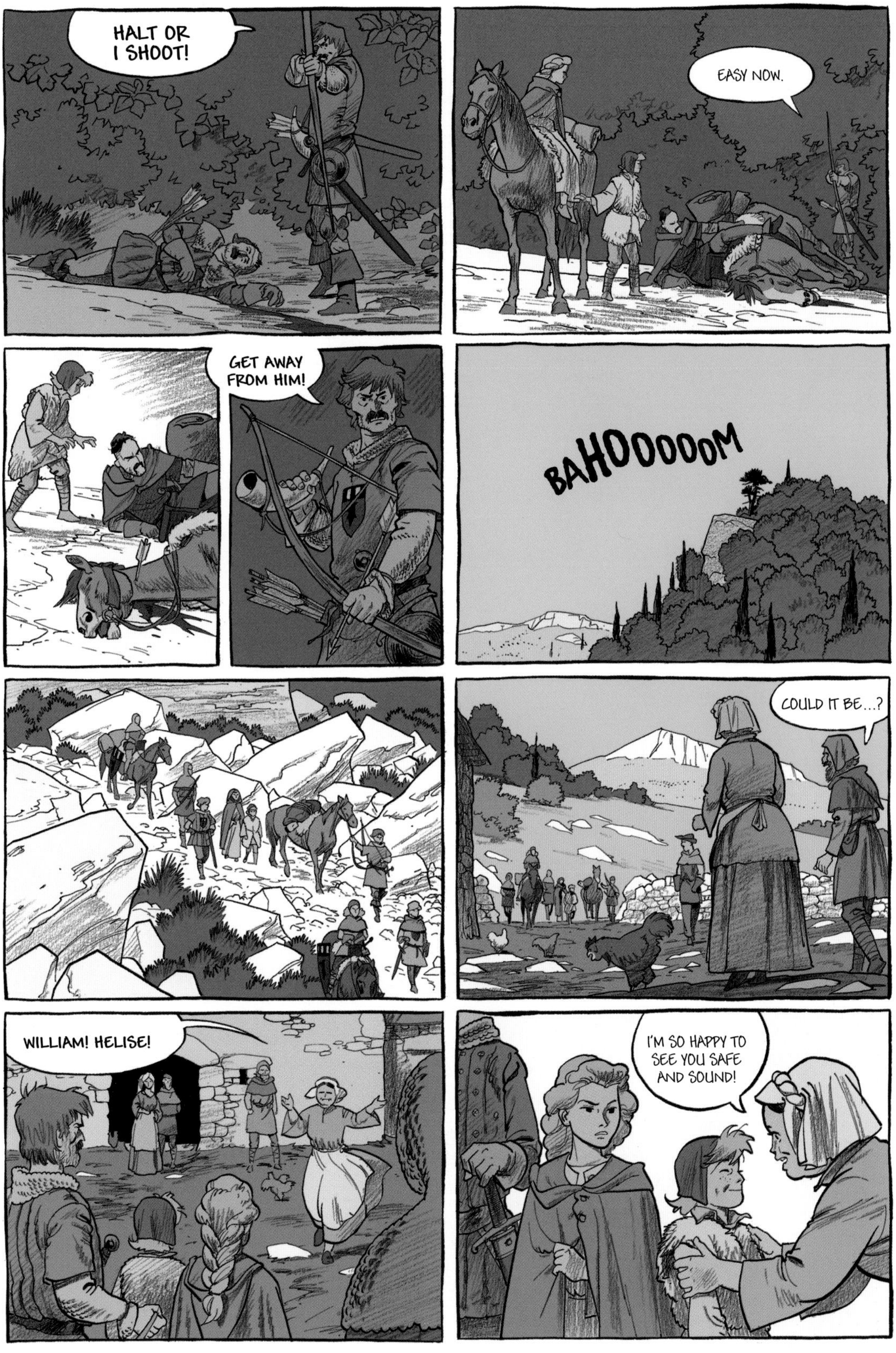
HALT OR I SHOOT!
EASY NOW.
GET AWAY FROM HIM!
BAHOOOOOM
COULD IT BE...?
WILLIAM! HELISE!
I'M SO HAPPY TO SEE YOU SAFE AND SOUND!

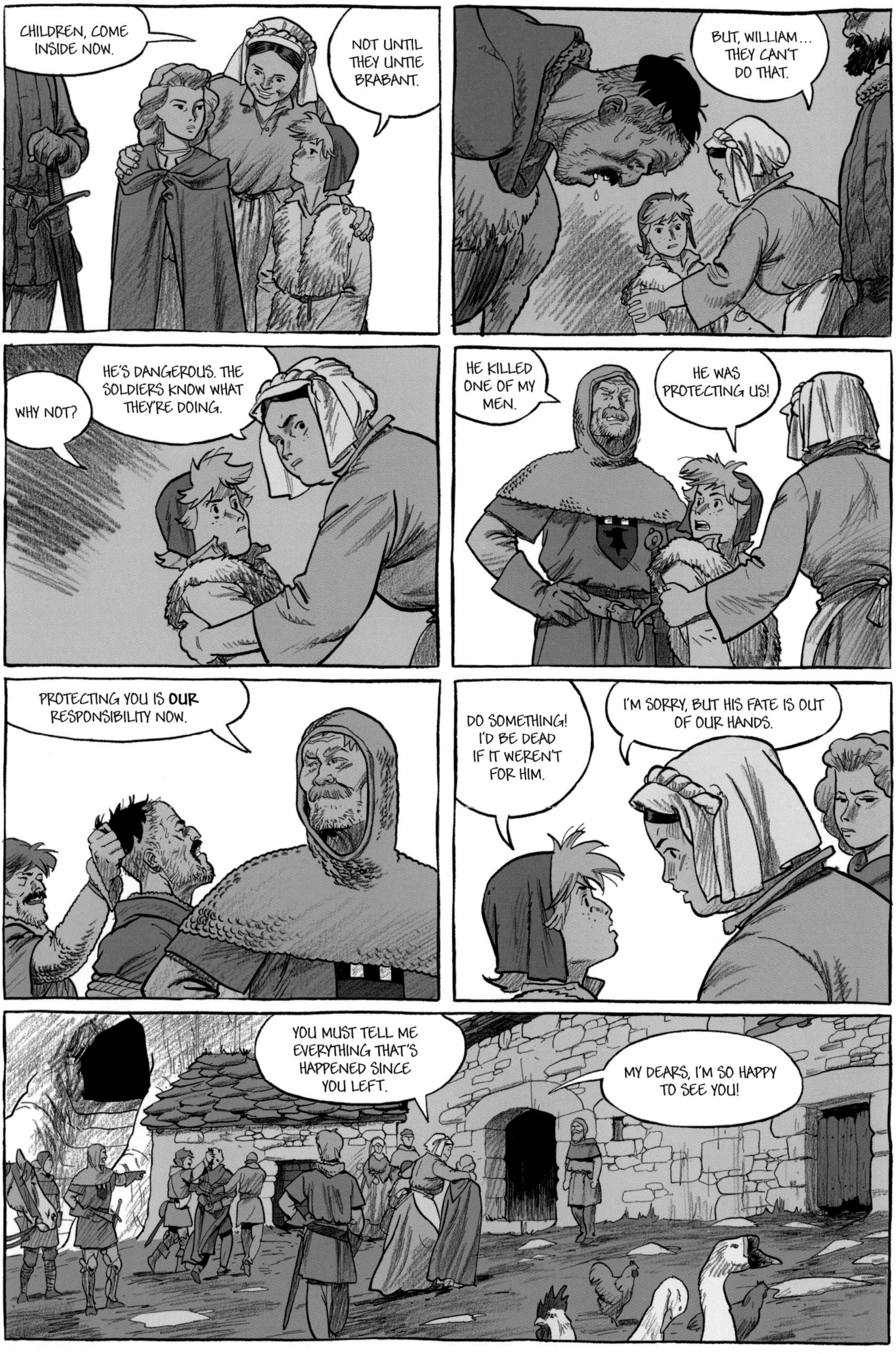
CHILDREN, COME INSIDE NOW.
NOT UNTIL THEY UNTIE BRABANT.
BUT, WILLIAM... THEY CAN'T DO THAT.
WHY NOT?
HE'S DANGEROUS. THE SOLDIERS KNOW WHAT THEY'RE DOING.
HE KILLED ONE OF MY MEN.
HE WAS PROTECTING US!
PROTECTING YOU IS **OUR** RESPONSIBILITY NOW.
DO SOMETHING! I'D BE DEAD IF IT WEREN'T FOR HIM.
I'M SORRY, BUT HIS FATE IS OUT OF OUR HANDS.
YOU MUST TELL ME EVERYTHING THAT'S HAPPENED SINCE YOU LEFT.
MY DEARS, I'M SO HAPPY TO SEE YOU!

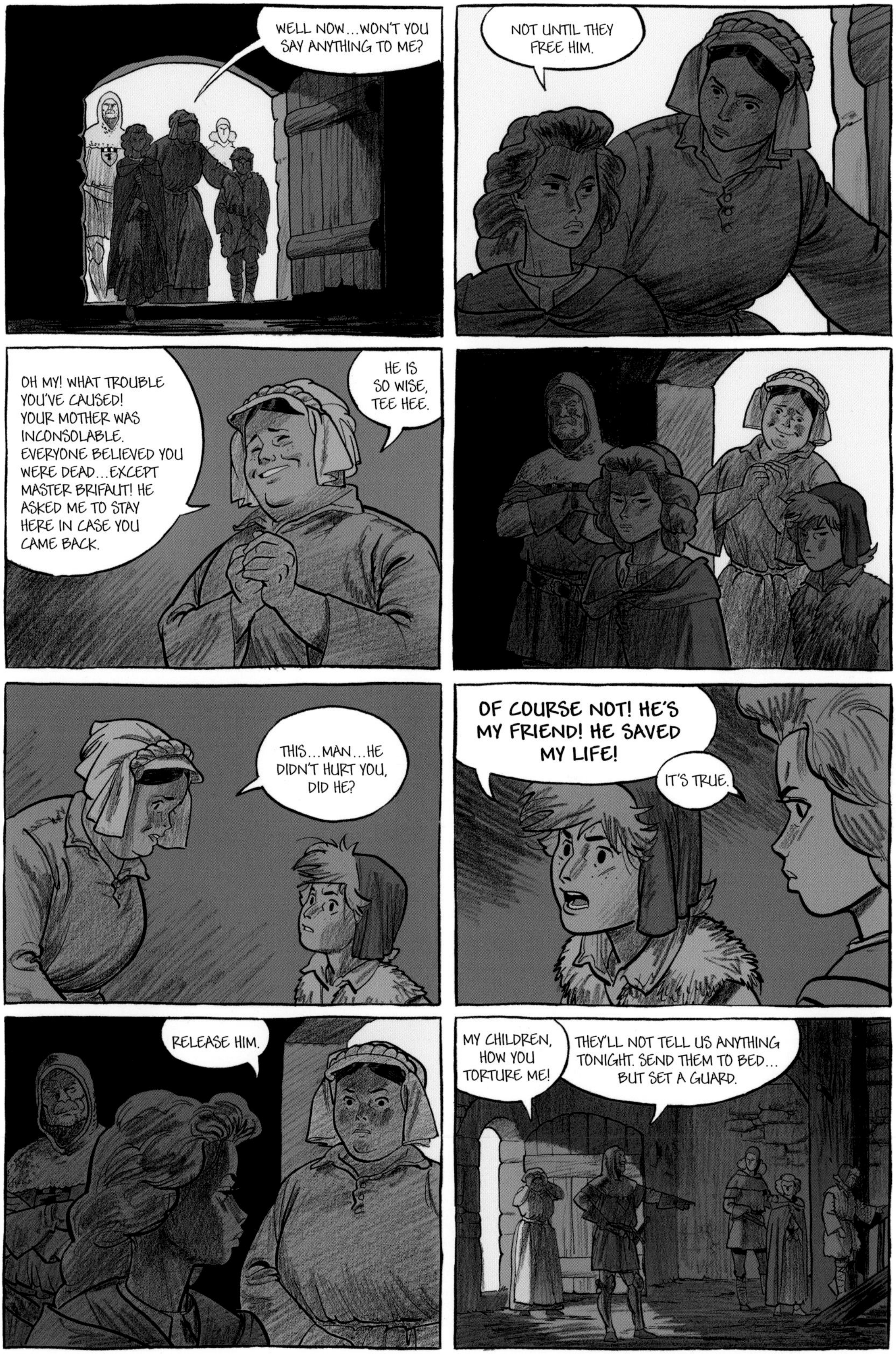
WELL NOW…WON'T YOU SAY ANYTHING TO ME?
NOT UNTIL THEY FREE HIM.
OH MY! WHAT TROUBLE YOU'VE CAUSED! YOUR MOTHER WAS INCONSOLABLE. EVERYONE BELIEVED YOU WERE DEAD…EXCEPT MASTER BRIFAUT! HE ASKED ME TO STAY HERE IN CASE YOU CAME BACK.
HE IS SO WISE, TEE HEE.
THIS…MAN…HE DIDN'T HURT YOU, DID HE?
OF COURSE NOT! HE'S MY FRIEND! HE SAVED MY LIFE!
IT'S TRUE.
RELEASE HIM.
MY CHILDREN, HOW YOU TORTURE ME!
THEY'LL NOT TELL US ANYTHING TONIGHT. SEND THEM TO BED… BUT SET A GUARD.

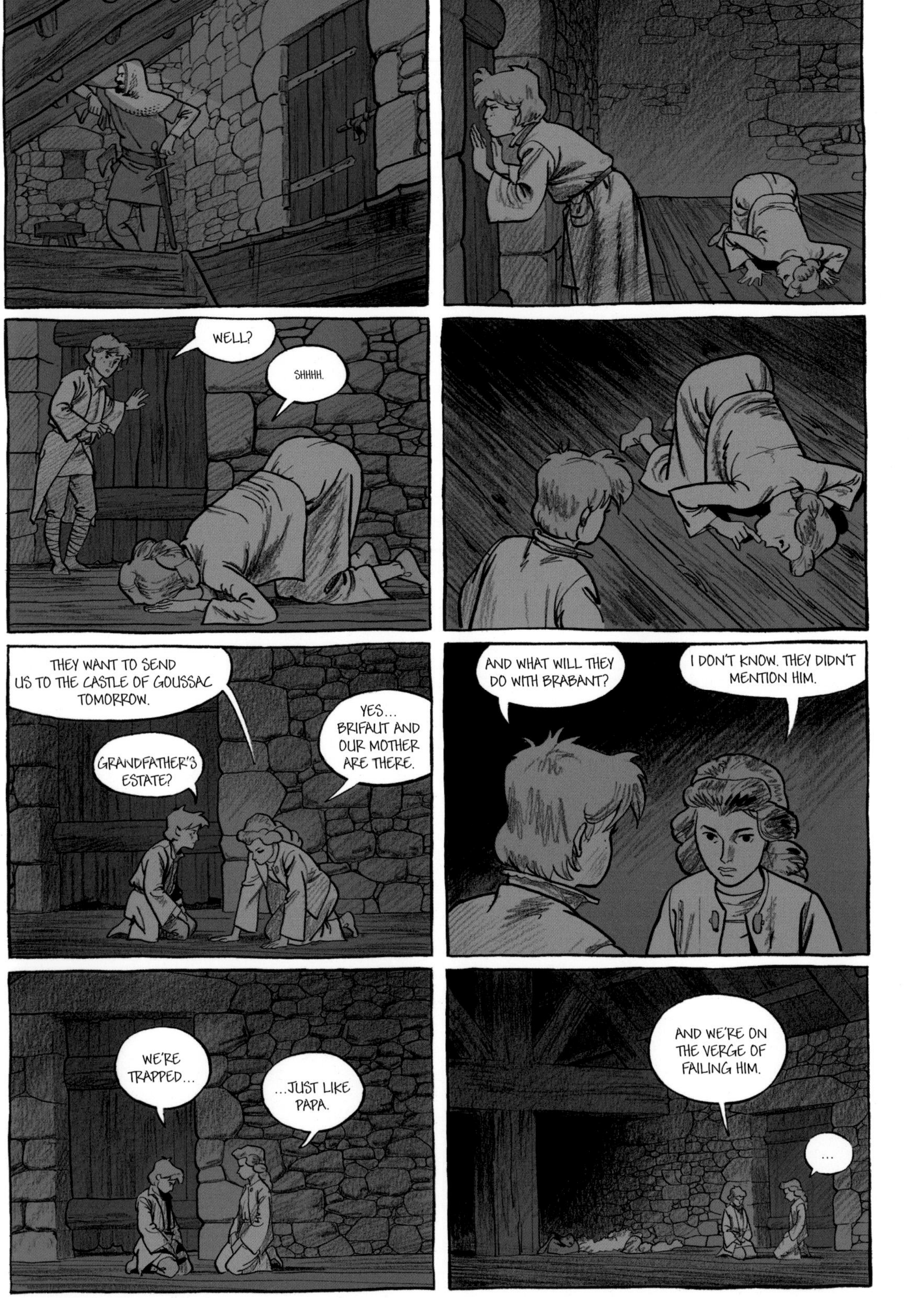
WELL?
SHHHH.
THEY WANT TO SEND US TO THE CASTLE OF GOUSSAC TOMORROW.
GRANDFATHER'S ESTATE?
YES... BRIFAUT AND OUR MOTHER ARE THERE.
AND WHAT WILL THEY DO WITH BRABANT?
I DON'T KNOW. THEY DIDN'T MENTION HIM.
WE'RE TRAPPED...
...JUST LIKE PAPA.
AND WE'RE ON THE VERGE OF FAILING HIM.
...

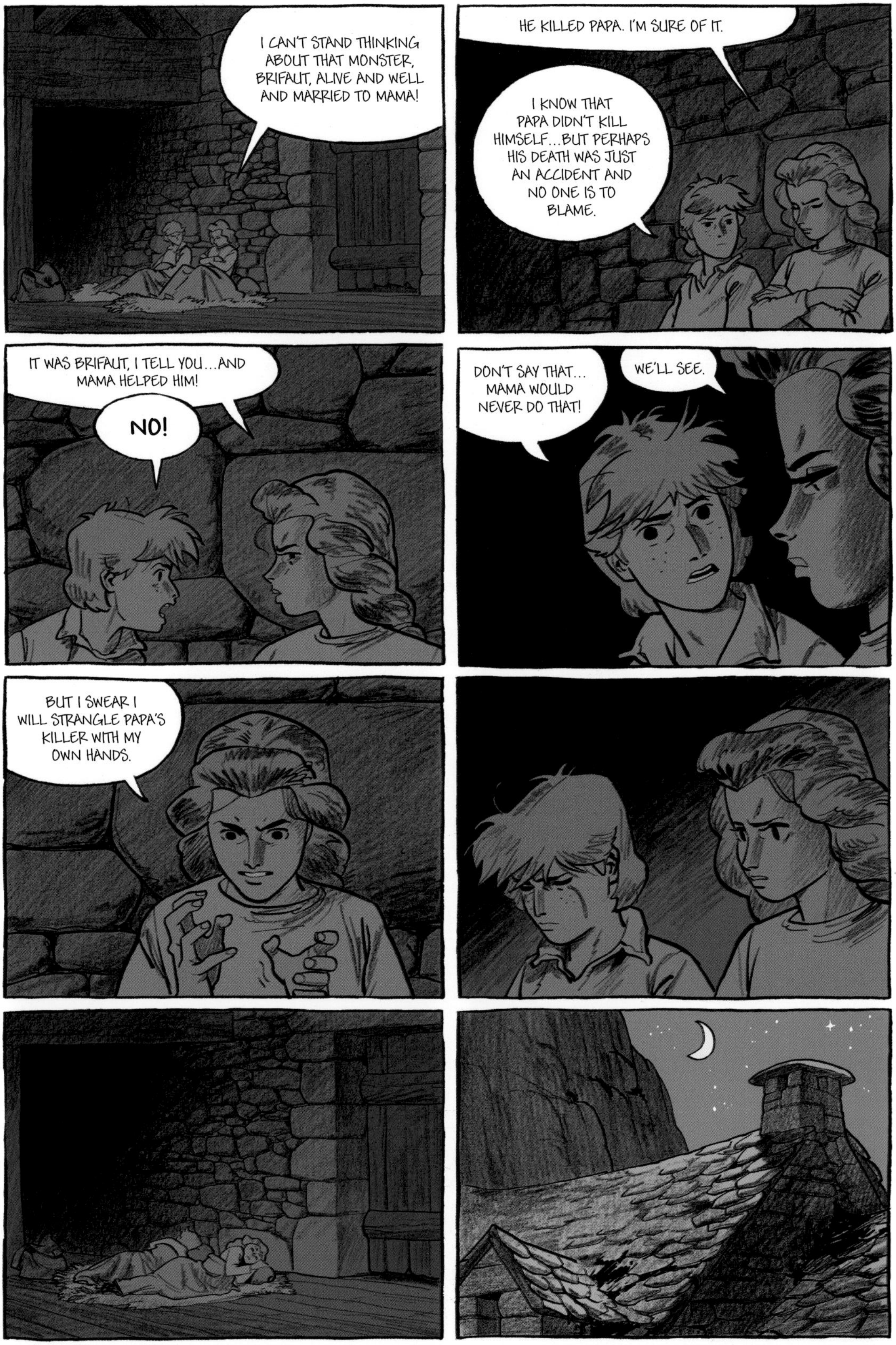

I CAN'T STAND THINKING ABOUT THAT MONSTER, BRIFAUT, ALIVE AND WELL AND MARRIED TO MAMA!
HE KILLED PAPA. I'M SURE OF IT.
I KNOW THAT PAPA DIDN'T KILL HIMSELF...BUT PERHAPS HIS DEATH WAS JUST AN ACCIDENT AND NO ONE IS TO BLAME.
IT WAS BRIFAUT, I TELL YOU...AND MAMA HELPED HIM!
NO!
DON'T SAY THAT... MAMA WOULD NEVER DO THAT!
WE'LL SEE.
BUT I SWEAR I WILL STRANGLE PAPA'S KILLER WITH MY OWN HANDS.

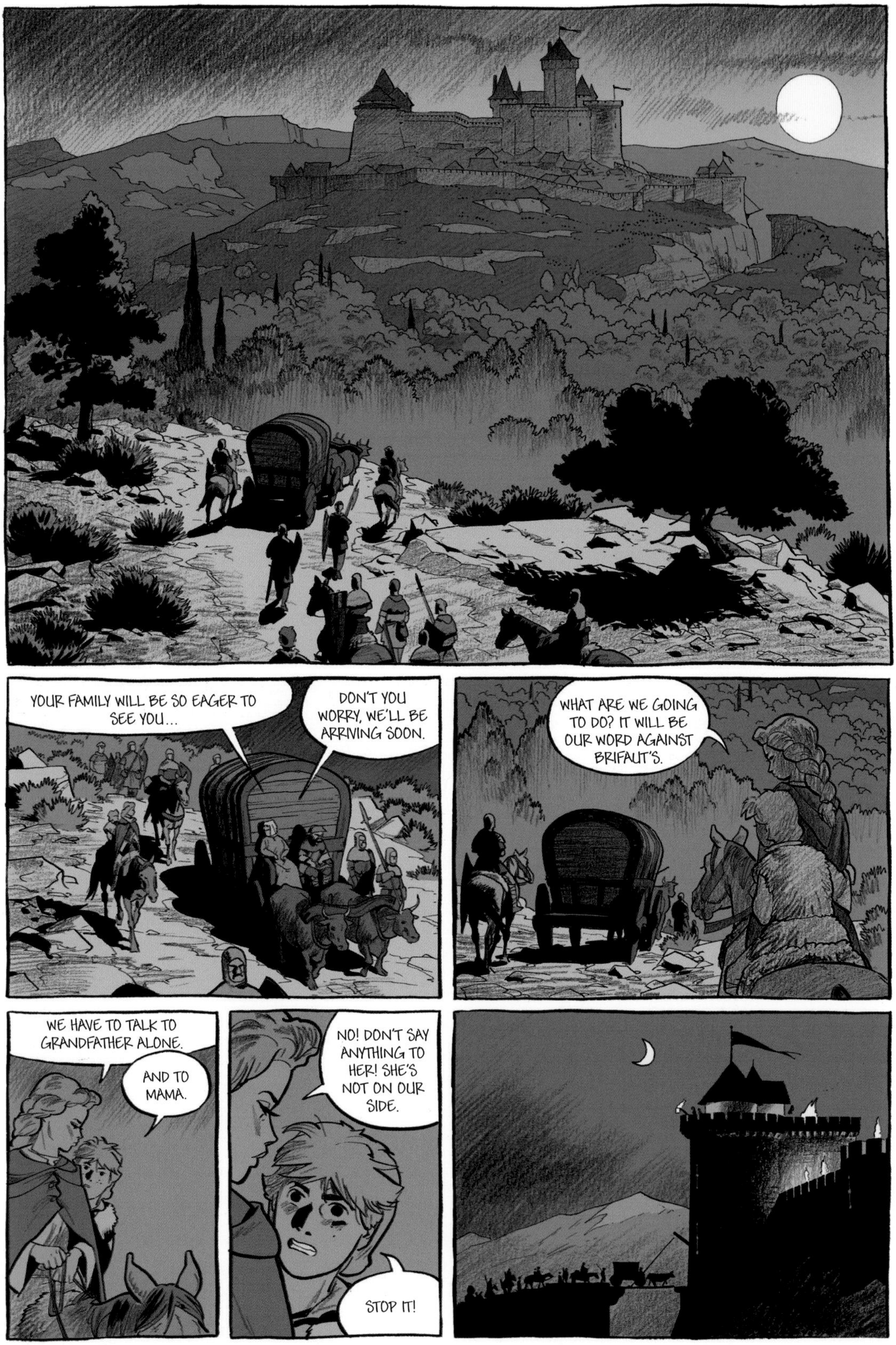
YOUR FAMILY WILL BE SO EAGER TO SEE YOU...
DON'T YOU WORRY, WE'LL BE ARRIVING SOON.
WHAT ARE WE GOING TO DO? IT WILL BE OUR WORD AGAINST BRIFAUT'S.
WE HAVE TO TALK TO GRANDFATHER ALONE.
AND TO MAMA.
NO! DON'T SAY ANYTHING TO HER! SHE'S NOT ON OUR SIDE.
STOP IT!

HOW HAPPY I AM TO SEE YOU, CHILDREN! WELCOME HOME!

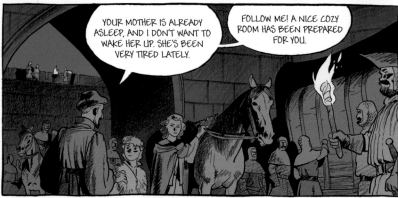

YOUR MOTHER IS ALREADY ASLEEP, AND I DON'T WANT TO WAKE HER UP. SHE'S BEEN VERY TIRED LATELY.

FOLLOW ME! A NICE COZY ROOM HAS BEEN PREPARED FOR YOU.

DON'T WORRY ABOUT ME!

I'LL BE FINE.

HE'S NOT WELL.

WHAT ABOUT GRANDFATHER?

WE'RE VERY WORRIED ABOUT HIM.

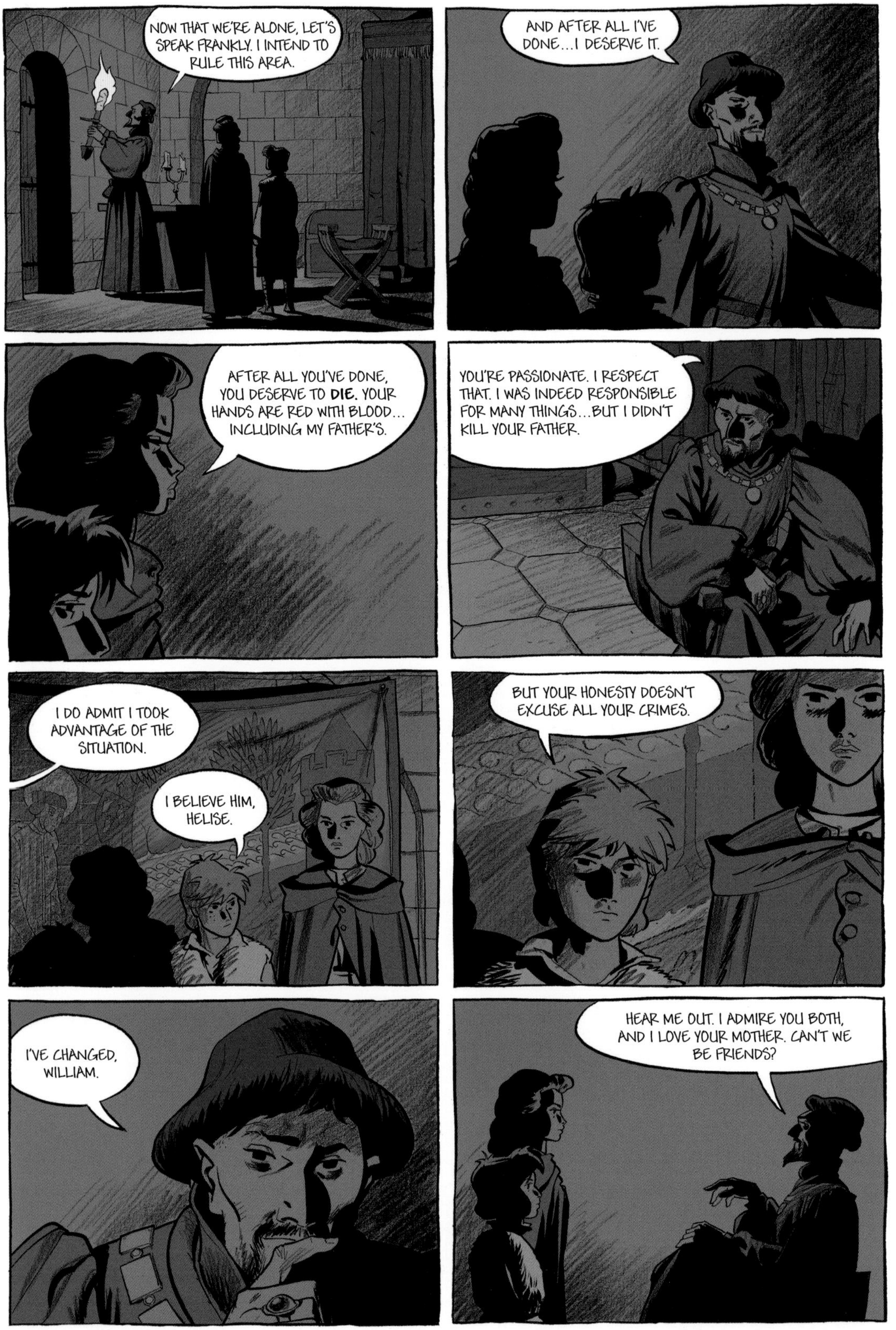
NOW THAT WE'RE ALONE, LET'S SPEAK FRANKLY. I INTEND TO RULE THIS AREA.
AND AFTER ALL I'VE DONE…I DESERVE IT.
AFTER ALL YOU'VE DONE, YOU DESERVE TO **DIE.** YOUR HANDS ARE RED WITH BLOOD… INCLUDING MY FATHER'S.
YOU'RE PASSIONATE. I RESPECT THAT. I WAS INDEED RESPONSIBLE FOR MANY THINGS…BUT I DIDN'T KILL YOUR FATHER.
I DO ADMIT I TOOK ADVANTAGE OF THE SITUATION.
I BELIEVE HIM, HELISE.
BUT YOUR HONESTY DOESN'T EXCUSE ALL YOUR CRIMES.
I'VE CHANGED, WILLIAM.
HEAR ME OUT. I ADMIRE YOU BOTH, AND I LOVE YOUR MOTHER. CAN'T WE BE FRIENDS?

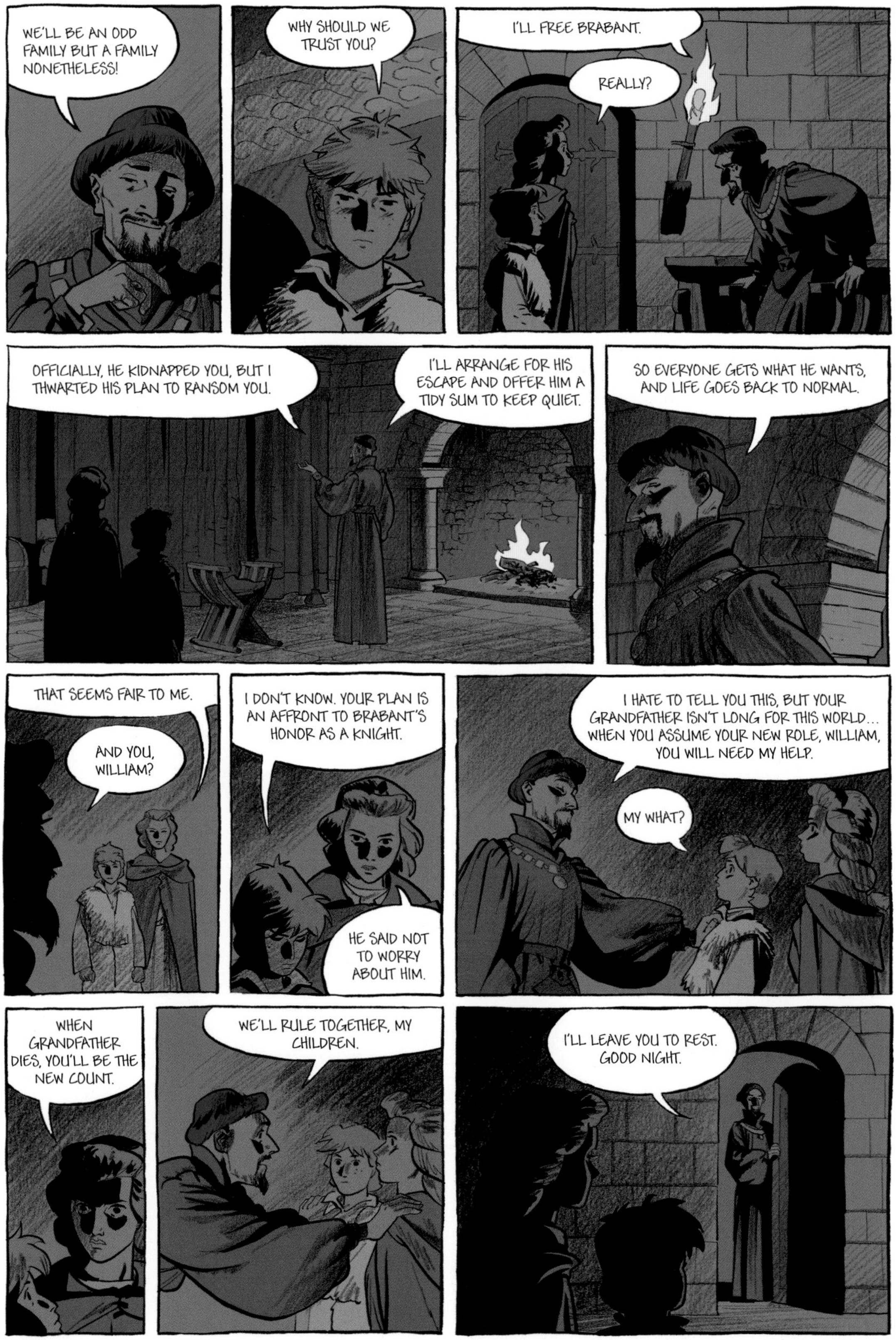
WE'LL BE AN ODD FAMILY BUT A FAMILY NONETHELESS!
WHY SHOULD WE TRUST YOU?
I'LL FREE BRABANT.
REALLY?
OFFICIALLY, HE KIDNAPPED YOU, BUT I THWARTED HIS PLAN TO RANSOM YOU.
I'LL ARRANGE FOR HIS ESCAPE AND OFFER HIM A TIDY SUM TO KEEP QUIET.
SO EVERYONE GETS WHAT HE WANTS, AND LIFE GOES BACK TO NORMAL.
THAT SEEMS FAIR TO ME.
AND YOU, WILLIAM?
I DON'T KNOW. YOUR PLAN IS AN AFFRONT TO BRABANT'S HONOR AS A KNIGHT.
HE SAID NOT TO WORRY ABOUT HIM.
I HATE TO TELL YOU THIS, BUT YOUR GRANDFATHER ISN'T LONG FOR THIS WORLD… WHEN YOU ASSUME YOUR NEW ROLE, WILLIAM, YOU WILL NEED MY HELP.
MY WHAT?
WHEN GRANDFATHER DIES, YOU'LL BE THE NEW COUNT.
WE'LL RULE TOGETHER, MY CHILDREN.
I'LL LEAVE YOU TO REST. GOOD NIGHT.

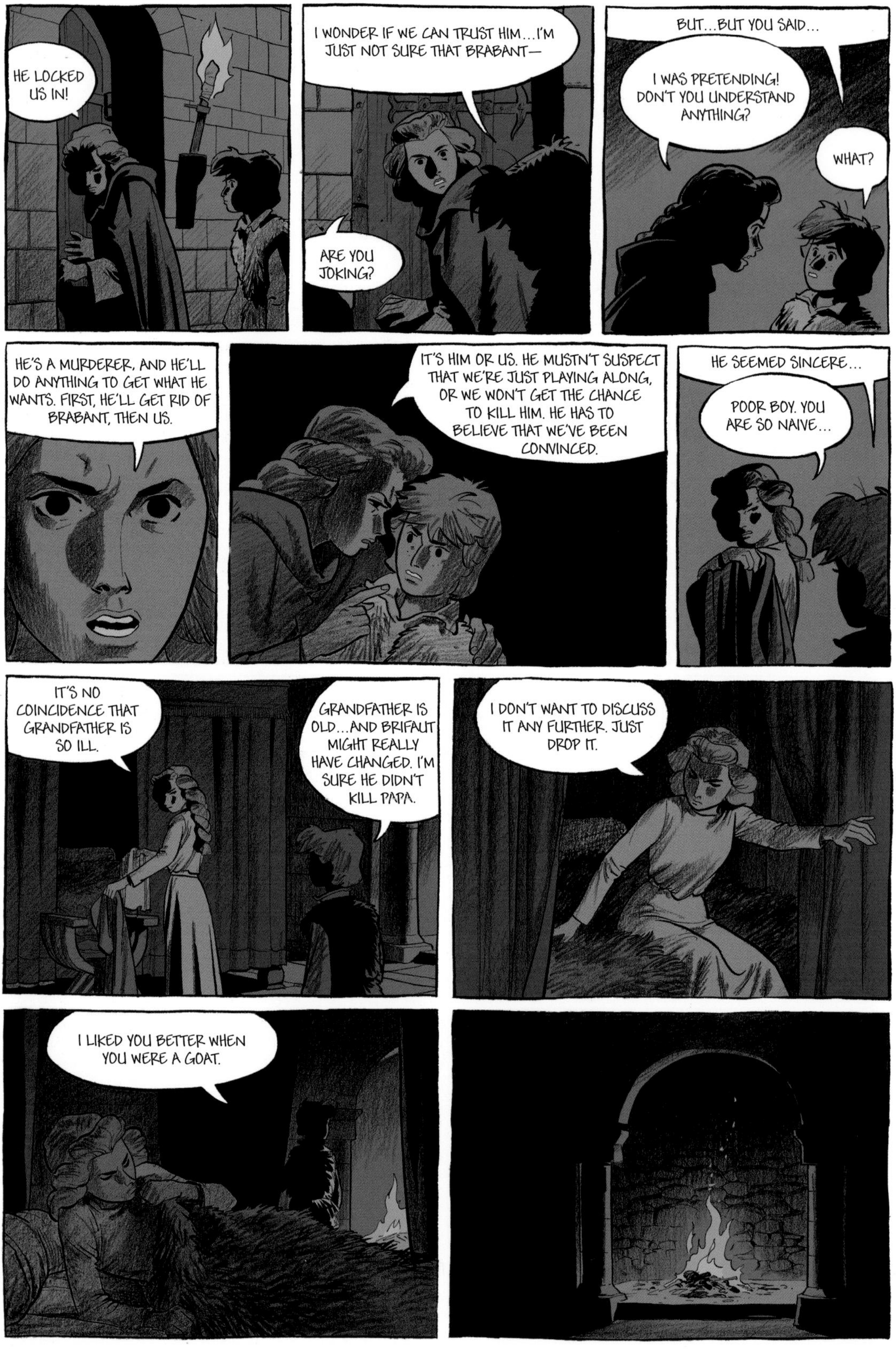
HE LOCKED US IN!
I WONDER IF WE CAN TRUST HIM…I'M JUST NOT SURE THAT BRABANT—
ARE YOU JOKING?
BUT…BUT YOU SAID…
I WAS PRETENDING! DON'T YOU UNDERSTAND ANYTHING?
WHAT?
HE'S A MURDERER, AND HE'LL DO ANYTHING TO GET WHAT HE WANTS. FIRST, HE'LL GET RID OF BRABANT, THEN US.
IT'S HIM OR US. HE MUSTN'T SUSPECT THAT WE'RE JUST PLAYING ALONG, OR WE WON'T GET THE CHANCE TO KILL HIM. HE HAS TO BELIEVE THAT WE'VE BEEN CONVINCED.
HE SEEMED SINCERE…
POOR BOY. YOU ARE SO NAIVE…
IT'S NO COINCIDENCE THAT GRANDFATHER IS SO ILL.
GRANDFATHER IS OLD…AND BRIFAUT MIGHT REALLY HAVE CHANGED. I'M SURE HE DIDN'T KILL PAPA.
I DON'T WANT TO DISCUSS IT ANY FURTHER. JUST DROP IT.
I LIKED YOU BETTER WHEN YOU WERE A GOAT.

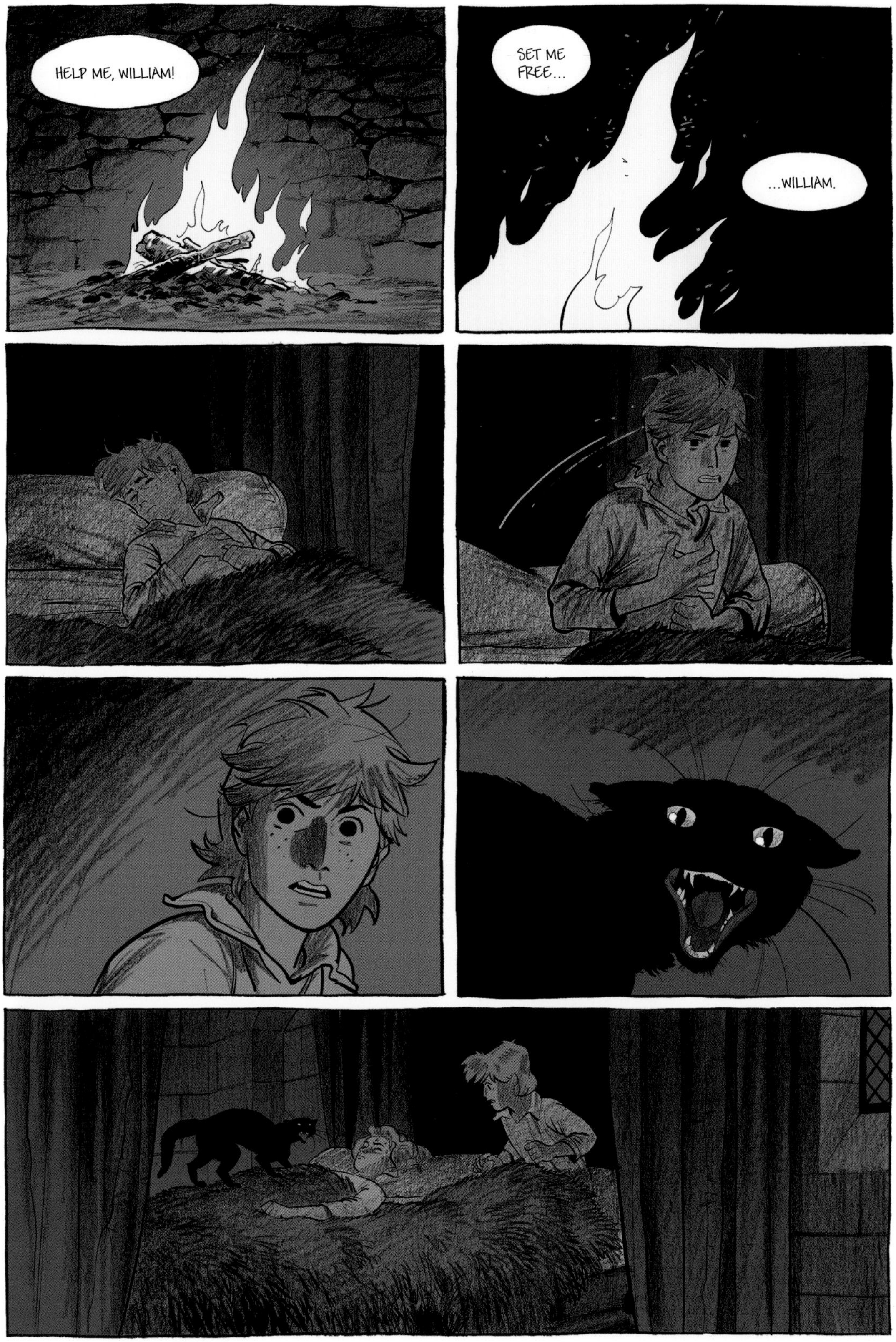
HELP ME, WILLIAM!
SET ME FREE...
...WILLIAM.

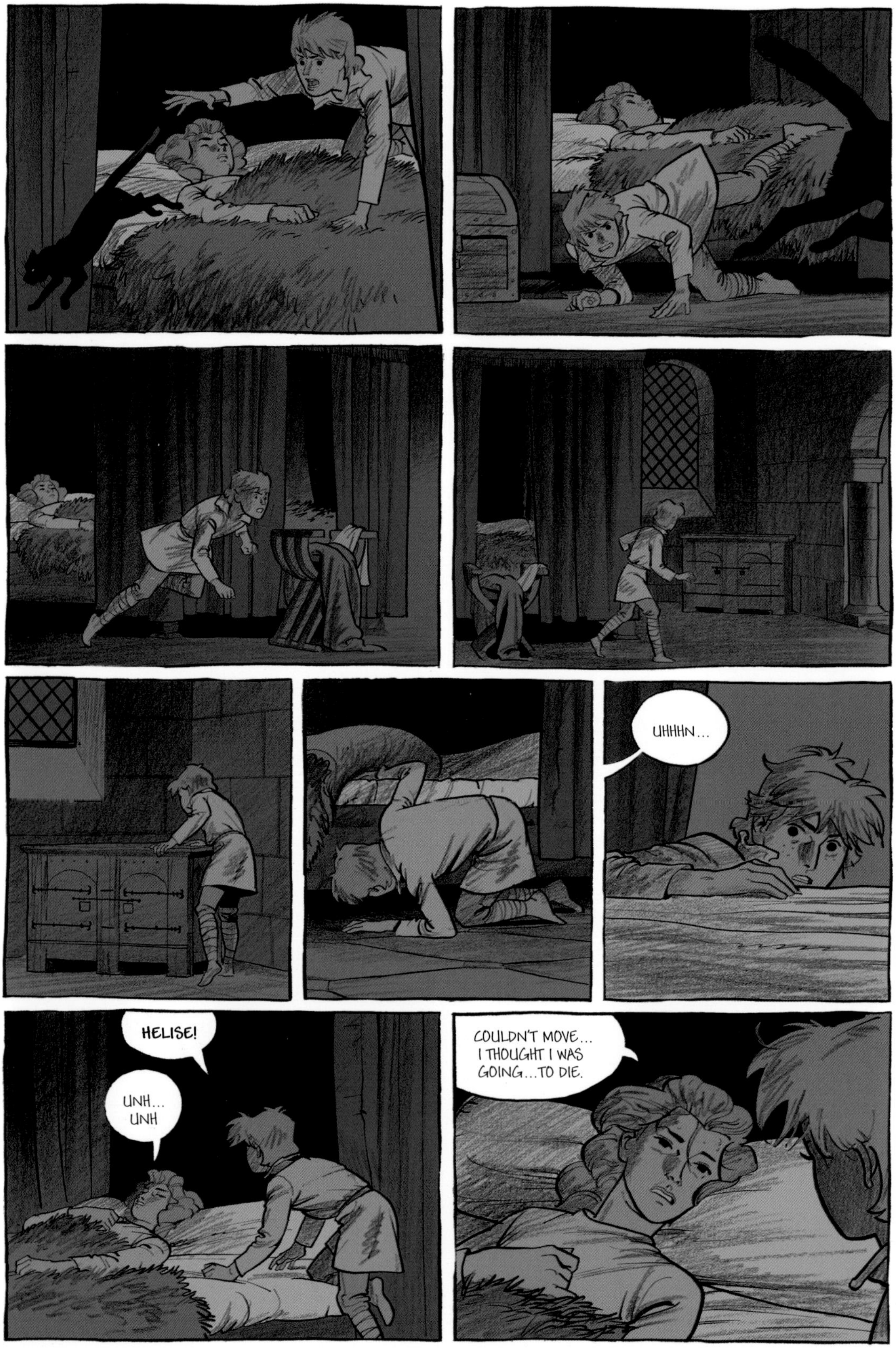
UHHHN...
HELISE!
UNH... UNH
COULDN'T MOVE... I THOUGHT I WAS GOING... TO DIE.

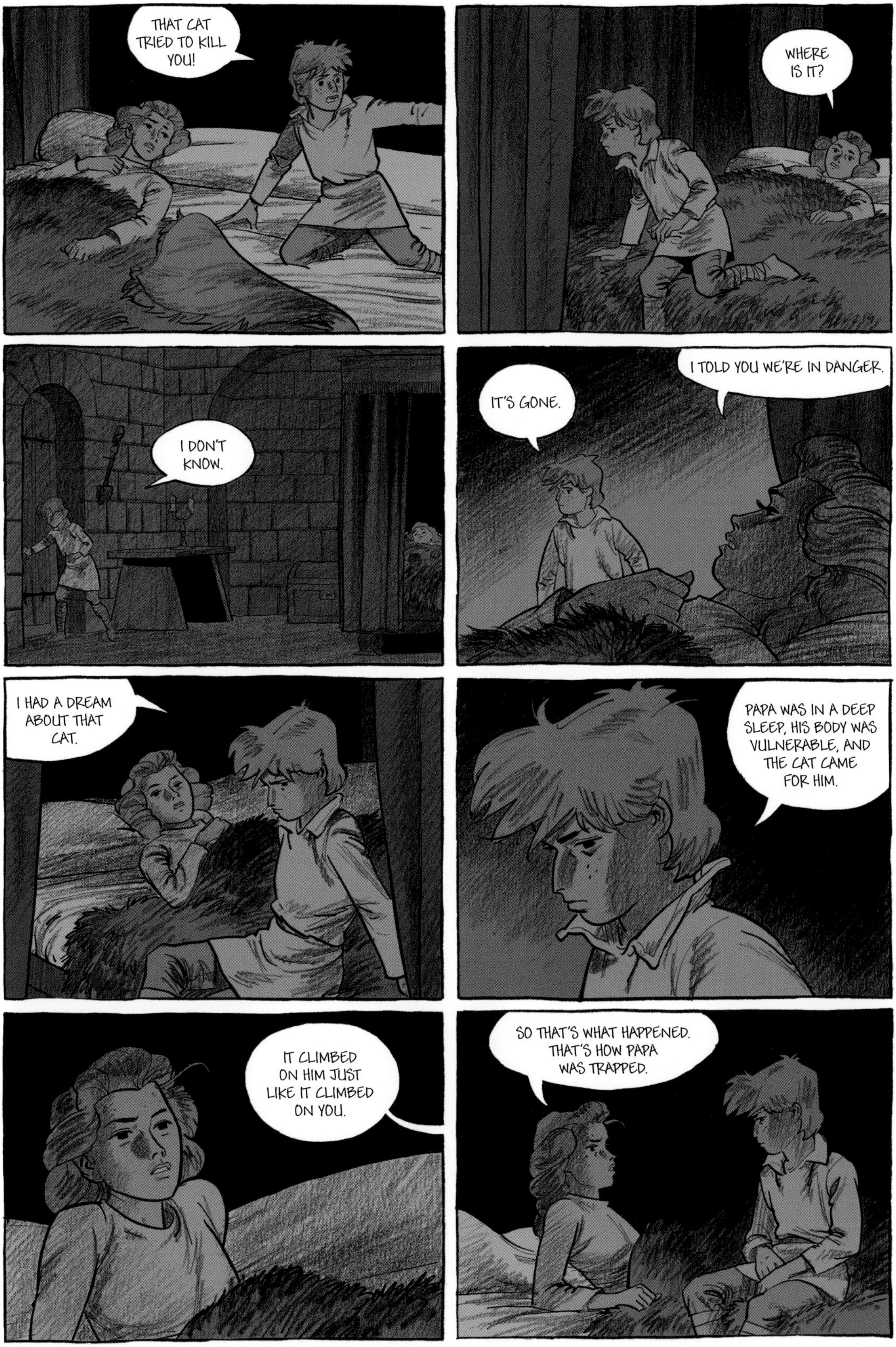
THAT CAT TRIED TO KILL YOU!
WHERE IS IT?
I DON'T KNOW.
IT'S GONE.
I TOLD YOU WE'RE IN DANGER.
I HAD A DREAM ABOUT THAT CAT.
PAPA WAS IN A DEEP SLEEP, HIS BODY WAS VULNERABLE, AND THE CAT CAME FOR HIM.
IT CLIMBED ON HIM JUST LIKE IT CLIMBED ON YOU.
SO THAT'S WHAT HAPPENED. THAT'S HOW PAPA WAS TRAPPED.

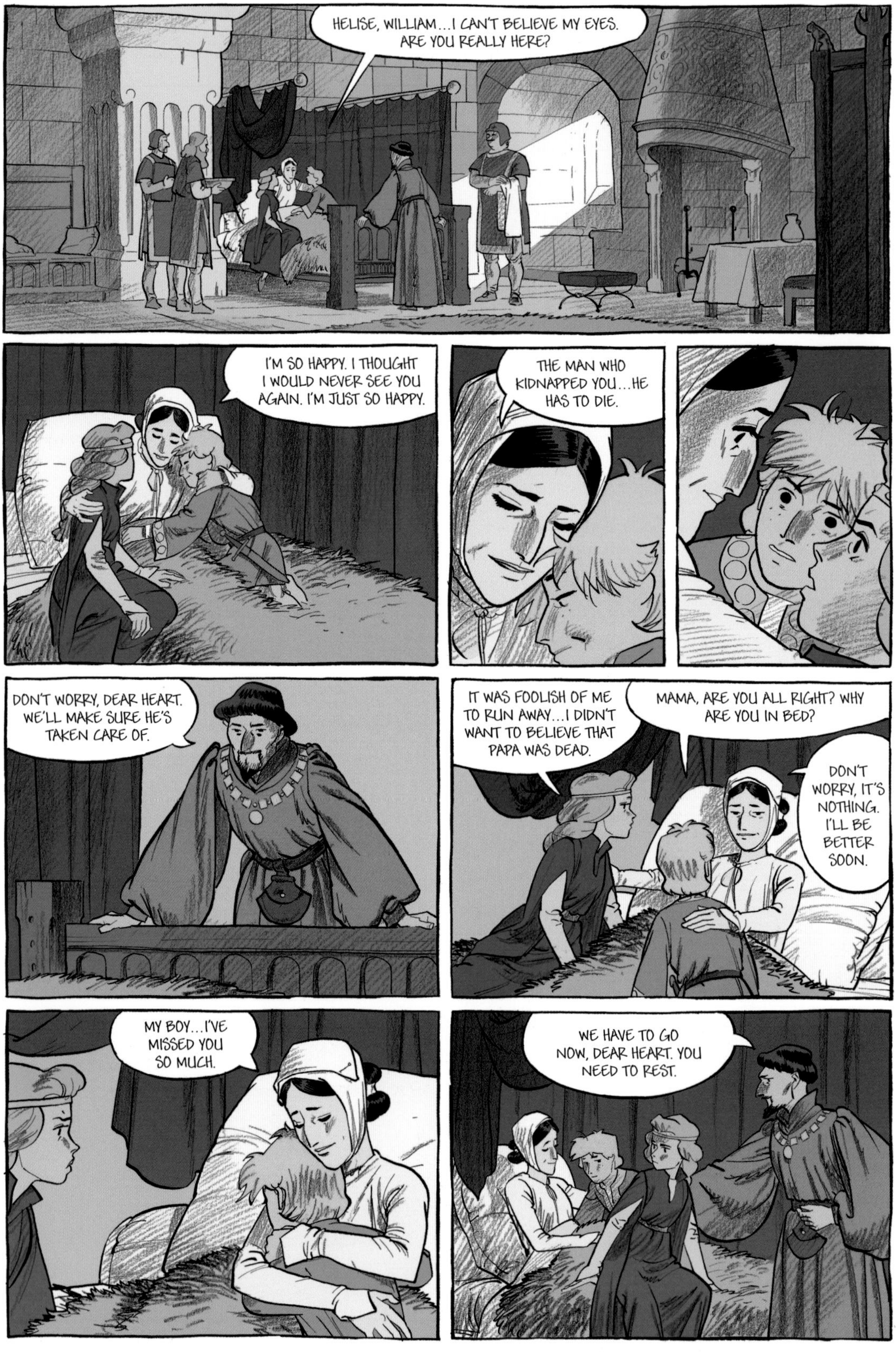
HELISE, WILLIAM...I CAN'T BELIEVE MY EYES. ARE YOU REALLY HERE?
I'M SO HAPPY. I THOUGHT I WOULD NEVER SEE YOU AGAIN. I'M JUST SO HAPPY.
THE MAN WHO KIDNAPPED YOU...HE HAS TO DIE.
DON'T WORRY, DEAR HEART. WE'LL MAKE SURE HE'S TAKEN CARE OF.
IT WAS FOOLISH OF ME TO RUN AWAY...I DIDN'T WANT TO BELIEVE THAT PAPA WAS DEAD.
MAMA, ARE YOU ALL RIGHT? WHY ARE YOU IN BED?
DON'T WORRY, IT'S NOTHING. I'LL BE BETTER SOON.
MY BOY...I'VE MISSED YOU SO MUCH.
WE HAVE TO GO NOW, DEAR HEART. YOU NEED TO REST.

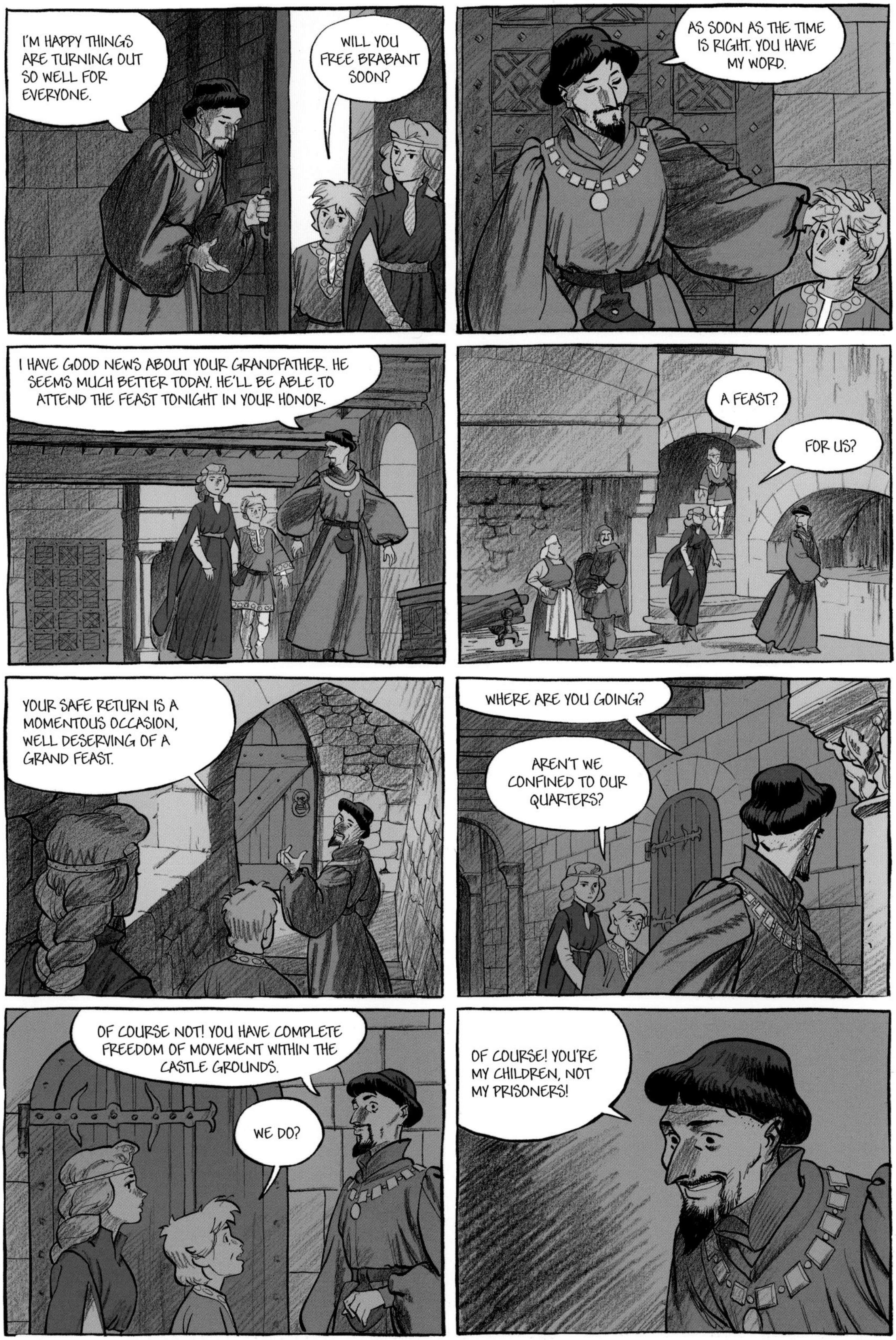
I'M HAPPY THINGS ARE TURNING OUT SO WELL FOR EVERYONE.
WILL YOU FREE BRABANT SOON?
AS SOON AS THE TIME IS RIGHT. YOU HAVE MY WORD.
I HAVE GOOD NEWS ABOUT YOUR GRANDFATHER. HE SEEMS MUCH BETTER TODAY. HE'LL BE ABLE TO ATTEND THE FEAST TONIGHT IN YOUR HONOR.
A FEAST?
FOR US?
YOUR SAFE RETURN IS A MOMENTOUS OCCASION, WELL DESERVING OF A GRAND FEAST.
WHERE ARE YOU GOING?
AREN'T WE CONFINED TO OUR QUARTERS?
OF COURSE NOT! YOU HAVE COMPLETE FREEDOM OF MOVEMENT WITHIN THE CASTLE GROUNDS.
WE DO?
OF COURSE! YOU'RE MY CHILDREN, NOT MY PRISONERS!

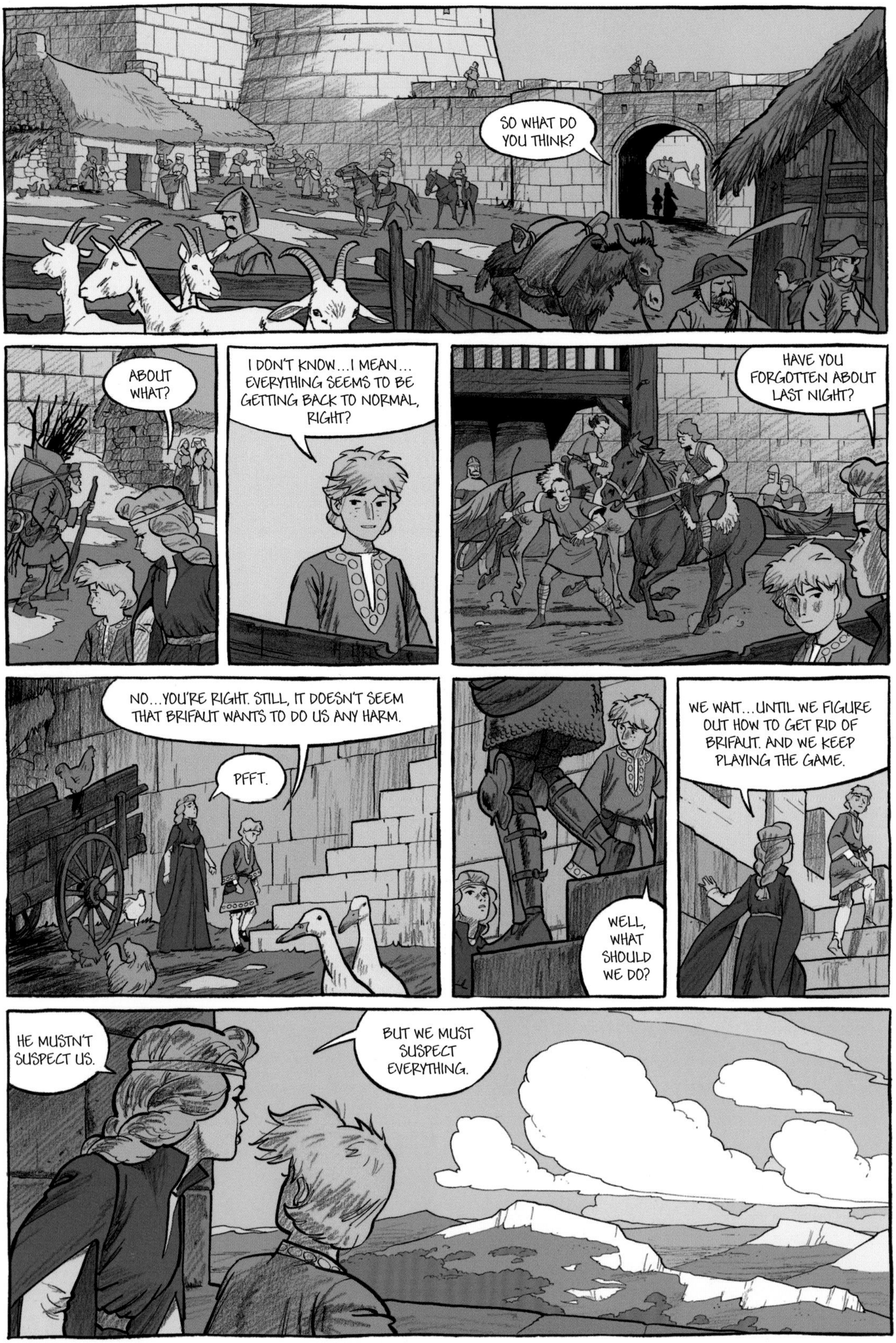
SO WHAT DO YOU THINK?
ABOUT WHAT?
I DON'T KNOW...I MEAN... EVERYTHING SEEMS TO BE GETTING BACK TO NORMAL, RIGHT?
HAVE YOU FORGOTTEN ABOUT LAST NIGHT?
NO...YOU'RE RIGHT. STILL, IT DOESN'T SEEM THAT BRIFAUT WANTS TO DO US ANY HARM.
PFFT.
WELL, WHAT SHOULD WE DO?
WE WAIT...UNTIL WE FIGURE OUT HOW TO GET RID OF BRIFAUT. AND WE KEEP PLAYING THE GAME.
HE MUSTN'T SUSPECT US.
BUT WE MUST SUSPECT EVERYTHING.

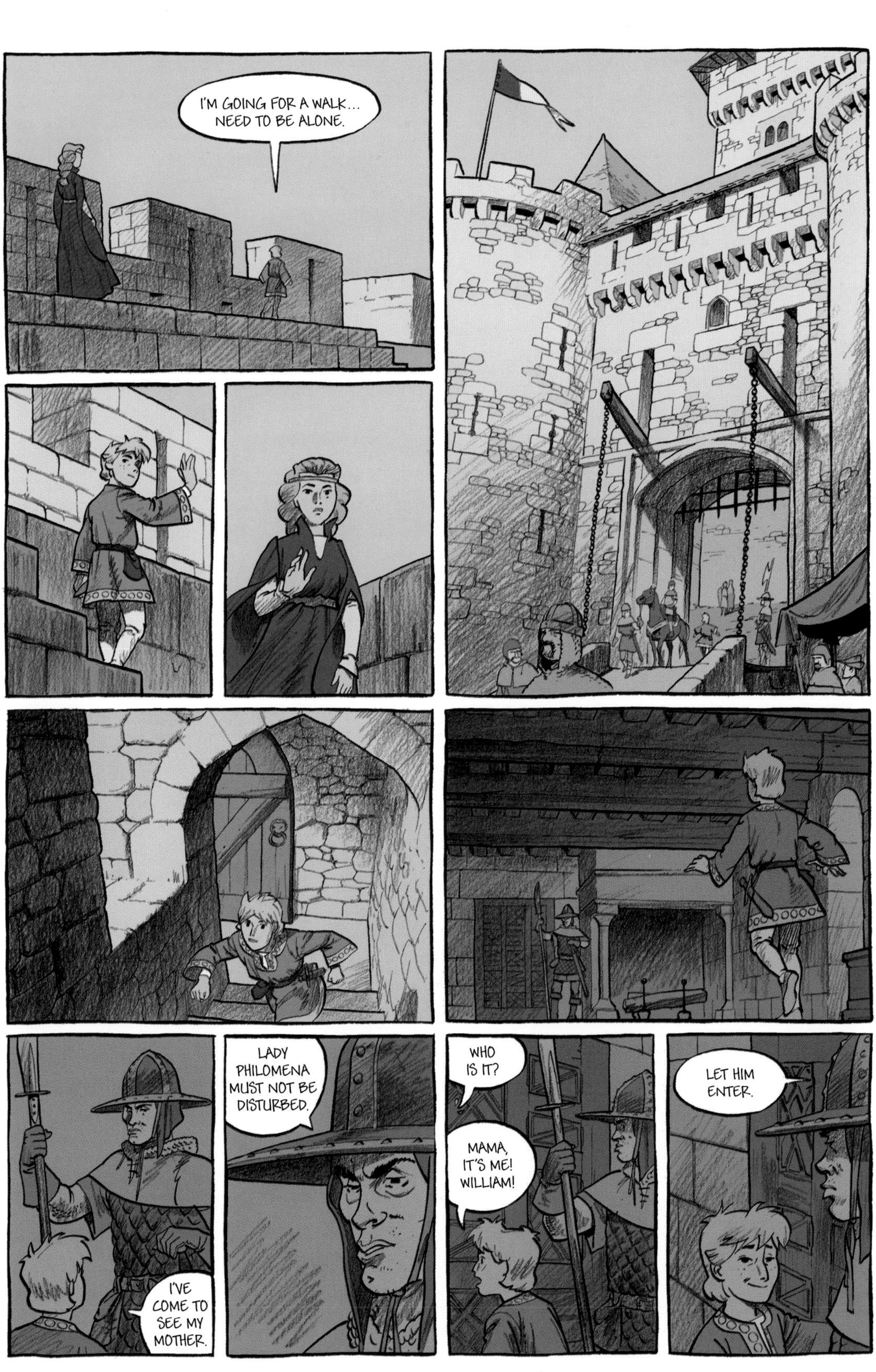
I'M GOING FOR A WALK… NEED TO BE ALONE.
I'VE COME TO SEE MY MOTHER.
LADY PHILOMENA MUST NOT BE DISTURBED.
WHO IS IT?
MAMA, IT'S ME! WILLIAM!
LET HIM ENTER.

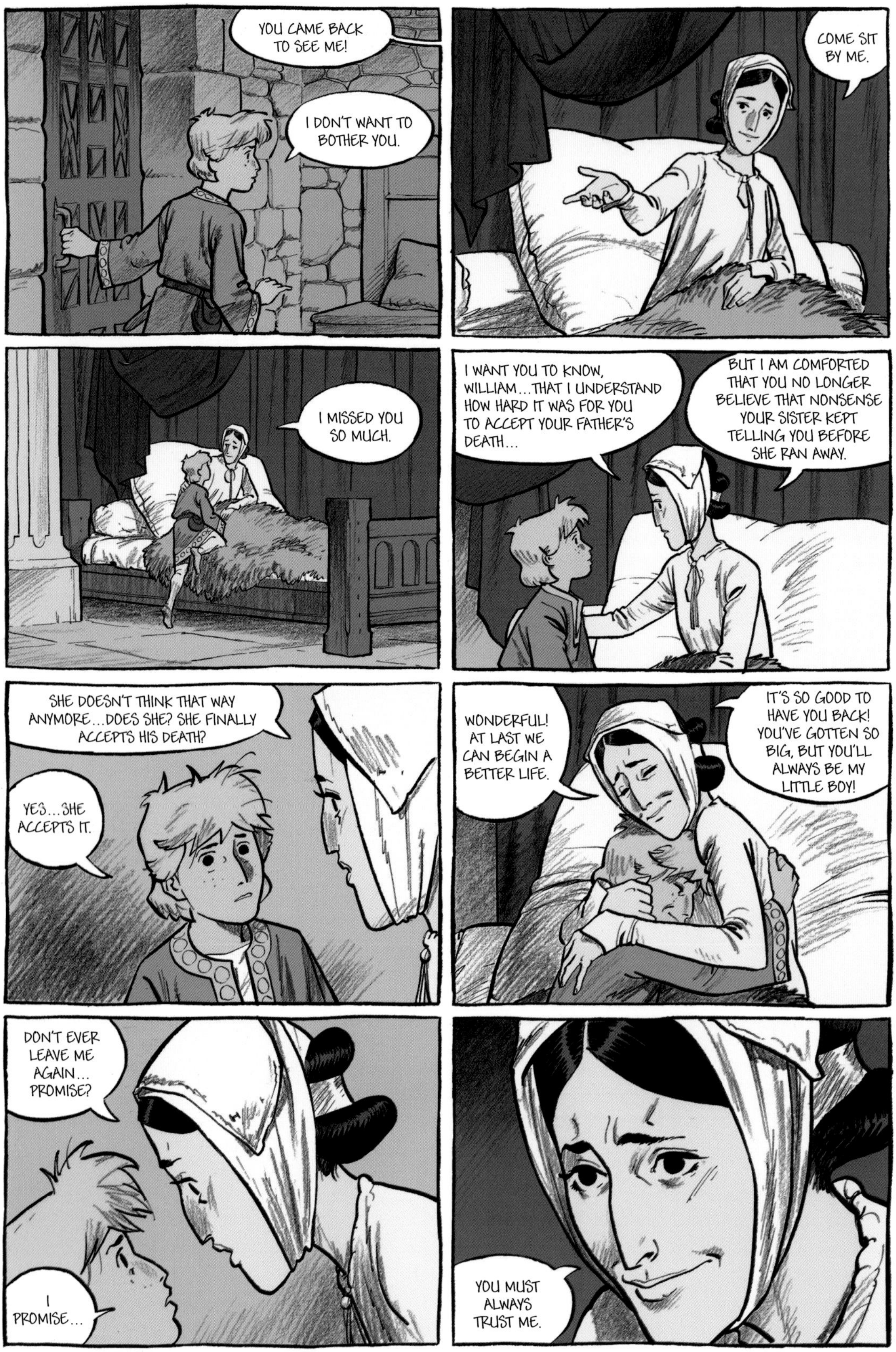
YOU CAME BACK TO SEE ME!
I DON'T WANT TO BOTHER YOU.
COME SIT BY ME.
I MISSED YOU SO MUCH.
I WANT YOU TO KNOW, WILLIAM...THAT I UNDERSTAND HOW HARD IT WAS FOR YOU TO ACCEPT YOUR FATHER'S DEATH...
BUT I AM COMFORTED THAT YOU NO LONGER BELIEVE THAT NONSENSE YOUR SISTER KEPT TELLING YOU BEFORE SHE RAN AWAY.
SHE DOESN'T THINK THAT WAY ANYMORE...DOES SHE? SHE FINALLY ACCEPTS HIS DEATH?
YES...SHE ACCEPTS IT.
WONDERFUL! AT LAST WE CAN BEGIN A BETTER LIFE.
IT'S SO GOOD TO HAVE YOU BACK! YOU'VE GOTTEN SO BIG, BUT YOU'LL ALWAYS BE MY LITTLE BOY!
DON'T EVER LEAVE ME AGAIN... PROMISE?
I PROMISE...
YOU MUST ALWAYS TRUST ME.

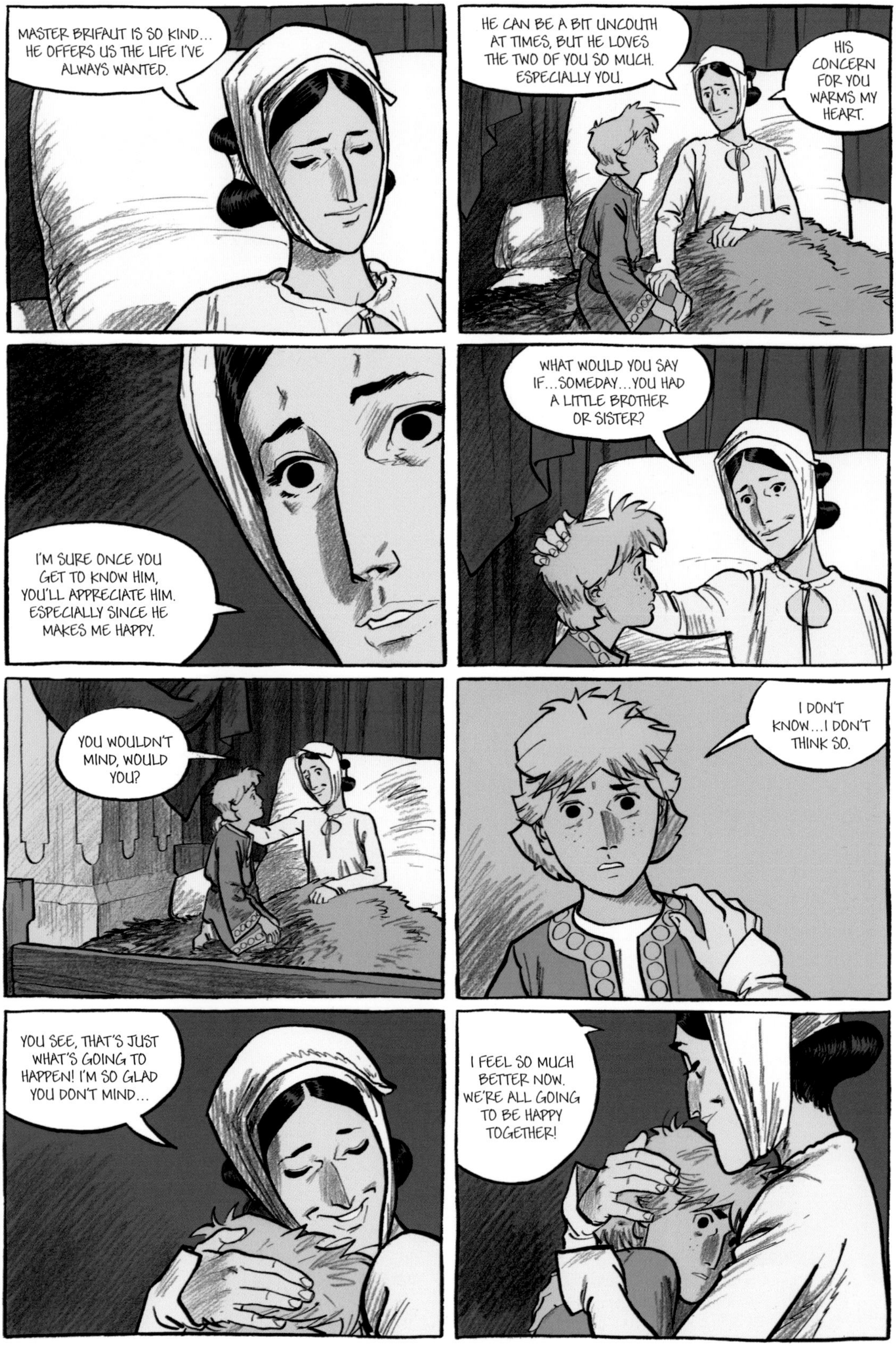
MASTER BRIFAUT IS SO KIND... HE OFFERS US THE LIFE I'VE ALWAYS WANTED.
HE CAN BE A BIT UNCOUTH AT TIMES, BUT HE LOVES THE TWO OF YOU SO MUCH. ESPECIALLY YOU.
HIS CONCERN FOR YOU WARMS MY HEART.
I'M SURE ONCE YOU GET TO KNOW HIM, YOU'LL APPRECIATE HIM. ESPECIALLY SINCE HE MAKES ME HAPPY.
WHAT WOULD YOU SAY IF...SOMEDAY...YOU HAD A LITTLE BROTHER OR SISTER?
YOU WOULDN'T MIND, WOULD YOU?
I DON'T KNOW...I DON'T THINK SO.
YOU SEE, THAT'S JUST WHAT'S GOING TO HAPPEN! I'M SO GLAD YOU DON'T MIND...
I FEEL SO MUCH BETTER NOW. WE'RE ALL GOING TO BE HAPPY TOGETHER!

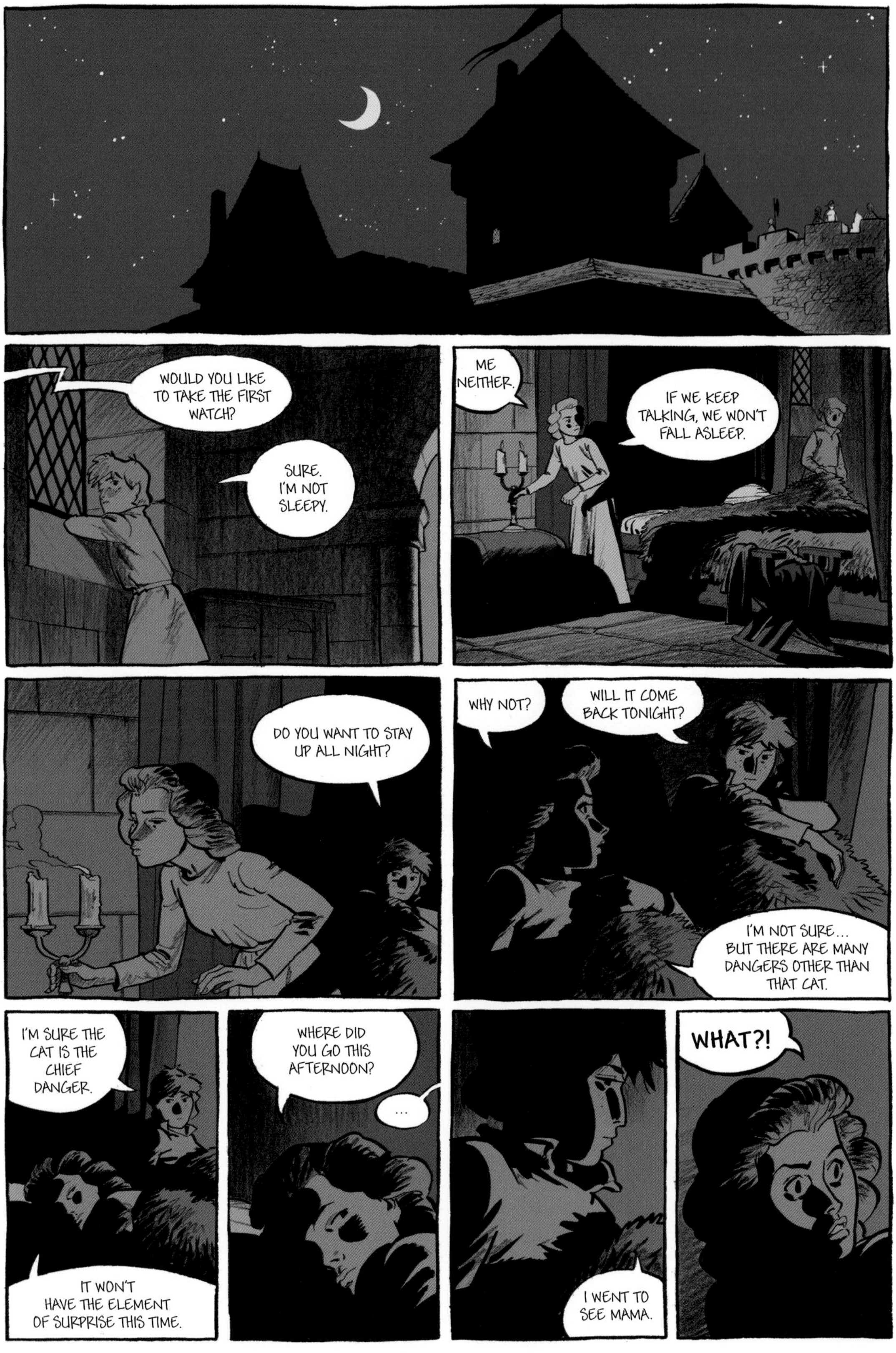
WOULD YOU LIKE TO TAKE THE FIRST WATCH?
SURE. I'M NOT SLEEPY.
ME NEITHER.
IF WE KEEP TALKING, WE WON'T FALL ASLEEP.
DO YOU WANT TO STAY UP ALL NIGHT?
WHY NOT?
WILL IT COME BACK TONIGHT?
I'M NOT SURE… BUT THERE ARE MANY DANGERS OTHER THAN THAT CAT.
I'M SURE THE CAT IS THE CHIEF DANGER.
IT WON'T HAVE THE ELEMENT OF SURPRISE THIS TIME.
WHERE DID YOU GO THIS AFTERNOON?
…
I WENT TO SEE MAMA.
WHAT?!

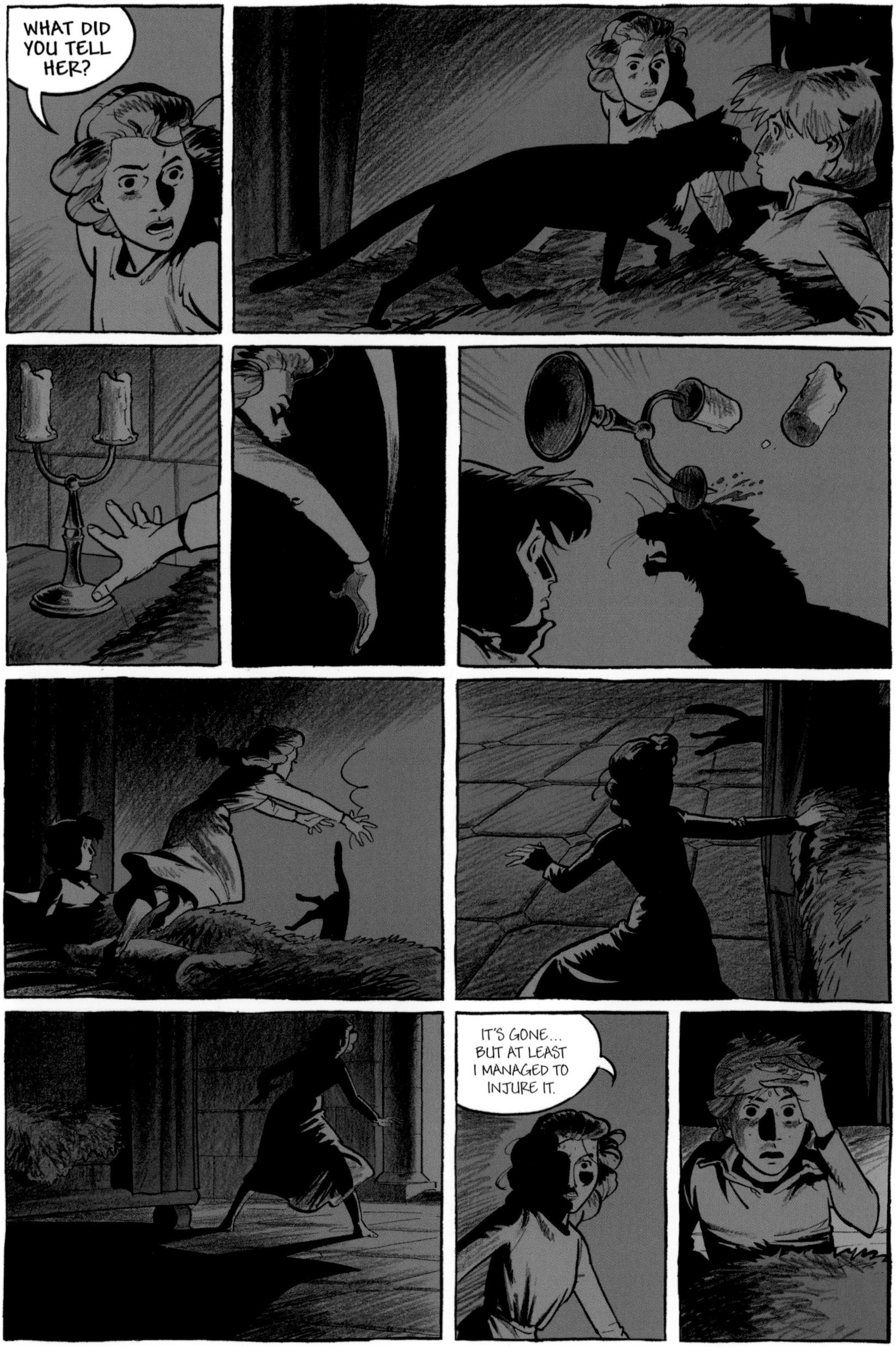
WHAT DID YOU TELL HER?
IT'S GONE... BUT AT LEAST I MANAGED TO INJURE IT.

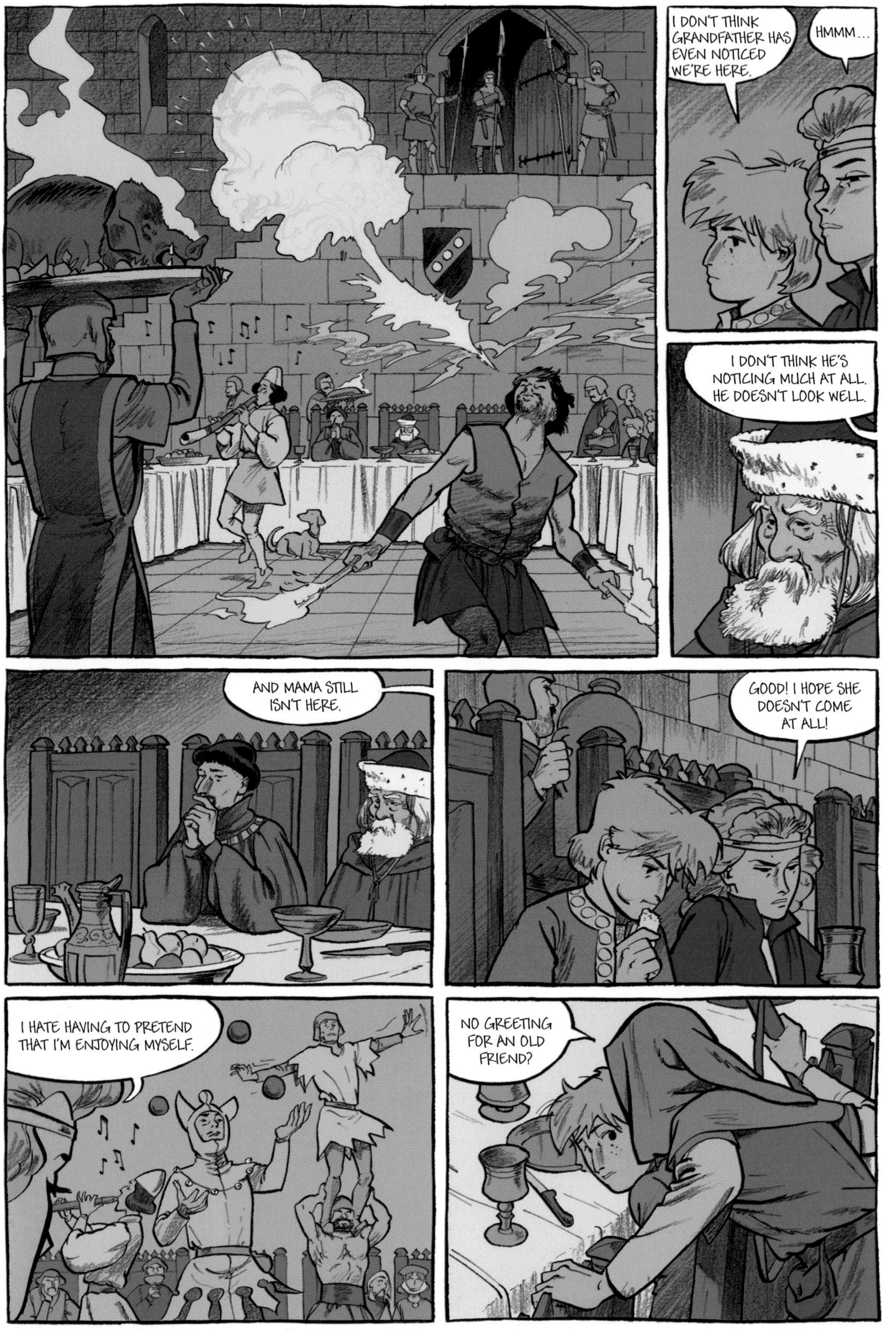
I DON'T THINK GRANDFATHER HAS EVEN NOTICED WE'RE HERE.
HMMM...
I DON'T THINK HE'S NOTICING MUCH AT ALL. HE DOESN'T LOOK WELL.
AND MAMA STILL ISN'T HERE.
GOOD! I HOPE SHE DOESN'T COME AT ALL!
I HATE HAVING TO PRETEND THAT I'M ENJOYING MYSELF.
NO GREETING FOR AN OLD FRIEND?

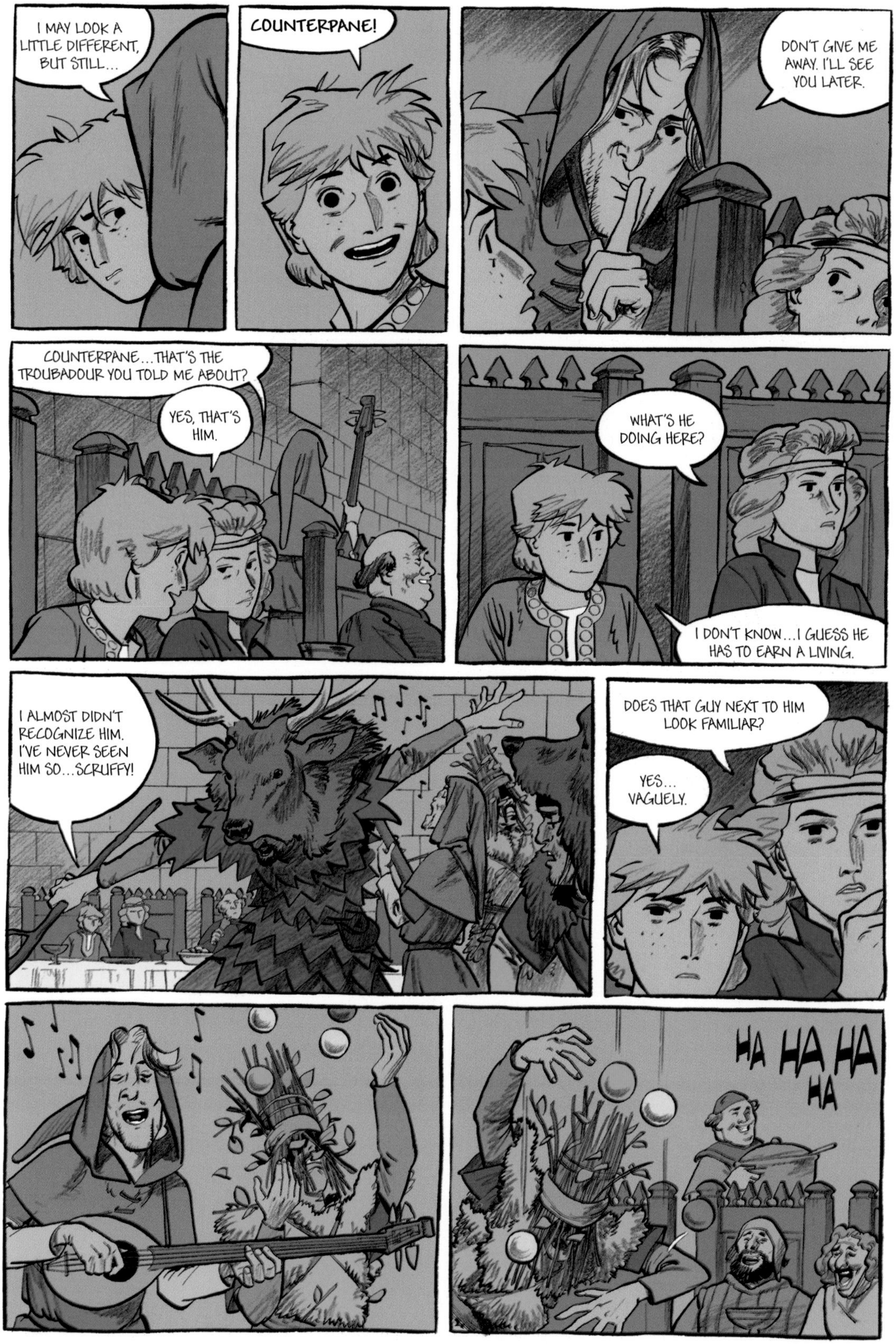

I MAY LOOK A LITTLE DIFFERENT, BUT STILL...
COUNTERPANE!
DON'T GIVE ME AWAY. I'LL SEE YOU LATER.
COUNTERPANE...THAT'S THE TROUBADOUR YOU TOLD ME ABOUT?
YES, THAT'S HIM.
WHAT'S HE DOING HERE?
I DON'T KNOW...I GUESS HE HAS TO EARN A LIVING.
I ALMOST DIDN'T RECOGNIZE HIM. I'VE NEVER SEEN HIM SO...SCRUFFY!
DOES THAT GUY NEXT TO HIM LOOK FAMILIAR?
YES... VAGUELY.
HA HA HA HA

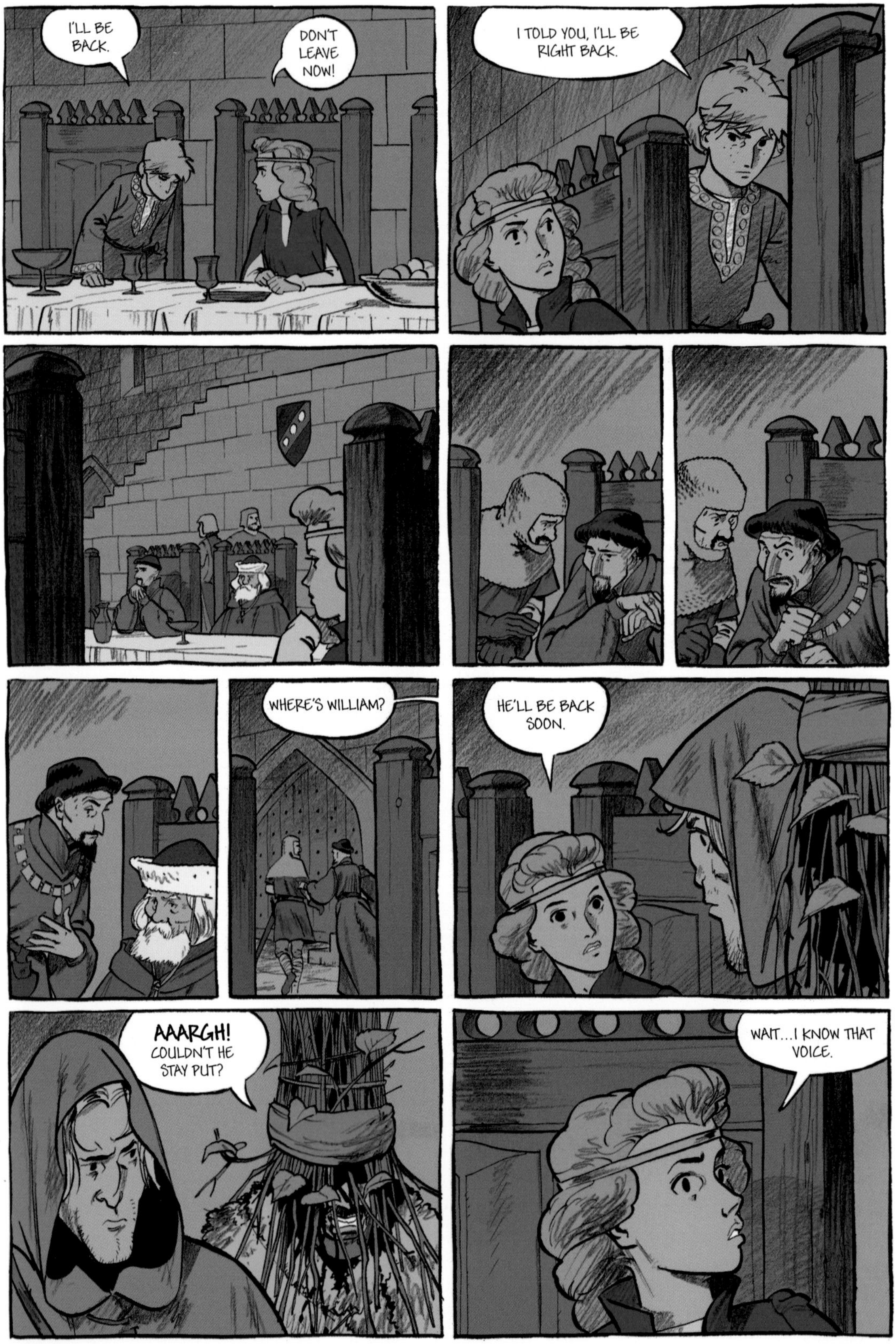
I'LL BE BACK.
DON'T LEAVE NOW!
I TOLD YOU, I'LL BE RIGHT BACK.
WHERE'S WILLIAM?
HE'LL BE BACK SOON.
AAARGH! COULDN'T HE STAY PUT?
WAIT...I KNOW THAT VOICE.

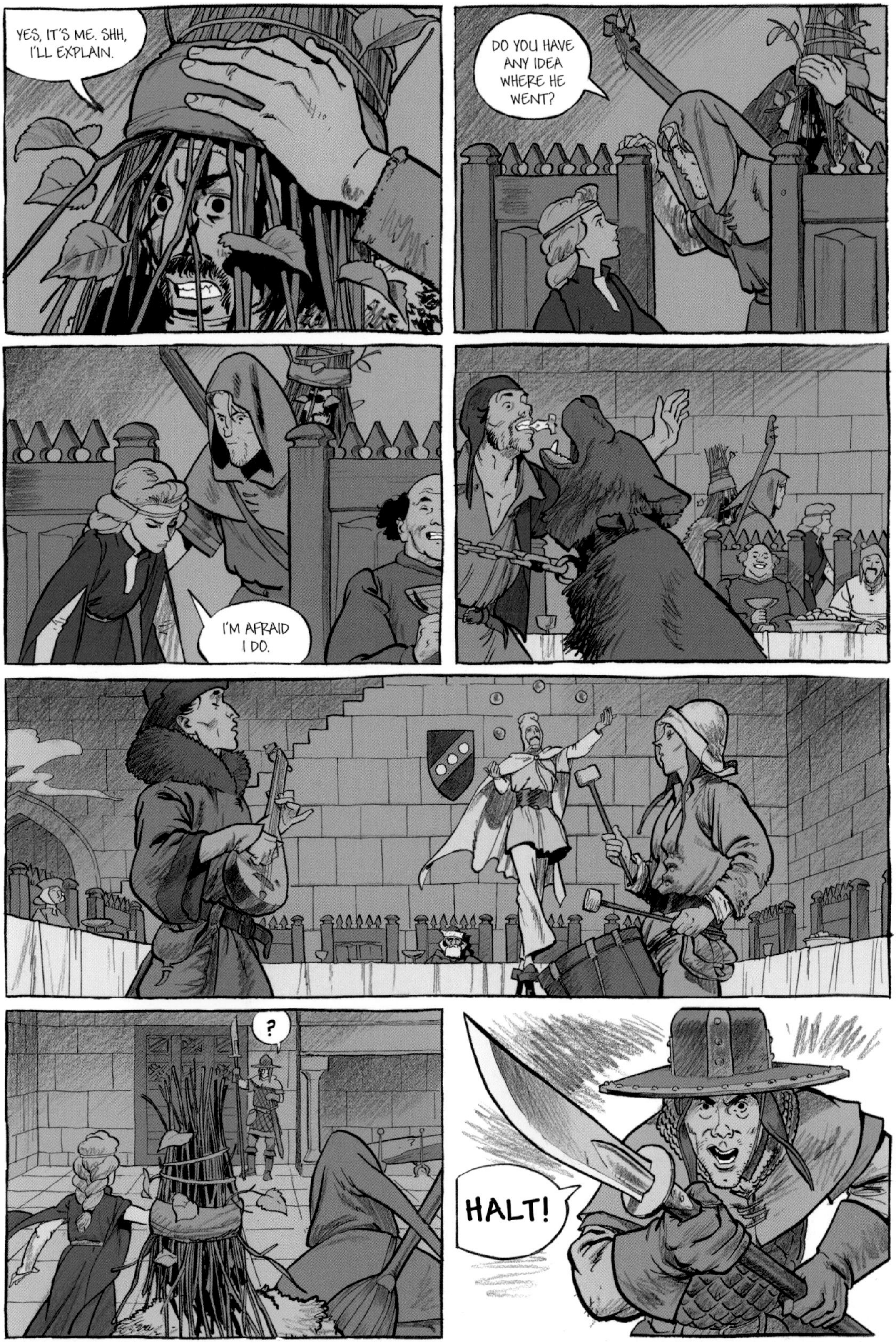
YES, IT'S ME. SHH, I'LL EXPLAIN.
DO YOU HAVE ANY IDEA WHERE HE WENT?
I'M AFRAID I DO.
?
HALT!

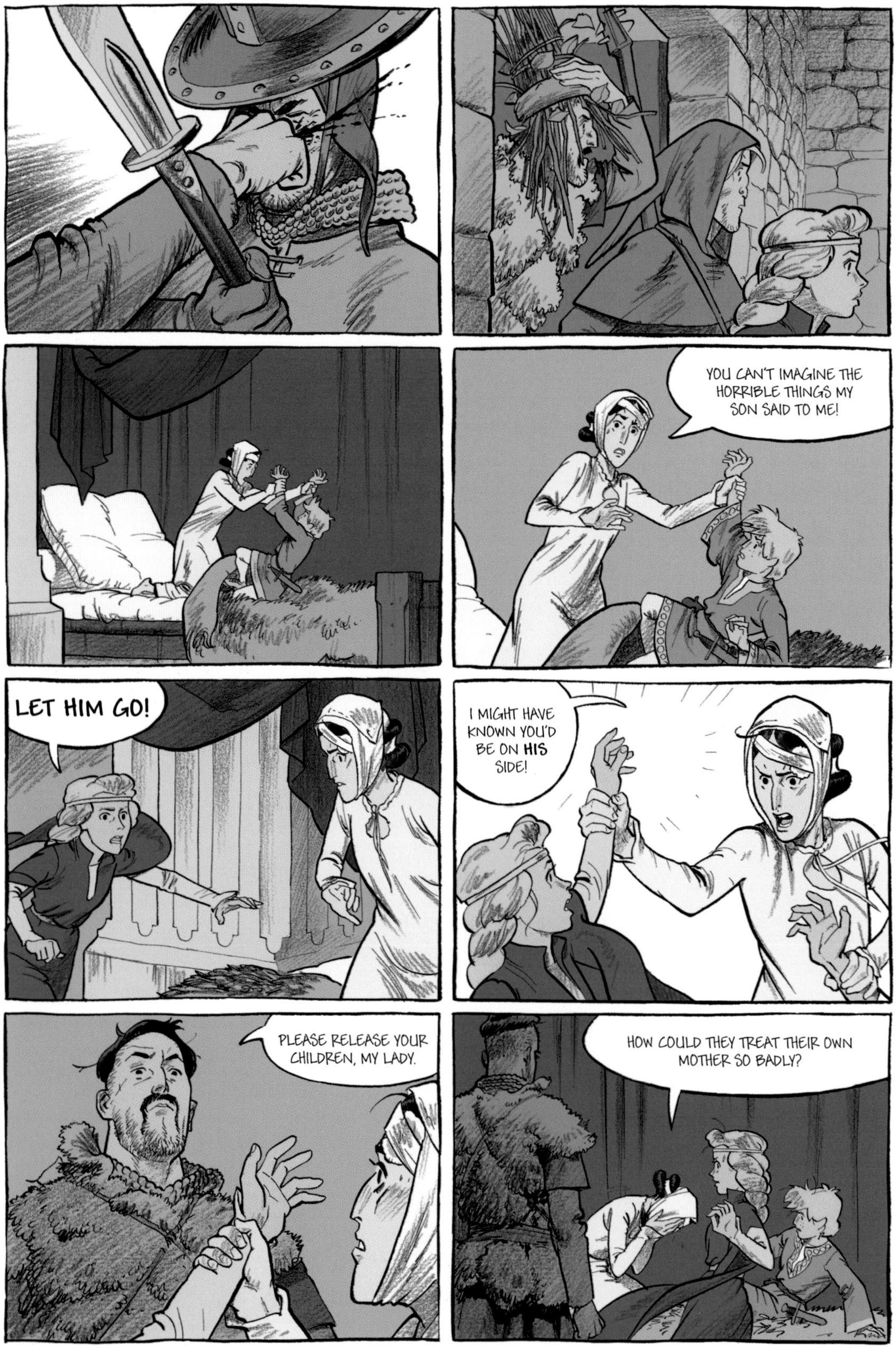
YOU CAN'T IMAGINE THE HORRIBLE THINGS MY SON SAID TO ME!
LET HIM GO!
I MIGHT HAVE KNOWN YOU'D BE ON **HIS** SIDE!
PLEASE RELEASE YOUR CHILDREN, MY LADY.
HOW COULD THEY TREAT THEIR OWN MOTHER SO BADLY?

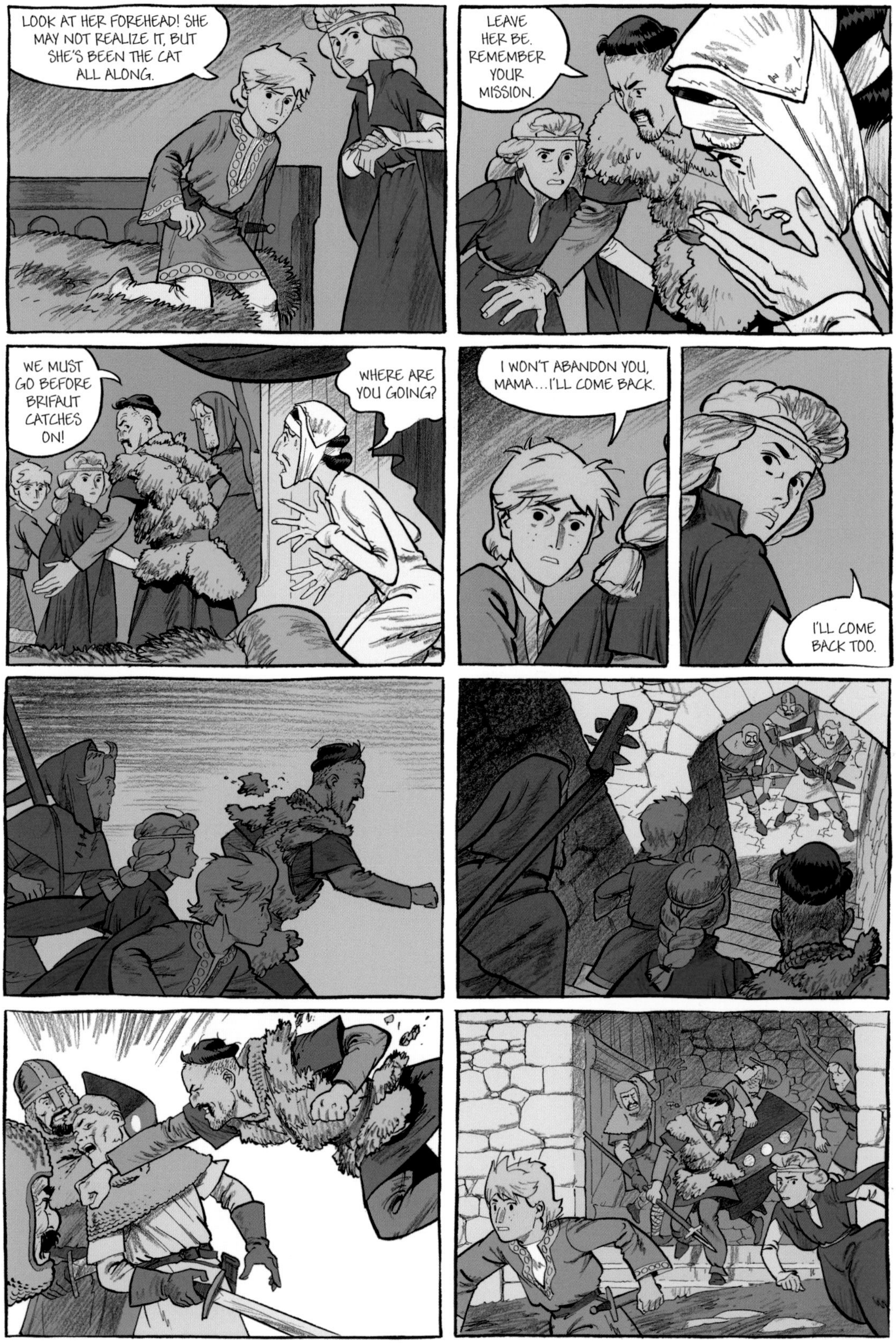
LOOK AT HER FOREHEAD! SHE MAY NOT REALIZE IT, BUT SHE'S BEEN THE CAT ALL ALONG.
LEAVE HER BE. REMEMBER YOUR MISSION.
WE MUST GO BEFORE BRIFAUT CATCHES ON!
WHERE ARE YOU GOING?
I WON'T ABANDON YOU, MAMA...I'LL COME BACK.
I'LL COME BACK TOO.

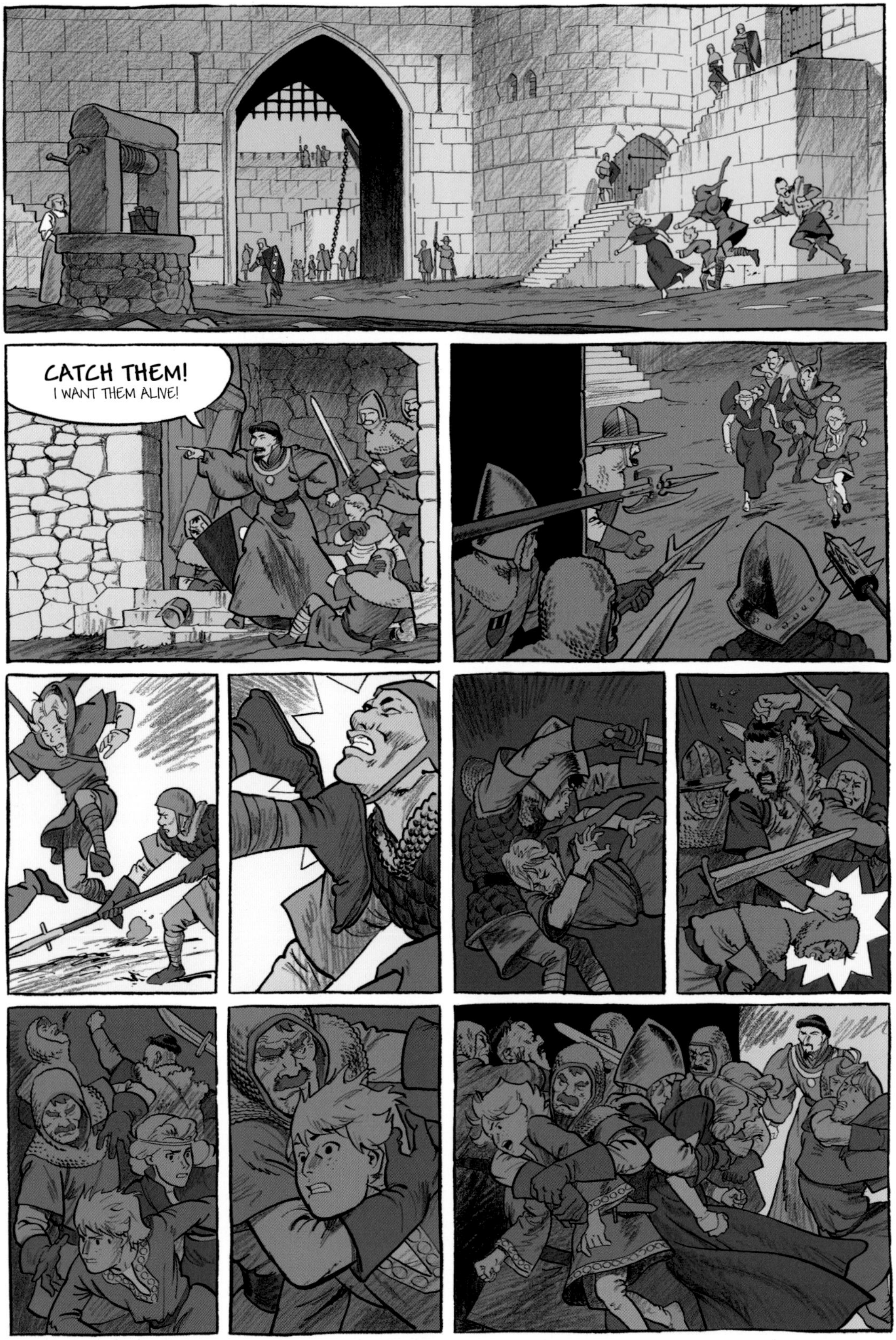
CATCH THEM!
I WANT THEM ALIVE!

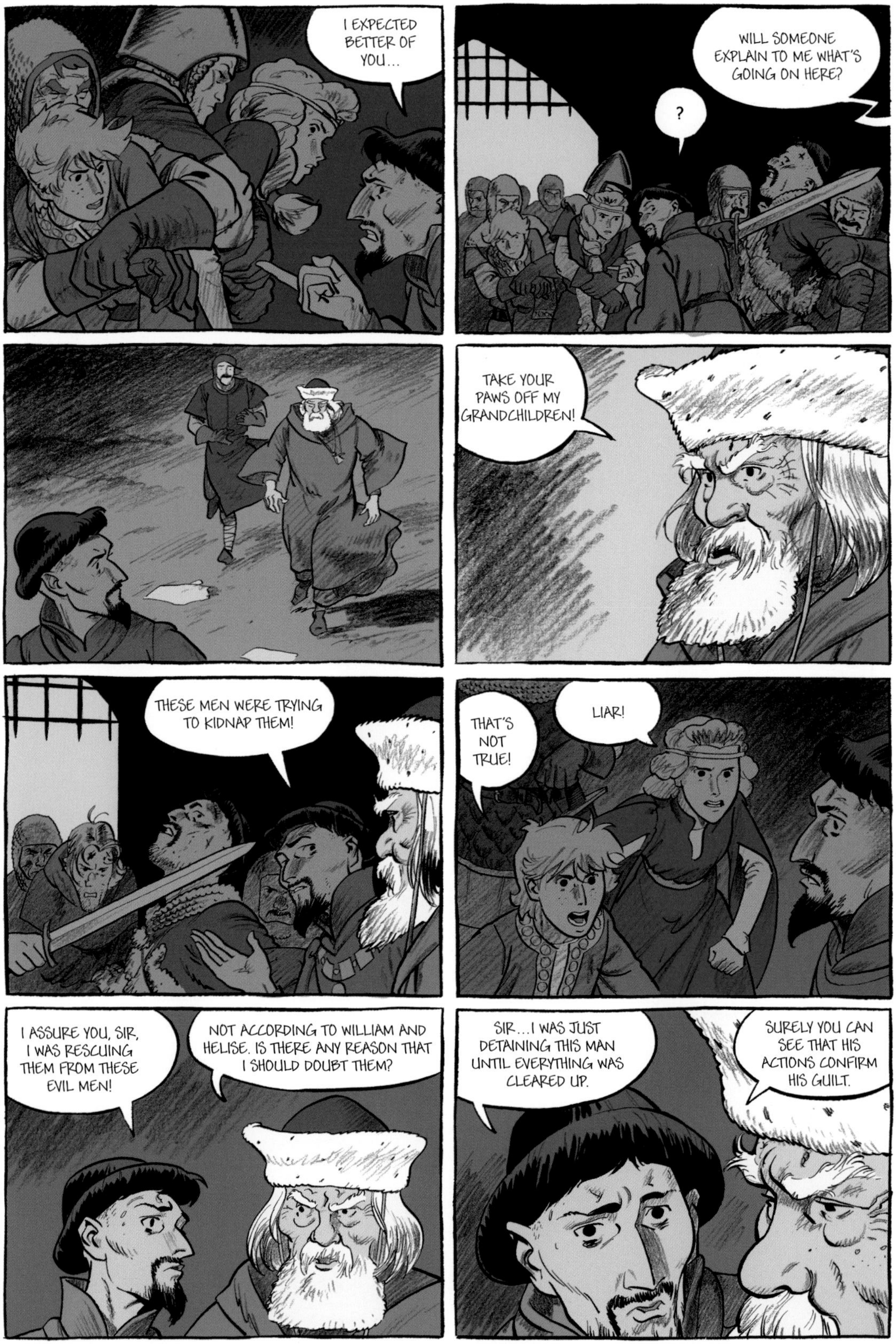
I EXPECTED BETTER OF YOU...
?
WILL SOMEONE EXPLAIN TO ME WHAT'S GOING ON HERE?
TAKE YOUR PAWS OFF MY GRANDCHILDREN!
THESE MEN WERE TRYING TO KIDNAP THEM!
THAT'S NOT TRUE!
LIAR!
I ASSURE YOU, SIR, I WAS RESCUING THEM FROM THESE EVIL MEN!
NOT ACCORDING TO WILLIAM AND HELISE. IS THERE ANY REASON THAT I SHOULD DOUBT THEM?
SIR...I WAS JUST DETAINING THIS MAN UNTIL EVERYTHING WAS CLEARED UP.
SURELY YOU CAN SEE THAT HIS ACTIONS CONFIRM HIS GUILT.

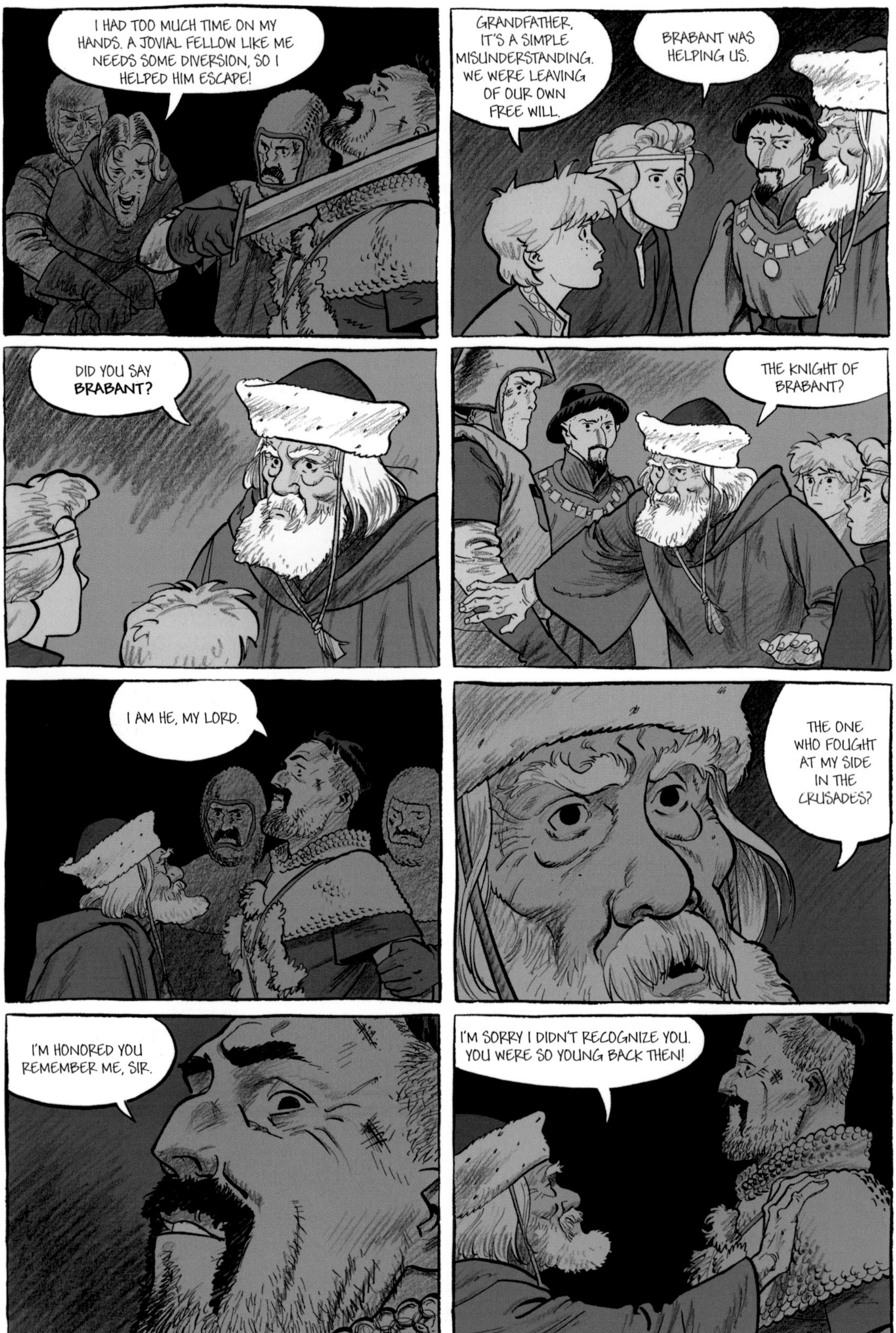
I HAD TOO MUCH TIME ON MY HANDS. A JOVIAL FELLOW LIKE ME NEEDS SOME DIVERSION, SO I HELPED HIM ESCAPE!
GRANDFATHER, IT'S A SIMPLE MISUNDERSTANDING. WE WERE LEAVING OF OUR OWN FREE WILL.
BRABANT WAS HELPING US.
DID YOU SAY **BRABANT?**
THE KNIGHT OF BRABANT?
I AM HE, MY LORD.
THE ONE WHO FOUGHT AT MY SIDE IN THE CRUSADES?
I'M HONORED YOU REMEMBER ME, SIR.
I'M SORRY I DIDN'T RECOGNIZE YOU. YOU WERE SO YOUNG BACK THEN!

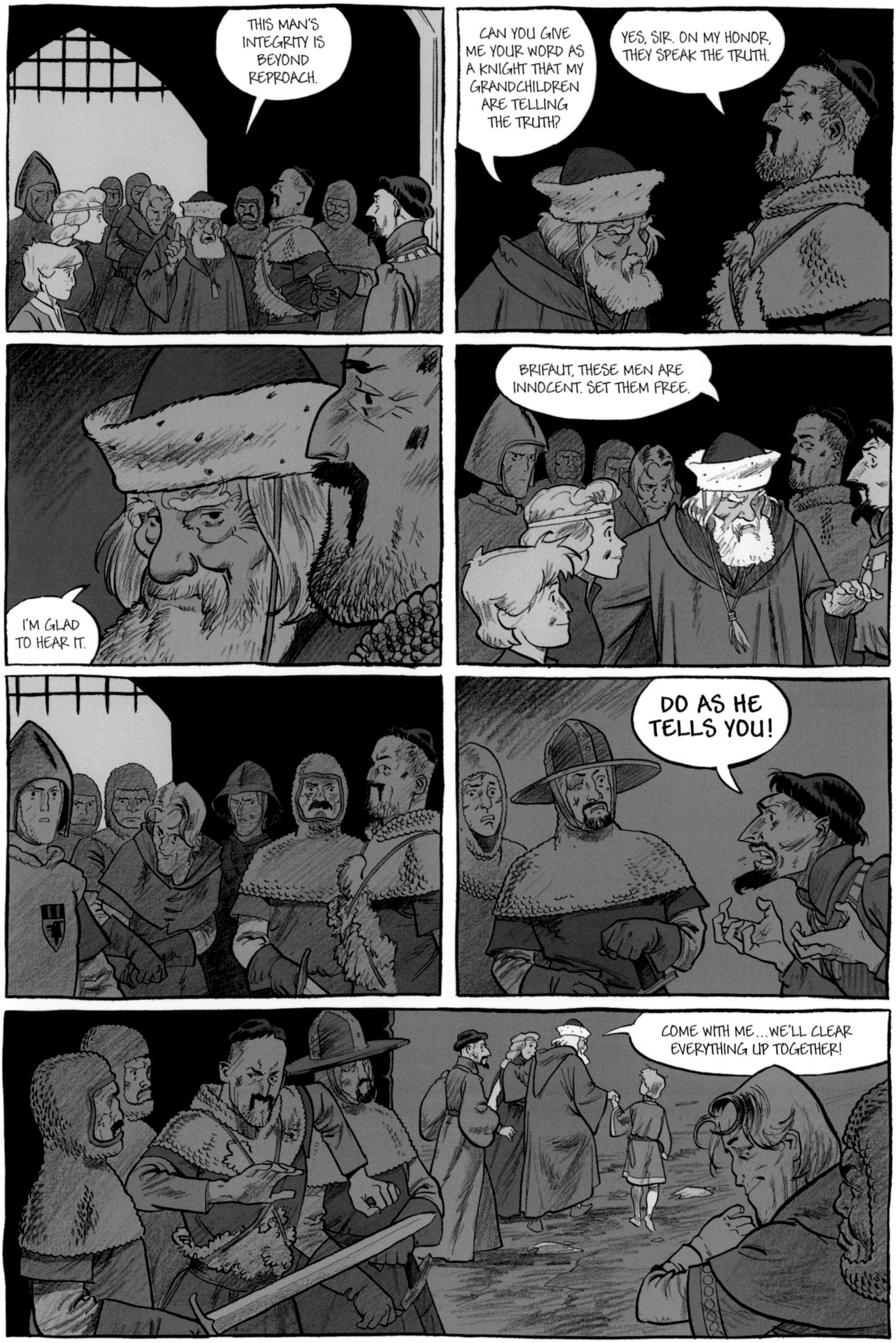

THIS MAN'S INTEGRITY IS BEYOND REPROACH.
CAN YOU GIVE ME YOUR WORD AS A KNIGHT THAT MY GRANDCHILDREN ARE TELLING THE TRUTH?
YES, SIR. ON MY HONOR, THEY SPEAK THE TRUTH.
I'M GLAD TO HEAR IT.
BRIFAUT, THESE MEN ARE INNOCENT. SET THEM FREE.
DO AS HE TELLS YOU!
COME WITH ME…WE'LL CLEAR EVERYTHING UP TOGETHER!

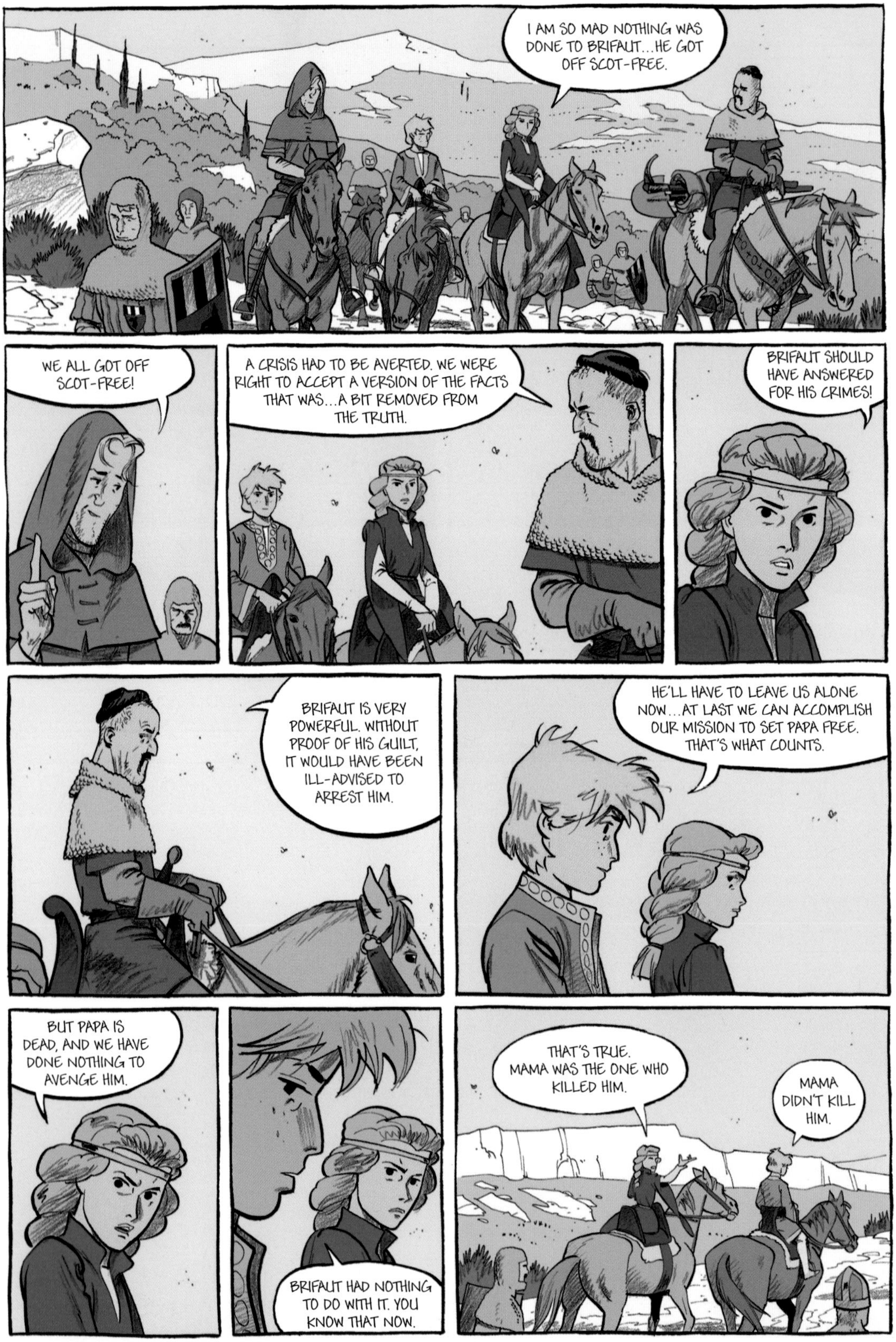

I AM SO MAD NOTHING WAS DONE TO BRIFAUT...HE GOT OFF SCOT-FREE.
WE ALL GOT OFF SCOT-FREE!
A CRISIS HAD TO BE AVERTED. WE WERE RIGHT TO ACCEPT A VERSION OF THE FACTS THAT WAS...A BIT REMOVED FROM THE TRUTH.
BRIFAUT SHOULD HAVE ANSWERED FOR HIS CRIMES!
BRIFAUT IS VERY POWERFUL. WITHOUT PROOF OF HIS GUILT, IT WOULD HAVE BEEN ILL-ADVISED TO ARREST HIM.
HE'LL HAVE TO LEAVE US ALONE NOW...AT LAST WE CAN ACCOMPLISH OUR MISSION TO SET PAPA FREE. THAT'S WHAT COUNTS.
BUT PAPA IS DEAD, AND WE HAVE DONE NOTHING TO AVENGE HIM.
BRIFAUT HAD NOTHING TO DO WITH IT. YOU KNOW THAT NOW.
THAT'S TRUE. MAMA WAS THE ONE WHO KILLED HIM.
MAMA DIDN'T KILL HIM.

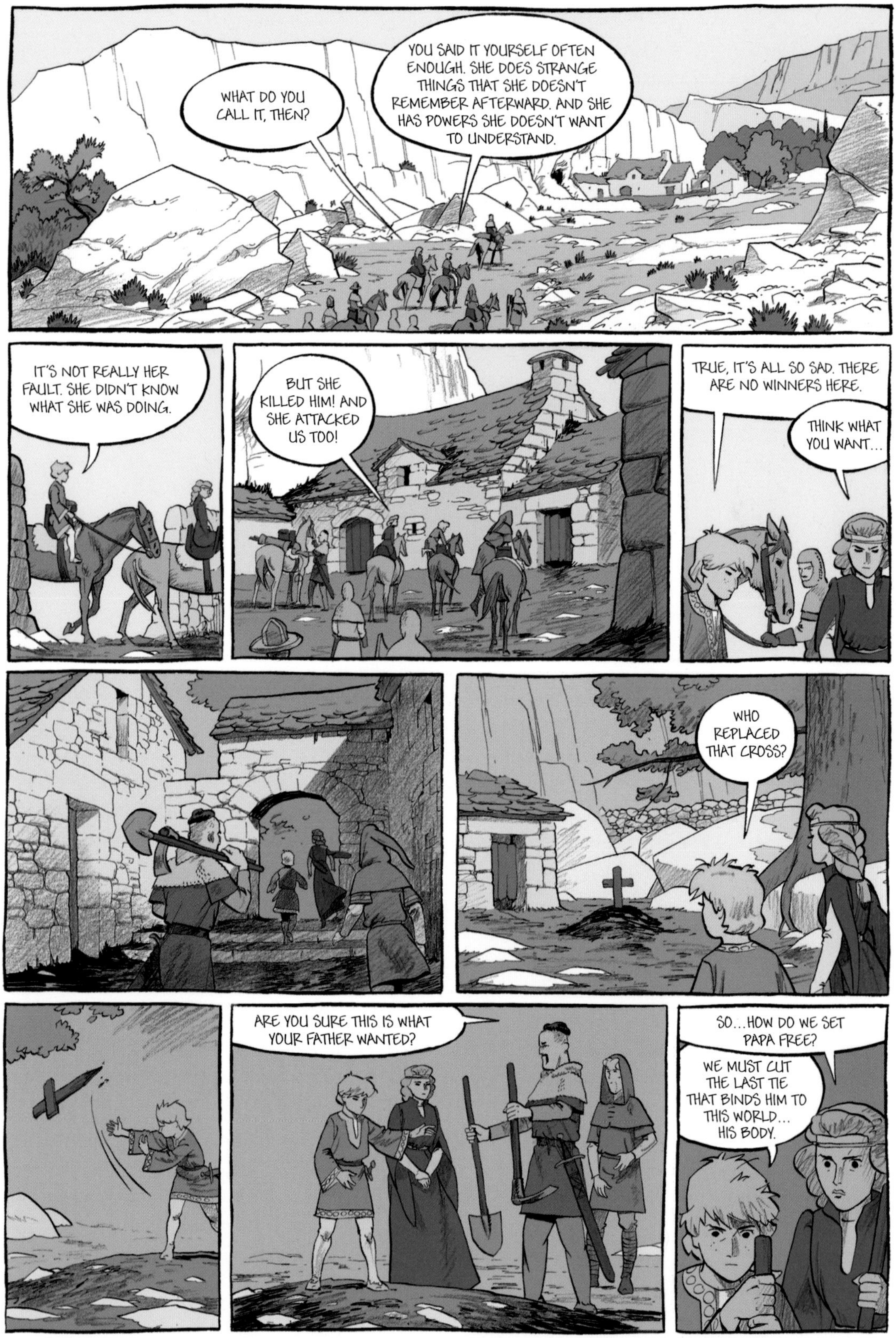
WHAT DO YOU CALL IT, THEN?
YOU SAID IT YOURSELF OFTEN ENOUGH. SHE DOES STRANGE THINGS THAT SHE DOESN'T REMEMBER AFTERWARD. AND SHE HAS POWERS SHE DOESN'T WANT TO UNDERSTAND.
IT'S NOT REALLY HER FAULT. SHE DIDN'T KNOW WHAT SHE WAS DOING.
BUT SHE KILLED HIM! AND SHE ATTACKED US TOO!
TRUE, IT'S ALL SO SAD. THERE ARE NO WINNERS HERE.
THINK WHAT YOU WANT...
WHO REPLACED THAT CROSS?
ARE YOU SURE THIS IS WHAT YOUR FATHER WANTED?
SO...HOW DO WE SET PAPA FREE?
WE MUST CUT THE LAST TIE THAT BINDS HIM TO THIS WORLD... HIS BODY.

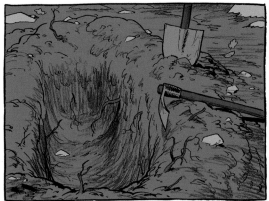

THE END

GWEN DE BONNEVAL
MATTHIEU BONHOMME

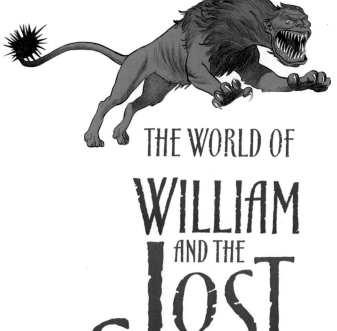

THE WORLD OF

WILLIAM
AND THE
LOST
SPIRIT

ROLES AND RANK IN THE MIDDLE AGES

BRIGAND

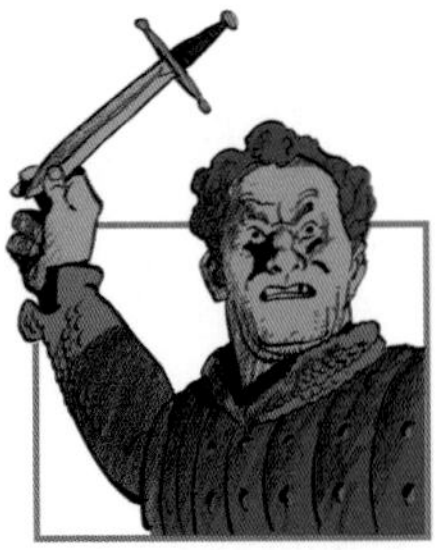

A person who made a living by robbing travelers and stealing from people's homes and farms. Brigands would also kidnap wealthy or important people and hold them for ransom. Brigands seldom worked alone; like Malart and his comrades, they preferred to work as a group. They had no scruples about killing anyone who got in their way.

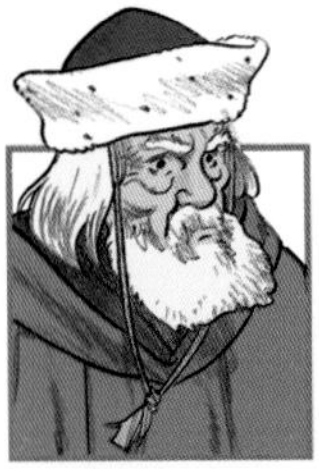

COUNT

One step lower than a duke, a count was a high-ranking nobleman who governed feudal lands assigned to his family by a king. The title was passed down to the eldest son in each generation. In this story, William will inherit the title from his grandfather. There really were Counts de Saunhac (Saunhac is the original French version of the name, which was anglicized to Sonnac). The Saunhacs were a powerful noble family in Southern France during the Middle Ages and Renaissance.

MERCENARY

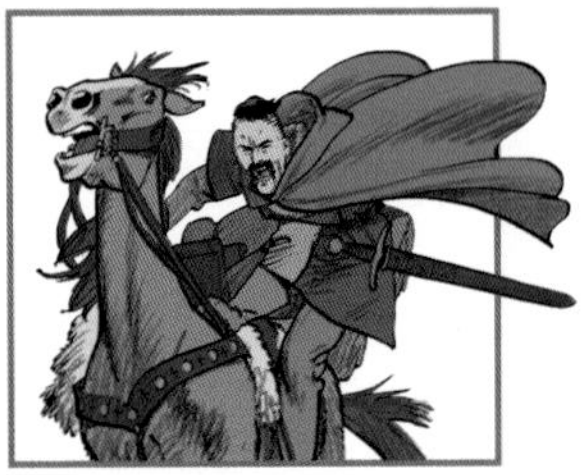

A soldier for hire, who will fight for any country or cause that pays him. At the time the story takes place, a particularly famous and successful group of mercenaries were from Brabant, a state located in parts of what are now Belgium and the Netherlands. Anyone who lived at the time of the story would wonder whether the Knight of Brabant was simply *from* Brabant or whether he was one of these mercenaries!

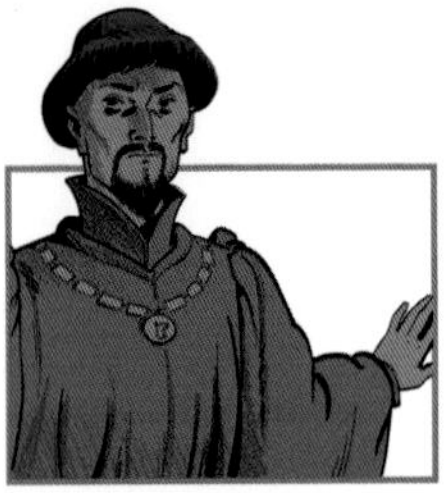

SENESCHAL

An important officer in the court of a nobleman, responsible for the day-to-day administration of the nobleman's lands. Becoming the seneschal for the Count de Sonnac gave Brifaut a great deal of power, especially since the count was ill and did not take an active role in governing the region.

TROUBADOUR

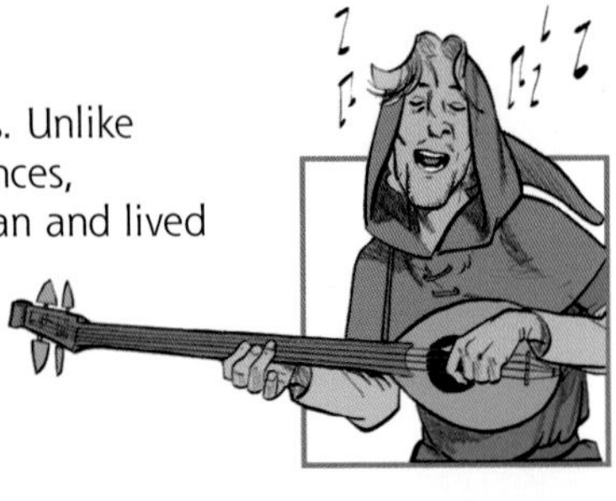

A lyric poet and composer who wrote and performed his own songs. Unlike minstrels, who wandered from town to town giving street performances, troubadours were usually sponsored by a nobleman or a noblewoman and lived at the sponsor's estate. In this story, the troubadour Counterpane is sponsored by a powerful sorceress. Like other troubadours, his songs deal with topics such as chivalry and romantic love.

MYTHOLOGICAL FIGURES IN THE FAR-OFF LANDS

BLEMMYES

The ancient author Pliny the Elder, who wrote an encyclopedia of nature, described a race of people who had no heads but had faces on their chests instead. Many other writers in ancient, medieval, and Renaissance times also wrote about these imaginary beings. As the story was handed down, details were added: some said that Blemmyes were cannibals, and others said they had neighbors whose faces were on their backs!

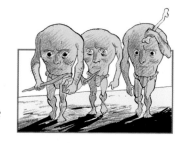

PRESTER JOHN

A popular figure in European legends during the Middle Ages and the Renaissance, Prester John was said to be the ruler of a far-off Christian land in the middle of a non-Christian part of the world. *Prester* is an old-fashioned word for "priest." He was seen both as a king and as a religious leader. The exact location of his territory changed from one story to the next but was always someplace far away that seemed exotic to Europeans, such as India, central Asia, or Ethiopia.

DOG-FACED PEOPLE

The notion of dog-faced people is found in many works from different places and different times, including an ancient Chinese text called *Liang Shu* and in the writings by the ancient Greek historian Herodotus. Dog-faced people are generally described as barbarians who live in faraway places. How far away? Well, the ancient Syrian author Lucian of Samosata claimed that there were dog-faced people who lived on the star Sirius (the Dog Star)!

GRYPHONS

The Gryphon is a mythical beast with the head, talons, and wings of an eagle and the body of a lion. Its symbolic meanings make it an especially appropriate mount for Prester John, who himself was called king of all kings. Since the eagle is the king of birds and the lion the king of beasts, the gryphon is a symbol of kingship. Moreover, Prester John claims to be a Christian. In the Middle Ages, the dual nature of the gryphon was often interpreted as a symbol of the dual nature of Jesus Christ, the eagle representing Christ's divinity and the lion representing his humanity.

GENDER ROLES IN THE MIDDLE AGES

As a knight, Brabant holds a position of authority that helps him solve the problems he faces. Moreover, when solving problems, he frequently uses technology (his sword). What problems do other male characters, such as Brifaut, Prester John, and the Count de Sonnac face? How do they use technology to solve their problems?

As a woman, Ysane has no formal position of authority and must solve her problems in a different way. By using her powers of persuasion, she can manipulate people into doing what she wants them to do. She is also an accomplished sorceress, who uses magical powers to achieve her goals. What problems do other female characters, such as Helise, Prester John's daughter, and Philomena face? How do they use persuasion and magic to solve their problems?

GENDER AND RELIGION

Reflect on the use of magic by the main female characters in the story. Are they always aware that they're using magic? Are they always successful in their use of magic? Do you approve of their use of magic? Why or why not? Overall, does the story present a positive or a negative view of magic?

Reflect on the ways in which the major male characters identify themselves with Christianity. To what extent do they use their association with Christianity to help them reach their goals? Are they always successful in their use of religion? Do you approve of their use of religion? Why or why not? Overall, does the story present a positive or a negative view of organized religion such as Christianity?

William is an unusual character who doesn't fit neatly into the categories we have discussed.

How is William like the other male characters in the book?

Does he use a position of authority to achieve his goals?

Does he use technology in solving his problems?

Does he ever associate himself with Christianity?

How is William like the female characters in the book?

Does he use persuasion to achieve his goals?

Is he able to practice magic?

In the story, how do male characters help William?

How do female characters help him?

DISCUSSIONS

PART ONE: THE FAR-OFF LANDS

The unexpected death of William's father places the main characters in a situation where they have to make difficult decisions. In making these decisions, the characters must balance two conflicting factors: *duty* (what they're supposed to do, especially in light of their social obligations and family expectations) and *inclination* (what they want to do, especially in terms of achieving happiness for themselves and the ones they love).

Each character in the book faces a conflict between duty and inclination. Consider the major characters in the book (William, Philomena, Helise, Ysane, Brifaut, Brabant, and Counterpane). What were their *duties*? What were their *inclinations*? Was there a conflict between their duties and their inclinations? If so, did they choose to act according to duty or did they follow their inclinations?

PART TWO: THE LAND OF TRUTH

William doesn't exist. His adventures didn't really happen. Everything has been made up by Bonneval and Bonhomme. This book is a work of fiction, and to enjoy it, you have to *suspend your disbelief* by pretending that the story (or at least part of the story) is true, even though you know it's not.

Even though you suspended your disbelief when you began reading the story, you are faced with important questions about truth and falsehood from the very beginning of this book. From the viewpoint of the characters in the story, are William's experiences in the far-off lands *true*? Did they really happen? Do the people he met really exist? Are the places he visited really there? Or are William's experiences *false*? Are the people he met and the places he visited some type of dream or hallucination?

PART THREE: MOTHER, LAND

It is important to be aware of the difference between the way something seems to be (its *appearance*) and the way it actually is (its *reality*). In nature, plants and animals often appear to be different from what they really are in order to capture prey or ward off predators. People can act the same way. In *William and the Lost Spirit*, characters use deception for selfish reasons, but it is also used to help others.

As a member of the story's audience, you too have to make decisions about the reality (true nature) of characters based on their appearance (the information that Bonneval and Bonhomme have chosen to reveal to you). When you were reading this book for the first time, were you ever mistaken about the true nature of a character by the way the character first appeared? How did you figure out that you were mistaken? Did you learn anything from making this mistake?

ABOUT THE AUTHOR AND ILLUSTRATOR

GWEN DE BONNEVAL was born in Nantes, a large city in western France. Early in his career he worked in newspapers and children's publishing. In 1998, he joined l'Atelier des Vosges, an acclaimed comics studio whose members have included Marjane Satrapi, David B., Christophe Blain, and Joann Sfar. There he devoted himself to his true passion: writing and drawing comics. With author Fabien Vehlmann, he created a graphic novel series called Samedi et Dimanche about two lizards. He also collaborated with Vehlmann on the science fiction comic *Les derniers jours d'un immortel* (published in English by Archaia as *Last Days of an Immortal*). Bonneval's solo books include *Monsieur Forme* and the Basile Bonjour series.

Bonneval founded the comics studio l'Atelier du coin with his friends Matthieu Bonhomme, Stéphane Oiry, and Hubert. With his studio mates, he developed *Capsule cosmique*, a comics magazine for children. *William and the Lost Spirit* was first released in France under the name *L'Esprit perdu*. In 2010 it received the all-ages award at the Angoulême International Comics Festival. Bonneval has also collaborated with Hervé Tanquerelle to adapt the writings of Danish author Jörn Riel. He is currently writing a graphic novel series called *Bonneval Pacha*, based on the life of an ancestor who fought for both Louis the Great and the Ottoman Empire.

MATTHIEU BONHOMME is from Paris, France. He began drawing at an early age and went on to earn a degree in applied arts. His work has appeared in numerous magazines including *Spirou*, *Je bouquine*, *Grain de soleil*, *Maximum*, *D-lire*, and *Image Doc*. Bonhomme's solo book, *L'Âge de raison*, received the award for best debut graphic novel at the 2003 Angoulême International Comics Festival.

Like Gwen de Bonneval, Bonhomme joined the l'Atelier des Vosges studio. At the studio he met the writer Fabien Vehlmann, with whom he collaborated on the graphic novel series Le Marquis d'Anaon. Shortly after this, Bonhomme cofounded a new studio with Bonneval and several friends: l'Atelier du coin. The studio's comics magazine, *Capsule cosmique*, features his first solo work, a series called Le voyage d'Esteban. Recently, Bonhomme worked with legendary cartoonist Lewis Trondheim on his graphic novel *Omni-visibilis*. Together, they also created the wild west graphic novel *Texas Cowboys*.

ABOUT THE TRANSLATORS

ANNE COLLINS SMITH, PH.D., is an associate professor of philosophy and classical studies at Stephen F. Austin State University in Nacogdoches, Texas. Her dissertation was on medieval philosophy, and her favorite class in graduate school was Douglass Parker's course on parageography (the geography of imaginary worlds).

OWEN M. SMITH, PH.D., is an associate professor of philosophy and classical studies at Stephen F. Austin State University in Nacogdoches, Texas. A specialist in philosophy of religion, he has taught philosophy courses on mysticism, Hermeticism, and Gnosticism, as well as study abroad courses in Greece.